# For Mist and Tar

Jinapher J. Hoffman

Wrathos Books

# ALCHE

SCORUS

# MIGHT

the unknown
DALBIAN'S ABYSS
The
BLOODY CLOTH
FRALES
RATHMORE MANOR
House of
STONE
CALIGARI

*ISBN 10: 0578989344*

*ISBN 13: 978-0578989341*

# Author Note & Content Warnings

I published *For Mist and Tar* in 2022. It was my debut as a fantasy author and the first book I ever published within Wrathos. It's remained silent but resilient while my other books took center stage. Slowly but surely, it's grown a cult following, the messages I've received from so many of you leaving me in tears and speechless (in the best way).

You will love these books or you will hate them. I've discovered there's no in-between with my readers over the last two years. You're not meant to root for every character. They're morally grey in a way that may drive you insane, and *For Mist and Tar* was written to be incredibly 'surface level' while *For Blood and Flame* is the far darker discovery of the characters and magic.

This was never a story I thought would sell remarkably well but a story I needed to be rid of. I needed it out of my heart. It means so much to me that it's finding homes with you all, and I can't thank you enough for taking a chance on me.

The Alchemight Duology consists of *For Mist and Tar* (FMAT) and *For Blood and Flame* (FBAF). While a completed set, they're two vastly different stories. FMAT is an origin story. You will meet the characters, the world, the magic, and you will see the darkness of the story evolve. FBAF is a finale. An end of an entire realm. It also has the most multiverse connections and lore of any of my books, including two cameos from FATES OF MIRROR.

In case you've missed any of the other warnings across Amazon summaries, GoodReads, my author website, etc...This is a tragedy, but it won't be the last time you see some of these characters. A select few will have character arcs that carry into new series across the multiverse. These books will hurt, but there *will* be more. I'm sending hugs. Take your time. Deep breath. Sink. Don't binge these. It's intended to be slowburn. Just. Sink.

***For Mist and Tar* is an epic, grimdark fantasy book. Readers should be aware of the following content warnings, but please be advised some of these could be potential spoilers:**

*Dismemberment and Beheading; Enslavement and Imprisonment; On-Page Hangings; Physical Abuse to a Minor; Domestic Violence, Heavy Imagery Related to Mental Illness, including but not limited to Post Traumatic Stress Disorder (PTSD) related to War and Parental*

*Abuse, Anxiety, and Depression; Characters with Suicidal Tendencies; Self-Mutilation; General gore and Violence; Morally Grey Characters; Murder; and finally, Tragic Backstories and a General Tragic Atmosphere.*

**In a realm starved of magic, power is the ultimate strength. The price? Your soul.**

**Readers can enjoy a Glossary at the back of this edition.**

BOOKS BY JINAPHER J. HOFFMAN

WRATHOS BOOKS

IN A MULTIVERSE OF FEMININE RAGE

ALCHEMIGHT

***FOR MIST & TAR***

***FOR BLOOD & FLAME***

MIRROR

***VEIL OF FATE***

***HEIR OF FATE***

***WARS OF FATE***

FIND NEW RELEASES AT
WWW.WRATHOSBOOKS.COM

TO THOSE WHO UNDERSTAND
WHAT IT IS TO BE DESPERATE
FOR A HOME, FOR SAFETY, AND
TO BE TREASURED.

NO MATTER THE COST.
NO MATTER THE BLOOD.
NO MATTER THE SCARS.

BECAUSE TO FIGHT IS TO LIVE.
TO LIVE IS TO FIGHT.

**ALCHEMIGHT IS
FOR YOU.**

ALSO, TO MY SISTER, FOR
BELIEVING IN ME, IN THIS
STORY, AND NEVER GIVING UP
ON MAGIC.

# PROLOGUE

# *ELEDAR*

### FIVE YEARS BEFORE

When his strings are cut, and his stifled rage shakes the clay beneath his skin—Eledar slaughters the first Imperial he sees. There is no hesitation in the power that bursts from his palms. Power that tears into a chest inked with the Rathmore crest. He tunnels his chemight in a clean shot. As lethal as a blade thrust through the heart, Eledar turns to kill another and another.

Until he stands before piles of bodies.

Until Golem join him in a joyous war cry.

Until he smiles through the blood spattered over his lips.

Because, for once, it is not his mud being leeched from his body. It is not his soul being ripped and torn and shattered. No. *No.*

It is theirs.

It will always be theirs.

Their blood on his hands. Their blood rolling through the streets.

Their blood that frees him of manipulation.

*Their blood* that will forever make him chase redemption.

# Chapter One

## *Vellene*

Lifeless bodies sway in the Scorian wind. Faces gray, cries echoed in the whips of a storm—they are a cruel conqueror's flag. Lives limp with decay, hearts rotted.

They were not fools. They did not seek death. They sought to end their hunger, to feed their families, to find warmth in a nation gone endlessly cold. They were Scraps, and for desperation, they hang.

For power, they hang.

Power ravages every great and glorious thing. Even the chemi beside Vellene. The chemi who kissed her forehead when she was small and scared, despite him being the reason. The chemi she's meant to call father.

She trembles as she stares at the hanging Scraps. Scared, like the way she can't breathe in the pitch black of a cellar. Scarred, like the way the mark down her left thigh sears with pain if she looks at it too long. Both are because of him. Every fear. Every cowardice. Him.

Scared and scarred, he must think of her.

What he cannot see, what she hides so well, is how each mark against her skin lit an ember in her veins. All she needs is a match, and Vellene will grant her father a final embrace. One wrapped in fire. One that burns them both into the mist and tar they were born from. An embrace to end all tyranny. An embrace to tear down his endless array of gray, limp, swinging flags.

She would burn the world if it meant turning Aquim Winloc to ash.

All she needs is that match.

Until then, she smiles. In the face of death. In the face of tyranny. For him for him for him—she smiles. Hollow and empty and brilliant, that is the role of an heiress to the source of all power: the source of all chemight. Chemight that flows through her veins—every chemi's—and rushes through her blood. Chemight that nourishes her hunger and starves a nation. Chemight that rips and shreds and cripples love.

If it didn't, then maybe she would have love. Maybe her mother wouldn't have been poisoned. Maybe her sister would laugh again. Maybe her father...*No.* No, there is no hope for love. Not in this family. Not anymore.

"To wield chemight is a privilege that belongs only to Imperials." Aquim's gaze trails from the bodies, slow and methodical. He relishes the way they dance, the way his daughter stiffens.

He reaches a gloved fist out and snatches a pouch from one of the bodies. When he pulls his hand free from inside the bag, he reveals a singular formulary. One. Identical to those settled in deposits along his chest, its formulary swirls with colored mist inside a glass orb.

“It’s not cruel to take back what they stole from me.” His navy locks lift with the roar of the incoming storm, then float in tune with the flap of his cloak and the creak of the bodies. The silver-threaded spideria on his cloak’s back shines with each curl of the fabric.

The creature’s spindly legs and double, diamond-shaped body mimics the one on his chest, on Vellene’s. Inked in careful black lines and indented with multiple bronze deposits, the spideria winks in the night. Formularies, like the colored glass orb he pinches, are pressed into each deposit. They swirl and sparkle and whisper with greed.

Some formularies are pressed into marvel deposits, becoming metal, chemight, and a wish to create, to heal, to explore. Others are clasped in nether, allowing metal, chemight, and a curse to seduce, to break, to kill. Each colored orb is power. Each deposit is a conductor. All of it, in Aquim’s grip, weaponized.

It's how Vellene learned it doesn't matter if a formulary is made with the best of intentions. Every wish can flourish into a curse, and every curse can wither into a wish. Marvel or nether, formularies are not a gift from Dally and Bian, the Guardians of Alchemight. Formularies are power, bound.

And power in chains is power with teeth and claws.

Vellene's fingers trail over her empty deposits. She may wear the same cloak as her father, even brandish the same Winloc crest across her chest, but she is as starved for power as the Scraps hanging dead before her.

She, herself, might as well be a formulary. Power bound in a pale body with wily hair and golden eyes. Power silenced, just like the rest of her nation, Scorus.

She looks away from the hanging Scraps, from her father's satisfied expression. *Perhaps they were hungry. Perhaps they wished to be happy. Perhaps they wished for more.* Vellene's lips sew shut. It's not that she doesn't want to speak, it's that she can't.

Her father rendered her speechless five months ago.

After her mother, Aurora, was murdered.

After Vellene's embers screamed until she found a spark.

Not a match. Not quite. But the pain of her mother's last breath was enough to send Vellene over the edge.

It was a moment of free fall. A moment.

But Aquim reaped her voice when she was two curses in, forever a million wishes drowning.

*Silgis entris*, he called the formulary. He purred like it was a pet name. It strung out of his palm in chemight wisps of teal, before it sank into her neck and stole her cries, even when she sits alone curled in her bed at night.

Utilities, the servants of Scorus, work around the clock to create new formularies, recipes only Aquim has. *Silgis entris* is one of those formularies. Otherwise, Vellene would have healed herself and screamed until her spark became a fire no one, not even she, could put out.

Now, she has no choice but to bite her tongue, to swallow down the bile that rises when her father displays bodies like trophies.

"I enjoy this obedience," Aquim says, a grin attached to his words.

Vellene lifts her chin in defiance, but she doesn't let go of her fear. For all the courage she pretends at, her father terrifies her. She felt shame for that fear, thought it meant she was a coward. However, like she learned the lesson of curses and wishes, there is no courage without fear. Courage, to steal blows away from her mother, when she was alive, and her younger sister, Mogaell. Fear, to save herself when no one else will. To let fear go completely in the presence of Aquim is to lie with death—and she cannot die. Not yet. Not without finding that match.

Sometimes, though, she worries.

She worries the flames will consume her from the inside out. That her embers will meld into sparks. That those sparks will blaze. That her heart will wither into mist, and her voice will remain trapped beneath sticky tar.

That she will die of pain. Pain of loss. Pain of burdens. Pain of desperation. Same as the Scraps hanging before her.

Movement at the hillside draws their attention. Her Surveillant, Idus, strides down the pathway from their estate, the monstrous building a black shadow at his back. His ceremonial robes flare around him in his haste. The garment is a singular tunic of navy, embellished with his affiliation to the Winlocs—the spideria matching the silver-threaded rope tied at his waist.

Idus's scraggly beard hangs as milk-white and severe as his eyes. Both are wild as his hunched-over body rushes down the rocky path toward them. He pulls to a stop a few feet away, the age lines around his nose wrinkled in distaste. "Sir Winloc," he addresses Aquim. His eyes slip past Vellene as if she is as nonexistent as her voice.

"Out with it," Aquim grumbles. His gaze remains transfixed on the bodies, intolerant to whatever message Idus must deliver.

Vellene crosses her arms. It draws a scowl from Idus, but she doesn't care. His acknowledgment reminds her she still has weight in this world, even if it is silent.

"An audience has been called." Idus tucks his spotted hands and curling black nails into the sleeves of his robes. He squares his jaw and presses his lips together as if he can seal away what needs to be said next.

Vellene straightens in curiosity. She tilts her head, drags her eyes over her Surveillant.

Aquim peers up at the sky's ominous clouds. "Who calls an audience on the cusp of a shard storm?"

The ice white of her Surveillant's eyes flash with an eerie thrill. "The Convocation of the Eternal."

The indent between Vellene's brows flares as confusion rakes through her. Her fingers clench her skirts.

Her father's face darkens. "They wish to beg on their knees, I assume?"

"They wish to fill the Rathmore seat." Idus grimaces. Every wrinkle falls in time with the weight of his beard. "It's his son. He's alive."

Vellene takes a measured step back as tension waves off her father—wrath on the verge of igniting. It's not every day a High Imperial is resurrected.

Aquim erupts with a frustrated growl. Chemight slices out from his palms and the bottom halves of the hanging Scraps thunk to dark soil. He recovers enough to breathe out, "Then, we shall hire an assassin," but Idus is quick to make a mess of her father again.

Bad news to Aquim is best when cleaved like a head from its shoulders. Quick. Painful. Victorious.

"They're here, sir," and Idusfalls in line with Vellene. "As well as, Dally—our Eternal and Guardian."

Vellene swallows. Darkness rises. A shadow of fear curls and slinks around her and Idus. Those words, she knows what they are.

Aquim Winloc, the wicked High Imperial of Scorus, has been summoned not only by a resurrected opponent but also by his maker.

## Chapter Two

# *Eledar*

A breath in and the warmest light dances over Eledar's fingers. He stretches his legs, back pressed into the cardboard wall of a Scrap shack—one of the few still standing—and squeezes a glass orb of *lumis*. It swirls in a twinkling periwinkle. A morph formulary.

The orb drains and the *lumis* sinks into his heart.

Or, at least, where a heart would be.

Eledar touches an indent in his cheek. Whether it's from a fistfight, a blast of chemight, or something he fell on in a stupor, he doesn't know. Nor does he want to know.

Pressing carefully, he pushes the clay beneath his skin back into its place and reforms his cheek.

*All this time.* He sucks in a short, painful burst of breath. *And I am still as malleable as the day I was created.*

He tilts his head to the side, cringes at the smoke that billows into his nation's sky. It blocks Alchemight's massive sun and casts a deep, unsettling darkness upon Frales.

Fire blazes into furious peaks every few miles. Chemibreakers set flame to shacks and shops as they hunt down Scraps and reap them of their chemight.

Only a block away, Scraps are strung up by their ankles and drained of their blood. Every ounce of their lives, their chemight, feeds the greed of the Imperials of Frales. Before Scraps, it was Golem hunted through these streets, melted back to clay as they chased freedom.

He can still hear their screams. The cries of those he was meant to lead. The deaths of everyone he failed.

Eledar rests his head against the wall. He stares at the heavy cloud of smoke wavering above him, listens to the symphony of screams that ring through his nation. The clang of armor. The yells of the poor and innocent. The madness of a nation without the very thing that keeps them alive: chemight.

He flexes his fingers, and the empty orb of *lumis* falls to the ground. It rolls toward a pile of bones. Chemi or creature, there's no telling who the skeletons belong to these days.

The *lumis* takes effect—what little he drained from the orb. Everything in him goes silent. The world shifts into a blurred hush. For a moment, all he knows is clay. He stretches his fingers, feels the way his joints don't exist.

He cracks his knuckles, feels the pop of each, yet no sound reaches him.

*Golem until the day I'm melted down and made into another.* His consciousness shifts realities. The *lumis* takes him back and back and back:

To a young female chemi—a certified Scrap with her greasy orange hair and shakily tattooed ink up one side of her body.

"Soffesa," he breathes as if saying her name will conjure her. As if his best friend, his sister of chance and circumstance rather than blood, never left him here to protect her family.

The family he failed to keep safe.

The father that may as well have been his.

Dead. *Dead.*

Eledar's eyes widen at the smoke. "Niam?" he calls to it as it shifts and folds into the elder chemi, bloodied and lying in an alley.

"Eledar, you must stop," the smoke whispers.

He licks his lips, struggles to his feet. "Niam, is that you?"

The smoke falls silent but for the faint wisp of laughter.

"Niam?" he tries again, this time frantic as he reaches a hand into the smoke.

It drifts between his fingers like the softest touch.

Eledar smiles at it, but his lips fall with a single inhale. His shoulders weigh him to the asphalt, to the pile of trash he sat upon. "This is where I belong," he argues with the smoke and collapses onto a broken chair.

Its wooden leg, snapped in half, jabs into his side. It tears his worn and dirtied shirt, grazes his torso.

"Abyss," he curses. He pushes a hand over the scratch as a bit of clay bubbles out of it. It tacks between his fingers, and he picks at the wound, opens it wider, deeper. Until it's a mouth of mud, rearing its ugly words.

*What about me is even real?* He closes his eyes as he curls against the ground. The *lumis* subsides, the dose not large enough. Never large enough. Not for his failures. Not for his faults.

He lies a hand over his chest. His heart beats. *But I have no heart.*

His blood quickens. *But I have no blood.*

A tingle of shame grapples him. It's smaller than years before when he felt smothered by the hollowness of his makings.

But it's still there, that doubt, always.

He swallows, his throat dry, and bursts into a fit of coughs. He braces himself as the *lumis* leaves him, as armor clinks and clatters at the opposite end of the alley.

Awareness trickles back, tries to warn him as Chemibreakers charge toward him. He's too focused on that empty orb. *Where did it go?* He drags himself across the alley, ignores the Chemibreakers that pull to a stop mere feet away as they watch him throw trash around.

Even without a formulary of chemight in it, an orb holds value. It can often be traded for small comforts but comforts nonetheless. Eledar grits his teeth.

"Looks like we missed a Scrap," one of the Chemibreakers growls. He leads the small unit of soldiers, teal hair slicked back with sweat. He brandishes a sword—not uncommon these days in Frales with the scarcity of chemight. Most of his buddies carry weapons too—daggers, bows, spears.

Eledar ignores them as he finds his empty orb and pinches it. He holds it up in victory. "Thank, Alchemight," he says with a laugh. Then, he tosses it into the air and catches it with a grin, turning to the Chemibreakers.

"What do we got here?" Eledar peers at their crests.

With the armor hiding their official ink, each of their cloaks are embroidered with the crest of the Imperial bloodline they serve. These Chemibreakers all brandish the rodenti, a smaller but fierce creature. Its impressive fangs and beady red eyes glisten with ruby-colored thread.

"Chemibreakers for the Stones." Eledar breaks into a slow clap. "Commend your service. Truly. I can't imagine this nation without the dead bodies."

"Watch your mouth," the leader hisses. "We need to drain you of your chemight, but I'm not desperate enough to allow you to insult my battalion."

Eledar raises a brow and pockets his empty *lumis* orb. His eyes narrow on the Chemibreakers lined at the back of the unit. All of them carry torches. "Gonna burn some more trash? If you don't mind me asking, what exactly does that accomplish?"

"It's a fresh start for Imperials. No Scraps. No trash." The leader takes a step forward. He extends his sword. "Come forward. Slowly. We can make this painless."

"I don't suppose we could come to some sort of agreement?" Eledar questions. No matter how much he wishes to slice these Imperial scum to pieces, he has no weapons. The only formulary he has left is one gifted by Soffesa's father, Niam, before he died.

Eledar hasn't been desperate enough to trade it for more *lumis*.

Not yet.

"Surrender yourself or be taken by force," the leader says. His blade flashes with the reflection of Alchemight's sun peeking through the smoke above.

Eledar heaves a breath and takes a step into the center of the alley. He scratches his beard, pretends to consider their offer. "Um, no. Sorry. I think I'll pass."

Fury flashes across the Chemibreakers' faces.

Eledar laughs and pivots on his heels. He works into a sprint, arms pumping, chest aching.

"Stop!" one of them shouts.

A cunning grin spreads across his lips as adrenaline bursts through his veins.

Armor clangs as the Chemibreakers move into a chase. A blast of chemight fires.

Eledar curses and bites back pain as the shot makes a gash in his bicep. Clay dribbles out and runs down his arm.

"It's a Golem!"

Eledar's breath falters, but he careens around a corner and shoots toward a line of Scrap shacks. *No no no no no—*

"Don't let him get away. He'll have more chemight in his veins than any Scrap," the leader commands.

Eledar braces himself as he leaps off the ground and latches to a dangling ladder rung off the side of one of the shacks. He grunts and pulls up the ladder to the roof, ignoring the sketched drawings of his face plastered to the side of the wall.

WANTED, they read, ELEDAR LIRIK.

He glances to the sky and steadies atop the roof. "I thought you were on my side," he growls at Alchemight's sun, wonders if the realm's Guardians, Dally and Bian, laugh down at him.

"That's him," a Chemibreaker says. They tear off one of the posters as others climb the ladder in pursuit.

Eledar strides to the other end of the roof, then scowls at the gap between this shack and the next. He sends a middle finger up to the massive sun, convinced it's mocking him.

"You're Eledar Lirik," the leader calls out. He tugs onto the roof with an amused expression.

Eledar folds his arms and sighs. He turns to the Chemibreaker. "Oh, you've heard of me?"

The leader chuckles. His eyes alight with dark rage. "You murdered Lazar Rathmore, incited the Golem revolt and turned the streets of Frales into a battlefield." The chemi looks Eledar up and down. "Now, you're living in Scrap trash, out of your mind on—what is it—*lumis*, if I had to guess by the dilation of your pupils."

As the leader talks, the others reach the roof. They take slow steps forward as if Eledar is one of the rodenti embroidered on their cloaks on the verge of scurrying away.

"I must say," the leader remarks, a smile growing on his lips, "I will enjoy cutting you open and draining you of your last breath."

Eledar prowls forward, careful not to get within snatching distance but giving him enough of a running start. "Fine," he says and matches the Chemibreaker's smile, "I'll jump, if I must."

Adrenaline sparks through him as he whirls around and sprints to the edge of the shack. He grits his teeth and tears through the air, arms and legs wild. A hysterical laugh bubbles up his throat, and he hums in contentment, wind whipping through the dark silver strands of his hair.

Bearing his weight forward, his false muscles threaten to snap with tension as he propels toward the next roof.

But his breath catches.

His momentum falters.

A lasso of red chemight latches to his ankle.

Eledar's eyes bulge. He looks down at the chemight and the several-foot drop to the asphalt it rips him toward. He tries and fails to grab the side of the next building, scraping down it with a cry of pain. He stares up as he falls, at the Chemibreakers who lean over the side of the roof.

"I'll kill you," he shouts and squeezes his eyes shut before his spine can crack against pavement.

But Eledar snaps to a stop.

He hovers above the ground, arms and legs splayed in surrender. The lasso around his ankle tightens and *tugs*.

A surprised yelp rips through his clenched teeth as he's yanked down an alley, then thrust into a shadowed alcove. He falls to concrete with a solid thunk, the lasso loosening around his ankle and curling into a gloved palm across from him.

Eledar wrenches into a fighting stance. His eyes scan the darkness and land on a hooded figure. "Clever trick. Another Chemibreaker, I presume?" he asks, fists raised in defense.

Without formularies, all he has is his natural chemight. It's not powerful enough to kill, but it's powerful enough to help him beat a face in. He summons it, the chemight's gray-colored mist steaming between his knuckles.

"Always the fighter, Lirik. I'd be impressed, but I've watched you lie in your own waste for days on end." The stranger's voice flicks between male and female, using a morph formulary to distort it. They step from the shadows and Alchemight's sun blazes across them. They're masked, cloaked, and gloved. Nothing, not even their eyes, shows. "At least that jump was valiant."

Eledar's brow furrows. "Who are you? Why have you been watching me?" Then, more assertive—"I'm not afraid to take a stranger's head."

They roll their shoulders and reach a gloved hand into the side of their cloak. They whip out a playing card. "I have a message from Equilibrium."

On the card, a crimson hourglass shines, each end shaded with a deep burgundy.

Eledar clenches his fists tighter. He doesn't dare let go of his chemight. "I want nothing to do with your so-called resistance group." He sticks his head out of the alcove, then shoves into the shadows as Chemibreakers march through the next alley.

"Strange." The masked chemi takes a step forward. Despite Eledar's wielded power and raised fists, they slip the playing card into the small, battered pocket on his shirt-front. "We're on the same side, Golem."

Eledar chuckles darkly, then slams his forearm into the figure's neck. He backs them into the wall. "Tell me who you are or die." He sharpens mist into a dagger and places it below their chin.

Their head tilts. "I think not."

A blade pricks his neck.

Eledar snaps his gaze to the side, frustrated at the sight of a weaponized formulary. Wielded as a curved emerald dagger, it's poised to slice his head clean from his shoulders.

"I can take your head, too, Lirik, and how messy that would be. All that wasted clay and potential." The chemi maneuvers from Eledar's grasp. They keep their blade extended as they step away. "Read the card. This is your only chance. We won't ask again."

Eledar launches forward when the stranger turns and sprints. He charges after them, his chemight sputtering in his fists, but they disappear in a plume of white light. He shields his eyes and falters three steps back before he releases his power.

Eledar frowns and plucks the playing card from his pocket. He stares at the hourglass and runs a thumb over the raised design. Then he turns it over.

*Dalbian's Abyss. When the moons rise*, the card reads in small, precise ink.

His frown deepens. He peers at the sky. The sun has reached its apex, about an hour from pinching into its three, nightly moons.

"Hey!" someone cries behind him.

Eledar swivels around and tucks the card into his shirtfront.

The leader of the Chemibreaker unit rushes toward him, sword outstretched.

"Oh, look at you. You found me," Eledar mutters and shoots the Chemibreaker an irritated glare. "Not in the mood," he says louder.

The rest of the unit rounds a corner and joins their leader. Some wield formularies along with their weapons, attacks waiting to spark off their fingers.

Eledar sighs and pivots. He darts between Scrap shacks on fire and lets the flames lick his skin. It will heal. Eventually.

In the distance, a sea of tar and mist roars. Dalbian's Abyss.

He sprints free of ruined shacks and burning debris, then clamps down on his tongue and runs for the abyss.

*Only because I'm curious,* he tells himself, spotting the outcrop of ruined ships lining the shore—the stronghold of Equilibrium.

## CHAPTER THREE

# *VELLENE*

The Convocation of the Eternal. Vellene dreamed of the day she would be introduced, dreamed of possible allies and freedom.

Then, five years ago, the two nations of Alchemight—Scorus and Frales—combusted with change.

Once, Aquim Winloc was nothing more than an egotistical High Imperial of Scorus thwarted by the Convocation of the Eternal, a delegation put in place to prescribe balance between the nations. In particular, it was Lazar Rathmore, High Imperial of Frales, who kept her father in check. They both wanted to conquer Alchemight.

Vellene guesses their want was so great, it was a matter of time before it corrupted them both.

In a night, Golem, the servants of Fralian Imperials, revolted. Lazar Rathmore, their Master, was murdered. His son and only heir disappeared—presumed dead. It was the perfect time to strike, and so Aquim did. While Frales fell to chaos, he stole the source of all chemight from its neutral location and hid it.

With Frales cut off, he knew the only thing standing in his way were the two other Imperial bloodlines of Scorus: the Vonners and Pineskys.

Their heads line Winloc Grove's front hallway.

When chemi die, their souls turn to mist and their bones ooze to tar. The chemight in their veins releases back into Alchemight.

However, if a chemi dies by a blade, their body will never be reclaimed by the realm. Unlike chemight or starvation, death by a blade isn't perceived as natural. It's not any worse than being pulverized by a formulary or caving in on your stomach, but the Guardians must frown upon it. Hate the violence of a blade.

So, despite all his formularies, despite having captured the source of all power in Alchemight—it was not chemight, power, or poison Aquim brandished; it was a steel blade. A long sword embossed with a crawling spideria.

With a smile, he claimed his prizes.

Trapped beneath polished glass, their mouths gape in silent screams, skin drooping with preserved sorrow. The heads rest atop pedestals. There are no plaques, no memoriam. Within the year, they will be skulls. Forever, they will be nameless. Nameless except to Vellene. The Vonners and Pineskys are whispers, gossip.

Perhaps, she shouldn't be envious of the dead.

But at least these mouths get to talk. Even if it is through the tongue-wags of others.

Near the end of the hall, an empty pedestal stands. There was a night not long after her mother died and her voice was taken that her father paralyzed her before it.

It stands taller than the others, crested in silver. A chandelier lights it from above. Her father's sword, crusted with the black tar of chemi blood he never dared to wipe away, is mounted to the wall behind it, sitting in the shadow of the spotlight like a dark promise. The pedestal sits pristine and empty. No head—just a whisper of her own.

"It will be yours," Aquim said into her ear. He stood behind her, hands digging into her shoulders. "Unless you obey."

It was hours before she could move. Her eyes went bloodshot. Her throat ached with an unfurled shout. When Idus retrieved her, he grabbed her behind the neck, set her feet free, and charged her to her room.

Vellene stands before her pedestal now. She eyes it at least once a day, challenges herself to look beyond it. To see a future where her head remains on her shoulders, a future where she is more than another nameless, open-mouthed scream.

Achievement flickers through her. Tonight is the first night she's won that challenge. With the Convocation gathered on the other side of the door across from her, Vellene knows all bets are off. New cards are being laid out on the table, and she needs to know what they are.

She sucks in a breath and enters the Reading Room. It's one of her places of peace at Winloc Grove. Her father and Mogaell were never readers, nor have they ever cared for research. If they need a tome, they send a Utility to scrounge around the towering shelves. But she enjoys the room, the soft tick of its clock, and the musty smell of old words. She hates that the meeting is being held here. It's as if the room knows it's been invaded by the most unjust, every shelf a dark leering beast.

Her heart slams at the sight of three familiar faces.

Just like Scorus had three Imperial bloodlines—Winloc, Vonner, Pinesky—Frales has Rathmore, Stone, and Caligari. On either side, a bloodline has an equal in power. Winlocs and Rathmores are High Imperials, gifted with more potent chemight in their veins. Then came the Vonners and Stones. Last, the Pineskys and Caligari.

Idus leans close and nods toward a stout man with a bald head and an emerald beard. "Xenos Caligari," he says in a low voice. Then, he tilts his chin toward a pink-haired woman. "Evanora Stone."

He doesn't bother to address the third.

The Guardian's presence is enough of an introduction. *Dally*. To see a Guardian—a being capable of creating worlds, creating living beings—is a sight Vellene wasn't sure she'd ever witness. Even her father and Idus look shocked to see her.

The Guardian is clad in gray and silver garments. Her hair falls to her spine in waves of rich silver. Her skin is dark, wrinkled, and spotted, yet she holds herself with confidence and youth. Beyond that, she glows. Like a silver flame, she exudes radiance. She is eternal life, and she is *angry*.

Dally's gaze flashes to Vellene's throat, and her lips curl in displeasure.

Vellene rubs an arm. Discomfort flings through her, but she rolls her shoulders back and tries to portray strength.

"Two cowards and an Eternal of our Convocation," Aquim growls, his voice ice. It snaps through the Reading Room and echoes between the crevices of tomes. "It sounds like the start of a joke, and it must be, as I see no Rathmore."

A dark chuckle creeps from beside the large, standing clock against the far wall, and a chemi drenched in plum suede and golden threads peels from the shadows.

Tall, broad-shouldered, and cheekbones as defiant as the jagged scar that runs diagonally across his face, a Rathmore strolls forth. The proof—the Rathmore crest inked across his chest, the ravian, a flight creature, exposed by the deep v of his black gossamer shirt tucked beneath his velvet cloak.

The cloak sweeps the floor as he walks, long legs prowling forward as if he owns the place, and the dark snarl on his face confirms just as much. Two, twin strands of yellow hair curl in at the caverns of his cheeks, while the rest is stark white and slicked back. His violet eyes—another Rathmore trademark—hold Aquim's.

He does not tremble, does not cower, as his words crawl through the room. "Thank you, Winloc. I'm one for grand entrances, and you provided the best."

"You will both hold your tongues, or I will take them from you," Dally snarls.

Aquim turns his rage toward the Guardian. "You are brave to come here. Even you do not overpower me, not when I have the source."

Dally's eyes flash. "I am here because I was called. I may not overpower you? I don't see the source in this room."

Vellene has never seen her father embarrassed, but in this moment, he flushes with heat.

He turns to Evanora and Xenos. "You have some nerve crawling out of your holes. You're lucky I don't take your heads where you stand."

"Oh, give it up," Evanora snaps and Vellene decides she likes the chemi. Very much. Evanora runs a hand through her pink bob, ruffling it with an annoyed expression. "We just want what's ours."

"You lost it." Aquim clenches his fists. "You were careless, and I took it." He looks to Dally again, this time with less rage and more certainty. "Don't pretend with us. You know I now hold the right to the source. They created those Golem abominations."

The Guardian's face sours, but she doesn't refute Aquim's claim.

Xenos' entire head scrunches, his baldness showing where the lines of his scalp ripple with nervousness. It makes sense. Of all the bloodlines in this room, his is the weakest.

Evanora, however, has fewer qualms about hierarchy. "Kadir is alive. The Rathmores have been the High Imperials of Frales since the beginning of time. He deserves what's his, and Frales needs a leader." She glares at Aquim. "While we do not wish to negotiate with you, we must. The war rages, and we are leeching what we can from Scraps but not enough."

*Leeching?* Vellene frowns.

"I can very well speak for myself, Stone." Lazar Rathmore's son props against one of the tall, leather-backed chairs. One foot tossed over an ankle, his expression is a perfect complacent. Everything about him is meticulously picked over.

*Kadir*, she whispers his name through her mind. He looks older than her by a couple of years, and when she peers at him closer, she notices another white scar across the length of his neck as if someone tried to saw his head from his shoulders. Maybe someone had tried, but something about the quiet violence behind his violet gaze tells her they didn't live to tell the tale.

She wonders if he wears his scars in the same way her father puts heads on pedestals. Victories. No matter how ugly.

"I'll put it simply," Kadir says. "I want my seat on the Convocation. I want to make choices for my nation."

"You are nothing but a boy," Aquim sneers.

"Whether the source is wielded by one or all, this Convocation is not disbanded," Dally interjects. Her voice commands the attention of the room, deeply magnetic. "Whether you like it or not, you have not sent an army to Frales. It is a nation. Their nation. Until you conquer all of Alchemight, as I know you plan to do, this Convocation will exist."

Her father cracks his neck. "My troops are preparing. It won't be long." He says it with a devilish sheen to his face, lips quirked and creating sinister grooves. His gaze sweeps across Kadir, Evanora, and Xenos, but only Xenos squirms under it.

Kadir clears his throat, the sound drawing everyone's eyes back to him. He must enjoy being a showman, his eyes glinting with mischievous desire as the room falls silent, waiting for him to speak. "I called this meeting to make a deal. Give me my seat, allow Frales to take a small percentage of the source's power, and we will not wage war on you."

He smiles then, but it's not a full smile. It climbs halfway as if he's baring his teeth. For a moment, his eyes reflect the sentiment—feral and wild.

Vellene remembers then that he's been lost—a chemi back from the dead. Where was the grave they dug him out of?

"We've spent the last five years building armies as Scraps and Golem revolted. We have grown in strength, prepared for every outcome." Kadir brings himself to his full height. "We melted Golem back to clay, bled our Scraps dry. We have talons now, Aquim. Don't underestimate a nation starved of power. We won't stop until we have it again."

The silence that follows is deafening.

Even her father, ever the chemi of never-ending threats, holds his tongue.

It fills Vellene with such a strange feeling. *Hope.* She's felt it once or twice before, but in the presence of Kadir Rathmore, of this strong-willed opponent to her father, she pictures a future beyond the pedestal—her father's head upon it, and Kadir's grip on the sword.

"Give us enough for electricity, heat, and nutrients. That's all I ask," Kadir continues after relishing the pause. "Then, our army will stay in Frales, where you will be free to attack it on your terms."

"I would be a fool to give you power," Aquim hisses.

Dally raises a pointed finger and Vellene's chest hollows. "Perhaps your heiress should get a say? She is only a few weeks shy of her 18th birthday, is she not?"

The pedestal glows at the back of her mind, her father's sword dripping with the ink-black tar of her blood. *Yours*, his words echo, *Unless you obey.*

Aquim looks at her then, as Idus sinks his sharp, dirty nails into her bicep. It's as if they both think she can speak.

"You have taken her voice," Dally barks. "Restore it."

Vellene's fingers twitch as the Fralian Imperials all look at her. It's Kadir's gaze that draws her attention. Despite his calm, calculated demeanor and cold face, the violet of his eyes flickers with a wrathful storm. She flinches away from it, casting her eyes anywhere else.

"Do it, Aquim," the Guardian growls. "I won't stand for such abuse."

Vellene's hands ball into fists. She hates the pity laced into those words as if she's a small, helpless child. What do they know of silence with their grand statements of war and pledges of power? Silence is one of the only weapons Vellene has these days, and as long as her power is bound within her, she knows it grows. *Feed the embers*, she tells herself when she looks in mirrors or bites her tongue before her father. It's been months without a voice, but it's been years with no way to fight back. Shackled in the cold cellars beyond their property. Locked in her room for days without sustenance. Beaten. Torn. Bled. Refused.

If they give her a voice now, she'll erupt.

And yet as mist streams from her father's palm and descends upon her throat to drench it with sound—

Vellene can't find anything but pressed lips and a trapped sob.

Her father's lips slide into the smile of a battle won. Their battle. He's trampled her into what he wants. Obedient.

The embers are stoked but silent. She waits for them to explode, waits for a rush of courage, but a daunting, horrible thought occurs to her. Has all her pretending to be subservient, to be quiet, left her a shell of herself? Did the screams for her mother's death root themselves into a void she will forever wander through, desperate to set them free?

The room waits for her to speak, but the longer she takes, the lower her head bows. It's as if her body isn't her own. Every bit of her was stolen and remade by her father's abuse and her mother's death. Her gut stirs with sorrow, a beast gnawing at the iron bars of an impenetrable cage, and her eyes burn.

Disappointment wafts off Dally before she states, "Very well. Aquim, name your price. How do you wish for Frales to pay for their slice of the source?"

*Pay.* The word lights her father's face. "How about I give?" His navy eyes turn to Vellene, dark and never benevolent.

Aquim does not give. He takes and takes until even what he borrows is stolen.

"A birthday present for my daughter." His eyes glint with satisfaction.

She imagines all the ways he could burn. How his flesh would melt and his mouth would crane back. So easily she could force a sword down his throat in that instant. So simple she could show him what it is to swallow a weapon and never let it free. But her throat clenches. Her fingers shake. She fills with the need to punish herself, to die, to never think ill of her father even if she has never wanted anything more. She stares at her boots in horror.

"Take her, Rathmore, and I'll never have to take her head."

For all his preciseness, Kadir looks stricken. His eyes widen with the request, and his lips slip into an unsettling scowl.

*Take me?*

"You want enough power to feed your Imperials? Stop reaping from the blood of Scraps and start taking it from her." Her father stands taller as he speaks. "If she remains here, she will die. You all know my intentions, and they don't involve an heir. Not for a few years, and I have Mogaell for that."

His soulless gaze drifts to Vellene's, not a sign of remorse among his hardened exterior. "Put her blood to use. Make her life meaningful."

"You want me to drain your daughter of her chemight and use it to fuel my nation?" Kadir asks, tongue sharp as a whip with accusation. His eyes are dark as he scans Vellene over. "What happens when she's dead?"

"Infuse with her, and she won't die. You'll feel when she's on the verge of death and be able to stop pulling from her. Then, have someone mend her and start the process over. She's of an original bloodline. The power will be enough to feed you."

*Infusion?* Vellene's fists ball at her sides.

Kadir opens his mouth, an objection ready to slide from his tongue, but the weeping, grieving thing inside her manages to slither up her throat.

"No," she hisses, but it's scratchy and half-there. She was afraid she'd forgotten the word, terrified it left her with the rest of her willpower. Her throat burns, and she throws a glare of steel at her father. "You cannot force me to Infuse. I won't link my life to another only to be leeched from."

But it's as if she's said nothing.

"I won't give you the source, but I will give you my daughter," Aquim says.

Vellene's tongue sharpens. She prepares to wield it, but Kadir steps forward.

His lips quirk into a grin of sin, and his eyes spark with wrath as they comb over her body. "I accept."

## CHAPTER FOUR

# ELEDAR

Alchemight's sun pulls apart into its three moons as Eledar reaches the edge of Frales. He crouches behind a pile of debris.

Scraps patrol the border of Equilibrium.

He glances over his shoulder. No matter how badly the Chemibreakers want Eledar's power, they aren't brave enough to face off with Equilibrium. Their cloaked and armored forms pace the resistance group's border, no doubt waiting for Eledar to make his way back to them.

*I don't see why they're so afraid*, he thinks as he surveys the Equilibrium recruits who patrol the border.

The Scraps, separating the shore of Dalbian's Abyss from the rest of Frales, are thin. Dark circles hang below their eyes. They wear used armor, chest pieces chipped and dented.

Equilibrium has more Scraps than Imperials have Chemibreakers. Without formularies on their side, Imperials use weapons and hand-to-hand combat like everyone else. Scraps, forever-starving, are adept in both. Plus, they're far more starved. That makes them dangerous, no matter their cause.

He plays with the edges of the playing card and sizes up the guards. He could take three or four of them with ease, but at least twenty are on patrol. He grips the card and stands, hoping it's enough to get him through the border without a fight.

The two closest Scraps raise weapons.

Eledar takes slow steps forward and lifts the card. "You sent for me," he calls.

They exchange a look, an hourglass inked on the side of their necks flashing in the moonlight. It's identical to the one on the card. "State your name," one of them calls, a female chemi.

"Eledar," he says and takes another step forward. "Someone in a mask gave this card to me. Told me to meet them here."

"It's the Golem," the Scrap beside her whispers loud enough for anyone within a five-foot radius to hear. It's a male, his voice lilted with youth. He lights up with excitement and scratches the back of his head, tousling a mess of forest green curls. He must be in his early teens, but he grips a broad sword with his free hand as firm as any expert. He slips the blade into its scabbard at his waist and hurries to close the distance between him and Eledar. He extends a wrist.

"Sir Lirik, it's pleasure." His voice breaks around the words as if he struggles to put them together in a way that makes sense.

Eledar stares at his extended wrist. "And you are?"

The warm olive of his skin flushes red. "Oh, I no one, sir. Just Scrap like everyone here." He nods to his friend.

Unlike the boy chemi, her face is wary. She keeps her sword drawn as she moves in and wraps a protective arm over the teen's shoulders. *Siblings*, Eledar realizes—her hair the same green. They even share the same caramel-colored gaze, flecks of gold littered throughout.

"I Thomae, and this my sister, Tatiania," the boy says. He bounces on his toes, and his extended hand tremors.

Eledar raises a brow but clasps Thomae's wrist. All wrist clasps are a sign of trust. He doesn't typically hand them out so freely, but the giddiness across the kid's face makes him grin. Then he offers Tatiania the same respect and holds his hand toward her.

Her chin-length hair slopes against the sharp angles of her face as she looks him over. She purses her lips but puts her sword away and clasps his wrist. "Call me Tat."

Eledar nods and drops his hand. He looks past them to Equilibrium's stronghold.

Four shipwrecks are stationed along the shore. Their hulls are battered, sails torn through. They're skeletons of ships patched with trash and strung together with rope bridges. They've been made Scrap, and from the second's mast hangs a burgundy flag with an hourglass embroidered. It whips in the wind as thick mist curls around it.

"You said you were asked to be here." Tat snatches the playing card tucked in Eledar's palm. She flips it over to the message before she peers at the moons. "You're late."

"I was a bit preoccupied when your friend invited me," Eledar grumbles and yanks the playing card back. "He forgot to mention his name."

Thomae opens his mouth, but Tat squeezes his shoulder to silence him.

She grins. "Nice try, but we know our leader wishes to remain anonymous."

"Then why am I here?" Eledar stuffs the card into his pocket.

Tat glances behind her.

The mist from Dalbian's Abyss swallows the ships along the shore, crawling forward to claim the night.

"Follow us," she says and tugs her brother toward the mist.

Eledar prowls after them, but Thomae slows and matches Eledar's stride.

The kid beams at him.

Eledar glances down but keeps his focus on Tat and the mist-covered path ahead. "Is there something you want?"

Thomae cracks his knuckles with a smile. "How you do it?"

"Do what?"

"Start uprising."

Eledar clears his throat. "I just did."

"That cool."

A laugh bubbles on the tip of his tongue. "You don't say?"

Thomae pushes up the sleeves of his black canvas shirt. "If not for you, then my sister and I would died from starvation. You gave us chance, sir."

"Call me Eledar. Please."

"Okay. Eledar." Thomae nods with a satisfied smirk. "You know, I never thought I see the day I meet you: chemi who freed Scraps."

Uneasiness squirms through Eledar. "I don't know about freed. Scraps are hunted through the streets now. Golem are dead."

Thomae waves a hand. "Because they stupid enough to stay out there. If they come here, they be fed and safe."

"How exactly do you remain fed?" Eledar asks.

Thomae licks his lips. "Well, our leader—"

"Thomae," Tat hisses, turning to them with wide eyes. "Shut your mouth. Now."

"So, the wrist clasp was for show, I take it?" Eledar directs toward the sister.

"What made you think that?" she replies with mock innocence.

Eledar offers a small smile to the boy. “Thanks, anyway.”

Thomae shrugs but he glares at his sister's back. “You freed us.”

“Right,” Eledar says, but the unease anchors in the pit of his stomach.

He slows as they reach the edge of the abyss, where the rocks of the Fralian shore fade into a bubbling sea of tar and the massive shadows of ships.

“Wait here,” Tat commands and grabs her brother’s hand. “If you move, then someone will kill you thinking you’re an intruder. So, keep your curiosity tamed.”

“You don’t want to invite me into your precious stronghold?” Eledar remarks and folds his arms.

Tat merely glares at him and drags Thomae up a wooden plank. It slants to the deck of one of the ships.

He runs a hand through his hair and blows out a breath as he scans the mist around him. He frowns and makes a slow circle to make out any shadows of guards.

“You came.”

He jolts and spins.

Before him stands his mysterious stranger. Outfitted in black, masked beyond recognition, voice distorted with chemight, the figure is a spirit of darkness.

“You shouldn’t sneak up on me,” Eledar warns. His chemight is sharp between his knuckles on instinct, his muscles tensed for a fight.

The cloaked chemi folds their gloved hands. "Maybe you should be more aware."

Eledar runs his tongue over his teeth. "Uh-huh. Okay. You got me here. What do you want?"

They tilt their head in consideration. "I want to save Frales."

"Sure."

"What if I told you I could give you new Golem to lead?" the stranger asks, their voice hard.

Dread sweeps through Eledar, and he grimaces. "I'd say you're a fool for attempting to make more and a greater fool for thinking I'd believe you could."

"I will." But they pause and their shoulders stiffen. Then they wave a gloved hand. "Or I won't," they reply simply, "when I have the source in my possession. That will be up to you." They gesture back to one of the ships, its bow poking through the mist. "This resistance needs the source, and we need it soon. I'm willing to offer you a deal if you help me secure it."

"Why should I help you with anything? I'm not part of your group, and I have no interest in joining."

They pace. "Everything you've fought for—Golem, your friend's family, yourself—is gone. Everything except the future."

Eledar barks out a rough laugh. "This is Frales. There is no future. Only tomorrow's misery."

Their head bobs with a slow nod. "I can understand why you have that mentality, but it's not what Frales has to be. Equilibrium is the future. It's not Scraps. Not Imperials. It's chemi as one unified kind. Equals in life. Equals in death."

"Oh, that's great." Eledar claps in sarcasm. "Idealism. I thought that died decades ago."

"This is not a joke, Lirik," the chemi snarls, their careful tone sharpening. "You once led Golem to revolt. You instigated the war. Gave Scraps the opportunity to uprise with you and your species. I am asking—kindly if I might add—for you to finish what you've started."

Eledar grows stiff from the painful, wrathful truth.

"Do you not care about the lives lost due to your actions?" the chemi presses. "Do you not wish to make right all the destruction you created rather than live in filth and rot, letting your life fade between *lumis* formularies?"

"Watch your tongue," Eledar growls as chemight steams from his palms. "I won't hesitate to cut it out." He steps toward the chemi. "You know nothing about me. What you think you've seen is not who I truly am."

The stranger matches Eledar's step forward, their mask close. "Then show me. Show Frales who you truly are. Be the hero I know you so desperately wish to be. Because let me tell you, Lirik, now is not the time for cowards and mourning. Now is the time to strike, and we won't get another chance like this."

His jaw tightens. "What would you have me do?"

They relax, their shoulders falling beneath their thick cloak. "We're building a proper ship, but we have smaller boats. Take one to Scorus. Secure the source, then contact us." They straighten. "We will retrieve it."

Eledar traces his gaze over the stranger's frame. "What will you do with all that power?"

"I will restore balance." They lift their chin. "I will remake the Convocation of the Eternal in the name of equality."

Eledar heaves a breath. He knows little about the Convocation, just that it's run by the heads of the six Imperial bloodlines. All decisions have always been made in the favor of Imperials. "You would give Scraps a voice?"

They nod. "Yes, as well as Utilities, a type of chemi over in Scorus, and Golem, as well. If any are left beside you. You could each elect a leader, someone to speak on your behalf and make decisions. It would be a true council."

"That's a lofty assignment. What makes you qualified to take on such a task?" Eledar persists, wary.

The chemi falls silent for a moment. Then, they say calmly, "I'm not qualified. But I do not seek power for myself. I do not wish for any kind of selfish gain. I want to put an end to a bloody and pointless war."

"How selfless of you," Eledar says. He clucks his tongue. "Mighty selfless. I don't buy it." Then he adds, "Also, I have no interest in resurrecting Golem. They deserve peace, and until you achieve your goal—if what you're saying is even true—I don't wish to bring more into this world only for them to suffer."

"Fine." The chemi clasps their hands behind their back. "Then how about we bargain with your freedom? Get me the source, and I'll give you your Master."

He freezes. "I have no Master. Lazar Rathmore is dead."

"And what, you believe Lazar fell down some stairs at precisely the right time to allow his Golem to uprise?" They shake their head. "Lazar Rathmore was murdered, which means—"

"That chemi now holds the strings to all Golem," Eledar breathes. "That can't be true. I haven't felt a tug on my strings in more than five years. If someone had that power, they would've used it."

"Perhaps they're waiting for the right time," the chemi continues.

"Who is it?" Eledar prompts.

The chemi behind the mask *tsks*. "That's not how this works. Get me the source, and I'll give you a name." They extend a gloved hand. "What do you say, Lirik? Do we have a deal?"

"You do realize Aquim Winloc has the source, correct?" Eledar pushes. "This isn't some easy task where I can just stroll in, grab it and get out. You're asking me to put my life on the line."

They tilt their head from side to side. "Yes, but how much of a life is it when you could be commanded by another at any moment?"

Eledar swallows. It's a selfish reason to help Scraps in need. Guilt fills him as he considers clasping the chemi's wrist. But how many years has he fought for everyone but himself? He won't be manipulated again. He presses his lips together and grabs hold of the stranger's wrist. "Deal."

They nod to the ships, all but faded by the mist. "Then welcome to Equilibrium, Eledar Lirik."

# CHAPTER FIVE

# *VELLENE*

Vellene strides down the hall. Her blood riles as she passes the pedestals of her father's conquests. The dead, soulless eyes of the Vonners and Pineskys drill into her. *Infusion.* She careens through the labyrinth that leads to her room and throws open her door. She locks it shut behind her.

She doesn't know when Kadir will claim her. All she knows is it will not happen. Not if she can stop it.

Vellene braces herself on her knees. She rakes in large, uneven breaths before she scrambles to the loose floorboard beneath her bed and pries it open. She fumbles for the little pile of keepsakes. Some are jewels she took from her mother's room before Aquim had it torn apart. Another is a small stuffed parduseus her sister gave her before they quit talking. Finally, she finds a small slip of paper—the same piece she's held onto since her mother's death five months earlier.

She unfolds it. The fear inside her falls silent at the sight of her mother's cursive. *Never forget*, reads one side, each loop of the letters drawn with a panic-stricken hand. Vellene wishes she knew what she's meant to remember. There are so many things she's forced herself to be rid of, to never seek out in the recesses of her mind. Life is easier that way.

Then, she turns the paper over and touches its singular word. *Run.* Her nerves rush at the thought of leaving. It would break every rule to leave Winloc Grove. Her attention pulls to the stuffed parduseus, it's whiskers crooked and feline eyes cold with lost memories. She would have to leave her sister. *Maybe she'll come with me*, Vellene thinks as she shoves everything into its place beneath the floorboard.

She and Mogaell are estranged. They've always been different. Aquim broke Vellene and molded her into the fearful daughter he prefers. However, Mogaell has a darkness to her, one Aquim likes. Her sister never needed a reason to disobey Aquim, because they share the same thirst for power.

*That doesn't make her any less my sister.* Vellene takes to the halls and ducks her head into each of Mogaell's haunts. When they were young, they'd play hide and seek, share secrets, love each other. Then, Mogaell learned Vellene would get their father's seat on the Convocation and continual favor for being first-born.

Vellene slows as she spots the shadowed, petite frame of her sister curled in a window nook. It's always a shock to see Mogaell, the stern resemblance of Aquim in all her features. Mogaell resents her for that, too. Vellene looks in the mirror and sees a piece of their mother anytime she wants. Mogaell has nothing. Only Aquim.

"You'd be a horrible spy," Mogaell says, her voice the perfect balance of soft and cruel. She turns her navy eyes to Vellene, the black of her hair slinking over her shoulders like oil. The orange light of the chandelier above highlights the blue hue of the dark strands. A Winloc, through and through. "You clomp when you walk." Mogaell crosses her arms and leans into the wall of her nook.

"I wasn't trying to sneak up on you." Vellene props against an archway. "I came to talk."

Mogaell sighs and runs a finger over the silk of her gown. It's far more intricate than Vellene's, crafted by a skilled Utility chemi. "Why do you want to talk to someone who hates you, sister?"

Vellene frowns but holds Mogaell's gaze. "I can't change being born before you."

"Nor can I change being born second. My resentment is a curse as much as your inexplicable fear of power." Mogaell snorts and rolls her eyes. "Still cowering with daddy? I see he gave you your voice back, at least."

"I do what I need to do to protect us." Vellene breaks their stare off and looks at her feet. "You don't know what I've been through to keep you safe."

"Save the chivalry, Vellene." Mogaell shoves out of her perch and straightens her gown. She's a foot shorter than Vellene but somehow manages to stand like a looming shadow. "I've never asked for your help, and I don't want it. Father and I have an understanding."

Vellene takes in a steadying breath, remembering why she's avoided Mogaell for the better half of a year. "I'm leaving."

Mogaell laughs. "Oh?"

"Yes." Vellene clears her throat. "Come with me."

Her sister tilts her head at that. "Where exactly are you going?"

"I don't know, but I'll find somewhere." She lowers her voice. "We aren't safe here anymore."

Mogaell scowls and waves her sister off. "If you want to leave, then leave."

Vellene's nails squeeze into her palms. "What?"

"I don't need you, Vellene. I never have. If your life is in danger, then leave."

"Both of our lives are in danger. Can't you see that? Mother is dead. He probably killed her."

"He didn't." Mogaell crosses her arms. Her fierce expression slips into something cold and unforgivable. "I did."

Vellene's heart drops.

"I killed her," Mogaell says. Her voice wavers, but she swallows and the next words come controlled and precise. "I proved myself to father. He wants threats eliminated, and Aurora was one of them."

"Aurora?" Vellene screeches. "You killed our mother?"

Mogaell's eyes flash. "Yes, and I'd do it again. She was going to ruin everything."

Vellene shakes her head. "You're lying."

"I'm not, and if you know what's good for you, then you will run, Vellene." Mogaell stalks forward. Her face darkens in a way Vellene has never seen before. The navy of her eyes turns wholly black. "I chose father. It's time you make your choice, too, but don't make it on my account." Her fists clench, knuckles white. "Months. We are months apart in age, and yet you have always looked down upon me as if I am some small, helpless child. I refuse to live in your shadow another day. So, yes, Vellene. Leave. I don't want you here. I never have. I never will."

"I never meant to hurt you. I wanted to protect you from him. I wanted to give you room to breathe because I've never been able to," Vellene whispers, her voice hoarse with grief.

Mogaell's darkness draws back for a split second, the smallest bit of remorse poking through. She sucks in a breath and shakes her head. "All you've ever done," she says, her voice soft but sure, "is suffocate me with your presence."

Vellene takes one long look at her sister, convinced maybe this is a nightmare. Maybe she's asleep, and if she digs her nails hard enough into her palms, she will wake. But only pain comes. It ignites where her fingers leave indents. It cracks through her broken heart.

Vellene shakes her head. "I'm sorry," she murmurs and leaves her sister behind.

"I'm sorry, too," Mogaell whispers to her back, "for everything that comes next."

Vellene frowns but hurries to her room. She wastes no time and yanks her orb pouch from her bedpost. She ties it at her waist, then she fills it with every formulary she has left of her allowance before she moves to the lamp by her bed, the chandelier in the ceiling, and the box on her dresser that pushes out heat. She frees them of their orbs, their formularies, and adds more to her pouch. She doesn't bother with anything else besides wrapping in her cloak, too furious, confused, and tired to think realistically about the journey ahead.

Standing before her mirror, she forces her uncontrollable purple, green, and blue curls into a bun. Then she pops formularies into each of her chemight deposits—three on either side of her neck, seven along her chest.

The last thing she grabs is her mother's note. She tucks it into the pouch, and her scavenged formularies clink at her hip as she lifts her hood and strolls through the shadows of her home. *This is no home*, she reminds herself. Her eyes meet those of the dismembered heads that line the hall to the front doors. *This is a prison, and I cannot stay*. Still, she hesitates when she reaches one of the large, double doors.

Somewhere deep within her, she knows there must be strength. It's hammered into submission, but it's there. *Please*, she begs it. Her hand hovers over the handle. Her father's pedestal—the one marked for her head—burns into her spine as if Aquim stands ready to strike her down with his sword. Her gaze roams the shadows for her sister. Instead, the hall sits empty but for the open, rotting mouths of the Vonners and Pineskys. Their screams are silent.

But hers doesn't have to be.

She grits her teeth and shoulders open the door.

Gusts of wind ram into her, Scorus raging at her side. A shard storm blasts through the night. Its black clouds drown the light from Alchemight's moons. Shards of tar have yet to thunder down from the sky. It's as if the storm, too, holds its breath, willing to slice her nation if she's willing to fight, too.

Vellene almost turns around. She almost says, *Tomorrow*.

But her mother's note burns from its place in her pouch. *Run.*

"Run," Vellene whispers to her feet.

Shouts of Chemibreakers and Utilities crowd the space behind her. With the door of the chateau slammed open by the wind, there's no turning back. This is it. This storm is what stands between her death and her freedom.

*RUN*, comes the command a third time.

Finally, she does what she does best. She obeys.

## Chapter Six

# *Vellene*

Wind wails against her ears, thrashes through her robes as Vellene charges through the downpour of the shard storm. Her heart gives frantic thuds as the storm's sharp fragments of crystallized tar thunk onto her cloak and wedge into its thick fabric. She pulls the thing tighter around her frame, head down to avoid cuts to her face. Quick glances to her left and right tell her she's the only chemi fool enough to brave the anger of Alchemight.

Vellene ducks into an alcove between two Scrap shacks and presses against one of their mismatched walls of stone, wood, cloth, tin, coils—whatever could be found on the street to slap together a somewhat formidable home. They tower around her, most several teetering stories high with rickety wooden ladders reaching various holes.

She peers down the path she came, at the wealth of chateaus and vibrant gardens blocked by a wrought-iron fence and gate. Dark shards pierce through the night, clink and clatter to the asphalt, then melt into puddles of tar. The black ooze splashes up her boots and clings to her shins.

Vellene slows and watches the gate. Her heart pounds in her throat. *No Chemibreakers. No Idus.* Her lips slip into a devilish grin. *I'm free.*

She crouches, relaxes. Every worry tucked between her brows smooths into a moment of bliss. Some shards nick through her cloak and make thin slices across her back and shoulders, where her simple gown leaves them bare and exposed.

The blood is warm. The pain warrants a hiss, but she keeps her smile. This pain—it's hers. It's not his bruises, his cuts and broken bones.

This pain? This pain is freedom.

Vellene burrows into her cloak, listens to the symphony of the shards as they crash into asphalt. Her smile fades. Her mind wanes toward the dark tendrils of sleep. Exhaustion of the day and its revelations weigh her.

Then comes the noise.

The final shard hits the pavement. The wind's wails quiet to their nightly whispers, and late-night Scorus awakens. Free from the day raids of Imperials, stew houses ring their bells for hot bowls and cold brews. Scraps and Utilities hit the streets, eager for fresh orbs—Scraps in their torn, dirtied clothing, and Utilities just as dirty but tucked into robes that blaze with the Imperial family's crest they serve.

Vellene sucks in a breath at their lean, almost-skeletal bodies. At the way many limp, beg, and hang onto life with desperation. She was never allowed beyond the Imperial gates. Never trusted to see the nation she's meant to make decisions for. She knew there was poverty and tension. But this? Vellene stands, legs shaking as tar dries to her skin and hardens.

Heads turn her way. *You do not belong*, their eyes scream. Her—with her crisp Imperial cloak, her Winloc crest and its diamond-shaped, spindly-legged spideria inked above her breasts. She realizes her mistake too late. Her chemight deposits swirl with vibrant formularies from the back of her ears to across her chest. She is the portrait of their greatest desire, and everything in her tenses as their faces warp with hunger and anger.

Vellene takes several steps back.

"Imperial out of its cage, come to play?" A Scrap chemi joins her in the shadows. His frame fills the entrance to the alley, shoulders broad and clad in tied-together rags. Ink wraps around his wrists, the needlework done by a shaky hand, maybe even his own. He smiles with rotted teeth, looks at Vellene with desperate eyes.

Another. This one small. A child forced to grow older with each blink of his bruised eyes, every breath through cracked lips. Tar from the shard storm clings to his hair and plasters it against his forehead. “Look at her. Bet she’d fetch a nice reward.”

“How many orbs, you reckon?”

“A dozen, I’d say. Of course, we could always just take the ones she stupidly flaunts.”

Vellene licks her lips, holds up a hand. “Don’t come closer.” Her voice shakes, and she wishes she wore more than her simple gown. The pale blue fabric hugs the curves of her body in a way that makes their eyes grow hungrier, vicious.

The Scraps grin at each other, then clench their fists. Orange chemight erupts across their knuckles.

“Pay up, princess, because you’re already costing us,” the larger one says. He raises his fists for emphasis. The chemight dances across his knuckles, sourced from orbs tucked in his fists.

*My father will hang you*, she thinks and cringes at the thought.

She wonders if these two Scraps knew the three hanging in her yard. She wonders if they care that her father is Aquim Winloc. Something about their viciousness tells her they know exactly who she is, and it’s all the more reason to strike her down.

Vellene reaches for the strength of her weaponized formularies. They vibrate in their chemight deposits. The unique conductors siphon the formularies from their orbs and into her bloodstream. However, she hesitates.

*How many fights will there be?* Vellene takes three steps back. *When will I run out of orbs? Be as desperate as them?*

She sucks in a breath, lets go of her chemight, pivots, and sprints down the alley. Protests clamor behind her, but she doesn't dare look back and stare death in the eyes. Or worse, be sent home. Vellene grits her teeth and pushes forward.

A sizzle zips through the air.

She yelps as a blast of their chemight hits her cloak. The patch blazes into flames. Vellene curses and reaches up.

She undoes her cloak, legs pumping beneath her, and lets it go. It flutters up and off her shoulders, just as fire consumes it, swallowing the silver threading of the Winloc crest in one fell swoop. Immediately, the cold, damp air of night sweeps over her bare shoulders and legs. She clenches her teeth to keep them from chattering.

Orange shots of chemight barrel past her, but without deposits to conduct their formularies, their blasts spiral out of control. They set flame to a pile of trash and the side of a Scrap shack. The stench of burning garbage fills the air.

Vellene veers into another alley, then right onto a street, fumbling through Scraps and Utilities as the city fills. She spots an empty orb stand, then grunts as she skids to a stop and ducks beneath it.

She squeezes her eyes shut as the shouts of the chemi chasing her add to the racket of the crowd on the street.

She runs through her options. One sticks. She needs to leave Scorus. Now. She chews on her lip, outlines in her head a sorry excuse for a plan, but a plan nonetheless.

Frales. The nation across the abyss. It's the only place she may be safe from Aquim.

Vellene crawls out from the stand and stays low.

A crowd gathers around a pair of street-performing Scraps. They fire off swirls of natural, gray chemight and use their fingers to manipulate the mist-like substance into shapes. Their shirts are off, flung to the side to display murals of Scrap ink across their torsos. The crowd erupts into a roar of approval as the duo storytellers drift the chemight into a scene of a Scrap-looking child taking down an army of Chemibreakers.

Vellene slows, watches, wonders. *A tale of the next generation?* Her eyes trail the natural Scrap chemight, something she's never seen before. She knows of it from her teachings with her Surveillant, Idus, but he always taught it as a dark, obscene craft. Her father added to that misconception, hanging any Scrap he found using it and explaining it to her as chaotic.

*But this is beautiful*, she recognizes, as the storytellers teach it to her in a new way.

Their movements are soft, their faces playful. The smoke flows in careful wisps, controlled and thoughtful.

Eyes gather toward Vellene, toward her exposed chemight deposits. Without her cloak, the orbs along each side of her neck and chest shine like beacons. She folds herself, hunching at the waist and hurrying to where the storytelling duo discarded their shirts. Carefully, Vellene plucks one from the ground with the toe of her boot, then kicks it up to her grasp and takes five long steps back into the crowd.

Shouts come from her left.

Vellene turns, heart in her throat. Her pursuers spot her, mouths ajar as they give orders to the Scraps surrounding them, fingers pointing straight at her. A frantic gush of air leaves her lungs as she thrusts through the crowd and slips the stolen shirt on. It hides the ink of her Winloc crest and the chemight deposits along her chest, but the ones on her neck are still visible. She slams her feet into the pavement.

The nation of Scorus slants, as all of Alchemight does, toward Dalbian's Abyss. The massive wall of thick vapor and ocean of tar curls and wavers before Vellene. She stumbles onto the main dock and searches for a ship. Any ship to Frales. But the harbor sits empty.

Shouts come down from the hill.

Vellene panics. Sweat pools in her palms, along her brow. She searches Dalbian's Abyss for any incoming ships, but the veil is too thick. She turns back to the hill—

and the shouts become a throng of shadows. More than the two who chased her. Five. Maybe eight.

Sidelining her fear, she drops over the side of the dock. She groans when she hits uneven rocks. The impact radiates up her shins, but she pushes the pain aside and darts forward. Runs until the shouts are faint, until her toe connects with something solid.

Vellene bites her tongue, keeps a shriek of surprise at bay, and hits the ground with a solid thunk. She shifts onto her elbows and looks back.

Ten shadows stand on the dock.

Vellene presses into the ground. She will die before she allows them to take her and be served like a feast on a platter to her father. She would be handed to Kadir, her blood and its chemight reaped from her body in slow, painful drips.

With the night, swirls of mist curl outward from Dalbian's Abyss. They knit together and form a veil of protection as they skitter over the jagged rocks of the shore. The fine, gentle fog slides over her skin with a sticky hush. Cold rocks grind into her cheek and scratch the formulary-filled orbs along her neck. She lies there, eyes wide as she stares through the fog at her search party, and holds her breath.

The Scraps pace the dock once, twice. Every echo of their boots in the night sends a wave of nausea through her.

Then one calls out, "She must have stayed on the street."

Vellene bites her lip when the group hurries up the hill, leaving her and—

A dark mass lies past her on the shore.

Vellene's eyes trace it, unable to will the strength to stand and approach it. She lets her heart settle, and the tension in her shoulders fades as the Scraps retreat. Then, she pushes up from the ground and steps over to—

It's a chemi.

She bends, stares at his back. A dead chemi?

Tar covers his body. The same tar that stretches from Scorus to Frales and bubbles in waves a few feet away.

Wary, Vellene pulls the sleeve of her stolen Scrap shirt down over her fist and wipes his face. The tar comes away in a thick sludge. She grimaces but wipes his nose as clean as she can. Then she lifts a finger beneath it and lets out a sigh of relief as breath from his nostrils tickles her knuckle.

She stands, steps back, then gives the chemi a nudge with her boot. "Can you hear me?" she tries. She reaches for his arm and tugs at it. Maybe it's naive to rescue what she assumes is a Scrap, considering they hunted her, but she refuses to be rid of her mercy. It's one of the only things that's kept her sane.

His eyes flash open, irises an impossible green through the tar slathered over him. He cranes his neck to get a good look at Vellene. She shivers when his eyes follow her booted feet to her torn and dirtied skirts, then to the foul-smelling Scrap shirt. They stop when they find the length of her full, wealthy chemight deposits on either side of her neck. He tenses. His fists clench around rocks.

Vellene reaches up to the braided bun of her hair and lets her curls bounce free, covering what's left of her exposed deposits with a grimace. She should've done it earlier.

Her stranger fumbles onto his feet. He shifts his weight, then groans and rests his hands on his knees.

"You're hurt." She reaches out to steady him.

He stumbles and raises a finger at her. "Don't touch me, Imperial."

"I was just trying to help."

"Imperials never help," he snaps. His voice is a deep, rough bravado—the kind that commands authority but speaks of darkness. His eyes reflect a similar sentiment, their emerald hardened with an emotion she feels an unsettling kinship to: fury.

She hugs her waist, unable to walk away from those eyes. It's stupid to stay here, stupid to talk to him, and yet a kind of trust awakens inside her. That kind of anger, she knows it so deeply inside herself that to witness it in the eyes of another makes her feel validated. As if the realm has been as cruel to her as it has to him. It's a gamble to latch to him, but as her eyes scan the mist for ships and find none, a gamble is all she has.

He grimaces and shifts his weight off his left leg. He looks around, and his face settles into uncertainty. "This isn't Frales."

Vellene's heart gives a hard thump. "Are you trying to get there?" She clenches her gown. "Can you take me?"

He trains his eyes on her. "You want to go to Frales?" He scoffs and wipes sludge from his brow. "What, daddy forgot to give you an allowance this week?"

She wavers at his hostility, but she stands firm. His words may hurt, but he isn't trying to grab her. He's far less of an enemy than those who chased her to this shore, but there's a desperate twitch to his movements. His fingers shake. He's injured. He needs a formulary.

And she has one.

With a ragged inhale, Vellene strides toward the dock and shoves past the stranger.

Boots scrunch against the rocky shore behind her.

A slim smile slides across her lips. She glances over her shoulder.

The chemi limps, brows drawn in thought, and tar-covered lips twisted with a grimace. He reaches a hand into his pocket before he draws his palm back. Then his shoulders relax at the sight of a single orb. The thing flashes auburn with yellow flecks. An oddity. Formularies are a solid, single color. Always.

Then he lifts his shirt.

Vellene's next step falters.

Her stranger is lean, his muscled torso lined with ink that makes the shape of a wing. Within the ink are several chemight deposits. They're empty, the bronze deposits shining in the moonlight—

But that is Imperial ink, and Utilities are never given that many deposits. She stops and turns to him. "Think twice before you insert that orb."

The chemi frowns.

Vellene licks her lips. "You should hide whatever you have if you want to live."

His brows shoot up in surprise. "So, it's true then? Scraps are hanged for practicing chemight here?"

She narrows her eyes. "Unless you're Imperial."

His face twists with disgust.

"You wear no Imperial clothes, yet your deposits are laid out in a traditional Imperial pattern." She nods to his abdomen. "So which is it? Imperial or thief?"

He inserts his orb into a deposit, a level of threat wavering in his eyes. "I'm no thief, certainly no Imperial, and you do not scare me."

"Why are you following me?"

"I'm not." He nods to the hillside where her pursuers disappeared. "Where I need to go is this way. Not that it's any of your business." He resumes his limp forward and makes his way past her.

Vellene nods to herself. "Fine."

He grins at that, but he keeps his attention drawn toward the city.

Her eyes trail him, unsure if he won't pivot and spark off an attack.

But as he leaves the density of the fog behind, tar slicks off him with each step, and the light of Alchemight's moons blazes against his back. His shirt is torn and gapes along his spine, where more deposits lie—these filled. His spine glimmers with swirls of color. Formularies. Power. Lots of it. More than she is. Enough to need his protection.

She turns her back to him and focuses on the dock, but her inner voice nags at her. She thinks of the Scraps that chased her, of what would happen to him, of the Imperials that would get him in exchange for orbs. It will be her father, and that—well, she'd never forgive herself for not preventing it.

Vellene clenches her fists, then spins and launches into a jog after him.

He hasn't gotten far. His hurt leg trembles with every step, and his breaths are ragged with the effort of climbing the hill into the city. He ignores her when she approaches, eyes focused on the lights of Scorus ahead.

Vellene pulls in front of him. "You can't go up there."

He presses his lips together, face creased in annoyance.

"I was chased down here because of my full deposits." She nods to him. "You won't get far with yours exposed."

His eyes light with confusion. Then, he reaches an arm back. His fingers find the tears in his shirt. He grumbles something foul, then looks at her. "I need to get to The Bloody Cloth."

"You won't." She looks at the lights of her nation, listens to the clamor of voices on the other side of the hill. "Not until morning, when Imperials make their rounds and Scraps head inside." And when it's too late for her to escape. Vellene focuses on the dock, begs for a ship to arrive. "Imperial Chemibreakers are still a risk, but they'll be easier to get past, their patrols five or six chemi to a group. Right now, Scraps are everywhere, and all of them are starving. They wouldn't think twice about killing you and taking your body to the first Imperial they find. You're a walking feast."

The chemi follows her gaze, then studies her face. "Imperials aren't out at night in Scorus?"

"Rarely. It's considered indecent." Vellene clasps her hands, twists her fingers. "We also aren't really supposed to go beyond the Imperial Gates."

He tilts his head, eyes her torn gown again as if seeing it for the first time. Skepticism fills his features and his brow creases. "Then why have you?"

Too many words, too many wishes rush to Vellene. They cram into her mind, her heart. She focuses on him. On those angry eyes. "It's none of your business." But she hesitates and points at his bad leg. "But I can fix that."

He looks down at his leg, then back at her. "You have a marvel remedial formulary?"

Vellene nods. "I'm surprised you don't with as many orbs you're carrying."

"I'm not here to do mending."

"Not even on yourself?"

He clears his throat. "In hindsight, I may have been too cocky."

"Seems so."

His lips slip into a small smile. It looks strange on his tar-streaked face.

Vellene nods to the dock. "Let's sit."

The chemi hesitates. "You're Imperial." Distrust drips off his words.

She shrugs. "I am." She stares into Dalbian's Abyss. "Hopefully not for long."

"Because you wish to go to Frales."

"I must go to Frales."

They walk toward the dock.

"You do realize it's a war-torn nation?" He says it slowly, eyes full of judgment. "Across a deadly sea of unforgiving tar and an almost impenetrable fog?"

"You got across." Vellene notes his surprise and rolls her eyes. "You're covered in tar. I don't expect you decided to 'take a dip'."

"Yes, I crossed, but it was incredibly dangerous. My ship capsized." He looks down at himself. "Hence this mess," he mutters. He clenches his jaw. "And there's a war over there. One I suggest you stay away from."

"At least they're fighting back."

"Typical Imperial, thinking putting down Scraps is the only way—"

"I'm not talking about Imperials fighting back." Vellene crosses her arms. "I meant the Scraps. I heard there may be a place of refuge there. My—" She cuts herself off before she can say 'father'. "An Imperial I know speaks of a resistance group. He hates them enough that they must be worth my time." She slides her tongue over her teeth. "If I can cross the abyss, then I'll take refuge with them."

He peers at her, eyes narrowed. "Who are you?"

The question is harder to answer than she expects. What is she besides a dutiful daughter or a broken heiress? Vellene clears her throat and goes for the obvious. "Vellene."

He considers it. His steps slow as they reach the dock, and he raises a tar-smothered hand. "Eledar."

She stares at it a moment, surprised. It's an offering of trust. Every wrist-clasp is. She swallows, then takes his wrist. They clasp for a few seconds, then she pulls her hand back and stares at the murk that clings to her palm.

"Abyss," he says. "Sorry."

She wipes the sludge off on her gown. "Sure."

They fall quiet as they step across the dock. It's silent beyond their breaths and the clunks of their boots on the wooden planks. Dalbian's Abyss has nothing to say, and neither do they.

Vellene settles onto a bench, and Eledar takes the place beside her. She leans her elbows on her knees, plays with her fingers as the light of Alchemight's three moons wanes. *Morning.* A heavy weight settles in her chest. To face her sister, her father—she wouldn't wish it on her worst enemy. Her mother's note burns into her thigh.

Eledar licks his lips. "You mentioned a remedial formulary."

"Oh." She straightens, flexes her fingers, then wavers. "Where on your leg is the wound?"

"Here." Eledar motions to his calf, but he doesn't lift his pant leg.

Vellene leans over to it and concentrates. Remedial formularies are tricky to pull from, especially when some are wrapped in nether and others in marvel. On top of that, it was rare for her to practice chemight. Even if formularies are allowed for Imperials, her father wasn't keen on her learning to wield them. She's thankful her mother disagreed and helped guide Vellene's chemight training in secret.

She focuses on the marvels, on their purity, their goodness. A buzz zings across her skin before pink mist radiates from her palms. She grips his pant leg around his calf and closes her eyes as the chemight surges.

Eledar sighs in relief. He stretches his leg. "Thank you."

Vellene pulls back. The light fades from her palms just as the color of the formulary drains from an orb on her neck. She nods. "Of course."

"Which family do you belong to?"

She tenses.

"Winloc?" There's a bitterness to her family's name.

Vellene's brain scours for the best alternative. A low-wealth Imperial family and a distant relation to the six bloodlines. "Shade."

Eledar's shoulders slump, and he leans back into the bench, relaxed. "Are you close with the Winlocs?"

"Not many are."

"Yes." He nods. "That makes sense. They probably wish to horde their power, then lord it over the other Imperials."

Her stomach twists. "Why are you here, Eledar?" She holds up a hand before he can object. "Remember, I just used precious chemight to heal your leg."

Eledar's eyes trace her face. Tar dried to his lids cracks. "Perhaps if I knew why you're running, I could tell you."

She measures her breathes, her words. Memories trapped in the darkest crevices of her mind fly forward. Glimpses of being trapped in one of her father's prison cells for weeks. Starvation. Weakness. Bruises as colorful as a piece of fine art. Screams from her own throat, from other prisoners'—unrelenting pain, *always*.

Then there's her pedestal and her father's sword. There's her sister's face when Mogaell admitted to murdering their mother. Finally comes the image she fears the most—her body strung upside down above a basin, the black tar of her blood dribbling down her neck. Her voice taken again as Kadir watches in the shadows, his life sustaining hers as he steals her power.

Vellene chills and crams the images back where they belong. She looks at her hands. She doesn't know how much she should reveal to Eledar. She settles on the thinnest of truths—a veil across the greater darkness. "My father."

Eledar sucks in a breath, then exhales through his teeth. "He hurts you."

"Yes."

"I'm sorry you've been dealt a cruel hand of fate." Eledar shifts his weight, rests his elbow on the back of the bench and leans his chin into his fist. The action curves his body closer to hers. His knee presses against her own, and the smallest prick of static buzzes through the thin fabric of her gown.

Vellene forces a swallow when he smiles. Maybe it's meant to be comforting, but the idea of comfort is too foreign to her. Any smile is to hide a beast. She's known it her entire life. Whether her father, her mother,

her sister—or herself. She moves her knee from his, her shoulders tense.

Eledar clears his throat. "Maybe I can make it right. I'm here to get rid of the Winlocs, but I could add your father to the list."

*Get rid of the Winlocs.* "You're going to kill them?" She stares at him.

Eledar flinches at the accusation in her voice. His brow furrows.

"I only meant, isn't that a suicide mission?" She bites her lip, hopes the redirect regains his trust.

Tar along his cheeks cracks into frown lines. Anger lights his eyes. "In Frales, I watched my family die. There may be more Scraps than Imperials, but natural chemight will never break through barriers of well-constructed Imperial formularies. The Winlocs are to blame for that war. If Aquim hadn't stolen the source, there may not be peace but there wouldn't be starvation."

"Is it really that bad there?" Vellene asks, uneasy.

"It's worse."

She tucks a loose curl away from her face. If she can't go to Frales, then where? Dread washes over her.

Above, the moons shatter. Their pieces scatter across the night. For a single breath, there are stars. Then all those broken pieces reabsorb into a large sun, the white of their light conforming into rays of warmth.

"We should get moving. I'm sure the Utilities that man this dock will be down soon," Eledar says.

Vellene studies him. "I can come with you?"

"Well, you can't stay here." Eledar pushes off the bench and tests his leg. He scratches the back of his neck. "And I need to get rid of this tar."

"You could use a primitive formulary."

"Only spoiled Imperials who have no worry for their chemight storage use primitive formularies to clean themselves," he sneers. His face twists. Annoyed, he walks toward the hillside. "Come or don't. I need to get to The Bloody Cloth before Scorus wakes up."

Vellene stands and stares at Dalbian's Abyss, searches for the shadow of a ship. *But is Frales still an option?* She clutches her gown. *I need time*, she realizes, *and I can't go back home*. She swallows, then turns to Eledar, to Scorus.

*He will kill my family.* The acknowledgment stirs something inside her. Killing her father would uproot the seat of power in Scorus, would leave room for someone new, someone better, to take his place.

As for her sister—Mogaell has become a shadow of Aquim. Vellene's not sure she will ever forgive her sister for murdering their mother. But Mogaell wants to survive as much as Vellene does. She hopes that's all it was, survival and desperation.

She blinks and shivers. Goosebumps rise across her skin. A warmth spreads. Hope. It clings to her, bursts through her bloodstream. Hope for a future without tyranny. Hope for a life in Scorus free from the grasp of her father.

Vellene closes her eyes, sucks in a breath, then takes a step forward.

## Chapter Seven

# *Vellene*

Trash litters the streets of Scorus, all the Scraps and Utilities who came out to play gone with Alchemight's sun high in the sky. Vellene follows Eledar between a set of Scrap shacks. These are top-heavy. The rotted shambles of their roofs curve into the alley and meet at a peak above, casting the alley into a dance of shadows.

A family of canisoss tuck beneath a set of old crates, their bodies skin, limbs, claws, and tail, bones peeking through. One of the creatures yips at Vellene. Its tail wags, and she has half the mind to bend and scratch its fleshy head. But there's something about its eyes, the four hollow holes of its skull, that glues her hand to her side.

She pulls her focus back to the Scrap shacks, listens to the snores of Scraps and the half-awake rush of Utilities. Some Utility chemi move past her and Eledar, eyes drawn to the ground, faces struck with their somber routine of the chores assigned by their Imperials. Utilities may wear nicer cloaks, even earn a weekly wage, but they sleep, eat, and live among Scraps.

Her Surveillant's lessons on Utilities come swimming forward. *As undesirable as any Scrap*, Idus taught. *Labeled differently for the sake of keeping them loyal.* A Utility chemi slips past Vellene, cheeks pink as a gust of wind tunnels through the alley. The young chemi eyes Eledar's back of full deposits, orbs glistening with chemight, but she says nothing. *Utilities bow to Imperials. They do not question.* Vellene's stomach twists with discomfort.

That obedience. It reminds her of herself.

"Your face looks strange," Eledar says, breaking their silence.

She blinks. She pulls her mind from the darkness of Winloc Grove. Still, the chamber Idus would lock her in as he taught her how to be a good Imperial haunt her. "We're getting further into Scrap territory," she whispers, afraid to wake those sleeping behind the makeshift walls of their shacks.

Eledar saunters forward. "And?"

"And it's dangerous. Scraps won't think twice about killing us for our orbs."

"I can handle myself."

Vellene frowns.

He looks at her. "What? Never had to fight?"

"I don't like the idea of it."

He scoffs. "And yet you want to run away to a war."

Her face reddens.

Eledar nods to a closed shop. "Don't worry. We'll grab some cloaks." He eyes the orbs that line her neck. Vellene's hair mostly covers them, but as they walk, their glistening formularies peek out. "Maybe one with a hood."

"I can't afford the orbs needed to pay for a cloak." Her fingers run over the formularies at her neck. She would rather freeze than give up her only weapons.

"You won't." He moves to one of the shop's windows and tugs at it. It doesn't budge. He grunts in dissatisfaction, then wraps his fist in the bottom of his shirt. "Shield your eyes."

Vellene lifts her arm as Eledar slams his fist through the glass. Her lips part in shock, brow creased in anger. "I am not stealing from this shop."

"Okay." Eledar ducks in through the window and disappears.

*So much for not being a thief.* Vellene glances down the alley, then peers through the broken window. The shop is dark, Eledar a shadow among the racks of clothes.

He scuffles about. Hangers clang to the ground. "Anyone?"

She hugs herself. "Not yet." She licks her lips. "What family do you belong to in Frales again?"

"I belong to no one," his voice carries through the dark shop.

"What about your ink?" Vellene asks, wary. "It looked like a wing."

Eledar clears his throat and searches a rack close to the window. "It's old."

"I know you said you aren't an Imperial—"

"I'm not."

"—but you have too many chemight deposits to possibly be a Utility, and—"

"Frales doesn't have Utilities."

Vellene frowns. "Then what are you?"

Eledar slips out the window and past her, two cloaks in his hands. "These should do."

He hands Vellene a gold one. The color belongs to the Imperial bloodline of the Vonners, but it's missing their crest—likely due to the fact their heads rot in her front hallway. Instead, the cloak is plain. Not too extravagant but also not torn, dirtied, and branded with poverty. It's new, not used.

Vellene holds up the cloak, studies it. "Shouldn't we lie lower than this?"

Eledar shakes his head, clasps his choice of a Pinesky bloodline, plum-colored cloak around his neck. "Wealth is still power, Vellene. We need a little bit of it to get by."

"Invading Imperials, maybe. But Scraps don't care how rich you are, just that you're rich."

Eledar chews on his lip, then he bends to a tar puddle leftover from the shard storm. He scoops tar into his palm, then smears it across his cloak in various spots. He raises his brows at her. "Go on. You made a good point."

Vellene dirties her cloak. Then, for good measure, she swipes some of the tar over her face.

Eledar smirks, his nostrils flaring with amusement.

She lifts her chin. "You didn't answer my question. What are you?"

He studies her, a hardness darkening the green of his gaze. "We should get moving."

Vellene blows out a breath. "I don't know where we're going."

He strides past her. "This way."

Their pace is brisk as they make their way from the shop and into the Scrap territory of Scorus. Every step forward leads to a new, broken-down home and an unrelenting quiet. With no Imperials to report to, Scraps don't care to be up this early. *It must be wonderful to have no obligation but to live*, Vellene thinks.

Then, she moves past two Scraps asleep on a street corner. They lie in the fetal position, backs to each other, eyelids slammed shut against Alchemight's sun. Dirt cakes their skin. Grease slicks through their hair.

She matches her stride with Eledar's. "What's this place called, again?"

"The Bloody Cloth." He picks dried, cracked tar off his cheek as he walks. "I need to meet with one of my contacts."

"Who would that be?"

He flicks his gaze to her, then back to the path ahead. "Soffesa Fedelis."

Vellene pulls to a stop, the name ringing every warning bell her father and Idus set for her. "The Silent?"

Eledar clenches his jaw but stops his charge and faces her. "That would be the one."

"She's deadly. My—Imperials are hunting her." Vellene gestures to posters plastered across the sides of Scrap shacks, Utility shops, orb stands. Several hold the etched drawings of the infamous Imperial assassin.

Eledar rubs his chin. "You do remember when I told you I was here to kill Imperials, correct?"

She cringes. "Yes."

"A deadly assassin is pretty useful in a plan like that."

"Of course." Vellene straightens. "Sorry, I'm just—"

"New to murder?" A grin creeps across his face.

A nervous laugh bubbles up. "Yeah." *Wait.* "Am I part of this now?"

His grin falters. "Well, yes."

"I don't get a choice?"

Without hesitation, Eledar steps into her, and her body goes rigid. Even behind his mask of tar, his face tightens, his pupils waver. His jaw and cheekbones sharpen into the kind of face warriors hone for battle. The change is so quick that she takes a trembling half-step back from him, but he follows, staying on her toes.

His grip goes to her shoulder. His fingernails curl into the bare skin beside the strap of her gown. "I don't want to kill you."

Chemight sparks in her veins. Vellene could slash him where he stands. She has the formularies, the power—but something stays her hand. Let him think her weak. For now. "I'm happy to remain alive."

He relaxes and turns away, picking up his stride. "Good. Then you'll help."

Vellene follows but her eagerness to escape the streets matches a new fear to get away from Eledar and his plan. Can she kill Aquim? Mogaell? Her blood tingles. What happens when he realizes she's a Winloc?

Eledar presses his lips into a low whistle. "What a beauty."

She follows his gaze and frowns.

Before them is the deteriorating frame of a Utility shop—a building that, perhaps in its prime, was a stomping ground for Imperials, a metropolis for gossip, and maybe even a gathering spot for couples' Infusion ceremonies. It sits lopsided, bears fissures, has the clear signs of a Scrap shack in the making. Mold-covered cardboard patches its bottom to keep wandering spideria from crawling up and inside. Halves and quarters of bricks, probably taken from Utility construction sites, stack and form the right, outermost wall. Tar collected from countless shard storms glues the pieces of brick together.

The second floor is a new addition, every inch of it constructed with materials found on the street. Walls of garbage. Windows that are nothing more than holes. Patch-worked fabrics strewn across wires and nailed into random pieces of wood to create curtains. It's a disaster, and how it remains upright is a mystery. Beyond its ready-to-collapse porch hangs a piece of wood with black lettering painted in tar that reads: THE BLOODY CLOTH.

Eledar steps onto the porch and gives one of its wooden posts a loving knock. It echoes, the wood rotting from the inside out. He takes a deep breath in and smiles. "Smell that? That's personality, character. Only great brew houses have that." He gives Vellene a playful wink, then looks at the saloon-style doors, rolls back his shoulders, and pushes inside. They groan on their hinges, shriek for refurbishment.

"All I smell is trash," she grumbles, then takes a timid step onto the porch. Vellene hesitates. *He's inside. I'm out here. Now is the time run.* But her feet glue to the porch. The hope she felt only a few hours before bows to her fear. She shakes out her hands. She hates this. Hates feeling so lost inside her own body and mind. Defiance pulses within her, matches the beat of her heart. Her hope claws to the surface and gasps inside her, shields her from the sharp sword of her fear.

Then she steps inside.

"I thought you left." Eledar stands to the side of the doors. He eyes the small crowd of the bar—mostly drunks who have overstayed their welcome.

She clears her throat. "I wanted to."

"Good."

The indent between her brows flares with confusion.

"You understand, then, that this won't be easy." Eledar gives her a small smile, something meant to be encouraging, but the streaks of tar on his face make everything about it cruel, conniving, and twisted. He turns his attention back to the tavern.

Dirty. It's the first word that comes to Vellene's mind as she analyzes the drunks, the tables, the floor, the walls. Even the ceiling is cast in strange splatters. There's an L-shaped staircase in the far corner. A rope with a sign blocks it off that reads: BOOK A BED.

A chemi descends the stairs, steps over the rope with grace—all the while tying thick, orange hair into a knot on top of her head. She's Scrap, her exposed skin free of chemight deposits. Instead, Scrap art is inked down one side of her body—from her face to the skin that peaks out at the bottom of her ruffled skirts.

"Felix, some idiots blew apart a door upstairs," she hollers to the bartender. She straightens her outfit, and Vellene admires its unique craftsmanship.

The skirts stop at the chemi's mid-thigh, then sweep into a pointed v between her legs to above her knees, where black, laced, and heeled boots begin. The bodice of the dress is made of thick, deep crimson leathers, long-sleeved on the side of her body that has no ink, while the arm covered in intricate designs remains exposed with firm, lethal muscle. At the neck, the top of the dress curves into a hood.

Despite the half of her face covered in Scrap ink, the chemi is stunningly beautiful, her face sharp angles and full lips. It doesn't take much for Vellene to recognize her, the chemi a spitting image of the drawings plastered around Scorus, of the description Idus fed to Vellene on a daily basis. *Soffesa, The Silent. Imperial Assassin.*

Eledar's face breaks into a wide smile. He crosses the room in three quick strides. "Soff."

The assassin freezes. Her breath catches when her eyes find Eledar's. "Tell me you're not a ghost," she whispers.

Eledar beams. "Hard to know, considering you'd be the first I'd haunt."

A strangled laugh of disbelief trembles from her lips. She closes the distance between them in a heartbeat and extends her arms. "You're really here." She wraps Eledar in an embrace, nuzzles her face into his shoulder.

"Hey," he whispers into her hair. His grip around her is tight, desperate.

They stay like that for a moment, arms clenched around each other, eyes squeezed shut against whatever comes next. It's more than a hug. It's as if they thought they'd never see each other again.

Then, Soffesa opens eyes as orange as her hair and finds Vellene. The moment shatters when the assassin's brow furrows. She pulls back from Eledar, her movement quick and eyes intense. Her palms light with lethal, gray chemight. It spirals with chaos, spikes into the air until it sharpens into each of her palms like knives.

Eledar presses a firm hand to Soffesa's back, "A friend."

Vellene takes a timid step forward, forces a smile. "Hello."

Soffesa tilts her head. "She's familiar." She closes the space between them. "Have I killed someone close to you?"

Vellene swallows. "Don't think so."

"You're Imperial, that's for sure." Soffesa looks back at Eledar. "Risky, don't you think?"

"Can you see my orbs?" Vellene asks. She tugs the hood of her golden cloak around her.

"I don't need to see them. You've got that look about you. Like this place is too unforgivable." Soffesa's face pulls into a sneer. "Naiveté."

"Let's sit before you scare off my only recruit." Eledar pulls out a chair at one of the tables.

Vellene reluctantly joins him.

The Silent douses her chemight, its sharp points fading into smoke before absorbing into her palms. "I don't like you," Soffesa says with certainty, voice hard and eyes trained on Vellene.

Vellene frowns. "It may be reciprocated."

Eledar lies his palms flat on the table. "Let's focus, shall we?"

Soffesa crosses her arms but nods. "You're here after five years. What changed?"

Vellene turns her gaze to Eledar. *Five years?* She frowns. That was when everything in Frales fell apart.

Eledar mulls over the question. He twirls his thumbs on the tabletop, expression pained.

Vellene saw the same look on her mother one too many times. The look of someone who wishes to share the weight of the truth but cares too much to ever do so.

He clears his throat and clasps his hands together, forcing his thumbs to sit still. Then, he reaches into his back pocket and pulls out a playing card. It's smudged with tar, but as he cleans it off, he reveals a symbol of an hourglass, both ends of it equally shaded.

"Equilibrium sent me." He places the card in the center of their table.

Vellene stiffens. She spoke of the resistance group, and yet he left out the fact he works for them. She grinds her teeth. He may carry a wrath like hers, but she can't trust him.

"The resistance group?" Soffesa asks, eyeing the card with suspicion. "What for?"

"They want the source of all chemight," Eledar says, lowering his voice.

His words from before—his mission to kill her family—click into place.

Soffesa scoffs at his admission. "Who doesn't these days?" She gives the playing card a flick of annoyance. "I've taken enough heads over that abyss-damned source."

Vellene eyes the assassin. Flashes of her father's prized hunts send a chill down her spine.

Eledar looks curious over Soffesa's words, but the assassin goes tight-lipped. He takes the playing card and stashes it back into his pocket with a grimace. "I was told Aquim Winloc guards it."

"He does." Soffesa leans back in her chair, expression bored. "He's outlawed natural chemight, calls it dirty. Keeps Imperials at a power threshold that can't be overthrown." She trails off, her eyes landing on Vellene. "He has two daughters that should be on your hit list."

Vellene stiffens. She grips the edge of the table as recognition flashes in Soffesa's eyes.

Gray chemight steams from the assassin's palms and wafts up her arms.

"What?" Eledar looks for a threat.

The Silent grits her teeth.

*No*. Vellene slams back as a slash of chemight arcs over the table toward her neck. Her chair tips over, and she crashes to the floor with a grunt, the air knocked from her lungs. Her eyes fly to the exit of The Bloody Cloth. She scrambles from the floor, but Soffesa catches her around the waist and slings her back to its grimy surface with a growl.

Vellene's head cracks against the dirtied floorboards and her lips part with a low groan. Chemight begs to break from her deposits, and this time, she doesn't think about it. She reaches for a chaos formulary wrapped in nether, and the weaponized chemight shoots through her veins before it blasts from her palms in waves of navy.

Soffesa gasps when the chemight hits her in the chest. It shoots the assassin across the room before she slams against a table. Her hands fly to her head in an instant, eyes wild with horror. A guttural screech seeps through her teeth.

Vellene flinches, understands what the mind-altering chemight shoves through the assassin's skull. The chaos formulary is a Winloc specialty, something her father uses on anyone who disobeys him. Including her. Vellene steps back as Soffesa writhes on the floor.

The assassin hyperventilates. She drags her fingers through her hair.

Eledar drops beside Soffesa and touches her face. "It's not real, Soff. It's okay."

Soffesa chokes on a ragged breath. Tears pool down her cheeks.

Eledar turns a glare to Vellene. "Make it stop."

"She attacked me."

"Make it stop!"

Vellene steps toward Soffesa as terror etches across the assassin's features. Guilt pummels her. *How many times have I been Soffesa, curled on the floor whimpering, wetting myself, wishing to be free of a chaos formulary?*

"Vellene," Eledar hisses. "Kill her, and I will slice you down where you stand." Chemight sparks from his palms, radiates up his arms, and scorches from his shoulders.

It's not lost on her that he isn't pulling from a formulary. Scrap chemight despite every sign pointing toward him being an Imperial. Vellene swallows and eyes the door again.

"Don't you dare run." Eledar turns desperate. He calls out across the bar, "Someone. Anyone. I need a chaos orb wrapped in marvel."

"I've got it." The bartender, Felix, crosses the room unamused. He's plump for a Scrap, belly and cheeks round. He opens a pouch at his waist. Then he pulls out a golden ingot and an orb pulsing with gray swirls. "But it will cost ya. It took me weeks to get my hands on these."

"I don't care." Eledar checks Soffesa's pulse as she fades into the oblivion waging war in her mind. He holds out his palm. "Hand it over."

Felix drops the ingot and orb into Eledar's outstretched hand. "I'll get a light."

Eledar ignores the chemi. He cups the ingot and orb, blows out a breath, then closes his eyes. He whispers a formulary, brows furrowed in concentration.

Vellene's lips part in shock as the ingot melts and molds over the orb between his palms—something that's impossible for Scraps, Utilities, and most Imperials. The orb accepts it, and its gray swirls color into a light green. Those who can forge their own formularies must practice for years, and most were snatched by her father, working night and day at Winloc Grove to create his specialized formularies.

Eledar lifts his shirt and presses the orb into one of his empty deposits before he channels it. Light green chemight blazes from his palms. He grabs Soffesa, hands pressed against her temples. He wills the chemight to wrap around her skull. She gasps when it streams into her nostrils.

Vellene clutches the torn skirts of her gown.

Soffesa snaps awake. She looks around in confusion, then her memory returns. She shoves Eledar away and clambers to her feet. Anger twists the beauty of her face into something of nightmares. "Winloc," she hisses between clenched teeth. "You could have killed me, you bitch—"

"Winloc?" Eledar cuts Soffesa off. His features pull taut with realization. His hands curl into tight, white-knuckled fists.

"Winloc. Yes." Vellene mirrors him. She prepares for another fight.

"She's Aquim's eldest. Next in line for a seat on The Convocation of the Eternal." Soffesa's lips transform into a snarl. "Our target."

Eledar stares at Vellene in disbelief. "You lied."

Soffesa scoffs. "I don't see why you trusted an Imperial in the first place."

Vellene holds up her hands. "I only lied because I wanted to protect myself, but I don't care about protecting my father."

"Liar." Gray swirls fan out around Soffesa. She lunges forward, but Eledar knocks her back with his arm.

"I'm excellent at hurting people." He measures his words, eyes glued to Vellene. "And you are now mine to hurt." He looks back at Soffesa. "My mess, my fight. Understood?"

Vellene's stomach hollows. Fear curls against the back of her neck. She takes a step back as Soffesa nods.

"Just make it painful," Soffesa says, voice bitter. Her words have a slight tremble, the effects of the Winloc chaos formulary still passing.

Eledar focuses on Vellene. "Block the door, Soff."

Panic laces through her. "I'm not with my family. I was running from them when I found you." Her spine hits the bar.

Eledar corners her, his steps slow and tar-streaked face a storm. "Give me one good reason why I shouldn't yank your heart from your chest."

Vellene trips over a toppled stool. She catches herself on a table before she sinks into a defeated crouch. Chemight tickles her skin, but she knows her advantage over Soffesa was blind, desperate luck. She has no fighting experience, and as rage tenses Eledar's body, she knows she can't win against him. *Death may be my only way free.* Her fingers tremble. Darkness pools against her shoulders.

Eledar must see it. The hopelessness. It's the only reason she can think of that softens his voice. "Tell me where the source is, and you will leave this tavern unscathed."

Vellene looks around at the drunken Scraps for help, but they've glued themselves to their tables and chairs, eyes bleary and minds elsewhere. "I don't know. My father hid it, and he's never trusted me enough to tell me where he put it."

Eledar crouches, levels his gaze at her bent head. "Look at me, Vellene."

She flinches, his words and breath close. She sucks in, then meets his eyes.

He searches hers for a moment. "Why did you leave?"

Vellene's stomach twists. "In a month, I'll turn 18."

"I'm going to need you to elaborate."

"I'll inherit my seat on the Convocation of the Eternal."

Eledar nods. "More."

"My father will kill me if I stay in Scorus, or—" She looks away, unable to stomach the next words.

"Or?" Eledar grabs her chin and yanks her face back toward his.

Vellene gasps at the touch, the warmth of it. Fire licks between her chin and his fingers.

Eledar's eyes widen and he lets go. He flexes his hand at his side with a confused look, and his eyes scrape over her.

"My father will sell me to Frales. Force me into Infusion with their High Imperial so they can reap the chemight from my veins." She forces herself taller. So long she remained quiet. So long she held herself back.

"My family is a problem. I wish so much they were different chemi. But, they're not, and for not being like them, sharing their views, they will kill me. One way or another." Her fists clench into her stolen cloak. "I have no desire to be added to my father's sick collection of heads."

The Bloody Cloth sits in silence at her admission. Eledar folds his arms, jaw hard. Sympathy settles in his eyes, and Vellene suddenly feels the intense need to smack it out of him. She pushes the heat rising within her into submission. Out of habit. Out of conditioning. Her body shakes with instilled fear, and Eledar's pity deepens. She wishes she could claw herself to pieces if only to put them together in a way that's of her making, not her father's. That version of her wouldn't cower or shake.

It would kill.

"I don't trust her. Not for a second," Soffesa says. The assassin stares daggers at Vellene.

Eledar runs a hand over his chin. He studies Vellene for another cold, silent moment. Then—"She's genuine."

"Just good at stringing words together," Soffesa snips.

"No." Vellene turns her anger on Soffesa. "I will give you that I lied about my name, but I won't allow you to write off the rest. I haven't lied about why I ran. I'm not afraid of you." She looks to Eledar and forces herself not to tremble, tries to be more than what monsters made her. "Either of you."

Eledar's seriousness breaks into a smile.

"Eledar," Soffesa recognizes the look, "no."

"Oh, come on. I like her," he says.

Vellene looks between them, unsure of what that means.

"And we could use someone on the inside," he explains. He eyes the assassin. "C'mon, Soff. We could get a

Chemibreaker at Winloc Grove, but wouldn't it be better if we had an actual Winloc on our side?"

"She'll betray us," Soffesa hisses.

"I don't think she will." Eledar nods to Vellene. "Will you?"

She shakes her head, but she hesitates. "You want me to go back?"

"Well, yes." Eledar gives Vellene an incredulous look. "What use is a Winloc if she can't pierce the devil's lair?" Excitement arches his brows. "Think about it, Soff. It's her father. She's near him all the time without Chemibreakers to stop her. She's our direct line of attack."

"I can't go back," Vellene protests.

Eledar's excitement halts.

"I told you. Worthless." Soffesa huffs.

Vellene glares at the assassin. "Actually you called me a liar, not worthless."

Soffesa scowls. "Same difference."

"You have to go back, Vellene." Eledar scratches his head. "You're more valuable to us if you do."

"And if I don't?" Vellene asks.

"Then we kill you. Now." Soffesa grins.

Eledar grimaces. "She's right. We can't have you walking around knowing we plan on assassinating your family." He brightens and claps his hands together. "So, that's settled. You'll go back."

Vellene presses her lips together. "It's the only way you'll let me help?"

"Yes."

"I don't know if I can do that," she grinds out.

His smile falters. "Right," he says as if remembering their conversation on the dock. His eyes darken, jaw clenches. "Vellene, it may be a lot to ask, but remember what comes at the end. He dies." Eledar raises a hand to touch her shoulder, but she flinches back. He holds his hand in mid-air before he curls his fingers and drops his arm. "I'm sorry. I know what it means to go back."

"If you did, then you wouldn't ask," she spits out. Vellene's fingers tremble. A terrifying heat lights her veins. "But fine. If it means the end of him, I'll endure." Her gaze flicks to Soffesa.

The assassin stands with her arms crossed, head tilted. Her furious glare withers into the smallest fraction of understanding. It's a margin better than pity.

Vellene heaves a breath and turns from them, grasping the ledge of the bar and finding the gaze of the bartender. "Just get me a brew. Please."

## Chapter Eight

# *Eledar*

Eledar's shoulders fall as he leans against the bar top. Vellene strides away, cheeks red with fury. She ordered a brew, then excused herself for the bathroom. She did both without so much as a glance at him or Soffesa, her lips pursed in a perfect scowl.

He grins as she goes. Admittedly, the heiress fascinates him. He likes her rage, wonders how long before she naps and whether it will be as pretty as those golden eyes. It's been ages since he's wanted more than *lumis,* but he knows her in the way he's known the closest in his life, Soffesa included. There are ghosts in Vellene Winloc's eyes. Ghosts among fire, sorrow, and agony. A desperate part of him wants to vanquish them.

He turns his head back to Soffesa, who scowls. He lifts a brow at his friend, "What?"

"Oh, nothing." Soffesa ducks her head and glares at the bar top. "I know you. That's all."

"Am I not allowed to look?" Eledar asks, but his head crawls with unanswered questions. There were small moments, like when she wrapped her hands around his pant leg to heal his calf, when he felt a shock. Small. Inconsequential. He thought it was nothing more than static.

But when he gripped her chin, there was fire. It seeped into his fingertips as hot as his palm above an open flame. It made him want to sink to his knees, to never let her go, to let her heat suffocate him. It reminded him of the same bliss he finds in *lumis*, only deadlier, heavier. Worthwhile yet destructive. Then he looked past her eyes at her shivering, frail body, and all he saw was a sacred, tired girl.

"I just got you back. I don't need you running off with the first chemi that catches your eye," Soffesa mumbles.

Eledar smiles. "Are you jealous?"

"I don't get jealous." She flicks a glare at him, but her lips curl into a grin. "And you look ridiculous with that tar dried to your face."

He laughs. "You seem a bit jealous, Soff."

She taps the countertop. "I'm allowed to be, okay? I've waited the last five years to see that ridiculous face of yours."

Eledar runs a hand over his forehead. "No need to insult me. Just trying to understand why my looking at Vellene has you all riled up."

"I'm not a fan of Winlocs." Soffesa averts her gaze and plays with her fingers.

"Canisoss?" Felix asks. The bartender lifts an empty mug to emphasize their orders.

"Yeah, that should do." Soffesa bites her lip, then pulls an orb out of a pouch at her waist. "Add this."

Felix raises a brow but accepts the formulary. "Can I keep the orb?"

Soffesa scoffs. "As long as you keep the drinks coming for free all night."

"Deal." Felix smiles, then cups the orb in his fist. He wields the chemight from the formulary into one of the mugs. When he opens his palm, the orb sits empty. "I infused it into the mug. Any brew you pour into it will mix with the formulary's chemight."

"And what formulary was that exactly?" Eledar asks.

"Something for our new friend. It will weaken her," Soffesa explains, voice dark and eyes wired with concentration. "I stole it off of a Winloc Utility. Fitting."

"Why would we want to weaken her?" Eledar questions. His fingers curl into his palms. Winloc or not, Vellene is hardly a threat to them. They overpower her tenfold, even if she does have a few formularies and an original bloodline on her side. She's never been in battle, never fought in hand-to-hand combat. That much is obvious.

"It's just in case, Eledar. A backup plan. If we don't need it, then your new partner in crime will simply think she drank too much. It's a chaos formulary, one meant to cause dizziness and fatigue." Soffesa sighs as Felix fills the mug and sets it aside for Vellene. "But, if she turns out to be as much of a pain as her father, then her inhibitions will be lowered enough to do something about it."

"I don't like this." Eledar straightens on his bar stool. "We need Vellene as an ally. Drugging her isn't going to help that."

"This is the only way I'll have a drink with a Winloc," Soffesa says. She snatches a non-formularized brew from Felix and takes a swig. "I won't sit here or be part of this otherwise. I don't trust her, and honestly, I don't know why you do." She frowns at her mug, then spits out a piece of creature to the floor in distaste. She sighs and looks at him. "Eledar, I've missed you, but I'm not the same doe-eyed, assassin-in-training you were friends with. I won't follow you blindly, and I don't like that, before there was a Winloc in this plan, there was Equilibrium."

Eledar twirls his thumbs.

"What aren't you telling me?"

"The chemi that sent me promised something in return," Eledar says slowly.

Soffesa leans an arm on the bar top and studies his face. "What would that have been?"

Eledar swallows and lets out a small laugh. "My Master."

Soffesa tenses. "Lazar is dead."

"But Lazar was murdered." Eledar glances at Felix. "My brew about ready, friend?"

Felix waves him off and takes an order from another Scrap.

Eledar chews on his tongue, waits for Soffesa to respond.

She grips the edge of the bar. "The murderer would have your strings."

Eledar nods once.

"Here." Felix passes Eledar a brew with an annoyed expression. "Don't holler at me when I've got other customers."

He lifts the brew in thanks but doesn't take a drink. Now that he has it, he's not sure he should. Brew leads to cravings. Including *lumis*.

Soffesa continues. "Wouldn't your Master have pulled your strings by now? It's been five years. Why would they wait to use that kind of leverage?"

"To be honest, I don't know." Eledar runs his thumb over the condensation on the mug. "But I'd rather know who they are than sit in the dark and wait to be commanded."

Soffesa takes a larger gulp of her brew, then wipes her lips with the back of her hand. "Abyss."

"Yeah." Eledar flicks his gaze to where Vellene disappeared. "Should we check on her?"

Soffesa rolls her eyes. "I'm sure she's just dealing with the fact that you roped her into assassinating her family." But her lips purse in thought. "You could've given her more of a choice."

"She could have left."

"Death isn't a choice, Eledar. It's manipulation." His sister exhales.

"And drugging her isn't?" he presses.

Soffesa grimaces. "We do what we must. To live is to fight."

"To fight is to live," he mutters, the old words creeping off his tongue from what feels like lifetimes ago. He eyes the bathroom. "You don't think she will actually help us."

Soffesa shrugs. "I do my best not to underestimate pain. Ours started a war, and hers feels deeper. It must be, living with a monster like Aquim." She tucks a strand of hair behind her ear, her nostrils flaring in discomfort. "But she also doesn't look like the type for vengeance."

"What type does she look like to you?" Eledar splays his fingers over the cool surface of the bar top.

"Like a third of a person," Soffesa admits. "She's nothing right now."

He nods. "Maybe we can help her with that."

"We have enough to worry about. We don't need to add a careless Imperial to the list." Soffesa rubs her temples. "Please, just slash her neck and dump her outside."

Eledar shakes his head. "I can't do that."

"Why not?" Soffesa frowns. "You've just met her. She couldn't have possibly made that much of an impression."

"I don't kill chemi."

"Oh, really? And how about all those Imperials you slaughtered during the war?"

He bristles. "That was different."

"What about the Winlocs you plan on assassinating?"

Eledar grits his teeth. "I get your point. I just meant I don't go around killing just because I can. That's not who I am." He gives her a pointed look. "That wasn't who you were, either."

"I do kill chemi. All the time. Just for power." Soffesa shrugs. "Orbs keep my stomach full, my mug filled with brew, and clothes on my back that aren't in tatters." She gives him a half-smile. "Don't knock the income of a good stab to the heart."

Eledar touches his friend's shoulder. Her muscles tense beneath his fingers. "I'm sorry, Soff. I never wanted you to have to do any of that. To worry about any of that."

"Yeah, well, it is what it is." Soffesa downs the last of her brew and passes the empty mug to Felix. The bartender adds it to his queue of refills.

"I just wish I could have protected you from having to sell yourself like that." Eledar rubs the back of his neck, and dried tar comes away in flakes. He grimaces but ignores the itch of the tar as he studies his sister. "How many jobs have you taken?"

"Enough." Soffesa licks her lips, eyes anywhere but Eledar's. "Didn't you get the orbs?"

"We did," he says carefully, not wanting to dive into her family. Not yet. "But that doesn't answer my question."

Soffesa grinds her teeth, bearing them in the dim light of the tavern. "I stopped counting after my first assignment."

"Why?"

She finally meets his gaze, her face hard and undeterred. "I hunted down every Vonner and Pinesky and led Aquim Winloc to their heads. I was forced to watch him torture them, and I was not allowed payment until I lugged each and every one of those heads back to Winloc Grove to be used as trophies for that sick bastard."

Eledar rubs his brows. "That's—"

"Don't make me work with a Winloc," she interrupts, and it may be the first time he's seen her beg. "I can't, Eledar."

"We need Vellene."

"We don't. We can get a Chemibreaker, a Utility, anyone else to help us."

"None of them will have direct access to Aquim." Eledar narrows his eyes in exasperation. "Don't you want him dead?"

"I do." Soffesa glares at him. "But not working alongside his daughter."

"Vellene doesn't give me the impression she would betray us. Not in favor of him." Eledar turns back to the bathroom, double-checking to ensure she isn't in hearing distance. "I just have this feeling about her. I can't quite explain it."

"You're going to need to," Soffesa insists, her anger growing.

He struggles for the right words. "From the moment she woke me up on the shore of Dalbian's Abyss, I could feel her. A connection. I don't know. But it was like a pull. Like I needed to walk away but I couldn't." He pinches the bridge of his nose. "You know me, Soff. I'm not an overly trusting person. I might play at being trustful, but I'm not."

She nods. "I know." She lowers her voice as Vellene emerges from the bathroom. "I just don't feel or see what you do."

Eledar blows out a breath. "You called her a third of a person. Good. We shape her until we can wield her."

Soffesa stiffens but manages a single bob of her head. "She's drinking that brew, and when she does, you better start thinking of a plan," she asserts.

Eledar eyes Vellene's formularized mug. "I'll think of something." He gives his friend's arm a small squeeze. "If I don't, then we kill her."

Soffesa's lips pull back into a feral grin. "That's the brother I remember."

## Chapter Nine

# *Vellene*

As Vellene settles at the bar, Eledar and Soffesa are quiet. She eyes the two with curiosity but decides whatever has made the two reunited friends so secretive is something she doesn't care enough to know about. She's spent enough time in her life being afraid. Being a coward. If she is meant to return to Winloc Grove, then she's determined to take something for herself. She'll start with a drink.

Felix slides a mug of strange bubbling brown liquid toward her. The brew behind the Imperial gates is soft-hued liquids in appetizing colors of rose, lilac, and honey. *But this.* Vellene crinkles her nose at the drink, bits of scumtis floating at the top.

Without access to nutrient-based formularies, Scraps are known for their stews and brews being infused with the chemight of creatures. The names of the brews written in tar on the wall reflect that—the bigger the creature, the more chemight infused and the more expensive the cost. Scum Rum is at the bottom of the list, the fist-sized scumtis beetles easy to find among the trash of Scrap shacks around Scorus. At the top of the list is a canisoss-based stew.

Vellene thinks of the four hollow eyes of the canisoss and shivers.

Eledar accepts a brew from the bartender, then knocks it back in a few gulps. He lets the mug hit the counter with a thunk as he wipes his mouth with the back of his hand. His tension is gone. His shoulders relax, and his lips turn up with an easy smile before he lets out a whoop of happiness. "I should have followed you to Scorus back in the day if it meant brew this good."

Soffesa sips on her brew, and a sad smile finds its way across her lips.

Vellene looks between them, the friendship that radiates between their expressions. Envy creeps through her, but she stifles it with a question. "You've known each other for a long time, then?"

Eledar slides his mug to Felix, who gives a grunt and refills it. "We worked together as children."

Soffesa purses her lips. "I don't see why she should know my history."

Vellene scowls. "*She* is right here."

"I see no one." Soffesa bats her eyes in sarcastic innocence. Then her face falls dark. "That I trust, anyways."

"I can vouch for Vellene," Eledar says.

"Based on what, your cock?" Soffesa spits.

Eledar balks. "Cruel."

"Well?" Soffesa persists.

Vellene sinks into her seat, her cheeks burning and chest seizing.

Eledar takes notice and a flicker of humor plays over his tar-streaked face. He gulps his refilled brew. "I just believe her."

Soffesa huffs. She reaches up and tugs her orange hair out of its bun in frustration. It falls and cascades around her face, shielding her from the bar as she sips on her drink.

Vellene clears her throat, wanting to steer the conversation toward anything *else*. She finds her composure somewhere between humiliation and wanting to, once again, run out of the tavern. "You worked together as children?"

"You asked me what family I belonged to." Eledar rubs his chin. "It was the Rathmores. Lazar was my…superior."

She remembers the curve of Eledar's ink along his abdomen, the clear definition of a wing. *Of course.* The Rathmore crest is of a ravian, a flight creature. She would've recognized it immediately after seeing Kadir if it weren't for the fact that Eledar's is placed differently from the Imperial's.

Before her father took control of the source, Kadir's father, Lazar Rathmore, attended The Drinking each year. The ceremony allows Imperials to drink from the source of all chemight. The refuel helps them control the most powerful of formularies.

"I met Lazar. It was years ago before he died." Vellene eyes the edge of Eledar's shirt, wonders if he was a Utility for the Rathmores. She blushes when he catches her staring and lifts her gaze to his. "Kadir, I met more recently." She clears her throat and wraps her hands around her brew. "As far as I can tell, both are equally distasteful."

All Imperials carry their ink over their chest, a clear signal of a direct bloodline. Most Utilities wear cloaks with the family's crest, but a select few are granted Imperial ink. It's a variation on the family's Imperial crest placed somewhere other than the chest.

*Eledar must have been important enough to claim*, she thinks.

"You didn't miss anything," Eledar says, face held in a grimace, but his jaw clenches. "Kadir is alive?"

Vellene takes a careful sip of her brew, desperate to do so at least once without making a horrified face. "Afraid so."

"I wish I'd been the one to kill them," Soffesa swears, voice soft with pain. She looks up from her drink and tucks one side of her hair behind an ear. "Where were you before you crossed Dalbian's Abyss?"

Eledar shifts in his chair. "I was protecting anyone I could."

Soffesa opens her mouth to ask for more, but Eledar cuts her off.

"I can't yet. Not here." His tone is stern, eyes plastered to his brew. He brings the mug to his lips and tilts his head back. He guzzles it—this time with less triumph and more need. A need to forget.

Soffesa's face falls, but she remains quiet. She leans her elbows onto the bar top, laces her hands around her mug.

Vellene senses there's something unspoken between the two, but she leaves it alone. "What is it like over there? I know you said it's bad but—"

"Why don't you go and find out?" Soffesa snaps.

Eledar blows out a breath.

"I was actually going to." Vellene frowns.

Soffesa laughs. "Good. Go."

"Soff, she'd be killed in a heartbeat." Eledar shakes his head in annoyance.

"That's the point, Eledar."

"You know, I don't have to help you," Vellene growls.

"I never asked for your help," Soffesa argues.

Eledar clutches the bar top. "Please, stop," he manages through clenched teeth as waves of chemight blaze up his arms—some swirls gray and others from colored formularies. Soffesa and Vellene both fall silent, and he takes a breath. “Vellene is going to help us complete our mission, Soffesa. You need to get on board.”

“I have no desire to trust an Imperial.” Soffesa sits back in her chair, arms crossed.

“She’s not an Imperial. She ran away,” Eledar counters.

“That’s not enough.” Soffesa hops down from her seat, finishes off her drink. “I need proof, Eledar, especially if you expect me to put my life on the line.”

Vellene grips the edges of her seat. “I don’t have any proof.”

“Then an oath.” Eledar heaves a breath. “That should do.”

Soffesa falls into silence. She shifts her weight, wary.

“An oath?” Vellene looks between them. “I’ve only seen Chemibreakers sworn in with oath formularies.”

“Scraps have their own formulary.” Soffesa crosses her arms. “It’s dangerous, but,” she shrugs, “I’ll definitely trust you more.”

Vellene’s stomach drops. “How dangerous?”

“As dangerous as the rest of our mission,” Eledar says. He clears his throat. “It will tie your life to our endeavors.”

Vellene sucks in a breath, grabs her mug of brew, and tosses it back. It burns her throat, far stronger than any of the brews she’s ever had. Her mind frizzes within a millisecond, picking up on a formulary within the brew. Her fingers tremor.

"That was a lot," Eledar examines. He stares at her half-empty mug. "For your body weight, I mean." He plasters his eyes to anywhere but Vellene.

Soffesa raises a mocking brow. "Your Imperial. Have you ever had a Scrap brew?"

Vellene shakes her head. She does it too quick, and the tavern spins. She gasps and clutches the bar top. "What is it?"

"Easy." Eledar latches an arm around her before she falls out of her chair. He jolts back for a moment, the same strange, electric sensation pulsing between them. He grimaces when she tenses against him.

Vellene sucks in a breath. Each heave of her chest thrusts her closer to him. Her veins ripple with heat. It's different from the embers she knows rest within her. She clenches his biceps and presses her lips together. Her face is too close to his, his ear only inches away. Between streaks of tar, his skin sparkles with the effect of the brew. She swallows, hard. No one has ever held her like this. No one has ever kept her from falling.

Their eyes lock, and Eledar's arms curl around her, tighter, relentless, as if the realm will shatter if he dares to let go.

"You can trust me," she whispers toward his ear, and she means it. She can't explain her draw to him or the heat that passes between them like a lifeline. All she knows is she doesn't want to let go either. She's been as starved for touch and care as Scraps have been for chemight. Eledar could be the end of her, and she would only step closer, latch tighter. She likes his heat, and she likes how it stirs her own.

His lips part with a heavy breath. His fingers glide down her forearm until his fingers sweep over hers.

She thinks he might take her hand, might kiss her, might help her rip herself to pieces and become something else.

Then The Silent clears her throat.

"I'll do the oath," Vellene says, and they break apart.

Eledar frowns. A muscle in his neck strains. "Well, now I feel bad." He helps her prop herself against a chair. Then he gestures to her mug. "We may have ordered you something a little stronger."

"What?" Dread fills Vellene. "You were going to force me into an oath unwillingly?"

He and Soffesa press their lips together.

Vellene glares at him, the heat she felt before shriveling into ash. "If you don't trust me to the point you need to drug me and force me into a life-threatening oath, then why not just kill me?" The words slur and it takes her a few moments to get them all out, but she manages it.

"That's what I was thinking," Soffesa points out. She eyes Vellene with suspicion. "Maybe I do like you."

Vellene squirms away from Eledar's arm. Its weight smothers her. She groans and leans into the bar, tries to put one foot in front of the other.

"I think she's trying to run," Eledar mutters in amusement.

"Formidable. I'll give her that," Soffesa says.

Vellene lets out a frustrated breath. "I can hear you," she drawls.

Eledar blocks her. He leans into the bar, elbow placed on its top, dirtied face resting on his fist. "Look, whether we like it or not, we need you, Vellene. You're our way into the monster's nest. Our plan was inspired to begin with. With you, it's successful."

Vellene's blood burns. The brew attacks everything in her, and she falls to her knees. She catches herself, palms flat against the floor, and a scream tickles her throat. A scream of fury. She chews on the inside of her cheek as the floorboards under her palms swirl. *I just wanted to be free.* Something hot runs down her face. She reaches a hand up and finds tears. She slams a fist into the floor.

"Yes," Eledar mutters. "Indeed." He motions to Soffesa. "I think now is as good a time as any."

Soffesa crouches in front of her. "I'd say I'm sorry, but this is actually quite fun." She grins as gray light shimmers from her palms. She lifts her fingers to her lips, concentrates. The gray seeps into her mouth and the fiery orange of Soffesa's eyes swirls to the solidity of stone. She opens her mouth to speak, and gray tendrils reach toward Vellene.

She backs away, but Eledar grabs her and forces her in place. She ignores the sensation that funnels through her at his touch. "I would betray my family willingly," she tries. Her voice fills with desperate trembles.

"I'm sorry." Eledar tightens his grip on her shoulders. "This is too important."

Vellene's body shakes when the first tendril collides with her skin.

"Vellene Winloc." Soffesa's voice comes deep, guttural—something from a world unknown. "You hereby enter this oath with a simple task: assassinate Aquim and Mogaell Winloc."

Vellene trembles. "Not my sister, I won't—"

"Complete this task by your 18th birthday, or you will die in your family's place." Soffesa leans closer, lips parted. The gray chemight pours from her and seeps into Vellene.

The mist hooks into her veins. First, there's only a tingle. Then, it stings. She convulses, coughs in exasperation. The pain takes its time to fade. She slumps further into Eledar's broad chest as it does.

The gray evaporates.

Soffesa pulls back. Her eyes revert to their normal shade of fire. She clears her throat, raises a hand to scratch her neck. "I think I did it right."

"You think?" Eledar asks.

Soffesa glares at him. "Yes."

Eledar loosens his grip. "Vellene?"

Vellene gnashes her teeth together. Scrap chemight is quite sobering. The effects of her brew dissipated the moment dread kicked in. Dread that there is no way out. Not anymore. She pulls up onto her feet.

"Vellene?" Eledar tries again.

"It's fine." Vellene turns to them, blows out a breath. "As I said before, I would have done it anyway." It's not fine. None of this is fine. Some part of her hates them. Another part of her is glad. The oath will keep her steady. The oath won't allow her to slip into the girl Aquim wants her to be. It will keep her true and honest.

Eledar relaxes.

Soffesa shrugs. "Okay. I will grant you a sliver of my trust for the time being."

Vellene hesitates. "I'm not saying I would." She chooses her words carefully. "But what happens if it's broken? The oath?"

"You die."

"How?"

Soffesa picks at her nails, bored. "The chemight won't leave your body until the task is complete, and if you don't complete the task, then the chemight will poison you." She glances up at Vellene. "Best you stay on task."

Vellene swallows. Poison. She strides to the bartender. All she can think about is escaping into one the rooms upstairs, hiding from Eledar and Soffesa, and figuring out what to do next. She looks Felix up and down.

He does the same.

"How much for a room?" she asks.

He raises a brow. "You can't stay here."

"Why not? I can pay."

"I'm sure you can, Imperial." His face twists in disgust. "I gave you your brew. You've had your fun. Now leave."

*Of course.* Vellene pushes her anger down, nods, and goes to the door.

Eledar chases after her.

She ignores him, steps outside and down onto the street. She careens into the shadows before anyone can see her. *What does it matter?* She shakes her head. *If I have to go back anyway?*

"You're doing the right thing."

Vellene finds a long crate stacked against a Scrap shack and settles onto it.

Eledar sits beside her. "Your family deserves to pay for the atrocities continuing in Frales."

Vellene drops her elbows to her knees, cups her face between her hands. She stares at her feet. "I barely know you."

Eledar swallows. "I know."

"And you've asked me to not only leap but to jump off an abyss-damned cliff, Eledar."

"I know."

She rubs her temples. "I ran away because I couldn't take another second trapped in that prison." She straightens and looks at him. "Do you get how much you've asked of me?"

Eledar stares at the square across from the Scrap shack. Utilities work to set up a stage and chairs, likely for an Imperial gathering. He leans into his knees and laces his fingers together. "Have you ever known a Golem chemi, Vellene?"

She knows the stories, their eventual outlaw after they rose against Imperials in Frales. They were dangerous. So dangerous they had to be taken apart in pieces, hunted and melted back down into clay, and dumped into the unknown depths of Dalbian's Abyss.

Vellene thinks of his wounded leg. When she healed it, he kept his pant leg down. She hadn't thought much about it at the time, but… She turns her gaze to him. He looks so normal.

Eledar peels dried tar from his skin, winces as it takes his arm hair with it. His eyes drift to hers for a moment. He tenses at her stare and quickly looks at his hands, plays with his fingers. "The Fralian Imperials got greedy one day and decided Utility chemi weren't obedient enough, said too much, could never fully be trusted."

He clears his throat, shifts his weight. "So, Lazar Rathmore used chemight to create the first Golem chemi. Males and females forged of chemight and only chemight. Malleable bodies. Malleable minds. Dummies meant to be directed to do an Imperial's bidding without question."

"It didn't work," she says. "The Golem evolved. Began to disobey Imperials."

"Yes." Eledar grits his teeth. "Because how dare they think. How dare they feel." He looks at her, and his face carves with an anger so potent, it drifts off him in waves. "How dare they wish to live."

"Your deposits." Vellene licks her lips.

"I'm a Golem." Eledar scratches the top of his tar-crusted head. "I was made to obey—and everyone I loved was built with the same obedience." His shoulders tense. "Until we began to want more, as every living creature does."

"You look no different from me."

"And yet every Golem chemi now faces hiding or execution." He shakes his head, a deep sadness in his eyes. "I could have left Frales with Soffesa five years ago, but I stayed to keep what was left of her family and the Golem safe."

"And now you're here."

He manages a terse nod. "Now I'm here."

She leans back into the wall. "Are they—"

"Yes." He grits his teeth. "Despite my best efforts."

Vellene hesitates, then places a hand on his shoulder.

His muscles tense beneath her palm at the zing that slices between them. It melds to nothing more than a warm comfort, and he relaxes.

"I'm sorry," she says.

"Don't be." His eyes trace her face. "I rather you do something about it."

Vellene's brow furrows. "How can I help a dead species?"

Eledar nods to three Scrap children playing in a puddle of leftover tar from the shard storm. They're the only Scraps awake, but they don't care, their laughter echoing between shacks and mounds of garbage.

"You can't, but you can help them. Scraps are next." He blows out a breath. "No, actually, they're now. The war in Frales is more than a war. It's an eradication, Vellene. You said so yourself. Every time Imperials feel threatened, they dispose of that threat."

He gestures to the children. "Even if the threat has a heart." He points to the Utilities working on the stage. "Even if the threat tries its best not to be one." He gives a bitter laugh. "I am going to kill your family, Vellene. Not just for Golem but for all chemi that aren't Imperials."

"I get it. I do." She bites her lip. "It's just that living with the enemy is like imprisoning myself." She measures her breaths. "I'm not ready to go back. I've only just gotten away."

"Yeah." He nods. "Of course." He stands, fingers twitching at his sides, face to the sky in thought. He brings his gaze to hers and manages a grin. "A few hours of reprieve then."

"Really?" She reaches for the calm.

"Yes." Eledar looks down at himself. "I'll get cleaned up." His lips slip into a sheepish grin. "Then we can share some brews with Soffesa." He glances at a clock. It hangs from a pole near the courtyard where the Utilities work. "Scraps should be waking up soon. The tavern is sure to get busy."

"I admit, I'm not much of a brew drinker." Her face reddens.

Eledar waves it off. "You will be with time." He laughs and juts his chin toward The Bloody Cloth. "Wait for me?"

Vellene nods. "Sure."

He claps his hands together. "Fantastic." Then he jogs up the steps to the tavern and vanishes inside.

Vellene places a hand over her chest, feels the beat of her frantic heart. Excitement. It flutters through her. Fear. It poisons her thoughts. Hope. It's there. Always. And that's a comfort. She stands, paces.

Some Scraps head inside, arms hung around each other, devilish grins on their faces. She looks to the sky, where the sun has begun its split into Alchemight's moons. It's stretched out, two portions tucked in as if someone stands behind it, pinching it into three spheres. She yanks her hood up as more Scraps fill the streets.

Despite the little pricks of the poison now flowing through her veins, Vellene knows she should try and enjoy the time she has here. It could be the last night of freedom for a long time. A veil of sadness cloaks her at the thought, and her feet turn leaden. *Going into The Bloody Cloth is to choose to move forward with this plan, and I don't know—*

The poison burns through her, clearly not liking her indecision.

Vellene squeezes her eyes shut. "Fine," she hisses between clenched teeth. "You win."

"I usually do."

She slams her eyes open at the sound of Soffesa.

The assassin stands in front of her, orange eyes trailing over her face, then the tattered remnants of her gown.

"What do you want?" Vellene crosses her arms and pulls her cloak tighter around her.

Soffesa sighs. "You didn't come inside with Eledar."

"So, what? You're my guard?"

Soffesa stiffens and frowns. "You know, I'm not always The Silent."

Vellene purses her lips in consideration. "Okay."

"And when I'm not, I'm Eledar's family. His only family." She studies Vellene. "I may be brash with you, but it's because he means everything to me." Her voice falters, and Vellene realizes she's struggling to say this—to open up past the rigid structure she's turned herself into. "I will protect him with my life until I've left this dreadful place in death."

Vellene watches her closely. "What does that have to do with me?"

The Silent smooths her hair. "I just thought you should know that, in case you do him any harm. Any."

Vellene twists her fingers together, and they stand in silence for a moment.

Soffesa's eyes run over Vellene's gown a second time. "So, you ran from home. In that."

Vellene grimaces. "During a shard storm."

Soffesa tilts her head. "That's brave."

"Is that a compliment?"

Soffesa's lips tip with a smirk. "I've been known to give them from time to time."

"I suppose I should consider myself lucky then." Vellene pinches the fabric of her gown between her fingers.

Soffesa clears her throat, uncomfortable as she throws a thumb over her shoulder toward The Bloody Cloth. "I have some spare clothes. If you want them."

Vellene touches a finger to her face, feels the hardened tar she swiped across it earlier in the day. "You wouldn't happen to also have a shower?"

Soffesa nods. "But you have to come inside for both."

Vellene's eyes flick to The Bloody Cloth. It's come alive with the beat of a symphonic, the music drumming out into the alley as Alchemight's three moons blaze overhead.

"Vellene."

She looks back at Soffesa.

The hardness of the assassin's face softens. "Death is not an admirable choice. That's what you were choosing when you wanted to run to Frales. That war would have taken everything from you. Then, it would have taken your life."

Soffesa's tan skin pales at the thought, her own past haunting her features. "I understand that the death oath may feel cruel. We had to do what we could to protect ourselves and this mission. If you want death still, I won't stop you." Her face turns to stone then, her shoulders rolled back with the decision. "But to fight is to live. To live is to fight, Vellene."

Vellene tucks a stray purple coil behind her ear. "That's where you're wrong," she whispers, unable to quite say the truth of it. She cringes at how timid she sounds, how fragile. Soffesa's right to an extent. Vellene never would have stood a chance in Frales. It was a foolish plan.

She would've died. Drowned. Or flayed for her power. But maybe that's what she wanted. Deep down. Maybe she didn't want to make it. Maybe she wanted it all to end. The flashbacks. The bruises along her ribs that still haven't healed. The long scar across her thigh from a fire wound that never faded. "To go back is death, as well," Vellene says, lifting her gaze to The Silent's.

Soffesa takes a careful step toward her, then she holds out a hand, her fingers slim but calloused and her nails painted crimson. "Then think of this place as purgatory." She offers Vellene an encouraging smile. It's strained, but it's enough to make Vellene accept her hand. The Silent guides her toward the porch of The Bloody Cloth. "Think of this night as a night to live between two deaths."

*A night to live between two deaths.* Vellene tightens her hand around the assassin's. "Thank you," she whispers, "for being kind."

The assassin swallows, her eyes dark with guilt. "Come," Soffesa says softly, then pushes open the swinging doors of The Bloody Cloth. "Let's get you cleaned up."

## Chapter Ten

# *Eledar*

Eledar steps out of a shower in the bathing chamber. Surprisingly, the tar was easier to rinse off than he thought. He tucks a cloth around his waist and leaves, the room nothing more than shower stalls and a large mirror. He wrenches his tar-covered rags and stolen cloak from the floor and stuffs them under an arm.

As he shoves through the door into the main area of the tavern, he runs a thumb over the orb nestled in the deposit on his torso. He should give it to Soffesa. It was a gift to her from her father, after all, but something about giving it up sends a pang of conflict through him.

Some portion of his mind—the part he has deliberately kept locked away—nags at him. *Grief*, he mulls over the word, the emotion he chooses to ignore every second of every thought that passes through him. *I'm not yours for the taking*, he thinks.

He passes a hole in the wall and glances outside to the alley. He spots Vellene and Soffesa near the crates and grins. If he stands any chance at procuring the source of all chemight, he needs every member of his crew to function with some amount of respect. Seeing the two together without him is a start in the right direction, but the warmth that spreads through him is more than a general sense of achievement.

To see Soffesa again, to know she's alive—his grin widens. *But how do I tell her about Niam?* He banishes the responsibility and takes the rickety stairs up to his designated room. *Don't think about that. Not now.*

He shoulders open a door and steps inside a small space. In the corner is a small table with a candle melted into its top. Nothing more than a hardened puddle of wax and a burnt-to-the-crisp wick, it beckons him. He steps to it.

Eledar clenches his teeth and wills the candle to light. Natural chemight seeps out of his palm in a fine, gray mist. He holds his breath as he directs the mist to wrap around the wick, pooling around it into the shape of a small flame.

Chemight is an art. Imperials have it easy with their formularies and deposits—both of which help channel the motive of the chemight in a way that matches their intentions. Manipulating natural chemight, however, requires a great amount of self-control, something Eledar lacks and continues to be the bane of his existence. If he were at war with this candle, if he had even the smallest amount of adrenaline pulsing through him, it would be a different story. As a Golem, he has more chemight in his veins than most, but he's only ever had true use of it in an emotional state.

He wishes he had the resources of an Imperial, the ability to have several primitive formularies on hand. Then, he could draw upon them and light the wick with the snap of his fingers. Unfortunately, Equilibrium supplied him with only twelve primitive formularies, most of which he used to sail the piece of wood they called a 'boat' through an unforgiving sea of tar.

His eyes narrow on the candle, and to his impatient delight, smoke curls up. A minute passes and a flame ignites. He rocks back on his heels with a smug expression as the flame gives him a flickering wave of hello.

Eledar dumps his old clothes next to a large bag that sticks halfway out from under the bed. He drags it forward and rifles through it for a pair of trousers and a shirt, grateful his best friend expected him to show up, even if it has been years. A metallic taste of guilt settles on his tongue, and his veins cry out for lumis. He blows out an unsteady breath as he pulls on the clothing. He pauses to run his fingers over the filled chemight deposits along his back.

After years of having little to no power, the rest of the formularies Equilibrium granted him overwhelm his senses. If he has so much as an itch to create a blade, an explosion, or heal an incurable wound—he could. But

Golem were built to hold power, not to use it. At least, not for themselves. Lazar Rathmore pulled their strings, commanded them to do his bidding. Free will was a concept Eledar knew little about, only dreamed of, as a young chemi. It's one of the reasons he had Vellene heal his leg. He needs to use his formularies sparingly.

When Lazar died and Eledar's strings were cut, he tasted freedom for the first time. He had plans. There wasn't a Golem who hadn't dreamed up some kind of glorious escape plan. None of them ever thought they'd get to use it. Until they could, and even then, they used most of their previously supplied formularies before the night was out to fight through the Imperials' heavily guarded perimeter.

Eledar spent the five years following his escape and the ultimate failure of protecting the Golem who decided—for some reason he never quite understood—he was a reliable leader, attempting to make it up with Soffesa's family. When that failed: *lumis*. As much as he could get his hands on. He told himself he would stay away from it in Scorus, that this would be a fresh start.

The burn in his veins continues its constant banging from the back of his skull: *Just once*, it screams, *a night of bliss, just once just once just once.*

Eledar runs a hand through his hair and leans into the frame of the room's window, if it can even be called that. It's more of a misshapen hole closed off by nothing more than a jagged piece of fabric. The makeshift curtain flaps around his shoulder, bats him on the cheek. He shoves it aside and stares out across the city.

Scorus, in many ways, is as Frales was before the war. He half-expects to see spirits roaming the streets with missing limbs and blown-apart smiles. Scrap shacks, he supposes, are all the same. He imagined Scorus to be something else, maybe even something better than the broken nation he left behind. Instead, it's a fraternal twin, close to broken and certainly beyond repair.

Eledar folds his arms across his chest and picks out a set of wild blue, green, and purple curls making their way into The Bloody Cloth. *Vellene.* The Winloc Imperial follows Soffesa into the tavern, her hair vibrant against the night.

He traces her frame as she disappears from view, her movements fragile, as if one wrong step will cause her to crumple. Or maybe the world. He hasn't quite figured out which it is. She fears. Greatly. It could be because of her past, but it could be her future. A death doesn't make for comfort.

He aches with guilt. *Lumis.* His fingers find a scab and pick open the wound. They plunge into the clay that pushes free. He hisses and clamps his palm over it. *Quit doing that,* he reprimands himself and shakes his head.

Then he jumps up when the door swings open.

Soffesa freezes in the doorway and lifts a brow. "Why do you look caught?"

His cheeks redden. "Nothing. I was just lost in thought."

She narrows her eyes on his blush but shrugs and reaches for the same bag he pulled clothes from. "I see you found my stash." She pulls out a piece of black fabric he thinks may be a dress. Then she grabs a clean cloth. "Vellene needs something, too."

He rubs the back of his neck. "I saw you being nice to her."

Soffesa shoots him a pointed look. "That doesn't mean I trust her."

"Why not?" he shrugs. "She's under a death oath, Soff."

She blows out a breath. "Yeah, I know. It's just hard for me."

"I remember." Eledar crosses to her, and she clutches the black garment and the cloth to her chest.

Her eyes flick over his face. "I still can't quite believe you're really here."

Eledar nods. "The feeling is mutual."

They fall silent, and he hates how awkward it feels. There was a time when their silence was a comfort. Now, it feels like a rift that may never heal itself.

"I should get this to her." Soffesa holds up the dress for emphasis. "You're coming back down, right?"

Eledar bites his lip, then takes her shoulder before she can turn away. "Soff, we'll get through this."

She shifts. "I know." She manages a half-smile. "I guess I just thought your homecoming would be more of a relief and less of a stress. With this mission..." she trails off and steps back from his grip. "We'll be fine."

Eledar shoves his hands in his pockets. "Yeah."

She glances up at his hair. "You should dry that more. You look like a mop."

He raises a brow.

She laughs and waves him off. "Whatever, just come down soon. We need to send Vellene back to Winloc Grove before the night ends."

"Alright." He waits for her to leave, for the door to close, before his shoulders and smile fall. He wonders when, if ever, he can quit pretending to be the strong one. *It's worth it*, he tells himself, but another, smaller voice echoes through his skull. The one of doubt. The one who knows the truth.

He can pretend to be the hero, the best friend, the brother. He can pretend the need to forget that thrums through him will pass into nothing more than a whim. But no matter what, he will crawl out of bed tonight, and he will hunt the streets of Scorus for *lumis* to keep the nightmares at bay. To push back the truth of why he's here.

*Pretend, pretend, pretend*—but it won't change the facts. Most, if not all, of his species is dead. He failed to protect his best friend's father and the last of her family. He is here, not to be heroic, but to save his own ass. Worse, he put an innocent chemi, one that fills him with a sense of calm he's never felt before, under a death oath.

What does that make him? Does he care?

Eledar dries his hair, then wipes away the mud that slipped from the wound he picked open. It hasn't healed, but it's begun to re-patch with a scab. Golem heal faster than most chemi, due to the ample amount of chemight that flows through their clay.

He frowns at the scab, and if it weren't for the blast of a symphonic coming to life downstairs and the bellows of drunken Scraps vibrating the walls, he would open the wound again and again and again.

To feel the pain. To feel anything other than the guilt, the grief. Instead, he drops the cloth, opens the door, and moves to the stairs.

*Brew will have to do*, he decides as he takes the steps two at a time and heads straight for the bar.

## Chapter Eleven

# *Vellene*

Vellene stares into the mirror of a bathing space downstairs. Dark bags hang under her eyes, and as she scrubs the streaks of tar from her face, she finds herself paler. She wonders if it's the poison. Silent but deadly. Just like the chemi who gave her it.

Soffesa appears then, a black garment folded in her arms, along with a cloth. She closes the distance to the counter, moving with the same litheness Vellene imagines a shadow would have. Then, the assassin plucks the cloth and holds it out.

Vellene grimaces as the water turns the dried tar on her face into a thick sludge. She hesitates but accepts the cloth from Soffesa. It's unreasonable to be scared of a cloth, but is it as unreasonable when it comes from a renowned, merciless individual? She flicks a glance up at The Silent, who scowls. Vellene swallows and pats her skin dry before she focuses on her hair.

It's as wild as it's ever been. *Untamed*, her mother always said. She attempts to push it into something prettier or, at least, smoother, but it disobeys her every swat, flick, and pull.

Soffesa pulls up onto the counter. She grips the ledge and swings her legs, watches her feet kick. "You should get dressed. If we want good drinks, we'll need to get them before the end of the hour."

Vellene pinches the black garment Soffesa brought her. It unfolds into a slim-fitting dress, a slit up to the thigh on the left side, and a deep v in the neck. It won't cover anything, especially her orbs. She raises a brow at the assassin.

Soffesa shrugs. "It's all I have."

"I'll have to keep the cloak on."

"Or take your orbs out."

Vellene freezes from fidgeting with the dress. "What?"

"No one will look twice at empty deposits," Soffesa explains.

"I'd be unprotected."

"You'd be safer." Soffesa reaches for a pouch attached to her waist. "You can put them in here."

Vellene eyes her. "You want me to hand over all my formularies?"

Soffesa grins. "You have to trust me at some point, Winloc. Why not now?"

Vellene runs her fingers over the formularies along her neck.

"There's no place safer to put them. No one would dare to steal from me."

Carefully, she pops one of her formularies out. Its power leaves her in an instant. She rolls the marble-sized orb around in her palm for a minute, then she sucks in a breath and drops it into Soffesa's pouch.

"Good job." Soffesa gives the bag a shake. "Now for the rest."

Vellene grimaces but pops them out, one after the other. Once she has, the loss of them isn't the only thing that makes her feel naked in the dim-lit bathroom. She slips into the borrowed dress, the fabric soft against her skin and more revealing than anything she's ever worn. Curves she's been lectured into hiding are accentuated, especially by the built-in corset she fastens at her waist, the leather and boning a matte black.

"Huh," Soffesa says, lips parted a bit in shock.

Vellene cringes. "Is it awful?"

The assassin shakes her head. "No. It's not that. You just look…greater."

"Greater?"

"Like something more than you were before."

"Weaker is more accurate." Vellene flexes her fingers. "I don't like not having any formularies to rely on."

"Vellene."

She looks at Soffesa. "What?"

Soffesa hops down from the bathroom counter, the light glinting off the Scrap ink on her face. "I don't have any formularies, either, and do I look weak?"

"No." Vellene glances at herself in the mirror. "But I don't look like that." It's true. Soffesa has an air about her, one that commands the attention of anyone she wants. It surprises Vellene, considering The Silent is exactly that. Silent. Invisible. Vellene never thought someone so in tune with the shadows could also be such a beacon of confidence in the light. If anything, it gives her hope for herself.

Soffesa must notice Vellene's internal battle because she clears her throat. "Roll your shoulders back," the assassin commands. She places her hands on Vellene's shoulders. Then she wrenches them back. "Great. Tilt your chin up. Just enough." Soffesa demonstrates with her own, and Vellene mirrors her. "Now tell me you don't look powerful."

Vellene stares at her reflection, and this time she sees a glimmer of something new. Gone is her discomfort from the dress and her missing formularies. In its place is someone more confident. Someone greater. Vellene manages a smile and turns to face the assassin. "You're not so bad, are you?"

Soffesa balks. "Abyss, don't ever say that in public," she swears as she opens the bathroom door to go out into the crowd. "Otherwise, I'll kill you. Slowly."

Vellene laughs and shakes her head as she follows Soffesa out, leaving her nightgown, her stolen cloak, and her fear behind on the bathroom counter. She gets one night to live between deaths. She won't allow her father's conditioning to ruin it.

Empty, The Bloody Cloth is a dirt-covered bar with little to brag about.

At its capacity, it's another story.

Scraps, Utilities—even some Chemibreakers—fill the little tavern. They order brews, hunker down at one of the tables, or stand about in conversation. A fight breaks out in the corner and a circle forms around the fighters. Playful jeers rise before they're devoured by the sound of a symphonic in the opposite corner. The band of instrument players draw out the first chords of a song, then rush the tempo as their lead steps up and belts the lyrics. Bodies move to face the symphonic before they writhe to the rhythm. Smiles on faces. Some covered in filth. Some wiped clean. All of them desperate to not think.

And it's beautiful.

Vellene loses Soffesa as she comes to a stop near the doorway. Chemi push past her, grunt curses for her to move, but Vellene plants herself to her spot, eyes wide with wonder. She doesn't care about the smell. Doesn't care about the drunken slurs slung her way. Doesn't care about anything except for the muddled mess that the tavern is. Nothing like this was allowed within the Imperial gates she was trapped behind.

Soffesa finds her a few minutes later. She carries two mugs and eyes Vellene with wariness. "You know you're in the way, right?"

"I don't care." Vellene's lips fall into a smile. "Is it always like this? All these different chemi?"

Soffesa raises a brow. "Aquim keeps you under lock and key, doesn't he?"

Vellene chills at her father's name. "Please, I don't want to think of him."

Soffesa's lips crook into a sly smile. "Here." She pushes one of the two mugs of brew into Vellene's chest. "This will help with that."

"Another ploy to cast more chemight on me?" Vellene cocks a brow.

The assassin scoffs. "I'm offended, Winloc. I wouldn't be dumb enough to try that twice."

She yanks the mug from Soffesa and brings it to her lips. Vellene ignores the chunks of scumtis and tilts her head back as she chugs. It sears down her throat, and she squeezes her eyes shut in an effort not to choke.

"Abyss," Soffesa curses. "Easy."

She finishes the brew and shoves it back toward the assassin. "A night to live, right?"

"Sure. Whatever." Soffesa stares at her, brows furrowed in uncertainty.

The brew takes immediate effect, but the difference between this one and the one used to force an oath on her is incredible. Her veins don't burn. They *sing*.

Everything in Vellene becomes fine-tuned to the music of the symphonic. It pulls her forward, traps her between swaying bodies. She sways, too, and The Bloody Cloth changes color.

Every chemi glows. Every movement of her body to the beat vibrates with energy. She rides the wave of color, of euphoria, throwing her head back. She's always loved to dance. It's always been alone in her room, humming to herself. Now she relishes the heat of the crowd and the pulse of the music.

Hands grip her waist, but she remains tuned to a frequency only she can hear.

A frequency of life. Of color.

Of zero obligation.

"Vellene?"

*I know that word.* Vellene hums along with the leader of the symphonic, eyes closed. *What is that word?*

"She chugged a brew," comes Soffesa's voice, and it slices through her.

The hands on her waist tighten. "Are you okay?"

*Vellene, that's my name.* She remembers it now. Her eyes flick open and she stares at the hands at her waist. They connect to wrists, to arms, to broad shoulders, to a neck, to—"Eledar," she mutters, and his name rolls off her tongue as sweet as honey. He's different. *Clean*, she realizes. Every streak of tar rinsed away.

She reaches a hand up and rests it on his face. His lips move. Words come toward her, but they fade before they reach her ears. She surveys this new him.

Before, tar matted his hair into an unrecognizable mess. Now, it shines in dark gray waves to his ears. The green of his eyes is still striking, but it warms against the light bronze of his skin. The playfulness of his brows makes sense now with the dance of freckles across the bridge of his nose. Her chest tightens, and a certain heat floods her.

Vellene runs her thumb over the inside of his wrist, several scars marring his skin. Her breaths are uneven, her steps unsteady, and she wants—him. She can't deny it. Attraction. She's sure of it, even if she's never had the chance to feel it before. Something inside her tugs desperately toward him.

He turns his face from her, speaks something to Soffesa, but The Silent gives him a wave of annoyed dismissal and disappears.

"Can you hear me?" Eledar asks.

Vellene blinks, and he *sparkles*.

Eledar swallows and peels her palm away from his cheek. He leans to her ear. "Are you okay?" His voice is soft but loud, breaking through the music of the symphonic.

Vellene's heart sticks to her throat. "My mother would have loved this place."

Eledar draws back, nods. "Sure," he calls over the crowd. "But *are you okay?*" he tries for the third time.

She runs her fingers over his freckles. "You're different."

Eledar's forehead creases. "Well, I'm clean."

"Yeah."

Eledar laughs.

The effect of the brew brightens his face as his head tilts back. His smile glows. His eyes twinkle. She's never seen anyone more breathtaking. She floats toward him, finds her body against his.

Electricity crackles between them. Then a moment passes, and the sting of their connected bodies swarms into a flood of warmth. This close, she can feel his lethality. He grew up in Frales. Golem or not, he was a soldier. Had to be. She feels the hard grooves of his arms, and her eyes trace the sharp jut of his jaw. He reminds her of a weapon, and she likes that. She wonders if he'll teach her how to be one.

Eledar's face dips toward her, his eyes reflecting with a dark conflict. Guilt. Terror. Sadness.

It makes her wrap her arms around him, tuck the side of her face to his chest—hold him as close as she can because no one has ever done so when she feels those things. Even if it's all she ever wanted. Simple. Loving. Touch. It's been so long since skin against hers didn't mean a bruise or a scar.

She sways, watches their feet step from one side to the other. She closes her eyes, breathes him in, and her lips form a slim smile.

She'll admit she's dreamed of this. To dance with a boy. A girl. She never cared. She wants love. She always has, and she's so tired of everyone around her making her feel as if that's a weak want to have. Why can't she be angry and soft? Why can't she be quiet and fierce? The greatest exhaustion of her life has been trying to be a monster or a girl. She wants to be both. Feared and wanted.

She's so tired of never having a choice.

They stay like that for song after song. *Or is it the same song?* She's unsure, nor does she care. She vanishes into the chords of the symphonic. With her ear pressed tightly to his chest, she listens for the beat of his heart but finds none.

Instead, his chest vibrates with the chords of the song, turns his body into a new kind of instrument. *No heart.* The thought floats through her, and the idea is somewhat difficult for her to comprehend. *No heart, just chemight and clay.*

His muscles tense as if he can hear her skepticism. She wonders faintly if she said her thoughts aloud, but even that fades away. She trails her fingers under the back of his shirt, finds one of his chemight deposits. She touches the smooth edges of an orb. The energy of the chemight within pulses against her fingertips. Then she spreads her hand, feels the ridges of his spine.

She can't stop touching him, knowing him, and she loves how everywhere she touches pushes his chest against her cheek with heavier breaths. It's powerful to affect someone so easily, to know her touch might mean as much to him as his does to her.

Vellene slopes her hands down his waist, and his cheek brushes her ear.

"Vellene," he murmurs, and her heart races at the gravel in his voice.

She closes her eyes. "I'm sorry." Slowly she pulls back, but he catches her hands.

"Don't apologize to me." He sucks in a shallow breath. "You've done nothing wrong."

Vellene stares at him. Such a concept feels like a lie. She is wrong. Everything about her is wrong wrong wrong—

"Is it enough?" he interrupts her thoughts, one of his hands scraping gently against the nape of her neck.

She shudders under his touch, and heat sprouts through her with keen want.

Eledar's fingers clench the back of her dress. His expression is hardened, eyes staring past her. "To go back, I mean."

She bites her lip.

He nods behind her. "They're here, Vellene."

Suddenly, the brew isn't enough. The dance isn't enough. Vellene swallows and follows his gaze.

Four Chemibreakers stand in the doorway of The Bloody Cloth, their silver and navy uniforms holed out in places to show filled chemight deposits. All of them wear the Winloc crest embroidered on their shirts. They scan the crowd. Blue chemight from weaponized chaos formularies steams between their knuckles.

"They're not here to drink," Eledar mutters.

Vellene tightens her arms around him.

His eyes trace her face. "You need more time."

She nods.

Eledar looks to the stairs. He pushes her gently and takes her hand. "C'mon."

Vellene follows him up the steps. With each she takes, they become more solid against the bottoms of her feet. Her heart aches as the brew seeps from her system and wafts to the dance floor. It leaves her skin clammy but cold, a sheen of sweat along her forehead while goosebumps litter her arms.

She tightens her grip on Eledar's hand as they leave the stairs behind and enter a narrow hall lined with doors. Intricate spideria webs sparkle in the rafters of plywood above their heads. Beyond that is the roof—a thatched thing of tarps, cloths, and certainly not enough stability to survive the calmest of shard storms. Fresh patches fill places where the shard storm of last night sliced open new wounds in the roof. She's surprised the rooms even have doors—a luxury for any Scrap shack.

Eledar pulls her past an open door. Scraps sit inside on a bed with brews. One practices dirty chemight. Gray sparks encircle his wrists before they spark outward, uncontrolled. All of the Scraps duck, eyes wide, before the gray chemight dissipates into nothing, and they burst into laughter.

She can't help but imagine them hanging in her front yard.

Eledar tugs her past them, stops at a door a few down. He pulls a key out of his pocket.

"They're here." Soffesa emerges from the stairs, face grim. "They're looking for Vellene."

"I saw." Eledar opens the door. "Get inside."

Vellene hurries in.

The room is dressed in dark tones. Navy curtains. Charcoal bedspread. Walls of oak and red brick. It's the least Scrap-looking part of The Bloody Cloth she's seen. Some trash is used to patch a few holes, but the curtains—though battered and draped at odd angles—are hung on an actual iron rod, rather than a string, and the bed has a sturdy wooden frame.

Eledar looks to Soffesa as she shuts the door.

"They'll check the rooms." Soffesa moves to the window. She draws the curtain, then flings it back in place. "There's five more outside."

Vellene looks between them. "I have to go, don't I?"

"That, or our oath can kill you." Soffesa shrugs. "Can't say I wouldn't be pleased if you chose the latter."

Vellene grimaces at how much those words sting.

"Soff." Eledar scowls.

Soffesa rolls her eyes. "Your affection toward her is nauseating."

A blush follows the trail of Eledar's freckles. "She's on our side. You don't need to keep harassing her."

"She's on our side for now, Eledar. What happens when she goes home? When she's surrounded by her life of wealth?" Soffesa glares at Vellene. "What then?"

Vellene sobers. Her moment of calm, of escape, wipes away. She settles on the edge of the bed. "Then I'll die."

A flicker of guilt crosses Soffesa's face before she tosses her pouch to Vellene. "Put your orbs back in."

Vellene does, shifting them out of the pouch and into each of her deposits. She tries to ignore how Eledar's eyes follow her fingers. How he watches as she pushes the orbs into their places above her breasts.

She lifts her gaze to his, and the faint blush from Soffesa's comment darkens. Her lips twitch. It's nice. To be wanted. The brew may have faded, but she still wants more. This night is hers. She decides when it ends. Not her father.

"Eledar," she says, his name hot on her tongue.

He studies her, and his blush wanes toward desire, the emerald of his eyes dark with curiosity. She matches it with ease, and he goes to the door. He yanks it open. "Go downstairs, Soff. We'll be down in a minute," he mutters, his eyes never leaving hers.

Soffesa crosses her arms. Hurt flashes across her face. "If they catch you with her, then it's over before it's begun." She steps into the hall. "Remember that," she snaps, then strides away.

Eledar heaves a breath and shuts the door. "I'm sorry. She's hard-headed, but you learn to respect and love it with time."

"I know." Vellene plays with her fingers. "I saw a bit of the nicer side earlier." She shrugs. "But I'm Imperial. We aren't trustworthy chemi. She has every right to be suspicious." She places the last orb into its spot behind her ear and continues to look him over.

Eledar takes wary steps across the room and sits beside her on the bed. "That's the same thinking that led to Golem being erased. You can't define an entire group of chemi based on your experience with a select few."

Vellene touches his hand where it rests on his knee. "Thank you." She turns to him. "For the time. It wasn't long, but I needed it."

His eyes hold her gaze. His lips part with a question but nothing comes.

"I want more time, but maybe that's selfish. I should go before anyone gets hurt by those Chemibreakers." She says it quick. Her heart flutters as she pushes up from the bed and away from him.

Eledar swallows, stands.

She takes cautious steps to the door, everything in her telling her to plant herself, to never face her family again. She touches the doorknob—

"Vellene."

—and it's all she needs to stay put. To root herself to the way he says her name. Like a wish. Like a curse.

Eledar steps close. He gently takes her shoulder and turns her toward him, sparks igniting where he touches. The toes of his boots hit hers, as he brings a hand to her face, runs his thumb across her cheek—*spark spark spark.* His chest puffs as he sucks in deeper breaths.

Vellene's stomach flutters. She blinks a few times as the electricity from his fingers pricks across her face.

"I'm trusting you." His eyes trail to her lips. "With everything I have to live for."

Vellene hesitates but leans into him, giving in to her inherent need to stay in this room, to never walk down those steps or give herself to those Chemibreakers. "So am I."

He sneaks his free arm around her waist and tugs her close. "We can't mess this up. It's too important."

Their breaths deepen. The heaves of their chests sync.

"I'll do my best." She tilts her face toward his. "I want to help you, to help all chemi, and if that means I also get my freedom—" her confidence wavers, lips tremble—"then my family's deaths are a sacrifice worth making."

He hovers his lips before hers. His hand moves from her cheek to her hair. He tangles his fingers in the coils of it, and the little pricks of feeling slide into a wave of lust.

"I must tell you." His lips brush against hers as he speaks. "I often do impulsive things I later regret, but somehow, this feels different."

"What is it?" Vellene wonders. Her heart pounds.

"I'm not sure." His fingers find her spine against the fabric of her dress. He runs them down it. "But I'd like to find out. If you'll let me."

"Touching you feels..." She shakes her head and flattens her palms over his chest.

"Right," he finishes.

Her eyes fasten on his mouth. She reaches a thumb to his lips and he kisses it softly.

"What do you want, Vellene?" he asks. "I'll give it."

"Something that's only mine." She leans close enough to brush her lips against his in the same way he did.

Her thighs shake as heat pools between them. Her breath hitches.

Then Eledar closes the distance.

*SPARK*—A fire spreads through her. She closes her eyes and sinks into his grasp. There is so much power in completely giving in. She hasn't felt this kind of trust in another in—ever. She's never trusted like this, never been given the opportunity.

Eledar cups the back of her head and the kiss deepens. His tongue swipes between her lips, and his arms shake around her. It's as if he fears letting go, too, but he's willing to try, and for that, she'll honor his wishes.

She parts her lips and twines her hands up the back of his neck into his soft hair. She tugs him closer with a fierce need. Then she claws his shirt up and off him until his chest is bared to her. She breaks their kiss to descend upon him, to trace the tip of the ravian wing on his peck with her mouth.

Eledar shivers, each of his movements as jagged and frantic as hers. His fingers hook into the laces of her corset. He tugs and pulls until newfound air fills her lungs, his eyes wild with the same starvation that lights her soul. He kisses her jaw, her neck, the curve of her breasts.

Then the world sinks away as he presses her into the door, his mouth hot on hers and their tongues twined with a unified groan.

It's an escape better than brew. It's real. Hers.

But he breaks away.

Vellene gasps and grabs his face. Warmth blazes through her. It's the choice of it. The lack of obligation.

Eledar shakes his head and rakes in a troubled breath. It's as if he's trying to reel himself in as if he thinks she wants him to stop.

"Don't," Vellene whispers, the word a ragged mess as her lips tremble. "Don't stop."

His pupils flare at the command. He wavers.

"Eledar—"

Then he bends and grabs her thighs. Vellene laughs in surprise as he lifts her into his arms and balances her against the door. His lips stretch with a wide smile—and the heat between them smothers something dark and cold within her.

She hugs him as he leans in and trails soft kisses down the column of her throat and over the chemight deposits there. Her head falls back against the door as she slides her fingers through the dark silver strands of his hair.

Every thought flies away. She closes her eyes. Listens to the steady thud, thud, thud of her heart. Her eyes flick open when Eledar carries her to the bed, lies her down. He hovers above her, then he gently presses his weight atop her. A nervous breath stumbles from between his lips, from hers. Neither of them moves, both frozen by the weight of each other. Then she kisses him. She kisses him like the realm is hers to ruin and he is her realm. She peers through her lashes at the furrow of his brow, then she moans when his teeth bite into her bottom lip.

His entire body dips closer with the sound, his hips grinding into hers. "Guardians save me," he murmurs into her neck.

"More," she whispers.

But he shakes his head and kisses her forehead. Then he finds her lips again and gives her something slow and sweet. "I can't do that. Not if I'm still meant to let you leave."

"Just a bit," she bargains, and she blushes when he smiles.

"A bit?" Eledar's eyes dance with mirth. "What is a bit, Winloc?" His hands find the top rim of her corset and drag it down until the slip covering her breasts is exposed. He traces his thumb over one firm bud, and her eyes widen. "Enough?"

Vellene struggles to find the right words. She shakes her head.

His eyes darken. "This is dangerous."

"This is what I want," she breathes and hooks her hand around the back of his neck, pulling him to her lips. "But I won't beg. I'm done begging."

"I want it, too," he admits and kisses her softly. "More than I've ever wanted anything. Being near you makes me feel awake. Like I haven't been for a very long time."

"I know. I feel it." Vellene weaves her hands through his hair and tugs him firmer between her legs. Her breath stilts at the hardness of him.

His nose lines with hers, his eyes closed and his breaths heavy as he rolls his hips. "Just a bit," he says.

"A bit?" she echoes with a smile and presses her hand over his, sliding his fingers to the edge of her dress.

Eledar chuckles. "*You* are dangerous." But the heat of his palm prickles over the slope of her calf. He slows at her thigh, traces the scar tissue of her old burn wound. The green in his eyes winks out as the warrior inside him takes the reigns. "They will bleed."

Vellene swallows and nudges his hand higher. "Yes. They will."

They crash together, their mouths vicious as they kiss and tangle and throb. His thumb finds her center, and Vellene arches into his palm with a sigh. His teeth leave marks along her thighs before they tease above his fingers. She cries out, her vision clouding with dark spots. Power hums awake inside her as every muscle in her body sinks into his grasp. The soft scent of smoke tangles up her nostrils, and her eyes flash open when his warmth leaves her.

Eledar sits back on his heels, his eyes dark with need as he stares at her bare and spread. Never in her life has she been looked at in such a way. It's as if she's being seen for the first time, and she doesn't feel any shame for it.

Color sparkles out of her peripheral, and they both blink out of their haze. For a moment, they only stare, share the same disbelief.

Like veins, chemight of every color strings between them. She shudders as her chemight deposits drain and fill, over and over. It's as if their chemight swims between them in intertwining wavelengths.

"What's happening?" he whispers, voice unsteady. He shifts his weight and runs his hand through the chemight. The waves crash around his knuckles, pulse against his wrist—but they remain strong. His eyes glimmer with curiosity.

"I don't know, but I have to go." The words leave her unwarranted, her mind kicking in while her heart rages to stay still. In this small moment with Eledar, she created her own world. One where she's strong, confident, and her surname doesn't exist. But fear inches its way into the forefront of her mind at the sight of the strange chemight. Even this isn't allowed to be wholly her own. Whatever this is, she can't deal with it. Not now, when so many problems are stacked against her.

Eledar frowns at her words. He dips his head to her left ear, brushes his lips against it. "I know, but I wish you didn't."

"You said we couldn't mess this up," Vellene breathes as his lips come back to hers.

"I say lots of things." He kisses the corner of her mouth. Little pricks of ecstasy spread outward from her lips.

"Eledar."

His chest heaves. "That solves nothing." He drags his teeth over her bottom lip.

A soft moan escapes her, despite her clenched teeth, and her back arches further. The chemight around them pulses and twines, every colored sting slowly building into a group of chains. Panic trickles through her.

His eyes waver with concern before he brings his forehead to hers. "You're safe."

"You have to let me leave." She says it, but even she can hear how her tone sounds otherwise.

He runs a hand over the chemight deposits across her sternum. He traces the long legs of the spideria inked across the tops of her breasts. "I didn't plan for this." His eyes find hers. "It complicates things."

Vellene locks her eyes with his. "It doesn't have to." She inhales sharply and—to his dismay and her own—manages to wedge herself out from under him. When she does, the chemight between them snaps apart and falls away. She gasps and braces herself on the edge of the bed as her orbs empty. Exhaustion overtakes her, but she can't deny she feels relief not seeing those chains anymore.

She looks at Eledar. All of his formularies have drained as well, except for the strange auburn-colored one with yellow flecks. He tugs it free from its deposit and brings it to his eye level, brow furrowed. "Very strange," he mutters.

Vellene chews on her tongue in thought as she pushes to her feet and presses a hand onto the wall for support. "Should we worry about whatever that was?" she asks.

"Maybe later." He sighs, runs a hand through his hair. "We've already got something unknown to conquer."

Vellene looks down at her feet. "About that. I have a request."

Eledar props up on his elbow, his eyes glittering in the low light. "Anything."

"Promise me you'll do it quickly. At least for my sister, Mogaell." Sadness grapples her. "She's always been given the short end of the stick. I just don't want her to suffer." She pulls her gaze to his with reluctance.

Eledar's expression darkens. His eyes trace her face before he focuses on the bedspread.

"Eledar."

He runs his tongue over his teeth.

"What?"

He sits up. "You're second-guessing it."

The indent between her brows flares. "No. No, I'm not." She steps to the bottom of the bed and forces herself into his line of sight. "I just mean she's a young girl being influenced to do a lot of wrong."

Eledar takes in a deep breath. Then he stands, grits his teeth, and nods to the door. "It's time to go, Vellene."

She sways. "What?"

"Go. Do your part. I'll do mine." He steps to the door, pulls it open. The hall beyond yawns into a deep darkness.

Vellene steps close to him, lifts a hand.

But he catches it, pushes it to her side, and the sparks that emanate from the action *sting*. He struggles to find words, forehead creased as his eyes trail over her face. "Soffesa is right. I shouldn't be so trusting of you. Not yet."

Pain. It slashes through her heart, poisons their shared moment. How could he say that after what they just did? Even if he's second-guessing her loyalty, she didn't think he'd be this cruel. Vellene presses her lips together in frustration and manages a single nod before she moves into the hall.

She stands there for a moment, fists clenched at her sides. Then she turns to him, uncertain of what to say. She wants to scream at him. She wants to scream at everyone.

Eledar looks at the ground, his boots—anywhere besides her. He grips the door knob, face grim. "We will send instructions with our next move."

"That's it, then?" she spits.

He winces.

Vellene shakes her head. *Fine*. She moves to the staircase.

"Goodbye."

She grips the rail, eyes cast to the steps.

"In case—"

"I betray you and die of poisoning?" Vellene snaps. She looks back at him, face drawn in anger. "Goodbye, Eledar."

His face twists. "Vellene, I'm sorry." Then, under his breath, he mutters, "I should've known it was a mistake kissing you."

A mangled half-laugh scrapes up her throat. "Good to know."

He cringes. "That's not how I meant to say it."

"Just forget it." She bites down on her tongue.

"That's not likely," he says, voice soft and pained. He clears his throat. "What I should have said is you're beautiful and extraordinary, and if we had the time, I'd give it all to you." He grips his doorway, knuckles white as if trying to hold himself back from her. "But we don't have that time. Frales and Scorus don't have that time. And I need to trust you. I need to avenge the Golem."

*Beautiful and extraordinary.* She captures his face in that moment, the clear grief written across it. It, too, is beautiful and extraordinary, and if she had the time, she'd give all of her to him if it meant lessening it. Even for a moment. Even if she never saw him again. Because she knows that written across her soul is the same grief. It's always there like a shadow, hungry to devour whatever warmth and light comes into her life.

But he's right. There is no time. There was only tonight, and it must be enough. She must will it to be. Until she can fix the atrocities her father has committed. Until she can cut her father's throat and tug free from her chains. Until she can face death knowing she did everything to stay alive. Then maybe she'll kiss him again. Not as a confused, desperate heiress, but with choice and power, and a body that is hers to own.

Because to live is to fight. Just as Soffesa said. Just as Vellene knew deep down when she ran out into the shard storm.

Then, she ran from life.

Now, she won't. Not after she's finally tasted it.

"We'll send word," Eledar promises, his voice strained as he keeps himself to his doorway.

Vellene nods, and—knowing if she doesn't look away now, she never will—she takes the first steps down into the noise of The Bloody Cloth, her chemight deposits emptied but her power strong and the poison in her veins feeling nonexistent. Even her death oath knows, her fire is stoked.

# Chapter Twelve

## *Vellene*

Vellene runs a finger over the slick, bronze metal of her empty chemight deposits. The orbs were drained after her moment with Eledar, but Idus made a point to remove them anyway. Now, her deposits stand exposed, their emptiness echoing in her veins.

She plasters her eyes to the streets of Scorus, a rock lodged in her throat. Part of her wants to rip open the carriage door, fall into the street, run away, and let the poison of her death oath with Soffesa and Eledar end this, all of this, for good. But her will to live pounds in her skull, vibrates through her chest. Her will to fight.

Her mind drifts to The Bloody Cloth, to Eledar's touch.

*I shouldn't be so trusting of you.* His words slam through her, knock her confidence down a million pegs. But then the rest, the words that sear across her heart like a brand: *You're beautiful and extraordinary, and if I had the time, I'd give it all to you.*

It's a terrifying thing: to want someone who actively manipulates her. She knows nothing of the Golem besides the pull she felt and the death oath he held her down for.

He. Held. Her. Down.

And she let him. She said it was fine.

Vellene's mouth dries, but she refuses to be embarrassed or to regret letting him touch her. Maybe it's wrong but wrong is all she knows. In some ways, she craves it. She seeks the control she felt when she kissed him. She wants to hold it in her grasp on her own. This realm doesn't have good. Even the best of the best have hearts tainted with permanent darkness. Eledar felt like a lesser of the evils, a warmth to him she's sought her entire life.

She frowns as the Scrap shacks beyond her window slip away and something more expensive takes their place. Small chateaus. Grand gardens. Chemibreakers lining pathways. Between all the opulence lies the burned ruins of the Vonner and Pinesky estates. Utilities tend the wreckage daily, pulling weeds at Aquim's request to preserve them like sick trophies. She prefers the burned homes to the rotting heads, but still.

Vellene strains to focus on what lies ahead of her, the deception she must commit, the lives—her family's lives—she must take. Then Eledar's lips against hers, his hands in her hair and hers in his, and—She doesn't know what to do with the war inside her. Half of her entirety wishes to die. The other wants to sink so fully into life that even misery is a lover.

Her fingers curl into her skirts, and she glances at Idus.

Her Surveillant is a chemi who has always looked old. Even as a child, Idus was hunched over, frail, eyes filled with worlds of knowledge. It's a facade. Strength remains in those wrinkled fingers, venom behind his parched lips.

He sits on the carriage seat across from her. He studies her empty orbs as he places them into a pouch tied to his waist. He wears his Winloc cloak over clothing made for battle, the fabric lightweight but secure, and armor stretches across his chest and groin.

*He expected a fight*, she realizes, and by his disappointed expression, she almost feels guilty not giving him one.

But then, there is also something strange about this chemi she's known all her life.

His face is not stern. Instead, it's curious—and Idus is never curious. He knows all. Or so he preaches. His curiosity is off-putting, as well as the braid he's put his long beard into. He's never cared about his appearance, yet he's made an obvious effort to tidy himself. The pleats of his beard knot the long, scraggly thing into a tame and structured look. It frames his lips, which open and close every few minutes, questions trapped on his tongue.

Which is also unusual. Vellene expected to be berated with his questioning by now.

Idus opens his mouth once more, then he draws back into his seat, unsure.

"What?" she snaps and crosses her arms. She's positive death or worse awaits her beyond this carriage, so she doesn't see the point in pretending at the good daughter until she's forced to be.

Idus gestures to her with a glare. "What exactly did you get up to during your recklessness?"

Vellene looks down at the revealing black dress Soffesa loaned her. Her face settles into a grim smile. "Wouldn't you like to know."

"Your behavior is inappropriate for a chemi of your age and caliber." Idus lets out a strangled noise, face scrunched in frustration. "I signed up to be your Surveillant, not your babysitter."

"You've fooled me." She pinches her forearms, grimaces.

Idus shakes his head. "I'm to prepare you for your rise to the Convocation of the Eternal." He scowls at her. "I will—"

"Is there anything else left to try?" Vellene interrupts. "What more could you possibly do to me Idus? We both know I will never inherit anything, especially not a seat on that council." Maybe she should be more careful. Maybe she should bite her tongue as she always has. Idus has inflicted just as many scars upon her body as her father has. But she is so tired of this. All of this. Her brow creases and the indent between them grows heavy with exhaustion.

Uncharacteristically, Idus hesitates. His eyes roam over her for a moment, and anger flares in his white, terrifying gaze.

Vellene straightens at the sight of it, wonders if for once Idus cares.

But he rebounds into his infamous sneer. With a flick of his wrists, green chemight swirls out from his palms—a primitive formulary weaponized with nether. *Latorial ssosum*. It lassos around her chest and biceps.

Vellene looks down. "What is this?"

"Your father believes a prison cell may help you come to terms with your lack of freedoms," Idus says, but he grimaces.

Her skin crawls. There's never been a time he hasn't enjoyed her pain. She should probably be relieved the elder grew a conscience, but his sympathy unnerves her further. "Why are you acting so strange?"

Her Surveillant ignores her. "I don't know what to tell you, Vellene." He reaches for the door and pops it open. He whistles to the Chemibreakers driving the carriage, and the thing rolls to a halt. "Start acting like a Winloc. Or, next time, run farther." He holds onto the carriage door as he steps down to the ground, the knuckles of his free hand white as he brandishes the chemight binding her.

She slides across the carriage, then hops to the cobblestone driveway of Winloc Grove. "I needed a night of fun."

Idus scoffs. "You're not built for 'fun', Winloc. You're built for power. I thought you would've recognized that by now."

Vellene crams her retort into the back of her mind. There's never any use in arguing with a chemi who's built his livelihood upon twisted vengeance. She looks up at the chateau before her. The monstrosity of her home.

Winloc Grove stands too large for comfort, too cold for happiness. Vines crawl across the home, bare and black like the thin, long nails of a reaper. It's as if they've held the chateau in its clutches since the beginning of time, sucking the life from anyone living within. Dark curtains cover every window and allow no light to escape. Or come in.

She swallows as Idus tugs her along. She thought she'd never be here again, thought she'd left this place and its horror behind her. Every step forward is weighted with obligation, the pieces of confidence she found at The Bloody Cloth are cut from her with every inch she dares closer to her father. She swears she bleeds as she's dragged between gnarled trees to where two vicious shadows await. Father and sister. Monster and monster-made. Her breaths come ragged, her rib bones a cage again, and the beast in her gut whimpering in submission.

*It's just a place*, she tells herself. *It's just a past.*

But a quiet rage filters through her. *They conspired and killed my mother.* Her hands ball into fists. Sweat trickles down the back of her neck despite the fresh sleet across branches. She stares at Aquim and Mogaell, and it truly hits her then what must be done, the life that must leave their eyes.

The two share the same brows, same eyes, same hair. Aquim stands with a face of stone, the dark navy of his hair slick and combed down to his mid-back. Mogaell whispers something to him, face grim, her own navy strands tucked into a tight bun of intricate braids. She purses her lips in judgment, but there's something colder beneath the facade. Vellene doesn't know how she ever missed it. The hardness. The darkness.

"Aquim, I believe this belongs to you," Idus says, voice hitched with annoyance as he draws to a stop before her father.

"Tonight, she doesn't." Aquim's face of stone cracks in disgust. "Take her to a cell like we discussed."

Mogaell crosses her arms.

Vellene lifts her chin. It's strange—the confidence that comes from hate. "Anything is better than living under your roof."

Aquim moves his eyes to her. He sees the challenge there, but he points his gaze back to Idus. "I believe our *silgis entris* formulary would do my eldest some good."

Her confidence falters. *Not again.* She opens her mouth to protest, but Idus is quick.

Maroon chemight wavers from the tips of her Surveillant's fingers to around her neck. It seeps into her skin, and the next words she tries to form never make it to her lips—only a strangled noise.

"Very well." Aquim waves them off. "Get her out of my sight."

Idus tugs on her.

Vellene stands firm for a moment, holds her sister's gaze. She's not sure what she hopes to find in Mogaell's eyes, but she never thought she'd see them glitter the way they do now.

Mogaell's pinched face flickers with amusement, before Vellene turns her back with a hard swallow.

"Move." Idus gives his lasso a soft yank.

Vellene stumbles. Her focus drifts to the cellars, the concrete dome to the north side of the property. In many ways, the prison is more her home than her room within the chateau. She knows what awaits within. The confinement. The thoughts. The cold. The hunger. She presses her lips together in resolution. She will not break. Not again.

Idus pulls her to the prison's door, stops a foot away from the iridescent wards cast over the dome. They sparkle with electricity—a warning to stay away. Then he presses his palm against the stone, and the wards slice open at his touch. The chemight peels outward until it exposes the door.

Her Surveillant leans into it with a grunt. It scratches open, and he drags her into the prison's dark chill.

Inside, the dome is divided into eight separate cells. They're all empty, which is rare. Vellene scrutinizes the floors. There are remnants of blood—some splashes faded with time and others as fresh as this morning. Aquim must have found and hung more Scraps since she left.

Idus opens the door to the first cell—her cell—then pushes her inside. He slams the iron shut, grips the lock, and a ward laces around her cage.

*Is that really necessary?* She wants to ask, tries to ask, but the words stick to her throat, scramble in her head. She exhales as Idus releases his lasso's hold on her. She stretches her arms, rubs her biceps where she lost circulation.

"I will fetch you in the morning. You're lucky we convinced Rathmore to stay in Scorus to do the Infusion. He's no idea you ran away, and we will keep it that way." Idus clasps his hands. He stares at her with the same strange hesitancy he had in the carriage. Then, in a lower, more careful tone, he says, "Consider your next moves, Vellene. A game is being played. Move your piece or be knocked down."

She frowns at her Surveillant but settles onto the ground, turns her back to him. He's always spouting cryptic nonsense, though this time it rings true. A game—maybe. But is it just a game if death is its end? She listens as he retreats, and the stone door slides shut.

Vellene scoots to the concrete wall at the back of her cell, runs her fingers over the rough ridges of the carvings she made as a child. They're mostly doodles, etchings to pass the time. It's been years since she's drawn anything, and it's been several months since her last stint in this cell.

As years passed, it was easier to lie down on the cool stone, to close her eyes, and to try and sleep the time away. Looking at the drawings, *remembering*—it hurt too much. Yet her brief escape beyond the Imperial Gates makes her want to remember, to give her all the ammunition she needs to take down her father and sister.

Vellene traces her inept depiction of a parduseus, then another of a purple flora that grows in the Winloc gardens. Of all the things she could have drawn, the child she was wanted to remind herself of reasons to keep going. Beautiful, small things—they were all she had in the darkness. Face twisted with a pained smile, her fingers freeze as they find two words etched near the purple flora. Her heart gives a frantic thump as she reads them once, twice, a hundred times.

*Never forget.*

It's her handwriting. The rugged markings of a young girl deprived of light. But they're also the last words her mother ever gave her.

Vellene reaches for the note her mother left, then remembers it's in the pouch Idus confiscated. She runs a thumb over the lettering again. Is it possible her mother saw these etchings? That her last words were Vellene's own at one point in her adolescence?

*Never forget*, she thinks, and the words light a fire through her. They reignite the flames that made her run in the first place, that led her into the arms of a Golem and the binding of a death oath.

*What can't I forget, mother?* Vellene wonders, tilting her head and breathing the words into the dark. The fire in her veins rages in response. It tingles up her spine, licks around the muscles in her neck. It's the fury she's tethered, bound, and left behind, *had* to leave behind. Because submission was peace. Submission was less of this prison cell.

Vellene brings her forehead to her knees. *Remember it all*, a small voice in the back of her head whispers. She squeezes her eyes shut. *I can't.* Pain prickles through her chest. *I can't I can't I can't I can't*—She sinks to the cold stone of her cell, listens to her heart thrum in her ears. She forces herself to let it all fade, even the fire awakening within her. She begs to rest, begs. Just for a while. Just for a night.

The nightmares come quick and fierce. Rampant and vicious and real. Memories long forgotten. Wishes never spoken aloud. Hopes turned as dark as the tar Alchemight slices down and the waves of Dalbian's Abyss that pummel the shores.

Sleep tugs her deeper into the black, and as her breaths run heavy and her heart cracks and cracks and cracks—everything splinters off, lost in the dark.

Everything except the smallest ember of her fire, waiting and dreaming for her to light a match.

Within the prison, there is no light. No shadows. Just Vellene. She's unsure how long she slept, if anyone cared enough to stop by. If they did, they didn't wake her.

She holds her knees to her chest, rocks back and forth.

Vellene was conditioned to the darkness, the solitude, but with her brief break, it plays with her senses in detrimental ways. Her eyes are wide or squeezed shut. Her lips are parched. Her stomach growls. The brews at The Bloody Cloth were the last form of nutrients she had. There's a tremor to her fingers, and her mind—it plays tricks.

A blink, and she's eight, in the cell for the first time, tears forming a puddle beneath her.

A swallow and she's fifteen, bruised and bloodied, slumped against the stone floor of her cell in defeat.

A breath and she's every version of herself that's been trapped here, helpless, alone.

Then there's Aurora, her mother. A ghost, a whisper, a hitch in Vellene's breath. Her mother was grace and beauty. She was discipline, viscious wisdom, and words wielded as sharp as any weaponized formulary. Aquim would torment Vellene, but Aurora was smarter than physical abuse. She had a way of pushing Vellene to be the perfect daughter, perfect heir—a way that often made Vellene hate her mother with every fiber of her being when she was younger. But it was the way Aurora stood up to Aquim that made Vellene stay.

All those years, Vellene took Aquim's vengeance with stride. There were screams in between—tears were a requirement—but she took anything her father threw at her if it meant he wasn't harming her mother.

Because when Aquim hurt Aurora, her mother would disappear.

And when Aurora disappeared, so did the small amount of light left at Winloc Grove.

Vellene tucks her chin against her knees, thinks on the small moments she chooses to remember her mother by—the summer Aurora took her to be fitted for new corsets, the weekly visits to decipher her mental health, the one night five months ago when Aurora came to her room.

It was the night before Aurora died, and looking back, Vellene wishes she'd seen the signs, the resignation painted over Aurora's features. She sat Vellene down and brushed her hair before braiding its wild coils into a smooth bun.

"You will be given a chance soon," her mother said, voice soft as she tied off Vellene's hair, then pressed her hands into Vellene's shoulders. "Take it."

Vellene didn't know what her mother meant, but part of her believes this is it—a quest to kill the ones who killed her mother. *But did she know it'd be Mogaell?* Vellene looks at the ceiling. Her doubt turns to pain—*poison.*

It started small, like a tingle in her veins. It was barely recognizable until she woke.

Now, the poison of her death oath is relentless.

Vellene clenches her teeth and stands when the stone door of the prison slides open. The moment it does, the pain dissipates. She makes a mental note. She can't be trapped or cornered. Somehow, the chemight that fuels the death oath knows when she can't fulfill her mission.

She steps to the bars of her cell, careful not to touch its wards. She needs to stay moving and out of this cell. If she doesn't, if she becomes ill, then Aquim and Mogaell will know something has changed. She must pretend to be okay, pretend to be dutiful. She clasps her hands in front of her as her Surveillant steps inside. Pretend and stay alive.

"Eager to escape?" Idus asks.

Vellene motions to her throat.

"No. Your father thinks it's better you don't speak during lunch."

Vellene crosses her arms as he opens the cell.

"Do I need to cast *latorial ssosum*?"

She takes strong strides out of her cage, her fingers ghosting over the bruises left by his last lasso. She shakes her head no.

"Fantastic." Idus moves into the daylight.

They walk through the grass, past the gardens, to a side entrance meant for the comings and goings of Utilities. Idus holds open the door, and they step into the kitchen.

The room is messy, alive with smells. Vellene smiles to herself, the kitchen a haven for her. She nods to the Utility chefs. They stand over large pots where they boil stew mixtures for lunch. She doesn't recognize them, she never does. Aquim has a habit of killing off the staff—a way to keep Winloc Grove's secrets.

"Come along. They're waiting," Idus pesters.

Portraits of her bloodline stare down at her as she steps down the hall, every face a scowl or a grin of deception. Her favorite is of a great-great aunt, Cicily Winloc. The chemi is in a portrait alone, unlike the others, lounging on a chaise, a crystalline glass of brew in her hand. She's maybe in her late thirties, dressed in a simple gown, navy eyes peering through thick lashes.

Despite the portrait's and Cicily's relaxed nature, there's something about her gaze that buzzes with power, defiance. Her chin is tilted slightly upward, lips curved into a dissatisfied expression. *Dissatisfied with the realm,* Aurora once said. *As we all should be.*

Vellene gives the painting a sad smile as she passes it, runs her fingers along the bottom edge of its frame. She hesitates when Idus stops at a pair of double doors and Chemibreakers. The guards give a small bow, then they push the doors open.

Beyond is the dining hall. It's a grand room with a grand table—Aquim at the far end with Mogaell at his left. Chemibreakers line the walls, hands clasped at their backs, faces solemn. A chandelier hangs from the ceiling. Orbs drip from it, light from candles refracting through each of the clear spheres. It casts the table in a glitter of warm-colored shapes and shadows.

Aquim stands at her arrival, pulls out the free chair at his right for her. "Daughter, you look better."

Vellene catches her reflection in a mirror on the wall—dark circles under her eyes, hair 48 hours unbrushed, face exhausted. *Not better*, the beast inside her screams. *Just to your liking.*

Then her eyes find her mother's empty seat. It sits at the opposite end of Aquim's.

Vellene yanks the seat out at the left of it, ignoring the one her father got for her. She's already dead. Maybe she has been for as long as she can remember. *S*o, why sit next to him? Why give him the pleasure? Mogaell likely told Aquim that Vellene knows the truth about Aurora. If she is immediately obedient, she worries they'll become suspicious. So Vellene narrows her eyes on her father and sister. Despite the race of her heart and the ample amount of fear setting her teeth on edge, she crosses her arms in defiance.

"We are over here, Vellene," Mogaell says, voice bitter, eyebrows drawn in scorn.

Vellene gives her sister a pointed look of distrust, then folds her arms on the tabletop.

"Right, I forgot. You can't talk." Mogaell leans back in her chair, twirls a strand of her blue hair around a finger in boredom. "It's fitting."

Vellene's blood boils. *What are you doing?* a small voice asks at the back of her head. It's the same voice that's kept her alive all these years, and yet she ignores it.

Aquim clears his throat. "Vellene, I have never been so disappointed." He gestures to a Utility, who then leaves. He studies her. "I presented you with mercy, and yet you ran away."

*Mercy?* She wants to shout back. *Is it mercy to become a blood bag?*

He clasps his hands. "All the freedoms you decided are not enough are gone. Chemibreakers will escort you to and from every scheduled event. Otherwise, you are to remain in your room." Aquim nods to Idus. "You may restore her voice."

Her Surveillant wraps his hands around Vellene's neck, then exhales as rose-colored chemight pools around her throat.

Vellene coughs, gasps. An extreme itch funnels down her throat as her voice returns. She covers her mouth as she hacks, and the Utility her father sent away moves into the room with three maids.

They carry in mugs of fresh stew and set one in front of each Winloc. Vellene looks into her bowl. The liquid is a soft green. It sparkles with the vibrancy of chemight. Her stomach grumbles. She shoved aside her hunger, along with her fears, when she left Winloc Grove. Now she grabs the bowl with both hands and gulps it back. Relishes the smoothness of the stew—uncorrupted by fragments of creatures like her brews at The Bloody Cloth were—as the warm substance slides down her itchy throat.

She guzzles it, doesn't take a moment to care about proper etiquette. She drains the bowl, then hands it off to the Utility nearest to her. "More, please."

The Utility nods and takes it.

She settles into her chair, the synthesized nutrients quickly making a difference. The tremble in her fingers subsides. The cramps in her stomach turn to a soft roar. She looks across the table at her father and Mogaell.

Aquim meets her gaze, his stew untouched. "You wouldn't be so hungry if you stayed."

"Perhaps." Vellene clears her throat. "But as I told Idus, I simply needed a night out."

"I could have thrown you a party." Aquim analyzes her.

She knows this banter is leading to punishment, knows her fury must be tucked away. Immediately. Killing her father and sister will require stealth. Throwing up arms too soon after returning from the city will force as much suspicion as being complacent. She must balance between the daughter she was and the weapon she must become.

Vellene nods. "I'll consider that next time, but I wanted to explore Scorus." Her eyes flick to Mogaell. Did her sister rat her out? Does Aquim know she's lying?

Mogaell sips on her stew, her navy gaze revealing nothing but contempt.

"You know my rules. I never want you or your sister going beyond the Imperial Gates." He leans back in his chair, brings his bowl with him but still doesn't drink. Instead, he weighs it in his palm.

"I'm sorry." The words are easy. They're hard not to be after 17 years of repeating them. She blows out a breath. "I've certainly learned my lesson," she lies.

"Good." He takes a sip of his stew. He still studies her, trying to pick apart every syllable she utters.

"My actions have been completely out of hand." Vellene peels herself out of her seat and stands. "I am sorry, and I know I betrayed you by leaving, but it opened my eyes. I have no desire to ever leave again."

Aquim considers it. “You will abide by my word and my word only?”

She nods. “Always, father.”

“You’re not actually going to give her another chance?” Mogaell asks.

Vellene manages a grin at the scorn in Mogaell’s words.

The promise of death sparkles in her sister's eyes.

Vellene tries to ignore it, but she makes a mental note to figure out what to do with her sister and soon. Aquim is pomp and frills. Abusive and brash but not as intelligent as Mogaell. Maybe Idus was right. This is a game, and they've all played it their entire lives. Vellene's remained a stagnant piece on the board but—she narrows her gaze on Mogaell—her sister's been making moves all along. The withdrawal. The killing of their mother. What else has she hidden? Become?

Aquim stands, rests a hand on Mogaell’s shoulder. “I promise you, my child, your day will come.” He pushes back his chair and takes slow steps toward Vellene like a predator closing in on his prey.

Mogaell yanks her bowl to her lips. She slurps her stew loudly in spite.

He extends his hands toward Vellene.

Vellene stares at her father’s outstretched, open palms. *Run.* She measures her breaths and lies her hands within his. She avoids her need to recoil, to light him on fire and dream sweetly of his end.

"Look at me, Vellene."

She holds back a grimace and lifts her eyes to his.

Aquim squeezes her hands. "I cannot forgive you. Not yet."

Mogaell sets her bowl down with a thunk and stands. "How about not at all?" she asks, voice up an octave.

Aquim ignores his youngest and focuses on Vellene. "But I will give you a final chance to earn that forgiveness." He squeezes tighter. "One. Last. Time."

It's a threat. She knows it in the way his words sting, in the strength he uses to send shocks of pain through her hands.

"I will do my best to appease you," Vellene manages. The bones in her hands throb. Tears prick at her eyes. She wills them away, but it's no use. She's never been one to hide her emotions, not well anyway—and he will forever use that against her. She needs to learn how to mask, and she needs to learn it fast. She'll never pull off the plan of the death oath if she's so easily readable.

Aquim stares, waits for the first tear to fall, then relinquishes his grip. His mouth curls into a grin. "If infusing with Rathmore isn't something you want, then perhaps you could simply get rid of him for me."

Vellene drops her hands, hides them behind her back. Confusion fills her, then dread as she realizes what he's asking. "You mean, kill him?"

"I'll give you until your birthday. At that point, I'll hand you over to him." Aquim presses his lips together. "You've always wanted choices. Now you have one. Get yourself cleaned up. Go to your room. Then find Rathmore. Earn his trust. Bind him to you." He motions behind him, expecting Idus to be awaiting his orders, but her Surveillant disappeared.

Aquim frowns but gestures to a random Chemibreaker. "Take her." He tilts his head at Vellene with curiosity, as if he's unsure if he can trust her but knows he will enjoy the torment of securing that loyalty again. "Your future awaits."

Vellene tenses. Her lips pull apart, an argument on her tongue.

But Aquim is quick to intercept it. "You will do it," he demands, eyes darkening to the black of a shard storm. "If you wish to stay in my good graces, then you will rid Alchemight of the final Rathmore. He thinks you are to complete the Infusion ceremony here, at Winloc Grove. We will hold several celebrations leading up to The Drinking, and we will use them to show our great, plentiful alliance with Frales."

Her father leans toward her, voice low and deadly. "He expects a good, obedient partner. You are to be a sign of faith." His fingers curl around her wrist, grasping it tight and digging his nails in. "Take him out. Do you understand, daughter?"

Vellene turns her focus to her feet, away from her father's darkness, from the daggers of Mogaell's gaze. Poison stings through her veins. "Yes," she breathes, the word laced with a deadly calm.

"Wonderful," Aquim hisses and lets her go.

Vellene leaves the dining hall with what's left of her strength and a new resolve, one that perfectly aligns with Eledar's and Soffesa's. The Chemibreaker her father assigned to her trails her as she climbs up the stairs and heads for her room. She longs for a plan.

A plan to end it all.

## Chapter Thirteen

# *Eledar*

Eledar stands, arms crossed. His stolen cloak flutters at his back, while the silver strands of his hair curl against his cheeks, tickle his nostrils. The wind comes from every direction, a shard storm on the way. Dark clouds fill the sky. They dim Alchemight's moonlight and his mood. Everything in him feels misplaced—his home an ocean of tar away, his mission without a solid plan and—*no, don't think about her*.

Dalbian's Abyss lies before him. The gray of its vapor seeps up the shore, tangles with his thoughts. He clears his throat, shifts his weight in discomfort as knots form in his stomach.

What he wouldn't give for *lumis*.

The back of his neck warms at the thought of Vellene's touch, but a hard lump lodges in his throat when he remembers his last words to her. He combs the memory from his mind, sucks in a breath, lets it go. *Let her go*, he tells himself. *You're not here for that.*

No, what he is here for is freedom. A selfish mission.

Again, he thinks of *lumis*, of getting its euphoric effects into his system, of turning every memory of battle and every thought of failing into bliss.

Vellene's face surges forward. The golden honey of her eyes. The softness to her face. He's never had someone make such an imprint on him. There were many female and male chemi over the years, but none of them stayed once they walked out the door. And they always leave, eventually. He picks at his wrist, heart thumping in his chest as he remembers the way Vellene clung to him as they danced, how she looked on her back, how she tasted—

He curses and drags a hand through his hair.

Eledar hadn't meant to, but he managed to memorize the rhythm of her heart against his chest, too. It was steady, yet thrummed with joy. Identical to how he believes—if he had a heart—his would be in every way. It felt like a kindred spirit against his chest, like the tune of a song he long yearned for. He wishes he could have stayed in that moment forever, feel her shiver as he ran his fingers down her spine—He bites his tongue.

"Stop that."

Eledar tenses, turns. Ears red—he's sure of it. "You need a bell."

Soffesa hops down from the dock, trudges across the rocky shore. She has the hood of her red leather ensemble pulled up to shield her Scrap ink, orange hair tied into a braided ponytail that falls over her shoulder and down to her elbow. "I can tell you're worrying about Vellene. Your eyebrows are doing that crooked thing they do when you're anxious." She sighs. "She'll be fine."

His sister stops next to him, her cheeks a soft pink against the wind. She grabs at his hand—the one mindlessly opening a small wound on his wrist—and shoves it down to his side. "I haven't seen you do that since we were kids."

Eledar fidgets, then brings his hand to his chin and scratches the uneven patching of his beard, a shave a couple days overdue, but the scraggly thing covers scars whilst acting as a barrier from his nervous tick. "Bad habits have a way of resurfacing for me." His fingers want to plunge into his skin, dig into scars. He forces his hands behind his back, clasps them. "You're optimistic for doubting Vellene as much as you did."

"I doubt that girl's ability to kill her family." Soffesa looks out into the abyss. "I don't doubt her passion."

"You were hard on her."

Soffesa snorts. "It's been a while, Eledar, hasn't it?"

He nods, and the memory of Vellene's face smooths into a memory of Rathmore Manor, of a younger Soffesa in a tree, of Chemibreakers casting formularies to shoot her down, of him climbing into that tree to shield her.

His lips press into a smile, a small quiver to it as he hears the echo of their thud to the grass when he was hit.

Soffesa healed his wound with the only remedial formulary she ever had access to. It was then she noticed the mud, knew what Eledar was in a time of great uncertainty for Golem. Yet, she simply wiped the clay from his wound, embraced him in a quick hug, and told him 'thank you', before she cracked her neck, let out a feral screech, and charged at the Chemibreakers that shot them down.

She was young, untrained in the art of assassination—but she managed to throw them off their guard.

Eledar and Soffesa got away, her hand clamped around his as they sprinted through the streets of Frales. It was his only time free from the grounds of Rathmore Manor. The next morning he was caught and lashed until his back was unrecognizable, but it was worth it.

Soffesa studies him, and her lips mirror his own—thoughtful. "You, at least, haven't changed."

Eledar grimaces at that. "You think of me as a naive, small boy with grandiose pictures of my horrid reality?"

"Hopeful, Eledar." She shakes her head. "You've always been so hopeful of our future."

"What else should I be?" he drawls and rolls his eyes.

She blows out a breath.

Eledar measures his own, then nods to the abyss. "I suppose 'grim' would be fitting, considering I lost our escape plan. Not that it was much of one. I think Equilibrium half-hoped I'd die on that boat."

Soffesa clicks her tongue. "We may be able to commission another ship." She reaches a hand out, moves her fingers through the vapor. "But it'd be faster to steal one, I think."

"That will be tricky."

She grins, looks at him. "Good thing tricks are my forte."

He wraps an arm around her shoulders and tugs her into him. He presses a kiss to the hood of her cloak. "Yes, I remember, sister."

Soffesa hugs him back. "I missed you."

Eledar nods, rests his head against the top of hers.

They stand there, eyes cast to the shroud of darkness beyond, until the ease of their hug turns to obligation. Their shoulders tense, jaws clench. They stare into Dalbian's Abyss as if they can see war-torn Frales, see the bodies that lie in piles along the streets, hear the screams of children as they lose their families, feel the crackle in the air of chemight, of shots being fired.

"I need to know, Eledar." Her voice is soft, timid, vulnerable.

His want to protect her shoves to the forefront, but he knows there's no way around the truth. Eledar hesitates, then tightens his grip around her. He couldn't tell her in The Bloody Cloth, not with Vellene there and a crowd. Now he must. She deserves the truth. "I'm sorry," he manages, and the words aren't enough. How can they be? He throws his other arm around her, braces her in the hope of caging the pain, of knowing just as she is the only family he has left, he's now hers.

Soffesa's face breaks. Its constant strength and determination cracks into grief and chaos. She sucks in a breath, rubs her throat with unease as her eyes glisten.

Eledar searches for the right thing to say. "I tried, Soff. I really did. But I was overpowered, and it's a mess over there, and I—" *I hate myself.*

Soffesa wipes a fallen tear in anger, then pulls from him.

The cracks in his soul rip into chasms. His arms hang loosely at his sides, useless. "I built them wards. I was going to bring them with me when I could cross to Scorus. But then I had no access to formularies. The wards fell. We tried to flee—"

"Stop." She squeezes her eyes shut, hugs herself. "Please."

Failure chokes Eledar. Five years he kept her family safe. Five years he fought back against Imperial formulary after Imperial formulary. Five years he protected the last of his reasons to stay in Frales. Yet, in those final moments, he failed.

He reaches a hand out to comfort her. *Forgive me.*

Soffesa bats his hand away and turns her back to him as the moons combust and combine into the daily sun. She looks up at it, and tears stream down her face. She wipes them furiously. "It's a new day." She glances at him, voice hoarse but stern. "And we have a job to do."

"Don't do that." He steps to her, grasps her face between his hands.

She goes rigid, frail.

"We will avenge their deaths, Soff, or we will meet them in the afterlife. Either way, this isn't the end. I promise."

Soffesa nods, sniffles. She clears her throat. "We should meet with Imaex. I said we'd be by yesterday."

"Right," Eledar says but keeps his hands on her face. He uses his thumbs to wipe her tears. "But I think we should talk about this."

"I—I can't." Soffesa's jaw trembles. "Please. I can't think about my family. Not like that."

He drops his hands. "They were extraordinarily brave. I finally got to see where you get that from."

Soffesa covers her mouth.

"Your father," he says and pulls up his shirt. "He wanted me to give this to you." He pulls the strange orb out of its chemight deposit and hands it to her. "I almost lost it. Had it in my pocket on the way over. I'm actually surprised it didn't fall out when I capsized."

Eledar hesitates. "Then something happened with Vellene. Drained all my formularies." His lips tug into a sad smile. "Not this one though. He was determined for you to have it, even beyond the grave it seems."

Soffesa analyzes the orb, turns it over in her palm. It pulses a deep auburn with yellow specks. "What is it?"

He shrugs. "I've no idea, only that he spent the last two years of his life stockpiling the orbs to trade for it."

Soffesa raises her brows.

"I was hoping you'd know what kind of formulary it is."

They walk down the shore.

She shakes her head, dries her eyes. "No, I don't know." She tucks the orb into a pouch at her waist. "But there's a lot I never knew about my parents, particularly my father."

Ahead, Utilities tend to the dock, a single ship in the bay. They lift cargo boxes off the ship as its captain shakes hands with the Chemibreaker watching over the Utilities.

Eledar lifts the hood of his cloak as he and Soffesa walk past, their heads down. "Do you think it's a formulary that could help us?" he asks.

Soffesa sucks in a ragged breath. "I wish I knew."

Eledar frowns at the tears glistening in her eyes. He shoves the subject to the back of his mind, suffocates his curiosity. Whatever formulary the orb contains, it's not worth her pain. His fingers itch to grasp her into another hug, but Soffesa hugs herself, as she always does. He slips his hands into his pockets as they make their way up to the streets.

"You really think this Imaex chemi will have information on the location of the source?" Eledar asks.

After Vellene was taken, he and Soffesa combed through each of the contacts she made through her assassin contracts. It was a dead end, and Eledar said as much when they ordered brews. Fortunately, their bartender wasn't above trading two of Eledar's empty orbs for a name.

Soffesa shrugs. "There's always the possibility that he doesn't, but Felix seemed pretty sure about it."

Beyond the hillside sits a quiet Scorus. Some Utilities open their shops, Imperials riding down from their mansions and chateaus for new clothes or to buy orbs. Otherwise, the streets are empty, Scraps retired to their shacks after a long night of brews and street entertainment.

A bitterness warms through Eledar at the sight of such peace. He yearns for these streets to be the streets of Frales, to see what's left of the Golem roaming freely and Scraps enjoying the daylight. *One step at a time.*

He follows Soffesa down a side street. Utility shops wane into run-down taverns. They pass The Bloody

Cloth and memories of Vellene prick like sharp knives in his skull. He pushes them away, picks up his pace.

Soffesa notices and slows her stride. "We can talk about it."

Eledar shakes his head. "We have more important things to worry about." He blows out a breath. "Like refilling my orbs."

"How did you drain them again?"

He presses his lips together.

Soffesa cocks a brow. "Will this be how it is forever? Us. Always deflecting?"

Eledar rubs his shoulder with a soft smile.

She nods. "Figured." She turns down a street and gestures ahead. "It's the house on the—" She pulls to a stop, eyes narrowed.

"What is it?"

She lowers her voice. "Something's wrong."

Eledar follows her gaze to a small box of a Scrap shack at the end of the block. An Imperial carriage sits out front. One with a Winloc crest on the side, the large spideria mocking them. "Is that where we're going?" he asks. Anxiety unravels in his lower abdomen.

Soffesa grabs his wrist and yanks him into the shadows.

A Chemibreaker in a navy cloak threaded with silver steps out of the home, a bag grasped in his hand.

"Vellene," Soffesa growls.

Eledar frowns. "We don't know Vellene sent him." He rips his wrist out of her fingers. "How would she even know about this contact? Did you tell her?"

Soffesa's anger falters. "No." She straightens. "I didn't tell her."

"Then it's not her." Relief passes through him.

"But it's still the Winlocs."

They flatten against a shack as the carriage passes. Chemibreakers sit in the driver's seat, foreheads covered in sweat as they maneuver the carriage forward with chemight. Eledar and Soffesa wait for the carriage to disappear around a corner before they both exhale.

"Let's go." Soffesa steps out of the shadows.

They hurry down the block to Imaex's. Eledar analyzes the front porch, looks for a trap of any kind. A gust of wind whips against the side of the house, and the whole thing shudders.

Soffesa stops at the front entrance. In front of a hole, where the front door would be, sits a large piece of driftwood. She grunts as she lifts it out of the way, then hurries forward. "Watch my back," she says.

Eledar tenses in the doorway. Inside is dark, quiet. Too quiet. "Be careful," he whispers.

"Imaex?" Soffesa calls out as she walks down the hall.

Eledar frowns. He should've known his friend would never choose subtly. Why would she when her mere stare is as lethal as any weapon? Soffesa has always been somewhat of a contradiction as an assassin. Stealthy, yes. Bold, always. Brave will never be enough of a word for her.

She disappears into a room. “Imaex?”

Eledar steps into an open space dressed as a living room. A couch of patchwork. A recliner with mold. Stacks of tomes line a hole in the wall meant to be a window. Its curtains whip with a breeze, and the smell of mildew encompasses his body. His eyes trail to the rug, to behind the recliner. His blood runs cold. His muscles tense.

A pale hand protrudes out from behind the chair.

Eledar stares, wavers with his next step forward. “Soffesa,” he calls out.

She strides into the living room, follows his gaze to the body. “Imaex.” Soffesa pushes past him. She drops to the carpet, lifts a hand to the chemi’s neck, and checks for a pulse.

“Is he—”

She nods. Her face creases in fury. She stands and strides to the front door.

“Where are you going?” His adrenaline surges. Eledar chases after her, grabs her shoulder, and pulls her to a stop. “Soff.”

“We know who it was, Eledar.” She spins toward him, fists clenched, gray chemight coming off her knuckles in waves.

“We aren’t ready to go after the Winlocs yet.”

Her eyes flash with hurt. "You want to do nothing?"

"I want to do everything." Eledar licks his lips. "But we need to tread carefully. We can't just barge into Winloc Grove. We'll get ourselves killed and then what?" He shakes his head.

Her lip trembles. She turns away before she breaks. "It's too much, Eledar."

"I know." Eledar heaves a breath. Seeing a dead body not long after finding out her entire family is dead? He swears under his breath, then stiffens when he spots a pair of Utilities across the street. They watch Eledar and Soffesa with intensity, documenting each of their identities. "We need to move."

Soffesa follows his gaze. She pulls herself together. "We need to know why they killed him."

"I agree, but look at their crests, Soff."

The Winloc crest blazes in the sunlight against the Utilities' abdomens—a sheer piece of fabric built into their uniforms to easily display the ink. The spideria has slight variations from Vellene's, particularly when it comes to the amount of chemight deposits built into it.

Vellene had several. These Utilities only have 3 or 4, at most. Still, they're dangerous. It's rare an Imperial family would claim Utilities in such a public way.

Eledar swallows, clenches his fists.

Soffesa stifles her chemight, pulls the gray swirls back into her skin. “They’ll report us back to Aquim. Go.” She grabs his wrist. “Now.”

They hurry to an alley, then move into a jog. They reach the end and pull around the corner to a halt.

Eledar peers into the alley and rakes in a labored breath. “They’re not following. Maybe I was wrong.”

“They don’t need to follow.” Soffesa curses. “They just needed a good look at us.”

“Maybe we could go back, bribe them.”

Soffesa shakes her head. She peers around the corner. “We need to save our orbs.”

“What’s the point if they report us?”

Soffesa grits her teeth.

Eledar clears his throat. “I have eight down my spine. They may be empty, but they’re still better than nothing.”

Soffesa scowls. “It’s not enough.”

“How many do you have?”

“None,” she scoffs. “I’m Scrap.”

Eledar runs a hand through his hair. “We have to do something.”

“Should we kill them?”

Dread fills him.

“It may be the only way.”

“They’re just hungry chemi trying to earn some orbs for their next meal, Soff.”

"And we're trying to end a war." She shrugs. "There's bound to be casualties."

His face twists in disgust. "Since when do you kill anyone beyond Imperials or Chemibreakers?"

She stares at him. "You don't get to judge me, Eledar. It's been five years out here. Alone. Hungry. Poor." Soffesa clenches her fists. "Look, I'll handle the Utilities. You go back to Imaex's. See if you can figure out why the Winlocs killed him."

Eledar hesitates but nods. "Be careful."

She turns to run back down the alley, then glances at him and shrugs. "I'm Soffesa The Silent. They won't even see me coming." She sprints away.

He stares after his friend, buries his concern. He's in no position to judge her. Not after all he's done and all that haunts him. He shakes his head and returns to Imaex's. Flashes of death trail after Eledar. Moments where he had to kill or be killed in Frales. He remembers every face, every drop of blood. He clamps a hand over his chest, shakes his head, and forces the images away. He slows as the alley ends.

The Utilities are gone and so is Soffesa.

Eledar peels from the comfort of the shadows and takes quick strides across the street to the withering Scrap shack. He steps inside, hurries past the living room, the dead body. He moves to the next room. None of them have doors, just arches. He stares into what appears to be the bedroom—a small box with a makeshift cot. Unlit candles litter the floor beside it, while sheets are strung from the ceiling and draped to form a tent. Probably to retain body heat.

He bends to the cot, pulls back its thin, woven blanket. He shifts the pillow, then stops when he finds a small, folded piece of parchment. He takes it gingerly between his fingers and unfolds it, the paper worn from being held onto for years. His breath catches at the sight of a list of names. He fumbles a hand into his pocket and pulls out a piece of paper almost identical to Imaex's.

It was common, growing up, for Golem to keep a list of their loved ones nearby, anyone they believed was still alive, so the Golem who finds them dead can reach out to those loved ones and let them know. Imaex's list is long, but all the names are crossed off or smeared and unrecognizable. Eledar looks at his own, at the names of his fellow Golem that vanished off the list in the last year alone. The only name left on his list is the name at the top: Soffesa Fedelis.

He tucks both lists into his pocket and swallows, hard. He drifts from the bedroom to what appears to be a riffled-through workspace. Torn papers from notebooks scatter the ground. Tomes sit open, face down, spines cracked. A makeshift desk of plastic pieces and tar-glued bricks lies on its side.

Eledar stoops to one of the tomes, lifts it from the ground. He flips through the pages, every margin filled with a familiar script. His heart skips a beat. Golem script. He runs his thumb over the frantic writing. Something in him lurches with pain. He reads the text, careful not to tear one of the fragile pages.

> They define the source as forever poisoned, yet we see the good chemight does. It mends. Gives breath to worn lungs. Tears down our enemies when we have been wronged.

He flips the page.

> Perhaps the source is darkness, but where there is darkness, there is undeniable light.

"I guess you had the information we were looking for, didn't you?" Eledar mutters bitterly. "Too bad the dead can't talk." He sets the journal down and moves to the toppled-over desk. He grunts as he lifts it upright, scoops its fallen notes off the ground, and lies them across it. "That is unless you wrote everything down." He fumbles through the loose pieces of parchment, all of them in Golem script.

Then he pauses when the hair at the nape of his neck rises. The floorboards behind him creak. He spins and reaches for his Scrap chemight. Gray swirls scorch between his knuckles.

Soffesa throws up her hands. “Relax.” Her palms are stained black.

Eledar douses his chemight, but his gaze flicks to her hands. Blood. He winces. His chemight fades, and he turns back to the notes. “Is it done?”

Soffesa steps beside him, nods. “Did you find anything?” she asks.

Eledar flips through a few more pages. “Nothing immensely useful yet.”

Soffesa picks up one of the notes. She frowns, unable to read the Golem script. “What is this language?”

“He was a Golem chemi.” Eledar points to the notes. “This is Golem script. It was never taught outside our species, a way for us to speak freely while imprisoned.” His gaze darkens, jaw clenches. “Aquim must have known. That’s why he had Imaex killed.”

“I had no idea there were any Golem in Scorus.” Soffesa shakes her head. "He must have smuggled himself across the abyss."

Eledar touches his pant leg over his thigh, where a twist of empty chemight deposits sit. “We all learn how to hide.”

"I get that he was Golem," Soffesa says, voice uncertain, "but he wasn't really a threat. He drank a bit too much brew at The Bloody Cloth, but he was mostly quiet, kept to himself." Her brow furrows. "Why would Aquim go through the trouble of killing him?"

Eledar lifts one of the worn notes. "It seems he was researching the source. If Imaex was trying to find it—"

"Aquim would kill him without hesitation, and I guess he did." Soffesa paces behind him, then she grabs his shoulder and pulls his face around to hers. Her eyes widen. "The bag, Eledar. That Chemibreaker had a bag when he left this house."

"You think Imaex found the source?"

Her eyes comb the room. "We need to pack this up. All of it."

Eledar looks at the mess. "What's the point? The Winlocs more than likely took the answer."

"The Winlocs may have taken any obvious materials from Imaex, but they can't read this script, and they probably assumed no one else can."

He nods. "You're right. Its research. He's bound to have at least mentioned his suspicions."

Soffesa collects tomes and papers and stacks them on the desk. "Let's hope Imaex liked to document everything."

Eledar runs a finger over the Golem script. He smiles to himself. It feels like freedom.

# Chapter Fourteen

# *Vellene*

Tar shards clatter against Vellene's window, smother it in black sludge before it slips away to the ground below. After once again emptying the lamps and heating box in her room, which Utilities refilled with formularies, her unease is at bay, four orbs of power now in her possession.

She wields a marvel primitive formulary, watches as tendrils of green waft from her palm to the window. They pierce the tar obscuring the view and wipe it clean. It may be a waste of chemight, but it's worth it to watch Alchemight erupt in displeasure. Tar clings to the trees, soaks the green of the grass, batters the small, weak buds of flora.

Enough of it, and Winloc Grove would be a fortress secluded by a lake of tar, trapping her forever but also trapping her father and sister.

What a victory that would be. Perhaps they would all drown.

She blows out a breath, and it fogs the window, distorts her reflection, but she jerks her hand back when her chemight fizzes out and snaps into her palm. Brow furrowed, she inspects her fingers. Had it been a specialized formulary, fizzing out would be common for her and her expertise level. But this primitive formulary? She's wielded it since she was a child.

Vellene reaches for the orb that held the formulary and pops it out of its chemight deposit. Holding it up to the light, she finds it empty, despite her using a small amount to clean the window. Confused, she rolls the empty orb between her fingers before she sighs and tosses it to her bed. It must not have been made correctly, or maybe it was some leftover effect from whatever transpired between her and Eledar. She runs an absentminded hand through her hair and its curls spring and snag between her fingers.

She made time to bathe, to change, but nothing about her feels right. She misses the stench of the brew that clung to her borrowed gown. With the stench came possibility—a different her. One that belonged to the streets, to Scorus, not to Winloc Grove. Clean, she's back to the version of herself she fantasized about leaving behind. Obedient. Serving. Dismal. She frowns and steps across the length of her Winloc-blue rug, a silver-threaded, double diamond-backed spideria across its center. She brushes her hands over her gown and sucks in a breath.

The outfit was on her bed when her Chemibreaker escort locked her in her room. The fabric is nicer than most of her other designs, and the corset reminds her of the ones Mogaell owns. It's a deep navy and fitted to accentuate her waist and breasts. It leaves her Winloc crest on full display, the spideria a constant threat each time she sees herself. Vellene doesn't bother to do her hair. She lets it be wild, lets it be free. It's the most she can give herself as she musters a false smile. It looks as hollow as she feels.

She slips what's left of the formularies she found about her room into the chemight deposits along either side of her neck, starting at the backs of her ears. With her hair down, they're hidden enough. Their power zings with soft affection, and some of her unease withers, but she startles as the lock on her door clunks.

The elegant wood swipes open, and the same Chemibreaker that locked her inside greets her. "He's here for you." The chemi's gaze is off-putting—irises the color of rubies—but they otherwise seem harmless. With their buzzed head and high cheekbones, they have a flight-creature's lithe grace as they hold open the door for her.

She inhales, shakes out her fingers. Then, she leaves her room and follows them. Goosebumps rise along her bare arms and shoulders, and nervous heat builds in her cheeks. Let the games begin.

"He's through there," the Chemibreaker directs, pointing to an archway.

"Thanks," she says, the word more bitter and cold than she intended. *Be the good daughter*, she reminds herself for the thousandth time as her guard disappears with a grunt. She chews on her lip, then steps through the archway.

Heads on pedestals shine before her, but her attention is drawn to where shadows filter out and around a tall figure. Her heart beats faster at the deception she knows must come next but also at the way Kadir Rathmore's gaze finds hers.

His violet eyes sparkle in the dim, flickering light of orb-encrusted chandeliers. His white hair is mused back, its pair of yellow strands draped on either side of his face and curling in at the hollows of his cheeks. "Well, if it isn't my promised partner." He takes a strong step toward her, the deep plum of his cloak waving off him. "I must say, you don't disappoint someone in desperate need of a beautiful thing," he mutters, his lips curling with the words.

Vellene stiffens as he lifts a gentle hand and runs a single finger down her cheek. It sends a shiver to her toes. It's jarring in comparison to the spark of heat and electricity she felt from Eledar's touch. Kadir's finger against her skin is as sharp as ice. She tenses, uncertain why suddenly each chemi she touches now comes with some sort of imprint.

Kadir swallows at her frozen stance. His eyes darken and his hand falls to his side. "My apologies."

"You don't have to pretend you want this," she says. She bites her tongue. *Pretend pretend pretend pretend.*

"Is that you calling me 'not your type'?" Kadir lifts a brow. The jagged scar that runs diagonally through his face lifts with the movement. A dimple appears as the corner of his mouth twitches into a smile. "That simply can't be true. I'm everyone's type, love."

Vellene levels her gaze with his and takes a step closer. Her confidence rises when his muscles tighten along his neck. Her eyes study the white lines of the scar that exists there, too. "Why accept my father's offer?" Someone cut him and he got away. She can't let that happen again. Maybe she should close her mouth, smile, and nod, but something about Kadir tells her he would rather her be blunt. Perhaps it's his calculating gaze. Maybe it's the clear indifference in the way he holds himself. He acts as if being here is nothing short of boredom, but—"What game are you playing?" she whispers.

His dimple vanishes and his lashes lower as he brings his lips down to her ear. "Yours, love. Call me curious."

Vellene frowns and takes a quick step back. A chill crawls over her chest and raises goosebumps along the ink of her Winloc crest. "Then you're losing, because I'm playing no game." Not true at all. But he doesn't have to know that. She adjusts her frown into what she hopes is a smile that tells him she is a demure creature. Something tamable, malleable.

Not something forged.

"Oh, but that's not true is it?" Kadir smirks. He reads her too easily, but his gaze skirts past her, and his left eye twitches. "You're both playing a game, aren't you?"

Vellene swivels around.

Mogaell stands at the front doors, hair a mess from the wind outside. She flings off her cloak into the arms of the nearest Utility, navy eyes flaring at the sight of Kadir. "Sir Rathmore."

Vellene narrows her eyes on her sister's perfect movements and flirtatious expression. Jealousy shudders through her. Not for Kadir but for Mogaell's ease and elegance in everything Vellene is baffled by.

Kadir takes Mogaell's hand, expression deviously charming as he places a small kiss to her knuckles. "Two beautiful things in a single day? I must have Alchemight's favor."

Vellene runs her tongue along the back of her teeth. She can't let Mogaell hijack this. "Let's go somewhere private," she suggests, hoping the words sound braver than she feels.

Kadir's attention draws away from her sister in a blink. His lips press into a tight grin. "Lead the way."

She decides she hates his voice, lush with stories to be told and mysteries to be solved, as she rigidly removes herself from the path of Mogaell's glare and into the direction of the gardens. Utilities file outside, the shard storm stopped, and their cleaning duties of the property begin. They carry ladders and pouches filled with primitive formularies wrapped in marvel. In an hour, the property will be spotless, all evidence of the shard storm vanished.

Vellene toys with her skirts, chews on her lip.

"Is there a reason you seem so ruffled?" Kadir asks, a hint of a smile to the question. With his long legs, he matches her hurried pace with ease.

Vellene throws open a door and sucks in a breath of fresh, crisp air. Alchemight's large sun blazes overhead, but the breeze keeps the air cool. "I'm fine," she says, and finally it's something she should say. Whatever confidence she had in her first moments with Kadir is traded for the familiarity of pretending. Pretend and live. Pretend and kill.

She finds her favorite spot, a trellis covered in various, thorned flora. Many are painted black from the shard storm, tar battering their color to oblivion. However, a few, particularly the ones hidden beneath the top layer, still shine with color. It's the same flora she drew on the wall of her prison cell as a child.

Vellene touches one, her shoulders tensing when Kadir steps beside her.

"You should be careful," he says and lightly wraps a hand around her wrist, pulling her hand back from the flora. "Those are poisonous."

Her brow furrows. She stares at the purple-petaled flora she's admired all her life. Then she turns her face toward Kadir. "Poisonous?" she breathes and her pulse races at his closeness, at a new him she sees out in the sunlight. Without shadows to accompany him, the white and yellow of his hair radiates with light. All the dark caverns of his face glisten. Even his scars are all but transparent. Never has a male appeared so perfect, so beautiful. He's sharp. So sharp she wonders what it would be like to be cut by him.

"Deadly," he says, face soft and serious. Much of the humor and mischievousness he had before vanishes into someone else entirely. Calm and calculated and precise. Even his grip on her wrist remains feather light, as if he knows anything more will make her fear him as she's feared so many others.

It's hard to look away from him, but guilt helps make it happen. At the end of this, he dies, and beauty—she shouldn't trust it. He is a High Imperial. He's grown up among the war of Frales. She can't let herself get tangled with him as she did with Eledar. There is nothing innocent or warm in his violet gaze, and even in the light of the garden, there is something impossible cold and withdrawn about him.

Vellene turns back to the flora, her mind wandering. She needs to pick him apart, learn his weaknesses, then use them against him. He won't be easy to sneak up on or simply assassinate. She'll need strategy.

But her thoughts hone in on her favorite flora. Kadir matters nothing to her as she stares at its thorns. Dread pools in her gut as realization claims her. "My mother was poisoned." Her heart thunders. She freezes when Kadir runs his thumb over the inside of her wrist.

Panic both recedes and rushes forward as something as tormenting as frost-bite blossoms where his thumb trails, where his fingers still capture her wrist. Vellene yanks it free, and the movement pulls Kadir out of a trance of his own. His eyes widen a fraction when she does it, hand left mid-air. He clears his throat and shoves it into a pocket, masterfully tweaking his expression into stone.

She thinks he means to insult her, to even redirect the conversation.

But Kadir's lips twitch between a well-practiced smile and a more permanent frown. "I'm sorry for your loss. I heard she passed not long ago."

"That almost sounded sincere," Vellene retorts, crossing her arms and turning her back to him. She stares at the flora, filling with more and more certainty they are responsible for the mother she lost.

Mogaell is smartly vindictive in that way.

"Are you cold?" Kadir asks after a moment.

"What?" She frowns. He shifts behind her, and she glances over her shoulder at him. "I'm not—" Her words fade as he shucks off his cloak.

Beneath, he wears a sheer, long-sleeved shirt, the fit loose but in a shade of plum like the rest of his attire. It sparkles with a lilac sheen in the sunlight. Her eyes snag on the chiseled and defined muscles beneath the fabric. She was right to think him sharp, to remember where he came from. She decides to hate him. She must. Even if she wishes to comb through the riddles of his many expressions, to puzzle out the chill of his touch and the shadows of his eyes.

But he steps to her and places his cloak over her bare shoulders. "You're shivering, love," he murmurs, his voice as decadent as the velvet fabric he drapes her in. His strange chill intertwines with her building heat. It's almost soothing. Like a balm to a burn.

She forces her eyes away from his chest, the dark ink of his ravian and the hollows of his chemight deposits. She peers at his face. "Thanks."

Kadir's face twists. It's not devious or careful or angry. Instead, it's—embarrassed.

Vellene's brow furrows, nose scrunching in thought. Why would he be embarrassed? Then his fingers reach for her again. They line along the side of her face before his thumb presses between her brows. Her chest caves. "What are you doing?" she demands, self-conscious beyond belief. She knows what he must see—her stupid indent. She attempts to smooth it.

Kadir yanks his hand back. He stares at her, his gaze severe, but she doesn't dare flinch or shy away. Instead she stands taller, her lips pursing with a challenge. He won't rattle her.

Kadir shakes his head and releases an unsteady chuckle. "I'm sorry. I think I may be exhausted. Traveling the abyss is quite the task." But he looks as confused as she does, as ready for a fight.

Vellene forces an exhale and steadies herself. It could be the truth. She imagines sailing Dalbian's Abyss is no simple adventure, and if he truly just arrived, he could be tired and worn. "Oh, that's alright. Let me show you to your room," she says. She measures her breaths until her shoulders relax.

Kadir nods with mirrored relief and waves her forward. "After you, Miss Winloc."

They walk wordlessly and hastily into Winloc Grove, both with the singular mission of getting away from each other. Kadir keeps his distance as Vellene leads him to a room a few down from her own. It's a guest room. One that, to her knowledge, no one has ever used. Her father never had a need for guests or for company besides his own.

Her arms curl around herself, hands gripping the sides of his cloak. *His. Cloak.* It's a small act of kindness, but it's a kindness she hadn't expected. This—them—it's a business deal. He owes her nothing. If anything, she thought he would be the one to be cruel and distant if he plans to string her up and bleed her dry. Her fingers sink beneath the soft velvet to the boning of her corset. Then she peeks at Kadir.

He walks with his hands laced behind his back. In the dim light of the hall, the ink of the Ravian across his chest is bold beneath his sheer shirt. Formularies swirl in deposits all throughout the flight creature's depiction. Unlike Vellene's, the deposits trail down either side of his torso as opposed to going up his neck. The placement is purposeful, lining the creature's two wings.

Eledar's must be a direct variation of the ink. While his Ravian was depicted as a profile, only one wing descending the length of his torso, Kadir's holds out both wings proudly. The creature's beak is opened wide against Kadir's left collar bone as if it's crying to the tune of battle.

"Is this it?" Kadir asks.

Vellene's eyes widen, realizing she stopped at the door and is staring at Kadir. She swallows and nods, throwing the door open. "All yours," she answers.

Kadir remains still. He watches her, a glimmer of curiosity and desire in his eyes. "Shall I continue to call you 'love'?"

"What?" she blurts. "Love?"

Kadir's lips tilt with amusement. "Yes, love." His eyes run down the length of her frame. "Your father promised you to me," he says, voice careful, "but I'm not a fan of forcing anyone to do what they don't want."

Vellene's heart sinks into her stomach. She doesn't want this, whatever this is. It's too much. She has a death oath to deal with, a Golem hanging off her back and an Imperial assassin just waiting for her to screw up. Seduction has never been her forte. What happened with Eledar was a fluke, and killing certainly doesn't make her list of accomplishments. The way Kadir watches her—sees *through* her—it's unsettling. It makes her second-guess everything.

"You don't wish to Infuse. That is apparent," Kadir explains. He steps closer to her. "So, why agree? Why are you giving up your seat on the Convocation? You could be better than him."

Vellene steps back and lifts his cloak from her shoulders, wanting to distance herself. "Please. Just take your cloak and get some rest."

Kadir's curiosity sinks into a scowl. "Is this all you are? An obedient puppet?"

"I'm a Winloc," she grinds out and grips his cloak.

His eyes trace her face. Then his gaze meets hers, and his next breath comes a bit ragged. "What will it be, Miss Winloc? Chemight or blade?"

Vellene frowns. "What?"

"Infuse with me or kill me." His violet eyes flash. "I imagine those were your options. Were they not?"

For a moment, her body turns away in cowardice. She thinks he may grab her, hurt her, but instead he projects his anger away from her.

Kadir sucks in a stiff breath and shoots her a glare. "I'm the price you must pay to keep your head on your shoulders."

Vellene stills.

Kadir laughs and shakes his head. "I have studied chemi like your father all my life. They never change, and they always want blood."

"You say that as if you aren't one of them," she argues. "As if you didn't agree to use me to feed your nation."

He scowls at her words, but he doesn't correct her. Instead, he approaches her again. "If you're going to kill me, you should do it now." He splays out his arms, exposing his chest to her.

Vellene sees the test in his gaze. He's right to assume she won't do it. She needs more time and training. But he's wrong to think she is nothing more than a puppet. A thought occurs to her. A dangerous one. She straightens and shoves his cloak into his chest. "Help me," she snaps.

Then she forces pain into her eyes and latches to the weakness that follows her through life. It's time it works for her rather than against her.

Kadir takes a step back, eyes drawn to her Winloc crest and the exposed tops of her breasts. He looks away, that same embarrassment from earlier creeping across his expression. "Help you kill me?" He forces a rough laugh.

"No, *help me.*" This time she says it with sincerity. The words radiate through her body.

Kadir frowns and stares at her. His severe look softens. "Vellene, I—"

"Help me kill him," she begs, eyes frantic as they roam his face. "Whatever you want is yours. Just please help me be free." It's meant to be a ruse, but the fear that rises inside her is plenty real. Some part of her wants to be saved by someone else. Another part of her knows she has very little weapons in her arsenal besides the way he flushes around her. He's attracted to her. She can use that. He kept her from touching poisonous flora and gave her his cloak. He has a savior mentality beneath that cold surface.

She follows his slow trail backward, his hands and hers clasped around his cloak as if it's an anchor between them. His back hits the wall, and she closes in. She releases her grip on his cloak and presses a hand to his chest, clutching the thin fabric of his shirt in her palm. Her eyes search his dilated pupils, and she relishes the genuine shock that breaks his placid mask. It feels like victory. "I'll be yours forever if you just give me a better life than this one," she says.

Of all the things she hates, it's this. The desperation. The need to be loved and taken care of. The want to simply be safe. Just once. That's all. But if it can work in her favor, if her desperation can keep her hands clean of the blood that must be spilled, she should use it. Ice sharpens between them, coils around her body and drives a chill down her spine. She trembles but she doesn't back down. This is how she'll fight. Doe eyes. Worried brow. Tears. All of it. Every weakness. Sharpened. Furious.

Kadir clenches his jaw. His shock wanes to realization and his eyes narrow. "Not so simple, are you?" His eyes glance down at her hand against his chest. Then his mouth twisting into a scowl. "Quit that."

Vellene laces a hand behind his neck, pressing herself into him. She shivers as the cold deepens, sinks into her bones. "Shove me away," she counters.

"Guardians save me," he curses. "I don't want to forcibly remove you, but I will if you don't knock it off."

Vellene wavers. "This is all I have to offer you." Her gaze dips to the scar across his face, and his hands tighten around her waist.

Kadir grits his teeth. "I don't need some sick bargain, Vellene." His cloak falls between them and he pushes her back. "I'm not your father."

The fire inside her licks against deep wounds. She hesitates. “You'll grant me my freedom without strings attached?” she asks, incredulous.

“No one has to grant you anything. You are free to leave.” Kadir peels from her and moves away.

“He will hunt me down.” Vellene's voice shakes. "If I leave, if you take me—it doesn't matter. He will find me. He will kill me."

His shoulders wilt. “I want to help you.”

She tames her smile. “Then help.”

“It's not that simple.” He looks away. Guilt fills his expression.

Interesting. Vellene takes a step forward. “You planned on killing me, too. Didn't you?”

He still won't look at her.

She growls in frustration, then shoves her hands into his chest.

Kadir stumbles back, stunned by her reaction. “Did you just push me?”

Vellene grits her teeth and does it again. “Go on, Rathmore. Kill me.”

His brow furrows.

“*Kill me.* What are you waiting for?” she cries and strikes him in the chest again.

“You're impossible,” he mutters, but one of his dimples—which he seems to keep under lock and key—makes an appearance.

"You think this is funny?" Vellene hits him harder.

"I think this is right," Kadir says, holding himself firm against her attacks. "You need to fight back, Vellene."

She halts her fists and glares at him. "Are you mocking me?"

"If I say yes, will you hit me again?" He smirks.

She frowns. "You want me to hit you?"

Mischief lights in his eyes. "I don't mind it."

Vellene turns from him in frustration.

"We have to kill each other. It doesn't have to be morbid or depressing. It could be fun," Kadir says, a hint of laughter in his voice.

"Fun?" Vellene's voice is a borderline screech. She grips her head. "It is not fun being pushed around from so many different angles, questioning whether you are anything but a card played on a table."

He steps around to face her and his face falls serious. "I can't save you, Vellene. I'm not a hero."

"Then what are you?" she hisses.

Kadir shrugs.

She narrows her eyes on the movement. "That's it? Just a shrug?"

He does it again.

"You're infuriating," she growls, but a smile tugs at her lips.

"And you're feistier than you let on," Kadir muses.

Vellene glares at him. "Why come and play the part of my Infusion partner? Why risk the danger if you knew my father would have me kill you?"

"I wanted to know which roles you are playing. Quite a few, it seems." He lifts his brows at her. "Distressed prisoner. Obedient daughter. Seductive killer."

A shiver arches up her spine. "Well, what now? Should we stab each other?"

"Don't be a tease, Vellene." His eyes twinkle, but his small smile vanishes at her clear distress. He rubs his chin. "I'll talk to your father."

Vellene's eyes widen. "No."

"Don't worry, I won't say anything about your lack of killing me. Although, me being alive will be evidence enough." Kadir touches the bare skin of her shoulder lightly.

Vellene flinches back from him. "What will you talk to him about exactly?"

He clicks his tongue. "Why would I tell you? That'd be no fun."

Vellene's brow furrows.

His lips quirk. "I think I love that."

"What?"

He lifts his hand to her face and gently brushes her hair out of the way. Then he presses his thumb against the indent between her brows like he had in the garden. "This."

Vellene pulls back in horror. *I have to kill him I have to kill him I have to kill him*—"Why?"

He doesn't answer. Instead, he smiles a lazy smile and moves his finger to her chin, lightly pulling her face up to his. "Goodnight, Vellene."

She sucks in a breath to steady herself as his lips softly kiss the indent in her forehead. It's brief and small, but it sends a shock of cold through her skull. She swears she sees a wave of blue extend from her forehead to his lips as he draws back, but it snaps into the darkness of the hallway.

"You kissed me," she says, the words tumbling from her in surprise.

Kadir chuckles and stoops to retrieve his cloak. Then, he steps away, moving to the guest room. "And you're intriguing."

*So are you*, she admits to herself, not sure what to make of him. "Are you going to kill me still?"

He steps inside his room, a glint to his eyes as he tugs on his door. "We'll see." Then, before the door can click shut, "Love."

## Chapter Fifteen

# *Vellene*

Orbs flicker light across her father's office as Vellene steps through the arched doorway and into the monstrous space. A lair fit for a devil, Aquim sits behind a massive black marbled desk. Veins of Winloc blue creep through the darkness—in the desk, his leather chair, the rugs, the walls. A large map of Alchemight fills the entire expanse of one wall, showcasing Scorus, Dalbian's Abyss, and Frales.

Vellene eyes it as she waits for her father to look up from his work. It's a pre-war map, Frales almost a mirrored replica of Scorus, with the exception of a few Golem encampments marked along the outskirts of the Rathmore property. Her stomach tightens as she thinks of Eledar growing up in one of those camps. She wonders if they were anything like her prison cell.

Idus wavers beside the map. His milk-white eyes trail her frame. "Sir Winloc."

Aquim pulls back. He turns over the paper he was reading and pushes his navy hair over his shoulders. "Vellene, I was hoping you'd stop in. How have things with Rathmore progressed?"

She smooths her dress and hair, then lifts her chin. "That's what I wanted to talk to you about. I'm not sure killing him would be wise." It took her hours to piece together a plan. It isn't much of one, but it's all she has. Until she can get her feet under her and figure out Rathmore, she needs to hold off her father's want to kill him. Her death oath is tied to her father and sister. It's them she needs to focus on—not Kadir. He's a problem, but she can't let him consume her.

Her father pushes up from his desk and moves to its side. He walks slowly, precisely, his eyes level with hers. He remains calm, despite the gravel of his voice. "I'm not interested in keeping another High Imperial alive." Aquim gestures to her, his ring finger twitching with the anger he manages to stifle. "This is also a test, daughter. If you are to remain alive past your 18th birthday, I need to know you're an ally, not an enemy."

She prepared for this, rehearsed this. "Sir Rathmore is sly, father. He will see a plot against him before I can ever make a move." Vellene sucks in a short breath. Her heart hammers. "Is there no deal to be made with Frales that could promote prosperity for your future empire, as well as peace for others?"

Idus straightens in the corner. A strange look crosses the old chemi's face. Apprehension, maybe? Surprise?

Vellene darts her focus back to her father.

Aquim cocks his head to the side. He stares at her as if he wishes to see all her riddles made whole.

*Try harder.* Her lips curl with a slim smile, the darkest pieces of herself slipping forward. She lets them have a victory, even if it is small.

"Those words sound like a ruler's," Aquim says. His voice sharpens the chill of his office. "Need I remind you of your power? You have none. I may have restored your voice for the sake of that Guardian, but I will take it away if you abuse it."

Vellene presses her lips together.

"Actions speak louder," Idus says from his corner. He folds his arms into his robes and nods to Aquim. "Sir, if I may?"

"By all means," Aquim answers with a tinge of annoyance. "You're her Surveillant, after all. You should have fixed this 'peace' nonsense decades ago with her."

"Vellene will never be me, father." Mogaell's voice haunts through the doorway.

Vellene angles between the three. Her eyes narrow on her sister as Mogaell emerges from a shadow in the corridor beyond. "Eavesdropping?" Vellene asks.

Mogaell grins and swishes into the room. She makes a point to bump past Vellene before she selects one of the two silver-threaded chaises in the office. She settles onto it and kicks her legs up, taking the skirts of her extravagant gown with her. "Not eavesdropping," she confirms. "I have an appointment."

Vellene frowns.

Idus clears his throat. "As I was saying, actions speak louder than your voice ever will." His long, bony fingers slip free from his robes and move to brush through his hair. Hair he doesn't have. He catches himself and moves to his beard. "If you want to prove something to your father, then you must prove it."

Vellene's frown deepens. It's unsettling getting advice from a chemi who never provided it before. More than that, Idus confirmed her suspicions. She figured talking her father out of killing Kadir would have little to no result, but she also knew it was worth a try. Plus, if word somehow gets back to Kadir that she attempted to save him, maybe he'll be open to an alliance. *Play all the angles*, she tells herself and rolls her shoulders back.

"I could kill Rathmore," Mogaell volunteers. "He's in our guest room, is he not?"

Aquim waves a hand in dismissal. "It must be Vellene. You have proven your worth, Mogaell."

*By murdering our mother*. Vellene's shoulders tense. She clenches her skirts. "Fine."

"Then go," Aquim insists. "Make a plan. Woo him. I do not care. Just get rid of him."

Vellene takes a step back, then hesitates. She eyes Mogaell. "What are you two discussing? Perhaps I can help."

Mogaell's eyes darken. Her lips twitch into a satisfied smirk.

"That won't be necessary," Aquim says. He rounds his desk and settles into his chair. He lightly fingers the paper he turned over and out of Vellene's sight. "Leave."

She bristles at the command but turns on her toes and stalks out of the room. She'll have to try for option two: making Rathmore more of a puppet than she is. She waits for the slam of the door, but instead, she hears the soft thud of leisurely steps. She glances back and slows.

Idus pulls the office door shut with a small click, then he follows her. He moves like a spirit, robes wavering around him and puffing up with each stride. The double-diamond body of the spideria flashes in the flickering light of the orbs that hang from the ceiling.

"Did I forget something?" she asks as he joins her in a stroll down the hall.

Idus eyes her profile. "You do have another option, Mistress Winloc."

Vellene's forehead indents with curiosity. "And what would that be?"

"You could choose to follow through with the original plan. Fail to kill Rathmore and, instead, Infuse with him. Join him in Frales."

They step behind a pair of Utilities and follow them into the Observatory. The hall of glass is filled with boxes of supplies for The Drinking. Several Utilities and some Chemibreakers work to set up a stage.

"Are you suggesting I deny my father's wishes?" Vellene asks. She slows on the outskirts of all the rush and activity, lowering her voice and studying her Surveillant.

"No." Idus heaves a breath and looks out upon Winloc Grove's staff. "I am merely insinuating your father expects failure, and—perhaps—failure is your only true option in this matter."

"You think he will still have me killed, even if I do his bidding." She studies him. "This is unlike you. Giving me advice."

Idus shifts his weight.

"You can't give me a reason as to why?" she wonders. "You've changed, or something has. I noticed it the moment I got inside that carriage with you."

He steadies and brings his gaze to hers. "My contract is as long as yours."

Vellene licks her lips. "You wish to leave your position? What about Mogaell?"

"Your sister doesn't need me. She never has."

"And I did?" she hisses. "I needed the prison stints, the slaps on the wrist, the abuse?"

Her Surveillant presses his lips together.

She peers at him, at the flash of fury that tightens the wrinkles around his eyes. Doubt shudders through her. It's possible, she guesses, that the elder has pretended all these years just as she has. It's hard not to in a place like this. She looks down at her fingers, fiddles with them. If that's the case, then he speaks the truth. His freedom will come when hers does.

"Just know you have options," he says after a long silence. Idus clicks his tongue in contentment, then pivots and takes slow, lengthy strides out of the Observatory.

Vellene rubs her forehead and leans into the wall. Her reprieve is short-lived, however. Three Chemibreaker escorts she evaded all morning find her. The one at the forefront is on regular rotation, their ruby eyes now a constant. Every corner she turns. Every meal she eats. They are there. Watching.

She sighs and steps around them. "I'm going to my room."

"You shouldn't leave your room without your escorts," one asserts.

Vellene ignores them and picks up her pace as she reaches a corner. Then she sprints toward the Reading Room. A small smile breaks across her face as she ditches her escorts. It's fleeting as she folds the Reading Room's doors shut behind her. Her chest heaves as she wracks in breaths. Her corset digs into her lungs. She moves her fingers to loosen it, then halts when she spots an unfamiliar chemi at one of the many tables.

"Oh." She clears her throat and fixes her hair. "Sorry, I didn't think anyone would be in here."

The chemi wears a Chemibreaker uniform with deviations from the Winlocs'. Vellene recognizes the pattern across his chest as the Rathmore crest. "Excuse me, Mistress Winloc. I was only taking a break. Sir Rathmore said this room is often vacant."

"It usually is except for me," she tells him. "You're a Rathmore Chemibreaker?"

"Arrived today. The rest should be getting in soon." He gives a small bow. "Geralt. Head of Sir Rathmore's guard."

"A pleasure to meet you." She skirts around a table and steps to a shelf.

Geralt strides past.

"You're leaving?" she asks.

He freezes but offers her a polite smile. "Sorry, Mistress. Was there something you needed?"

Vellene shakes her head. "No, I just didn't want to be the reason you ended your break. You may stay if you'd like."

Geralt straightens. "Thank you, Mistress. That's very kind of you, but I should report back to Sir Rathmore."

Vellene nods, then moves to him. "Actually, could you check the hall outside for any of the Winloc Chemibreakers?"

Geralt raises a brow. "Hiding?"

She gives him a sheepish smile. "It's hard to get privacy these days."

He fidgets with his uniform then shrugs. "Yeah. Sure. Let me check."

Vellene waits as he strides out into the hall.

He returns quickly and peeks his head back into the Reading Room. "The coast is clear."

Vellene relaxes her shoulders. "Okay, thanks."

He tilts his head and studies her. "I admit, I didn't expect a Winloc to even acknowledge my presence."

Vellene shuffles to a shelf filled with the colorful spines of tomes. She scans them and shrugs. "My sister and father probably wouldn't have."

"But not you?"

She glances up from her search and cocks a brow. "Not me, although you're quite chatty for a Chemibreaker."

Geralt stiffens as if he's been caught. He clears his throat. "I'm sorry," he blusters.

Vellene offers him an apologetic smile. "I didn't mean to make you uncomfortable. I didn't mean anything by it, actually. It's nice to talk to someone." She turns her attention back to the tomes and swipes her finger over the spines. She stops and selects one on poisonous flora.

"Doing some gardening?" Geralt asks, his eyes scanning the cover.

Vellene blows off the dust on the tome's cover and tucks it under her arm. "Truth-seeking."

Geralt nods, but his eyes remain on the tome's cover.

She inwardly curses. "I'm not going to poison, Kadir," she quickly asserts.

The Rathmore Chemibreaker slowly raises his gaze to hers. "Shall I escort you, Mistress Winloc?" He tugs open the door and peers outside.

Vellene walks into the hall. She hesitates but accepts Geralt's arm. Suspicion riddles his features. If she tries to leave him behind now, he'll suspect the worst.

"Where to?" Geralt asks.

"The garden," she answers, hoping her openness will deter his suspicion, and hugs the tome. "I have some research to do."

## Chapter Sixteen

# *Eledar*

Wind nips at Eledar's ears as he sits on the front steps of The Bloody Cloth. He grasps his forehead as he scans through one of Imaex's journals. He stumbles over the words, his eyes tired and mind weary. Reliving the life of another Golem is too much. His past is enough for his fingers to itch for a drink, for his veins to scream for *lumis*. The last thing he needs is to take on another's trauma.

His eyes wander from the page.

Scraps gather further from the alley, but many Utilities stop through after a long day of work.

He raises his brows as he spots three Chemibreakers. He assumed, like in Frales, Chemibreakers were recruited from the Imperial population. Here, well-trained Utilities are good enough. They shuck off their Chemibreaker uniforms, throw on tattered cloaks, and join the night festivities of the streets.

Eledar smirks at one, and he gives him a nod.

"You're new," the male chemi remarks.

Eledar's eyes trail over the male's frame, but he waves him off. While he could certainly use the distraction, the scorn of one lover is problem enough. *Vellene.* He rubs between his brows and closes the journal. He stands, prepares to step into the tavern, but stops when he spots a hooded figure and a couple of teen Scraps on the corner.

It's brief, but the orbs passed between them flash a familiar periwinkle.

*Lumis.* Eledar wets his lips and tucks the journal into his back pocket. He crosses to the dealer and catches them by the sleeve of their cloak. "How much?"

She pulls back her hood and stares at Eledar. She's taller than him—taller than most. Blue hair as light as ice runs in a sleek line down one side of her face, the other half of her head buzzed down. Eyes that match her hair comb over Eledar's face, then dip to his shirt.

He nods with understanding. "I can trade." He lifts the hem of his shirt, displays his three bottom deposits filled with empty orbs.

The chemi scoffs. "No formularies?"

Eledar takes a small step toward her. "I'll give you all three for just one *lumis.*"

She shakes her head and clutches the pouch at her waist tighter. "No formularies, no deal." She steps around him.

Eledar grabs her wrist. "No, please—"

She spins on him and nails her knee into his crotch.

He stands firm as pain radiates up into his abdomen. He clenches his teeth. It's not that it doesn't hurt—it does. His upbringing as a Golem slave, however, forced him to no longer be vulnerable in the ways most male chemi are.

The dealer curses and yanks on her wrist.

Eledar keeps a firm hold on it. "I need *lumis*."

"You don't. You're just a junkie." Mist drifts from between her fingers and toward his hand. The natural chemight pries at his grip with surprising strength. "Let go of me."

"Look, I can work for it. What do you need? Maybe you have some debts that must be collected on past transactions?" Eledar loosens his grip on her as her chemight sharpens and sticks toward him. He yanks his hand back as one of the needle-like blades nicks him, and the smallest speck of clay goops out. He hides his hand behind his back, but the chemi brightens.

"You're a Golem," she says. She pulls her chemight back. "I could use that kind of power to anchor to."

"Anchor?" he questions. Discomfort trickles in.

"I'm a weaver and a messenger Utility for Imperials," she trails off and shrugs, "and, well, those who don't want to be found."

Eledar lifts a brow.

She returns the look. "You wouldn't happen to be the Sir Lirik my pals at Equilibrium told me about, would you?" Her lips slip into a grin. "Very handsome. That chiseled jaw, that body. Well, I'd say you deserve some proper attire. Let me weave something for you."

He stiffens. "You work with Equilibrium?"

"How do you think I get *lumis*? We don't have a war here in Scorus, and that formulary was created for soldiers." She looks him up and down. "I guess maybe you do need it, huh? Is past trauma of a certain Golem uprising hounding at your back?"

"You could say that," he mutters. His fingers twitch at his side. How hard would it be to snatch her pouch and run? He eyes it. "You have a name?"

She pops a hip and rests her hand on it. "Nivia."

"What's a weaver?"

"I make things." She adjusts her grip on the pouch. Her gaze flicks to a tear in the right sleeve of his shirt. "Here, I'll show you." Then, she narrows her eyes. "But don't grab my pouch. I know you're name. I will find you."

Eledar presses his lips together, but his inner Scrap flares with approval.

She gradually pulls her hand from her pouch, then opens it and pulls out a primitive formulary. She grips it in her palm before she reaches out and takes his shoulder. He flinches back, but she tightens her grip. "It won't hurt," she promises and digs her nails into him.

His nostrils flare. "I beg to differ."

She grins but sucks in a breath and channels the orb pressed in her palm.

Eledar braces himself, expects her chemight to blast chaotically outward. Without deposits, most chemi can't control a formulary. Instead, his body warms as if brushed by a breath of hot air.

Nivia slowly pulls her hand from Eledar's shoulder. As she does, a dark emerald wave of chemight seeps and stretches with the movement. It protrudes from his shoulder.

"What are you do—"

"Shut up," she grumbles, then twists her fingers around in the air. A second wave of green branches off from the first. It glides over Eledar's chest and reaches for the tear in his shirt sleeve. Nivia's eyes narrow in on the cut, and the chemight swamps the opening. It pools and mends. Threads loosen, then pull taut. Nivia blows out a long, steady breath. Her fingers dance in the air as she weaves with her chemight, her other hand never letting go of the orb and its formulary.

"You're quite talented," Eledar notes.

Finally, Nivia lets go of the chemight. Its waves of emerald ripple backward. One branch sinks back into Eledar's shoulder, while the other snaps to her palm. When she opens her other hand and reveals the orb, three-fourths of its primitive formulary remain.

"You used me like a chemight deposit." Eledar gives her an appreciative nod. "Smart of you."

"I prefer crafty." Nivia smiles. She nods her head behind her. "Come back to my shop. We should talk."

Eledar runs his fingers over his beard.

Nivia shrugs. "I have a message from your boss. Want it or not?"

An image of the cloaked stranger from Equilibrium materializes in his mind. "Why didn't they send it to me directly?"

"Like I said, Lirik," she says and smirks at the way his jaw tightens with his last name, "I send messages for those that don't want to be found. That means I send the messages when an opportunity presents itself. My clients don't pay me for timeliness. They pay me to be discreet."

"And this is your way of being discreet? Selling *lumis*?" he argues.

"I got your attention without a paper trail, didn't I?" Nivia moves down the street. She lifts her hood, then nods to his. "Cover yourself and follow me. We have an hour before we lose the cover of night."

Eledar begrudgingly tugs his hood up. Their cloaks billow with the wind as they move through the streets and dance around crowds. He leans toward her. "Your Chemibreakers use natural chemight off-duty. Shouldn't that mean they hang themselves in the morning?"

Nivia glances at him but continues blazing a path forward onto a narrow street. "Sometimes they do." She grimaces. "But we all live two lives these days, do we not?

Me, I'm a messenger and weaver for Imperials by day. At night, I do the biddings of the cloaked and masked." She looks him over. "And you?"

Eledar shakes his head. "What you see is what you get."

"A lie if I ever heard one." Nivia snorts and shakes her head. Her hair waves with the movement. "How many of your friends and family know about your *lumis* addiction?"

He looks down.

"Exactly." Nivia stops outside of a small Utility shop. It resides on the edge of a bundle of Scrap shacks. "This is it." She shoots him a shining smile. "Time to get that pretty face of yours something suitable to match it."

Eledar blinks. "You truly want to dress me."

Nivia nods with barely contained eagerness. "It's my thing." She holds her hands up as if in surrender. "Don't get me wrong, sending messages in dramatic ways is always a good time, but helping a chemi reach their full potential? That's a high better than your sweet, sweet *lumis*." She shoulders open the door to her shop and waves a hand. Natural chemight flings outward with the movement. It darts forward to the various places candles rest throughout the shop and lights each one. Nivia claps her hands and moves to a squat desk in the corner.

Eledar takes a small step inside. The door falls shut with a soft click behind him.

The walls, the ceiling—letters cover every surface except the floor, where vibrant rugs overlap each other. Two plush chaises face each other in the center of the room, a few feet from where Nivia's desk rests.

She rifles through the letters and envelopes on her desk's top, then she plucks a playing card from it all.

It's the same type of card that brought him to Scorus, Equilibrium's hourglass crest plated in raised crimson on its front.

Nivia hands it to him, and Eledar flips it over.

Contract terminated.

Eledar reads it once, twice, before his eyes drift up to Nivia. "Is this real? They sent me across Dalbian's Abyss just to—"

"Are you an idiot?" she hisses and yanks the card out of his grasp. She thrusts a finger over her lips, then tears the card into small pieces. Her eyes dart around the room, then she grabs his bicep and tugs him into a small back room.

It's obvious the space is where she does her weaving work. Fabrics, metals, corset-boning, and ribbons drape and cascade across the room. In the corner is where she must sleep—a small bed done up with pillows and found quilts.

Nivia presses a hand to the door and scoops back her hood with the other. "Out there is my official workplace. I don't know that Imperials have bugged it with a primitive formulary or two to listen in on me, but it wouldn't surprise me. On top of that, you were on a secret mission by an equally secretive resistance group."

"Exactly. Past tense. What's that about?" Eledar growls and steps further into the studio. "Equilibrium and I had a deal. They can't just call that off."

"The situation changed," she says but won't give him more. She gestures to him with an exhale. "Consider yourself a free Golem. Go on about your life."

Eledar laughs darkly. "I am anything but free. I was promised the name of my Master."

Nivia rolls her shoulders back. "I see."

"If they can't give me it, then I will need to resort to my own methods of finding who it is."

Her eyes darken. "To stand in the way of Equilibrium is to sentence yourself to death."

Eledar shakes his head. He rips Imaex's journal out of his back pocket and grits his teeth. "I have been torturing myself to find that source. The least Equilibrium can do is offer me payment."

Nivia crosses her arms. "I was told they sent you here with months' worth of formularies. You may now keep those as payment."

Eledar slaps the journal to the floor. "I used them."

"All of them?" She lifts her brow. "How many dealers did you trade with?"

"Dealers?" Eledar shakes his head. He grimaces. "Tonight was the first night I even considered trading for *lumis*, and that was because all I have are empty orbs."

"Again—all of them?" she insists. "How could you have possibly used that many formularies?"

He looks away. There's no way to explain his empty orbs without ratting out Vellene in the process.

"Fine. Don't tell me. But it's really not my fault you used them all. They were ample enough payment for your services up to this point." Nivia picks up Imaex's journal and flips through the pages. "What Golem wrote this?"

Eledar blows out a breath between his teeth. He runs his hands through his hair. "You can read Golem script?"

"Of course. I'm a messenger Utility. It's kind of my job to be able to communicate with any chemi that walks through my door." Nivia's eyes scan the words. Her jaw tightens. "It's never happiness for you lot, is it?"

"No, never." Eledar balls his fists. "I'm sorry, but if you have nothing more from Equilibrium—and considering they've terminated my business—I'm getting out of here." He moves to the door, then freezes as a knock comes from the other side.

"Nivia?" a familiar voice calls through the door.

Eledar's brow furrows, and he yanks it open.

Soffesa's eyes widen at the sight of him. "Eledar?"

"Oh, my beautiful assassin," Nivia beams and crosses the room. She shoves Eledar out of the way with ease and takes both of Soffesa's hands. "How are you?"

Soffesa laughs nervously. "Eledar, why are you here?"

Eledar crosses his arms and studies the two. His eyes narrow on the blush trailing up Soffesa's neck. "I could ask you the same."

Soffesa clears her throat and wrenches her hands from Nivia's grasp. She gestures to her red leather dress. "Nivia's my weaver."

"And happily so," Nivia adds. She runs a playful finger over Soffesa's exposed bicep.

Eledar pushes aside his frustration and grins at his friend. "Are you two together?"

Soffesa tugs on a strand of her hair. "Well—"

"We see each other from time to time," Nivia finishes. "It's very casual." The chemi doesn't seem bothered by Soffesa's awkwardness. In fact, she plants a kiss on his friend's cheek with a smile. "I caught her torturing a—what do you call them, dear? Clients? Soon-to-be-dead?—because they were trying to short her two formularies." Nivia laughs and the ice blue of her eyes sharpens with delight.

Eledar's lips press into a pleased smile.

"We will never talk about this," Soffesa whispers fiercely as Nivia steps back into her room to pull out various fabrics.

Eledar bumps his shoulder into hers. "I think it's great, Soff."

Soffesa blushes and looks at her feet. "What she said is true. It's casual. We both see others."

"What's that like?" he asks, voice laced with longing.

Soffesa laughs. "Not as fun as it sounds."

"Maybe you'll settle down," he whispers and gestures to Nivia.

She gives a gentle shake of her head. "Nivia is fantastic, but there's always been something missing between us. We're too different, I think." She runs her fingers over her dress. She offers Eledar a sheepish smile, her cheeks reddening. "But, I can't say I don't like the clothes."

Eledar laughs.

It draws Nivia's attention, and the chemi throws her hair over her shoulder. She stoops and picks up a bin of dark-colored leathers. "You better be whispering about how unworthy you both are of my friendship."

Eledar leans into the door frame. "We just met."

"Fast friends, then," Nivia amends. She holds up a dark green leather. "Yes, this is the one." She steps up to Eledar and gives the side of his face a couple of small slaps. "Brightens your eyes."

"What's wrong with my clothes?" Eledar insists.

"Well nothing, unless," she trails off and grabs both Eledar's and Soffesa's hands, tugging them into her room and shutting the door. She grins. "Unless you plan on beating Equilibrium to the source of all chemight."

"I'm sorry, did I miss something?" Soffesa balks.

"They terminated my contract," Eledar confirms.

"But you still have that pesky Golem problem, don't you? You know, the whole strings-could-be-pulled-at-any-time-and-turn-you-into-a-puppet-of-clay thing?" Nivia waves the green leather in the air like a flag. "What do you say? I bet having the source in your possession would be enough leverage to get the name of your Master."

"I thought you worked for Equilibrium?" Eledar questions.

Soffesa laughs.

Nivia looks horrified. "Alchemight, no. I work for no one but myself, honey."

Eledar rubs his neck. "Sorry."

"I'll forgive you when you're out of those rags and in something with my brand," Nivia explains and pulls up a black cotton fabric. "Word-of-mouth is how my business thrives. Ask your stunning assassin."

"It's true," Soffesa says and smiles broadly, a devilish glint in her eyes. "I had a mark ask me where I got my dress from. I let them go just because I knew Nivia would kill me if I took out a potential customer."

"You're a trained assassin, and you're afraid of a Utility?" Eledar points out.

Soffesa shrugs. "You haven't seen her angry."

"I'm positively feral," Nivia agrees. Then she waves the fabrics around again. "I suggest you strip, Sir Lirik."

"I'm not in the market for playing dress-up," Eledar says. He takes a step back and raises his hands. "I won't be stripping for anyone."

Soffesa snorts. "Yeah? So Vellene—"

He levels her with a solid glare, and she chokes on her words with a laugh.

"You can't storm Winloc Grove looking like that," Nivia asserts.

"I never said I was storming anything," Eledar reminds her.

Soffesa crosses her arms. "Why not? Screw Equilibrium. Our plans really don't have to change."

"We don't have any plans, Soff," Eledar says. "We barely have a hint as to where the source is located."

"Then maybe it's time we use our contact," Soffesa answers.

Nivia smiles. "Oh, do you need to send a message to someone?" She wiggles her brows. "What a coincidence."

"I don't want to involve her if we don't have to. We've done enough to her," Eledar explains.

"Screw that. If she's one of us, then she won't mind going out on a limb," Soffesa returns, her voice sharp.

She looks at Nivia. "How easily could you get a message inside Winloc Grove?"

Nivia drops her fabrics and settles on the edge of her bed in thought. "We'd need a way to transport it, but I could put a formulary on the letter to keep it invisible except to the transport and the receiver."

"You need someone who can get into Winloc Grove undetected?" Eledar asks.

Nivia nods. "Not easy to do."

"But not impossible." Soffesa cracks her knuckles. "With the right persuasion, we could get a Chemibreaker."

Nivia brightens as darkness fills Soffesa's features.

Eledar frowns at Nivia's apparent awe for his best friend's viciousness, but he replies, "If we're sending our contact a message, then we need to know exactly what to say."

"We plan for a time to meet her in person and grab the source," Soffesa explains. "It must be at Winloc Grove. Aquim wouldn't let it too far out of his sight."

Eledar nods in agreement. "I'll keep looking through Imaex's notes, but I think we've hit a dead end with them. The Winlocs took whatever evidence of the source he had."

"Then we go in blind," Soffesa says, "but we're going to need recruits. Other chemi that can help us get in and out undetected. Multiple times."

"I can help with the message," Nivia inserts, "but I'm no good at sneaking." She unclasps her cloak and reveals an elaborate gown. "I'm your grand entrance."

"Then we find others," Eledar says. His gaze meets Soffesa's. "Are you sure you want to help me with this?"

Soffesa gently takes his hand. "Eledar." She gives his palm a squeeze. "Your freedom is just as important to me as it is to you. It always has been."

He stares at their hands. "It will be dangerous."

"We were already moving in that direction to begin with." She offers him a sad smile.

"But we could end it." He squeezes her hand back in earnest. "We could be done. If we move forward now, we're choosing to walk into danger because we want to."

Soffesa's lips curl into a beautiful snarl. "We are nothing but dangerous, brother."

His chest warms and his itch for *lumis* subsides as a fresh wave of adrenaline pumps through him. "Then let's find our Chemibreaker and recruits."

# Chapter Seventeen

# *Vellene*

A clock in the Reading Room chimes, and Vellene's eyes flutter open.

She fell asleep in a chair situated between two towering shelves of tomes, one of her favorites lying stuck between its pages on the ground. With the strange angle of her body, she assumes it fell from her hand when she dozed off. She spent the better part of the last two days between her room and the garden only to find Kadir was right. Her favorite flora is, in fact, incredibly poisonous.

At that point, all she wanted was to disappear. Stories help her do exactly that.

Her eyes flick to where she left her red-eyed, Chemibreaker escort on the couch—a spot she can make out through one of the shelves, a space open between tomes—but they're gone. She brings her gaze to the clock on the wall and groans. She did more than take a quick nap. She's been out for almost the entire day.

Vellene grimaces and peels from the leather of her chair. She blinks a few times, then goes rigid when a shadow moves across from her.

Kadir steps into the sunlight. It peers through the window at her back and highlights his darker attire's plum sheen.

For the most part, she's done a remarkable job avoiding him. This spot in the Reading Room always brought her solace, protecting her at times from even Aquim and Idus, as they were never able to find her or didn't care enough to look longer than a few minutes.

It appears Kadir wasn't as deterred.

Her eyes drift to a notebook tucked in his right palm. "Writing?" she asks and smooths her hands over her gown.

This morning, she found it in a box at the end of her bed. She was happy to find it less revealing than her first gifted outfit from her father, but she was less thrilled by the color palette. Plum. As if color association would be the thing to win over a Rathmore.

"No," Kadir answers, but it's all he gives her. He leans into the side of a shelf. He's dressed less formally than his first evening at Winloc Grove but still far more extravagant than most. Every detail of his outfit fits like puzzle pieces—a dark violet shirt that dips to display his Rathmore crest, and tailored black trousers marked with faint lilac-colored stripes. Pomp and frills. A disguise if she's ever seen one.

His head falls gently against the shelf, his twin strands of yellow hair gliding over his brows with the movement. His face reveals nothing but a calm, cold indifference, except his eyes. Their violet gleams in the sunlight. Magnetic. Mischievous. "I figured you'd play hard-to-get, love. Not hide and seek."

The growl of his voice. The pet name. She rolls her lips together and bends to retrieve her tome from where she dropped it, all too aware of the way he tracks her movements. She needs to understand him but no one has felt more impenetrable.

She sets the tome in its place on the shelf closest to him, keeping her eyes glued to the array of colored spines. "I guess I thought hiding was better than a knife in the back."

"You were asleep for some time, and yet you're alive. I think I should get a prize." Kadir raises a hand and picks up one of her curls, the rings accenting each of his fingers shining in the sunlight.

Vellene glares at him and smacks his hand away, cringing when she hits the metals that grace his fingers. She notices the array of necklaces he wears, too. She scowls. "Back off, Rathmore."

Kadir smiles, and it seems genuine, every tooth on display. "There she is."

"If you're not going to help me, then I should kill you," she murmurs and she means it. She stalks past the shelves and into the open seating area—the same place she first met him during the Convocation meeting.

Kadir follows her, but he does so lazily, running his fingers along tome spines and looking at the paintings on the walls. "I thought we talked about the teasing, love," he drawls, his violet gaze finally finding hers.

She crosses her arms. "I've decided I don't want you to call me that."

"Hmm." Kadir considers it then shrugs. "I've decided I like it too much."

Vellene runs her tongue over her teeth. "I don't like you."

Kadir raises an amused brow. "Yes."

She raises her own. "You don't care?"

"Do you want me to?" His eyes glimmer.

Vellene presses her lips together.

His eyes trace her frame.

"Stop looking at me like that," she hisses.

"Like what?" he asks, playing at innocence.

"Look, if I don't kill you, I will die." She drops her arms and clutches the skirts of her gown. "But you could also just quit asking my father for the source. Leave. Go back to Frales. Save yourself."

Kadir's face drifts into a mask.

*He's good at that*, she thinks, and she wonders if she's ever seen his true face.

"I can't leave." Kadir's shoulders tense.

"My life is on the line," she argues.

The muscles in his jaw flicker with tension. "So are the lives of the chemi left in Frales." He slowly moves his gaze back to her. "I want to ask you something."

Vellene rolls her shoulders back.

Again, he tracks the movement, but his face remains cold, determined. "Have you ever fought for anything?"

The question hits her like an accusation. "Yes," she snaps.

Kadir tilts his head. "Really?"

"I fought for my mother," she says, "and my sister, although I don't think it mattered."

"How did you fight?" he wonders.

Shame tingles up her spine. "I did what I could."

"You did nothing."

Her head snaps up at that. A fire blazes to life within her. "If nothing is taking a beating so they didn't have to, then yes. I suppose I did nothing."

One of Kadir's brows twitches. "Aquim beats you."

He doesn't word it like a question, more like an answer to a question he's always had. Still, she responds. "He breaks me." Vellene's fingers tighten around the fabric of her gown. "Just like he breaks everything and everyone."

"Why don't you use that?" Kadir asks, taking a small step toward her.

"Use it?"

He nods once, taking another step forward. "A broken weapon is still a weapon. It may only need to be wielded closer to the chest and with less forgiveness."

Vellene swallows. "I'm not a weapon." Pieces of her, maybe, but not her entirety—not in the way she wishes to be.

Kadir's cold mask breaks enough for a sly smile. "We are all weapons, Vellene."

She chills at his words and avoids his gaze. Instead, she purses her lips in thought. "Why is it I somehow know nothing about you?" she wonders.

"There isn't much to know," Kadir responds, lacing his voice with boredom. He steps over to the Reading Room's double doors.

"Where are you going?" she asks, striding after him. "I'm not done talking to you."

Kadir shrugs. "I have things to do."

"What things are more important than living?" She wedges between him and the door. "If you want to leave Winloc Grove still breathing, then we should discuss some sort of plan."

Kadir takes a small step back in retreat. Unlike his first night here, he makes an effort to put far more distance between them. His fingers twitch anxiously, and the hand grasping his notebook tightens.

"You could help me get rid of my father," Vellene whispers. "Then we could both live." Not to mention, she'd be halfway through with her death oath. Maybe she could manage to get Kadir to slit her sister's neck, too. She recoils at the thought, but it's her reality. Mogaell must die.

Kadir clasps his notebook behind his back and levels his gaze with hers. "I do not fear death, Vellene."

"You should," she insists, "especially by my father's hand."

"If you'd seen what I have, you'd know death in this realm is a privilege." His nostrils flare as he moves an arm around her, pushing the Reading Room's doors open and stepping past her into the hall. He's careful as he does so, movements precise enough that only his forearm brushes her shoulder. Still, a surge of cold zaps across her shoulder and over her collarbone.

Vellene shivers and follows him. "If you're not interested in living or killing me, then what do you want? Why are you here?"

Kadir glances back at her with a wicked smile. "Killing you was never taken off the table, love."

She scowls as he looks away and continues through the halls. Her eyes find the notebook he clasps, and everything in her narrows in on it. Vellene picks up her pace. A quick swipe of her hand forward and she manages to get a single finger on the notebook before Kadir whirls around.

In an instant, he traps her against the wall, arms like a cage on either side of her and the notebook pressed to the space beside her head. His eyes flare with venom. "I didn't peg you for a thief."

Vellene glares at him. "What's in the notebook, Rathmore?"

He sucks in a steadying breath, frustration wiggling itself over his features. "It's nothing."

She rolls her eyes at that. "Fine, don't tell me, but at least answer my initial question."

Kadir's lashes lower. "What do I want?"

Vellene's stomach flips at the way he says it, but she nods.

The hand free of the notebook moves to one of her curls. This time, she doesn't swat him away. She stills, her pulse beating loud enough she's sure he can hear it.

"I'm not here to live," he mutters and drops her curls with a keen look of displeasure. "I'm here to conquer." He pulls back and straightens his shirt before tucking his notebook against his thigh. "Perhaps you're familiar with the concept."

Vellene stiffens against the wall. Conquer. It's the same word her father utters in every selfish, despicable sentence.

Kadir's face tightens at the sight of her anger. He runs a hand through his hair, sending the yellow strands that frame his face up and over with the white of the rest.

"You want Alchemight," she says softly.

Kadir looks away but nods. "In a sense."

She's not sure why it surprises her so much. Maybe it's because she thought him to be different from the other Imperials, to be less selfishly motivated. But he said from the beginning he came to kill her. He wants the source—not to share it with Scorus but to obliterate her father. Part of her relishes the idea of Aquim having an opponent. Someone to challenge her father into submission. At the same time, she finds herself looking at Kadir differently.

What makes him any better than her father? Who's to say Kadir won't be worse? She swallows, fists balling at her sides. Chemight seeps down her neck and into her palms. It weighs heavy as it sharpens into twin daggers of crimson—remedial formularies wrapped in nether and as sharp as steel. Vellene's hold on them shakes, but her decision is firm. He must die. Before he can kill her. Before she becomes collateral damage. Again.

Kadir stares at her wielded chemight. He stashes his notebook into the waistband of his trousers, freeing his hands as she takes a step toward him. "Brave of you," he says, voice filled with threat and warning.

Vellene continues to grasp the chemight. She has no idea how to kill him with it, how to properly slice an artery, or force him to his knees. “No, I’m not,” she answers simply, tone even despite her nerves. “I’m a coward.” She tremors. "But I'm a coward set on living. At least for a time."

His violet eyes light. “Then let me teach you how to be brave.”

She grits her teeth.

Kadir’s right palm ignites with a dagger that's a triplet to hers but in sapphire—a weaponized chaos formulary. He not only means to maim but for his wound to inflict endless pain.

Vellene’s eyes narrow. It’s the kind of blade her father would draw.

For a moment, they circle each other, eyes locked.

His hair falls around his face as he readies himself, one foot trailing behind the other.

*I have no courage*, she reminds herself, *so there’s no point waiting on it.* Vellene rams a dagger toward his chest. Heat licks up her neck as his blade easily knocks hers away.

“Faster,” Kadir instructs, a small smile on his lips.

She tenses. “This is not a lesson.” She whips to the side, breath caught in her throat when Kadir’s dagger shoots where her head was. Her lips part in shock.

“Everything is.” His smile widens, and he lunges for her again, this time wielding his dagger toward her stomach.

She knocks back, but the tip of the blade shears a fine slit across the waist of her gown. The fabric droops, but she doesn't have time to feel modest as Kadir jabs his dagger toward the vulnerable, exposed skin. She grunts and shuffles back, Kadir on her toes as he takes advantage of her retreat.

Then he traps her, their breaths heavy as he presses the dagger into her stomach. "I could gut you," he whispers, drawing himself down to her ear. "See if your insides are as pretty as your outsides."

Thrill ignites. Dangerous, foolish thrill. Ice shoots between them, but the beast inside her is ready and willing. Her embers brighten and spark, her vision clouding with a haze of orange. She thrusts her twin daggers along either side of his neck without hesitation. "I could cut off your head. Add it to my father's collection." She presses the blades against the white scarring that brands his neck. "See if you still talk so mightily."

A breathy laugh escapes Kadir, his dimples showing for a flash of a second. "Here I am teaching you to be a weapon when you already are one, aren't you?" He narrows his eyes. "That pretty face and perfect innocence—a ploy." A wildness tips his lips into a tight smile. "What else are you hiding?"

His reaction unnerves her. "I'm about to kill you," she insists.

"As am I," he whispers, and his dagger nicks her stomach.

A dribble of blood runs free, and a wave of chaos tunnels through her torso and presses into her skull. Her vision dots with streaks of blue, and she blinks them back with a gasp. Dark shapes threaten to take her. Memories of her childhood she never wants to relive.

Kadir's gaze darkens, and he gently wipes the blood away with his thumb. The touch chills the wound, and she shakes. "Wouldn't want to ruin the gown. A rip can be sewn, but blood is impossible to remove."

Her indent flares as his fingers creep over her stomach, settling upon the curve of her waist. Pricks of ice scrape over her skin. They branch from the places he touches her like chains, the fire inside her seething to be free. But her confusion outweighs her rage. "You're worried about my dress?" She lowers her daggers from his neck. "Why?"

Kadir tips her face toward his, his eyes on her mouth. "Well, it was quite expensive."

She lets one of her daggers go, the chemight disappearing into a puff of mist, but she grips the second tighter. "You're the one who's been dressing me?"

Kadir's smile falters. "You don't like them?"

Vellene's eyes widen. "I'm not some doll you can dress up to your liking," she spits, a new kind of fury zipping through her.

His gaze hardens. "They're gifts. I wasn't trying to—"

"I don't get you," she cuts him off and glares down at her blade, still unable to let it go. "You won't save me, but you won't kill me. You want Alchemight, but you're taking time to dress me like a plaything." Vellene sucks in a breath. "Is that all I am to everyone?" She hesitates but brings her gaze to his. "A toy? You like pushing me, Rathmore? Like seeing what will make me tick and write it down in that journal you won't let go of?"

His gaze turns thunderous, every muscle in his face chiseling into something dark and grim. "Stab my thigh."

Vellene exhales. "What?"

"Stab me. Make it look as though you tried to kill me and failed." Kadir lowers his voice to gravel. "It will allow me to bargain with your father."

"Why?" she asserts and presses onto her toes, forcing him to look at her.

Kadir's jaw clenches. "I can't save you. No one can but yourself." His chest heaves. "But I will try anyway."

Her knuckles go white around her chemight dagger. "I don't believe you." She studies him. "I don't believe anything about you."

Kadir swallows, and the muscles in his neck threaten to burst. "Call it a favor."

"Favors often have to be returned," she whispers.

He gestures to his thigh. "Stab me, and I'll name my terms."

Vellene runs her tongue over her teeth. "Do you think I'm that stupid?"

He's quiet for a long moment. Then—"I want to know you." He grasps her waist tighter. "I want to meet the girl behind the pretending. I've seen glimpses of her, and I think we could be friends." Kadir gives his thigh a tap. "What are you afraid of, Winloc?"

*You*, she realizes. She's afraid of the way her stomach flutters in anticipation. Afraid of the smiles he reserves for her. Afraid of the way her head spins when she thinks about him. But most of all she fears how the chill of his touch soothes her in a way nothing ever has. Nothing.

"You asked for my help." He tangles a hand into her curls, and her lips part with a sharp breath. "You were desperate for it. If you want it, stab me. If you don't, then I will leave Winloc Grove this evening."

"You'd give up trying to conquer Alchemight?" she breathes.

"No," he amends, "but I'll find another way. I'll leave you to your fate, whatever you wish it to be." Quieter, darker—"I know what it is to be choiceless." His jaw hardens. "To sell yourself for a chance at freedom."

They tense as footsteps echo at the forefront of the hall. A pair of shadows pull around the corner.

"The dresses," Kadir whispers fiercely. "It was to give you something of your own, not to lay claim to you." He swallows, and his throat bobs. "I thought you might want something that wasn't his."

Vellene sways. "That's—" Selfless. Kind.

"Stab me, love." His voice wavers, emotion tucked behind his cold exterior slipping free. "I'll survive."

She raises the dagger, eyes trained on his thigh.

"*Vellene.*"

Then she drives the blade into his flesh.

A harsh breath rushes from between Kadir's teeth. "Hold onto your chemight. Let him see the blade," he mutters.

"What's going on here?" Her father's voice booms with the perfect hint of betrayal as if stabbing Kadir Rathmore was never on the agenda.

Vellene lets go of the dagger but keeps hold of the chemight making it corporeal and staggers back. A bit of horror fills her as blood pools around the blade and soaks Kadir's pant leg. He shudders, and her stomach squeezes. She shouldn't care, but she does. She cares if he dies.

"A plot to kill me, Aquim?" Kadir growls, his face the picture of violence. He grabs her dagger and rips it out. Blood drips from its tip and splatters in thick black droplets against the hall's silver and blue tile.

"I assure you, I had no part in this," Aquim says. His cold gaze rakes over Vellene.

On his left is Mogaell. Her sister stands with her arms crossed, dark eyes surveying the scene with suspicion.

Quickly, Vellene reaches for pain and forces tears to her eyes. "I'm so sorry, father. I failed."

Aquim's fists clench.

"You had no part in this?" Kadir counters and wields a marvel remedial formulary. Pink mist wraps around his thigh. The blood slows, and the wound seals. He lets her dagger clatter to the ground, and Vellene releases the chemight. The blade disappears in a puff of mist. "I suggest we re-enter negotiation, Winloc. Now," he growls.

But her father ignores Kadir, his sights set on Vellene. Her entire life, she's seen him angry. The smallest mistake, and her father erupts. Now he's quiet. There is no sneer, no venom. Instead, his next movement is calm, collected, and certain. A gloved hand whips forward, and navy chemight blasts out of his palm into Kadir.

Kadir stumbles back, shock breaking his careful mask of wrath. His eyes go wide, their violet slashing to a deep, sorrowful darkness. His entire body shakes as he tries to fight off the war waging in his mind. Slowly, he crumples. Slowly, he loses all sense of reality. A feral, heart-wrenching scream tears from his chest, and he slams to his knees.

"Kadir," Vellene shouts. She falls beside him and clutches his shoulders before she can think it through.

Every instinct needs her at his side. She doesn't understand it, but she knows it's right to help him.

"Finish him," Aquim snarls. He steps behind her, towering over her shoulder like a dark shadow.

Vellene turns to where her sister was, hopes to implore her for help, but Mogaell recedes into the shadows. She, at least, looks shocked, her skin pale and lips parted in surprise.

Kadir convulses. He grasps his skull and clenches his teeth. But then—he shuts down. He bites off his scream, his face falling still, even as tears wet his cheeks. His shoulders relax, and when his eyes find hers, she sees a boy who has bled long enough to not feel it anymore.

Something in her breaks. She understands that placidity, that need to become stone despite the pain inside. "Make it stop," she says, her voice brash as she turns to her father. "Now."

Aquim's calm dissolves. The vein in his forehead throbs. "You dare order me?"

Vellene rises. "I said stop," she bites out, the taste of smoke on her tongue. "He has nothing to do with this. Your anger is toward me. Not him."

Her father's eyes flash with amusement.

But he can't feel what she feels. He can't know the fire raging in her veins. He can't feel the way it seeps into her palms like a searing serpent, the beast inside her craving to sear him into submission.

"A few conversations and Rathmore's won your heart it seems." Her father gives a cruel laugh. "How many more seconds before he loses his mind completely? How many more years will you continue to disappoint me? Time—a foul mistress in the face of expectations. Just. Like. You."

A fit of rage shakes her body. She vibrates with pain. Years and years of unforgivable pain. For once, she does not bury it. For once, she sets it free.

Flames burst from her palms and circle around her wrists, dancing with pleasure. Power awakens, and her eyes widen. Fire. Real fire. Not chemight. The smoke on her tongue—it seeps between her teeth. The embers she's always felt tucked inside her like resilient friends—they spark across her knuckles.

Her father takes a step back, a wildness to his gaze.

"I won't ask again," Vellene says. She lifts her hands and shoves her flames forward. Fire whips toward her father's chest, but she wavers. There's something in Aquim's eyes she's never seen.

Pride.

He sidesteps her attack, his lips hooked with a dark grin. Then he flicks his wrist toward Kadir.

But Kadir remains calm. His eyes are pits of black, violet winking out like swallowed stars, and his lips—

Kadir smiles.

Aquim wavers. "What are you?"

Soft enough only she can hear him—"A broken weapon," he returns, his voice strained but his smile sharp. His gaze flicks toward her, a warning there. He wants her to be silent, to let him hurt, and to protect herself. He wants her to know she can take it. That he has before and will do it again.

No. She refuses to remain dull and quiet, to never claim wounds but always receive them. Vellene steps between them. “Let him free,” she hisses.

Her father’s jaw tightens with rage, but surprise flickers through her when he follows her command. Blue mist pools from Aquim's palms.

It sinks against Kadir’s nostrils before his hands twitch at his sides and his calm stare drifts toward a severe victory. He lifts with ease, and his gaze sharpens on the fire she wields. “Kill him,” he murmurs.

Flames ripple through her, licking from her inner core to her fingertips. But they’re waning. The formularies at the backs of her ears and along her neck are hot in their deposits, burning the skin around them. She exhales sharply as their formularies drain, and her fire sputters into golden wisps. Exhaustion takes her into its cruel, relentless hands, and her power dies against her palms, burrowing inside her and digging itself back into the hole it came from.

She wills it to return, but she wavers on her feet, black dots clouding her vision. It's too much. So much. Aquim,

Kadir—they turn into shadowed figures, then blurred lines.

"Don't—" Kadir shouts, and it's the last thing she hears before pain slams through her gut, and the hallway goes dark.

## Chapter Eighteen

# *Eledar*

Alchemight's moons rest in the sky as Eledar and Soffesa move the last of Imaex's research to their room at The Bloody Cloth. The boxes and papers litter the ground and rattle as wind whips through the curtains. Eledar grunts and sets a box of journals and tomes beside their bed. He moves to the curtains and ties them together at the bottom before grabbing a stool in the corner and pressing it up against them. It blocks some of the chill, but the room remains frigid. He tugs his cloak around him, his breath coming out in clouds. "Abyss, it's freezing."

"Shard storm." Soffesa sets her box down, raises her hands to her hips, and blows out a breath. "Always gets like this right before one hits."

"It gets so warm in Frales before them." Eledar ducks his head past the curtains and looks at the sky. Monstrous black clouds stream across the moons as they had in Frales. It's a wonder how places are so similar yet forever different.

He closes his eyes and listens to the roar of the oncoming storm, pictures himself in Frales. Like bolts of lightning—pain, blood, and screams resurface in his mind. He throws his eyes open, shuddering against the cold and the creeping anger that tenses his shoulders.

"It took a while for me to get used to it, but with time, you will." Soffesa grabs a brush from their nightstand and runs it through her hair.

He blinks away the fury from his vision—the blood-lust that overcomes him and wishes to break free. His fingers itch to wield chemight, to stride into Winloc Grove and cut Aquim's neck. *Patience*, he reminds himself. He sucks in a steadying breath, fingers gripping the windowsill. "Doesn't seem to stop the locals."

Down in the streets, crowds of Scraps venture into the night.

"Never does. Not when orbs are at stake. Imperials don't make rounds until the morning, so Scraps use the night to trade for formularies." She sets the brush down and clears her throat. "You staying up?"

Below, a trio of Scraps light each other on fire. They scream in hysterical madness before two of them break into a fistfight, the third struggling to pull them apart with a wide smile on her face. That smile alone is enough to render Eledar sleepless.

He can't recall the last time he saw friends messing around, or the last time he saw genuine smiles on

Scrap faces. Even his night with Vellene was a culture shock. Dancing with her. Kissing her. Feeling her against him—he rolls his shoulders back and shakes his head as if he can shake away the thought of her.

"Eledar?"

He turns, realizing he never answered Soffesa. "Sorry?"

Her eyes narrow. "Your ears are red."

Eledar curses. He rustles his hair around until it strikes his cheeks and hides his ears.

Soffesa's lips lift with amusement.

He clears his throat. "I'm going out."

She studies his face for another moment, then she shrugs. "Alright, well, I'm crashing." She flops onto the bed and tugs the comforter over her.

"In my bed, it seems."

"Seniority dibs." Then, she shrugs. "Besides, I can't afford a second room."

Eledar frowns. "You're like a day older."

"Four days older," she counters with a devilish smile.

He folds his arms with a laugh. "Need anything while I'm out?"

Soffesa yawns and curls into herself. "I never need anything from anyone."

His heart breaks at that. He wants to ask her about her family's deaths. He wants to hold her and tell her the worst is over. But that would be a lie. Instead, he steps up to the bed and places a quick kiss on her forehead. "Sleep well, sister."

She manages a soft, sad smile, eyes shut. "Be safe."

Eledar sighs and leaves the room in quick strides, securing the door behind him. Scraps lounge in the hallway, brews in hand, and the nightly festivities in full swing. A symphonic blasts downstairs. He fumbles his way through the hall and down the steps to where the dance floor is packed, Scraps and Utilities tucked close in an attempt to keep away the cold.

Eledar stops at the bar and nods to Felix, who slides over Scum Rum, his scumtis-based brew. It's the only drink Eledar can buy with empty orbs. Then, he shoves his way through the crowd and outside. Alchemight greets him with a howl as he steps onto the street. The wind chants rhythms of a faraway war, echoes of Frales. He tilts his brew back and downs the sludge before letting the mug clatter to the pavement.

A Scrap nearby rushes to it and throws the mug into a bag before sprinting off.

He gives the Scrap a salute and takes a weary lunge into another crowd. His teeth chatter, and he lifts his hood. He weaves through Scraps and Utilities with no real direction to his forward momentum. He stops at a stand of cardboard boxes and a barrel of homemade brew, and he decides to drown a bit further. The Scrap behind the makeshift counter accepts an empty orb with a gleam in his eyes before shoving brew into Eledar's hands.

He savors it and drifts.

Each group splits off at some point, depending on what they're watching. At the head of some groups are Utilities showcasing their latest crafts. Many have a knack for molding and making, which is what elevated them from Scrap to Utility in the first place. That, and undeniable loyalty.

At the head of other crowds are Scraps performing in a symphonic. Some sit on crates and babble about fiction. Another group encircles two burly Utilities who unleash two equally burly canisoss. The creatures erupt into a fight, growling and darting and thrashing. The crowd places wagers until one of the canisoss goes down, its head torn off by the other. Its dead body is immediately thrust onto a spit and rotated above a fire, the meat soon after passed to anyone who waged it would lose.

Eledar slows and listens to one of the tales of the storytellers. The chemi weaves fine, natural chemight, the gray mist lacing into shadowed figures as he sings:

> Once we were unlabeled, free to roam and
> do as we pleased,

But at our core we sought power, and hate grew from small, overlooked seeds.

Over time, we separated ourselves, as some grew with wealth and power,

And the Convocation of the Eternal turned everything sour.

Imperials grew greedier with each passing day,

Collected wealth like they stole our will and strength away.

But greed always has its consequence,

And for those wicked Imperials, that greed turned to offense,

Over the very things they created,

Golem wishing no longer to be sedated.

Eledar takes a gulp of his brew and trails past the storyteller, not needing to hear the rest. Not wanting to listen to tales of a war they have never seen. A war he barely escaped only to relive it daily. He sidesteps a herd of spideria that crawl through the crowd to wherever the night takes them. He stares at their long legs and robust, double-diamond-shaped bodies—the diamonds stack in line with one another to form a sharp-edged hourglass. They're larger than his booted feet and make a fearsome hissing sound as they dart from the stomping of drunkards. It's the same creature inked over Vellene's chest—the same creature flown on the Winloc crest.

Eledar's stomach twists, and he downs the last of his second brew before tossing its mug to a begging Utility. He lifts his head at the sound of cheers.

A large crowd gathers where Scorus begins its slope toward the docks and Dalbian's Abyss.

"Absolutely incredible, I'm telling ya," a Scrap remarks.

He startles and looks down at her, the woman short and squat with scraggly gray hair. She would be rather unremarkable if it weren't for the silver of her eyes. They glow in the night with what Eledar can only assume is power. *Strange.*

She smiles a toothless grin. "The performance. It's what you're here for, aren't ya?"

"Right." Eledar looks over the crowd.

They encircle a young Scrap chemi, maybe fourteen. She paces and addresses the crowd. Her voice is too small to hear from where Eledar stands.

"What's so special about her?" he asks, but the spot where the older Scrap stood is empty. Curious, he shoulders his way to the front.

The performing Scrap drops into a crouch. Hair, braided into pigtails of pink and purple, sits at the top of her head. Tar from the last shard storm paints her eyes with large wings. Her lips are smothered in black. Despite her torn, dirtied skirts and simple top, she holds her chin high, eyes sharp with a dazzling magenta. She places her hands on the asphalt, lengthens a leg out to the side. Her lips pull into a smile, cheeks pink from the cold, as gray chemight sparks off her frame like lightning. Mist whirls off her skin.

Eledar takes a step back, fearing she means to strike the crowd, but the chemight stretches toward them for only a moment before it careens to the sky.

The female chemi jumps up, raises her arms, and the chemight branches into little fireworks.

*Amazing*. Eledar crosses his arms as Scraps cheer in approval.

She draws her chemight back into herself with a slow, steady breath. Then, she looks behind her. "Father, the warded box, please," she shouts over the crowd.

A middle-aged Scrap steps through the throng of viewers at her back, a box in his hands. He sets it on the ground, then shoves his hand toward it. In an instant, he's thrown back, his glasses cast askew. The crowd gasps, and those behind him lunge for his body. He falls limp in their arms, but his daughter is unphased, eyes wild with amusement.

"As you can see from my father's test, this box is heavily warded with chemight." She walks around the box in a slow circle, eyes trained on the crowd. "In the next five minutes, I will have it open."

Murmurs rise through the crowd. One Scrap shouts, "How?"

She points her finger in the direction the voice came from. "That's a secret, my friend." She stops before the box, cracks her knuckles, then glances at the crowd with a sly grin. "Unless, of course, you're the highest bidder."

Nervous laughter rises.

She spreads her arms out. "Behold!" Gray swirls steam off her arms. They slide into the air and form sharp shards of iron gray. She measures a breath, then brings her arms together in a clap that resounds through the air.

The shards slam into the box. In a blink, the invisible wards explode into a million iridescent specks before they vanish into thin air. Her smile glimmers as she reaches for the lock.

Several in the crowd step forward, prepared to catch her as they did her father, but she touches the lock with no repercussions. Two swivels to the left, four to the right, and the door to the box clicks open.

The crowd erupts into cheers of amazement. They swoon forward with questions.

"Is it a formulary?"

"How did you sharpen your chemight like that?"

"Are you naturally gifted?"

"What's your secret?"

She raises her hands. "If you want to know, you'll have to bid for the answer!" She gives the unlocked box a nudge toward the crowd. Her smile falters when no one steps up to bid.

*Wrong street to perform on, kid.* Eledar looks around. Every poor scrap next to him is just that—poor. He waits for the crowd to thin, then reaches under his shirt to his waist. He pulls a single, empty orb out of its chemight deposit, and steps up to her box. Then he drops it in with a soft smile.

The female chemi stands off to the side. She whispers with her father, then she straightens at the sight of Eledar. She eyes him and moves to her box, pulling out the orb.

She turns it over in her fingers. "Don't have any with a formulary?" She smacks her lips in discontent. "Or one with chemight in general?"

Eledar shrugs. "Why would I do that? I'm the only bidder."

She blows out a breath. "Yeah. Sure."

He slides his hands into his pockets. "What's your name?"

"What's yours?" She gives him a stern look.

Eledar grins. "If I tell you, can I learn the formulary you used to break those wards?"

She crosses her arms. "Maybe."

He pretends to think about it. He extends his hand. "Eledar."

They clasp wrists. "Ferula," she says.

"Well, Ferula, I would like to purchase that formulary from you. I assure you I can pay a fair price."

She narrows her eyes. "I don't sell to Imperials. I'm not looking to hang."

"Neither would I want you to. I'm no Imperial."

Ferula glances back at her father.

The male chemi steps up, expression grim. He runs a callused hand over his shoulder-length hair, raking back its greasy strings. "Who are you?"

"Eledar."

"I didn't ask for your name. I asked who you are." Her father's voice is stern. Behind his glasses, his ruby-colored eyes focus on the orb Eledar dropped into their box. The chemi plays with the rags of his shirt with a nervous tremor. Wind whips the purple strands of his hair back into his face. They frame the gauntness of his features, the sharpness of hunger in his eyes.

Eledar locks his gaze with the father's and settles on honesty. "I'm on a mission to assassinate the Winlocs." He gestures to the box. "I could use a formulary like that in my arsenal. Winloc Grove is notoriously well-warded."

They still at the mention of the Winlocs. Ferula grabs her box, hugs it to her chest, and her father shakes his head. He wraps a protective arm around his daughter. "It's not for sale."

Eledar cocks a brow. "I beg to differ. I gave you an orb for it."

Ferula reaches into the box, grabs the orb, and chucks it at him. "We're not interested."

He catches it against his chest and slides it into his pocket. "I need you to be." Eledar studies them. Neither look like they've eaten in days. Nor do they look like they've had access to water for bathing. "What about for ten?"

They freeze in their hurry to escape. The father scoots his glasses up the bridge of his nose. "Ten? To be culprits in an assassination of the highest-ranking Imperial family?"

"Fifteen," Eledar amends.

"No." The father pushes Ferula into a hurried walk.

Eledar frowns as they go. His shoulders slump in defeat.

"Who are they?" Soffesa's voice slinks over his shoulder.

He jumps at the sound of his friend. "You really are Soffesa The Silent, aren't you? Abyss."

"Sorry, I couldn't sleep. Figured I'd come find you." Soffesa stares at the father and daughter. "Do I need to kill them?"

Eledar's eyes widen. "Soff, no."

She scans his face, then scrunches her own in annoyance. "You told them."

Eledar crosses his arms. "They have something I want."

"Our secret mission is not a bargaining chip, Eledar." She grits her teeth. "I have to kill them."

Eledar shakes his head. "Why don't we work on getting them to come to our side before we choose blood lust."

Soffesa lifts the red leather hood of her dress and strides forward.

He matches her pace. "You're following them."

She clenches her fists and a sword of gray chemight lengthens from each palm. "Watching them."

"They're not going to tell anyone," he insists. "If I thought they would, I wouldn't have said anything."

"Like Vellene didn't tell Aquim of Imeax?" she snaps.

"She didn't. You know she didn't. They were after Imeax for looking for the source."

"What about having sex with her within the day of knowing her, then?" Soffesa grimaces. "Does that prove my point that maybe not all your ideas are the best?"

Eledar stops, confused. His ears go hot, and he's thankful he pulled his hair over them earlier. "Where did that come from? I didn't have sex with Vellene." He scowls. "I don't just go around grabbing chemi and taking them to my bed."

She keeps her brisk pace, then calls back over her shoulder, "Fooled me."

Eledar jogs to catch up. He grabs her arm, forces her to stop. "We kissed Soffesa. Maybe a little more than that, but it wasn't a big deal."

She pulls to a stop with a huff and lets her chemight swords fade into mist. "I don't care."

He searches her worried gaze. "You obviously do, Soff. I'm sorry. I got lost in a moment. That's all."

She avoids his gaze. "I just feel like you haven't been taking this as seriously as you should be. Our lives—my life—are on the line."

"Is that what you're worried about? That I'll choose Vellene over you?" Eledar shakes his head and wraps her into a hug. "You're my family. I love you."

"And if you love Vellene, could you honestly say you wouldn't choose her?" Soffesa pushes away from him.

Eledar flushes. "It was only a kiss."

She exhales. “I saw how you looked at her, Eledar, and I know you, how you get attached to people. You fall easily, and while I've always loved that about you, it's a weakness in a situation like this.”

“A kiss, Soffesa. That’s it.” He tries to make the response sound solid, but his moment with Vellene thrusts forward. The feel of her skin. The strange way their chemight surged between them. It was more than a kiss. He knows it was.

She manages a sympathetic look. “A kiss with a Winloc, Eledar. That means something.”

Eledar looks to the sky, begs for the right words to say, then drops his gaze to hers. “You can trust me. I know it’s been years, but I will always have your back.” He nods in the direction the father and daughter duo disappeared. “And those chemi are worth having on our side. The young one—the female—she broke a complex set of wards within a minute.”

They resume their trail.

“Really?” Soffesa asks after a moment.

His shoulders slump in relief at the topic change in their conversation. “It was incredible.” He shrugs. “It could have been a trick, but I watched the wards fling her father into the crowd.”

“He could have been acting.”

“I don’t think so.” Eledar tilts his head from side to side, considers it.

Soffesa cracks her knuckles. "Let's hope it was real."

He glances at her with a frown. "Persuasion before killing. Understood?"

She gives him a slim smile. "Sure."

# Chapter Nineteen

# *Eledar*

They fall silent as they catch up to Ferula and her father. The two chemi performers step up to a Scrap shack. It's wedged among twelve others—built to be nothing more than a room with a roof and some questionable walls.

Eledar slows, and he and Soffesa hide at the corner of the street.

Soffesa licks her lips. "Vellene."

He clenches his jaw. "What about her?"

His sister clears her throat. "She looked upset when she came downstairs. Angry."

Wariness fills him. "Of course she did. She was turning herself in."

"But you kissed her?"

Eledar hesitates. "Yes."

"And you didn't see her off?"

He thinks of Vellene's resignation over Mogaell. His doubt in her creeps forward. Telling Soffesa wouldn't help anything. He clears his throat. "I didn't want the Chemibreakers to see my face." He eyes the ground as Soffesa tries to read him.

"So, you kissed her, then ditched her?" Soffesa releases a low whistle. "I thought I was cruel with my conquests." She folds her arms. "That's very un-Eledar of you."

"Vellene was not a conquest." He scrapes his hair back in frustration. "Quit analyzing me."

She side-eyes him. "You should probably apologize to her."

He presses his lips together with a grimace. "Yeah, sure. Let me just walk up to Winloc Grove and knock on the door. Maybe I'll buy a bouquet of flora while I'm at it."

She laughs under her breath. "I can picture it now: 'Oh, hi, Aquim. First, I want to say sorry for taking your daughter to bed before kicking her promptly out of it. Second, I should also apologize for the immense pain I'm about to put you through'." She shrugs. "I'm sure the flora will soften the blow though. You should go for it."

Eledar snorts, then flicks her shoulder. "Focus. We need to recruit these two, especially after losing Equilibrium on our side."

She gives him an expression of alarm, flying a hand to her chest. "Wait? So you did throw Winloc out of your bed?"

Eledar laughs at her expression and gives her a solid push. “Knock it off. I'm not above torturing you in return about that weaver.”

She tenses. "You wouldn't dare."

"Oh, I would, Fedelis."

She stifles a laugh. “Fine, fine." She clears her throat. " So you haven’t found anything in all those journals and notes?”

He shakes his head and tugs out of the shadows. He crosses the street as Ferula and her father go inside their Scrap shack. Soffesa stays on his heels, and they settle outside a hole meant to be a window and peer inside.

Eledar lowers his voice. “Once we recruit these two, I think it’s time we scope out Winloc Grove.” He eyes his friend. “I know you’re familiar with their property, but we will all need to be.”

“That sounds a lot like you have a plan in mind.” Soffesa’s eyes brighten.

He gives her a playful smile before their focus is drawn to the Scrap performers.

Inside, Ferula sits on her knees in the cramped quarters of her Scrap shack. Her father settles onto a cot across from her and takes off his boots. Gray chemight swirls out from Ferula’s palms. It folds over her box, wards it.

“I thought she used a formulary but she didn’t. It’s all her,” Eledar mumbles. “She’s so controlled for her age.”

"Chemibreakers wouldn't give her a second glance. That could be useful," Soffesa admits.

The father stands, pushes his glasses in place, and closes his eyes. He sucks in a breath as gray blazes from his fists, up his arms, *surrounds* him. He throws his arms out, and the gray shrouds the shack, explodes out from every crevice. It slams into Eledar and Soffesa and knocks them to the ground.

Eledar grunts, eyes wide. He sits up and rubs his head in confusion.

Soffesa stares at the emptiness before them, the Scrap shack vanished. "What the abyss?"

Eledar runs his fingers over his jaw. "We're still on the same street."

"I think he just cloaked their house." Soffesa's eyes widen. "I've only seen Imperials—and I mean extremely talented Imperials—do something like that. Only with formularies, too."

He looks at her. "That was Scrap chemight."

She shakes her head in disbelief. "We need them. Both of them. To break wards and cloak ourselves? That would be invaluable."

Eledar nods in agreement. "We just need to persuade them." He pushes onto his feet. Before he can think better of it, he shouts, "Hello!"

Soffesa grabs his wrist. "What are you doing?" she hisses.

Eledar pulls out of her grip. “They’re cloaking themselves. What better way to get them to let us in than to draw attention to what they don’t want seen?” he asks. Then he turns to where the house sat. “I know you can hear me.” He waves his arms and jogs back and forth in front of the invisible home.

Soffesa drops her forehead into her hand. Her face folds with a cringe. “I revoke my friendship.”

Eledar nudges her with his elbow and smiles. “It worked.”

A sliver appears as if the father’s chemight unzips to let them pass through. Eledar steps onto the piece of porch that appears, and Soffesa follows, Scrap chemight swirling from her knuckles. “Just in case,” she whispers.

Eledar nods and the father’s shield reseals. He steps into the open front entrance of the shack.

Ferula and her father stand at attention. Both look equally disturbed to be found out. The father’s brow creases as he recognizes Eledar. “You followed us, didn’t you?”

Eledar clasps his hands. “Your daughter was too important to let go.” Then he nods to the shield. “We had no idea you're just as talented.”

“Get out of our house,” Ferula hisses. “We didn't invite you here.”

Soffesa smiles at her. “I like your grit, young one.”

"And who are you?" the father asks, gesturing to Soffesa.

Soffesa offers him a menacing grin.

"We're not here to hurt you," Eledar explains quickly. "We wish to recruit you for our mission."

"To murder the Winlocs." The father grows grim. "I already told you we aren't interested."

"Unfortunately, that's not an answer we can work with." Soffesa tilts her head. "You can work with us, or I can kill you."

Fear spreads across Ferula's features.

*Abyss-damned assassins.* Eledar gives a nervous chuckle. "We won't kill you." He glares at Soffesa.

She shrugs.

"I want you out of our home," the father asserts.

"I'm sure you do." Eledar clicks his tongue. "But that's not happening." His eyes roam the room. "Why do you shield your shack?"

The father gestures toward them. "The likes of you."

Eledar waves it off. "Fair enough, but I know that's not the real reason."

Ferula crosses her arms, face stern. "We don't like chemi just walking in."

"Why?" Eledar persists.

Ferula looks at her father, who purses his lips in discontent.

"Alright, don't tell us." Eledar eyes a large chest in the corner. The thing is gilded in gold and looks to belong in an Imperial chateau rather than a Scrap shack. "We'll just have a look around." He points to it. "Maybe open that guy up."

The father steps between them and the chest.

Soffesa raises her brows. "Seems like there might be something important in that chest, Eledar."

Eledar crosses his arms in amusement. "Yes, Soffesa, seems like maybe you're right."

The father raises his hands in surrender, face fearful. "Okay, we'll help you."

Eledar shares a surprised look with his sister and scratches his chin. "Well, now I want to know what's in the chest."

"Same." Soffesa stares at the thing.

Ferula moves next to her father. "It's none of your business."

"That's true," Eledar agrees. "But maybe, whatever it is, we could help with it in exchange for you helping us."

Ferula shakes her head. "We're not working with you."

Soffesa shrugs. "Okay, then you won't mind us letting some Chemibreakers know you're hiding a rather wealthy-looking chest in your Scrap shack?"

Ferula scowls and her father smooths his greasy purple hair back. His fingers tremble with nerves. "It's only research," he says.

"Research?" Eledar asks.

"Father, don't," Ferula hisses.

Her father squeezes her shoulder. He licks his lips and looks at them. "You won't turn us in?"

"You have to help us," Soffesa reaffirms.

"And you'll give us orbs, too?" The father focuses on Eledar. "You said fifteen."

"Let's double that." Eledar motions to the chest. "Now, what's in the box?"

Ferula and her father straighten at the word 'double'. They share a look, then Ferula nods and her father pulls her out of Eledar's path.

Eledar eyes them with suspicion, but he goes to the chest and pulls it open. *Impossible.* He grips the edge of the chest. His knuckles go white. His breaths turn sharp.

"Eledar?" Soffesa asks, her voice filled with concern.

He swings his head toward the Scraps. "Where did you get this?"

Ferula stands taller. "An abandoned Winloc carriage."

Soffesa pushes Eledar aside. She frowns and stares at the chest's contents. "Clay?" She pokes at the blocks of brown that line the inside of the chest. "Why would this at all need to be protected?"

Eledar swallows and runs his fingers over his eyes, unable to look at the same clay that runs through him. The clay he could easily be melted back into, his screams silent for the rest of eternity. "It's Golem clay, Soff. The

Winlocs probably wanted to use Imaex as a resource for creating their own."

"Like," she hesitates, "you?"

Eledar manages a slow nod. "I'm starting to think that Winloc Surveillant didn't kill Imaex. I think Imaex killed himself. He probably didn't want to aid the Winlocs." He shakes his head in disbelief. "This clay shouldn't exist. The last of it got thrown into Dalbian's Abyss when the creation of Golem became outlawed." His brow furrows, and he directs his next question at Ferula and her father. "Why did you take it?"

"You're a Golem?" the father asks, eyes bright with curiosity.

Eledar hesitates. "Yes."

Ferula takes her father's hand. "Then we'll help you, but we don't want orbs."

Eledar frowns. "That's all I have to offer."

"Help us make one." The father nods to the chest.

Eledar's heart gives a frantic pulse. "What?"

"My wife." The father sucks in a breath. "Help us make Ferula's mother."

Eledar blows out a long breath. "That's—That's nearly impossible. This clay is incredible, but creating Golem is more than molding them. You need an extraordinary amount of chemight, as well as a very specific set of formularies—things only Imperials have." He grimaces at the pain and grief that flashes across their features. "And actually, they wouldn't even have that much chemight stored. That was altered around the same time this clay was thrown into tar."

"What about the source?" Soffesa asks.

"Source?" the father repeats. Then, his brow raises. "The source of chemight?"

Eledar points a glare at Soffesa.

"What?" She gives him a mocking, innocent look. "You're the only one that gets to shout vital information to strangers? We want them to help us, don't we?"

Eledar measures his words, then nods. "Yes, the source of all chemight."

"Unbelievable." The father steps toward them, his daughter on his heels. "You've found the source?"

Soffesa frowns. "Well—"

The group startles as the floorboard gives a groan by the front entrance. A bag drops to the floor, and Eledar and Soffesa spin around to find a third Scrap doused in an emotion somewhere between anger and fear. The chemi shares the same ruby eyes as Ferula's father, but their head is shaved. If it weren't for that, Eledar's unsure he would be able to tell them apart. Another exception, however, is the lithe build of the newcomer and their Winloc Chemibreaker uniform.

"What is this?" the Chemibreaker questions.

Gray mist sharpens into points in Soffesa's palms.

"Brother," Ferula's father says, his voice breathless, "you scared us."

"Maybe I should be scary, Ulrich. Who are these chemi?" The newcomer strolls in and unclasps the cape from their shoulders. All the while, their eyes never leave Eledar and Soffesa.

"This is my twin, Uzax." The father clasps his brother's wrist in greeting. "As you can tell, they work at Winloc Grove."

Soffesa's shoulder bumps into Eledar's, and he looks down. She gives Uzax a pointed look.

Eledar rolls his shoulders back and smiles. "I'm Eledar. This is my fearsome assassin, Soffesa." He gives his friend a playful pat on the head, and she bares her teeth.

Uzax folds their arms. "Why are you in my family's home?"

"We're going to help bring your brother's—Ulrich, was it?—wife back to life in exchange for a little bit of help." Eledar motions to the chest of clay. "How would you also feel about a pay upgrade, Uzax?"

Their brow furrows. "You want to infiltrate Winloc Grove."

"A fast learner. That's always a good thing." Eledar shifts his weight. "What do you say?"

"We'd do anything to get Ester back," Ulrich says.

Ferula nods vigorously.

*It's impossible*, Eledar wants to tell them, but he forces a smile.

Uzax straightens and steps between their brother and niece. "What will you use us for?"

"Assassinating the Winlocs," Ulrich answers.

Uzax pivots toward their family. "You can't be serious?"

"We have a contact on the inside," Eledar says in an attempt to persuade them. "We will need you, Uzax, to deliver a message to her."

"We have a friend who can cloak the message and ensure you don't get caught with it," Soffesa continues.

"We need to send it soon," Eledar continues. "We haven't sent her word in some time. We're concerned she could have made other plans by now."

"If that's the case, then why would I be caught delivering a message to her?" Uzax argues. "I will not do this. We will not do this."

"Brother," Ulrich says softly. "It's one letter in exchange for Ester."

"That's a pipe dream," Uzax hisses. "I don't care who these chemi think they are, no one has the power to resurrect the dead. Whatever you mold from that clay will not be Ester."

Eledar holds up his hands. "I can tell you three have much to discuss. If you wish to join us in taking down the Winlocs, then I suggest you meet my partner and I at The Bloody Cloth tomorrow."

"See? He evades the truth, Ulrich." Uzax turns a glare to Eledar. "We will not help you," they say again, this time more assertive.

Soffesa takes a step forward, fists balled and chemight wielded.

Eledar pulls her back by the shoulder, but he holds Uzax's glare. "Do you believe the Winlocs deserve to rule Scorus as they do, Sir—sorry, I didn't catch a last name?"

"No 'Sir'," Uzax corrects, "Just Uzax Eni. Chemi. Brother. Uncle. Sometimes friend, if I feel like being unwise."

"Fine." Eledar clears his throat. "Uzax Eni, as a Chemibreaker, can you honestly say the job you do protects your nation?"

Uzax licks their lips.

Eledar turns his glare to Ulrich and Ferula. "Is this a Scorus you would even want to bring your wife and mother back to life in?"

Ulrich wraps an arm over his daughter's shoulders.

"While I can't say for certain with the source in our possession we will be able to resurrect Ester, I can say no matter what, Aquim Winloc will be dead. Now, you can either choose to help us and then help make decisions on the future of Scorus, or—" Eledar shrugs "—you can be a bystander to change. Either way, it's happening."

"You can't trap us with words," Uzax insists. "We are Scraps, not doe-eyed Imperials."

"Then let me trap you with passion," Eledar answers. "Let me trap you with a desire to be free." He looks Uzax up and down. "I know why I want the source. I know why your brother and niece wish for it. But what about you, Uzax? Is there nothing you would use the source of all power for?"

Uzax closes the distance between them. "You're playing a dangerous game. I work in those halls. I see Scraps lynched on the front lawn and am forced to help remove the bodies. Aquim won't take kindly to being double-crossed. You're asking me to give up my family's security—our only income—to assist you, whom we barely know."

Eledar nods. "I understand, and that's why we're leaving." He takes Soffesa's elbow and tugs her toward the entrance of the shack. "I will tell you all about myself, Uzax. I will help all of you with whatever you want. I'm just asking for some faith."

"Faith?" Ulrich scoffs. "There's no such thing."

"Then we should reinvent it." Eledar nods outside. "The Bloody Cloth. Tomorrow. Early. Until I know you're willing to give us the smallest amount of trust, I can say no more about our plans."

Ulrich and Uzax cross their arms, the stance eerily similar between the brothers. Twins.

Ferula takes a stride forward, pushing out from behind her family. "We'll be there," she says, voice firm.

Her father and uncle exchange a concerned look, but Soffesa shoots the young chemi a winning smile. "We know."

Chapter Twenty

# *Eledar*

Their room at The Bloody Cloth is dark—candles unable to remain lit with the strong gusts of a shard storm billowing through the window. Eledar attempts to wade through the jumble of his thoughts. He sits at the center of Imaex's texts, journals, and scribbled-on parchment strewn over his lap and plastered about the room.

There's a knock on the door, the shuffle of boots, the curses of his friend as she kneels and touches his shoulder.

He remains still, cold, tired.

Soffesa lifts a hand and smacks his face.

Eledar squeezes his eyes shut, groans, and collapses backward. He covers his face with his hands in exasperation.

"Have you slept?" Soffesa grumbles.

He peers through his fingers. "I don't think so."

"You're not sure?" She looks down at him, orange hair cascading around her. She holds a mug of brew in her hands.

Eledar takes a breath and sits up, raising his eyes to hers. "Is that for me?"

She sighs and shoves it toward him. "Only because you asked so pitifully."

"Thank you," he manages between two large gulps. His body sparks with newfound energy as the nutrients of the brew flow into his system.

Soffesa picks up one of the journals and flips through its pages. "I don't see why you don't give up on these. We already have a plan."

The Drinking. A ceremony held for Aquim's closest circle of Imperials. Usually a lavish event and also masked. Imperials are encouraged to veil themselves and make new alliances or thwart old enemies. It's the only time the source is used by any chemi besides Aquim. Each in attendance gets a chance to drink directly from it, enhancing their abilities for the year to come.

Meaning, Aquim must take the source out of hiding. Even if only for a moment.

"Our Golem friend wrote a lot about the abyss, but most are entries on talks he had with others—stories passed down from one generation to the next on the origins of the abyss, of Scorus and Frales." Eledar blows out a breath and shakes his head. "A third of them conflict with the rest. None of it is hard proof, let alone a map that says, 'Hey, the source is here', but I don't see why he would write so much about Dalbian's Abyss for it to be a dead end."

"There's no land between here and Frales. Just mist and tar." Soffesa crouches and tosses the journal she picked up back on top of a pile of papers. "Look, we don't need to worry about where it's hidden. We'll just grab it when Aquim brings it to The Drinking."

"What about the bag that Winloc Chemibreaker took?" He runs a hand through his hair. "We could reach out to Vellene and ask her to look for it."

Soffesa's lips twist with reluctance.

"We put her under a death oath, Soff."

"I know." She shakes her head. "Okay. Fine. But we need to secure her alliance further before we send her after it."

A knock comes from the door—once, then twice.

"Guardians help us, that's them." Soffesa eyes the mess. "Hurry, clean this up."

"I knew they'd change their minds." Eledar hops up, gulps down the rest of his brew, and tosses the mug out the window. He grabs papers and journals, shoves them into boxes. Soffesa helps him push the boxes into the corner of the room as another knock resounds from the door.

"Hello?" a voice comes through.

Eledar strides to the door and wrenches it open, chest heaving, eyes wild. "You made it." He smiles at Ulrich.

Ulrich wavers in the hallway, an arm wrapped protectively around his daughter. He combed his greased, plum-colored hair back into a loose bun, a few strands free from the brash wind outside.

Eledar peers into the shadows, but Uzax doesn't accompany them.

"Hello, Eledar." Ferula lifts her hand toward him. She wears her pink and purple hair down around her in messy waves, a patchwork blanket wrapped around her shoulders and tied at the neck as a makeshift cloak. Her expression is wary as she extends her hand, but more confident than Eledar perceived her to be.

He clasps her wrist with a genuine smile. "Ferula, always a pleasure." His gaze drifts to Ulrich's. "Where's your brother?"

Ferula ignores him and shoves into the room. She strides to Soffesa. "So, I've been wondering how you got into the assassin business," Ferula tells her.

Soffesa's brows shoot up. "That's a long story."

Ferula places her hands on her hips. "Tell me."

"Ferula," Ulrich says sternly. He gives Soffesa an apologetic look, but he moves his focus back to Eledar. "You've got Chemibreakers outside this place on patrol. Uzax couldn't afford being seen." He clears his throat and nods to the room. "Nice place. Warm."

Eledar looks down at the goosebumps across his skin.

Ulrich amends his statement. “Warmer, I should say.”

“Cozy,” Ferula agrees as she runs her fingers over the bedspread.

“Yes, well…” Eledar trails off, unsure of what else to say. He crosses his arms. “Are you two okay to get started?”

Ulrich runs his fingers through his beard. “I want to know the plan.” He looks at Soffesa. “When do we attack the Winlocs?”

She frowns. “It’s not going to happen today.”

“Then when?” Ulrich paces. “I’ve got stolen Golem clay in my house. The sooner the Winlocs are taken care of, the sooner I can rest knowing they won’t barge down my door. Or hurt my daughter.”

“I understand. I do.” Eledar flicks his gaze to Soffesa.

She shrugs. “It’s really not our problem that you decided to steal Golem clay.”

Ulrich looks stricken. “We agreed to this partnership because you said you would help us.”

“And we will,” Eledar says. “But we can’t just walk into Winloc Grove.”

“Then we’ll use the source. Where is it?” Ulrich persists.

“We’ll tell you that when you hold up your end of the deal,” Soffesa answers. She pulls from the corner of the room and steps up to Ulrich, eyes narrowed.

"Trust goes both ways," Ferula says, the young chemi standing in the middle of all of them, arms crossed. She looks at Eledar. "If we need a plan, then let's make one."

"We plan to attack during The Drinking," Eledar says. He shuts the door and lowers his voice. "We'll need your brother's help to send word to our contact."

"Uzax is reluctant, but they did agree to help," Ulrich confirms. "I told them to come by Nivia's at the end of their shift to pick up the message for your contact."

"How did you know we were working with Nivia?" Soffesa asks. She cracks her knuckles, brow cocked in suspicion.

"I didn't. I was going to suggest today that we use her," Ulrich answers. He laughs and adjusts his glasses. "I suppose she has a way of knowing everyone, doesn't she?"

"Seems so," Eledar agrees.

Ferula tucks her hair behind her ears. "Where do my father and I come in? What do you need our abilities for?"

Eledar nods. "The Drinking. If Uzax has agreed to meet us at Nivia's, then you two can stay here and relax. Soffesa and I will meet them."

Ulrich shakes his head. "Moving forward, we wish to do everything together. If Ferula and I aren't there, then my brother won't do business with you."

Eledar rubs his forehead. "If we've got Chemibreakers outside, it's going to be harder to go unseen in a group." He blows out a breath. "When's the end of Uzax's shift?"

"Should be soon," Ulrich answers. "They had a morning shift."

They leave the room and head downstairs, crossing through The Bloody Cloth's newest drunkards. Eledar pushes the front doors open, then pulls to a stop, arm outstretched to keep the others from pushing through.

Out front is a set of Chemibreakers. Each has a clear panel sewn into their uniforms, much like the ones that watched Soffesa and Eledar at Imaex's. The ones Soffesa killed.

Eledar grimaces as they use chemight to form a protective barrier around them.

As tar shards slice from the sky, they shatter against their shields. The Chemibreakers hold pieces of paper and question a Scrap huddled under a cardboard box.

Eledar curses under his breath. He nudges Ulrich. "You could have mentioned they're hunting someone."

Soffesa peers over his outstretched arm. "Someone could have given up my location."

He scans the street. "We're going to need to split up and meet at Nivia's."

"They could be looking for us if they know we stole the Golem clay," Ulrich admits.

Eledar stares at him. "Did someone see you take it?"

Ulrich grimaces, then nods.

Soffesa pinches the bridge of her nose.

"Okay, they've seen me around with Soffesa, and they've seen you around with your daughter. So, Ulrich, you're with me. Soffesa, go with Ferula."

Ferula grasps her father's hand. "I'm not leaving my dad."

Ulrich kisses her forehead. "You said it yourself, Fer. Trust goes both ways." He looks up at Soffesa. "Protect her."

Soffesa hesitates, then lies a hand on Ferula's shoulder. "C'mon, you'll be safe with me. Remember? I'm Soffesa The Silent. I don't take that name for granted."

Eledar stares at Ferula's pink and purple hair. He pulls up the bottom of his cloak and grunts as he tears a wide piece free. He hands it to Ferula. "Wrap your hair up in this. It's too recognizable."

The chemi takes it. She sticks out her tongue in concentration as she folds her hair within the cloth, then ties it at the top of her head. Her roots are still visible, but it's less noticeable.

"Okay." Eledar looks to Ulrich. "Follow me." He lifts his hood.

Ulrich does the same, then gives Eledar a sharp nod.

Despite the storm, the street is busy with Utilities. They slip and slide across tar puddles, gripping boxes wrapped in plastic, likely to keep the contents from ruining. Ulrich and Eledar join the back of a passing group, and Eledar eyes the supplies the Utilities carry. "Is there something happening?" he asks.

"The parade," Ulrich says. "Imperials put it on every year. Usually, it's a week before The Drinking. Uzax mentioned it being bigger this year. Some kind of announcement." He slows as Utilities push past, hands full.

"A parade?" Eledar grumbles in distaste.

Ulrich shoves his hands in his pockets. "There are rumors that the eldest is to Infuse."

Eledar's blood chills. He shuffles through a throng of hurrying Utilities. "The eldest?"

"It's a sickening parade of power," Ulrich says, ignoring Eledar's question. He grinds his teeth. "Ester always despised it, too, but Ferula finds it fun. As Scraps, we were never allowed to attend, so we would create a makeshift parade. Collect discarded trash from the actual parade and use it for our own."

Eledar glances at him. "Did Ester pass recently?"

"It's been a few years, but it feels as fresh as yesterday." Ulrich nods. "Ferula still can't sleep alone."

Eledar nods in understanding. "Can I ask how it happened?"

Ulrich slows his stride, face conflicted.

"You don't have to," he adds.

"No, I want to talk about her. To keep her alive, at least in that small way." Ulrich hesitates. "I've never really had to say it. I'm not sure I'm ready to."

Eledar veers them to the right, spotting a trio of Chemibreakers ahead. "It's fine."

"We were so young when we had Ferula." Ulrich manages a sad smile. "I was your age."

Eledar winces. "I can't imagine. A child? In this world? All this strife?"

"When you're in love, you'll understand." Ulrich eyes him. "The loss of someone, however, I think you may be able to relate better to?"

Eledar directs them into an alley and under the cover of an awning. "Is it that obvious?"

"Only to those that have gone through it." Ulrich stops beside him. "It's nothing you've said or even anything you've done. It's always the eyes." He shakes his head with a grim expression. "Once you see death, it shatters you." He nods to a pair of Utilities smiling and gossiping. "You see happiness, and you see it for what it is, every flaw that makes it into smiles and laughter." He looks back at Eledar. "Those untouched by loss will look at that same happiness and see a moment of peace. Others—" he pauses, swallows, "—us—we see the pain that brought them to that moment."

Eledar grins. "You're wise."

Ulrich chuckles. He tilts his head to the side in consideration. "I'll take what I can get."

Alchemight gives a low groan, and the shards of the storm stop. The wind settles into soft whispers.

"Let's keep moving," Eledar says as Scraps venture out of their shacks to patch any holes the storm caused in their shacks.

Ulrich nods, and they move down the street.

Eledar hesitates. "Your wife—"

"Ester."

"Yes, sorry." Eledar tries to find the right words. "What made you feel for Ester in the way that you did?" He clears his throat. "If you don't mind me asking?"

Ulrich studies his profile as they walk, curious. "Ester was stunning." His lips twist into a tortured smile. "It was love the moment I saw her, and after our Infusion, we never left each other's sides."

Infusion. A way for couples to exclusively dedicate themselves to each other. More than that, it allows two chemi to share each other's power. Not everyone can do it, and over the decades, the ceremony has become more and more rare. The details of how an Infusion can even happen are murky.

*And now, Vellene may be Infusing with a stranger.* Eledar studies Ulrich. "Really? You Infused?"

"Infusion is tricky. It's not always a choice." Ulrich sucks in a breath. "It was quite painful when Ester died, not just mentally, but the Infusion broke. Her chemight was stripped from me." He stretches out his fingers. "I'd never felt so powerless."

"Most chemi skip the Infusion. The risk of being tethered to another." He frowns. "I'd probably do the same."

Ulrich looks at him. "You can't just Infuse with anyone, surely you know that. I mean, yes, it can be forced with a formulary, but it never ends well."

"I know the stories." Eledar slows his pace. He heard the tales of chemi going mad, of the natural chemight in their veins turning against them and their Infused.

"It's been misconstrued over the years." Ulrich sighs. "It's a shame because true Infusion—there's nothing like it."

"True Infusion?" Eledar wonders.

Ulrich nods. "It's as if Alchemight smiles upon you. You can't really go wrong when you have the entire realm on your side."

Eledar hunches his shoulders as they pass two Chemibreakers sitting on a doorstep. "I don't understand."

"It's a connection, and it doesn't happen with everyone. A transference of power is once in a lifetime."

*Transference of power.* Eledar blinks. Something in his gut twists with recognition. "Sorry, but what exactly does that look like?"

Ulrich smiles. "When it happens, you'll know." He laughs at Eledar's concerned expression and pats his shoulder. "You look like you just saw death, Golem."

Eledar swallows. He lifts his fingers to his elbow, picks at a scab. "I think it may have happened. There was this strange array of chemight between us, and when we pulled apart, both of our orbs were emptied."

Ulrich drops his hand from Eledar's shoulder and shoves it in his pocket with a knowing smile. "And you let them leave you?"

Eledar looks at the sky, the storm clouds dissipating. "I had to."

"Shared power isn't something you want to skip out on." He smiles as they round a corner and find Ferula and Soffesa waiting outside Nivia's shop. "Especially when you have a child to protect." He glances back at Eledar. "My advice: next time, don't let them go. Ever. You're connected to that chemi now. Perhaps not fully, not yet—but enough."

Warmth spreads through Eledar's chest. It feels like hope, at first, before it settles into something more dense. A wreckage of flames he can't possibly barrel his way through. He bites his tongue, then nods. "If I get a next time, I won't let her go." It's a false promise—the kind he makes to Ulrich because he fears the heavy weight in his chest. It's the weight of knowing, even when he takes his strings back from his Master, it won't be enough. A piece of him, small but certainly consequential, is now Vellene's, and he may never get it back.

"Hey," a rough voice shouts behind them, and Eledar spins.

Four Chemibreakers rush toward them. The one at the front holds up a poster with a sketch of the last face Eledar would have thought they'd be looking for: his own.

His eyes widen, and Ulrich glances frantically at Ferula.

Soffesa grips the girl's arm and tugs her inside Nivia's shop. Concern flits across his best friend's face, but her survival instincts kick in as she whips the door shut.

"We should run," Ulrich whispers.

Eledar cracks his knuckles. "They're right there, Ulrich."

"Yes, and we can hear you." A green-haired Chemibreaker rolls her eyes. She nudges her pal with her elbow. "Scraps and their idiocy, am I right?"

The other three chuckle. Unlike the Chemibreakers who are Scraps, these are cleaner, dressed nicer. Clearly, they came from a pool of Imperials.

"Why are you following us? We've done nothing wrong," Eledar tries, teeth gritted.

Green Hair snorts. "Why do you think we're following you?" She nods to his cloak. "I recognized your cloak. It's from Zedrick's. He's an old friend." She feigns mock realization, eyes wide, mouth agape. "Wait, you're not the one that robbed him, are you?" She gestures to his cloak. "That looks exactly like one of the items stolen." She looks at the poster, then back at Eledar. "And I gotta say, the Utility who saw you and that female chemi run off definitely got your face right."

"I bought this." Eledar straightens, projecting as much confidence as he can.

She narrows her eyes. "Artemis, is this our guy?" She tugs on her friend.

Artemis, a blue-haired chemi, focuses on Eledar. "Drop your hood, Scrap."

Eledar's blood rushes.

"I think you're right." Artemis steps closer, and Ulrich fidgets. She studies Eledar's shadow-covered face. Then she snaps her hand forward. Light green chemight from a primitive formulary shoots out of her palm. It swishes toward Eledar and draws his hood back with a crack of the fabric.

Eledar scowls. "Okay," he mutters. He bumps his shoulder into Ulrich's. "Time to run." There's no room for hesitation. Eledar turns and sprints, Ulrich at his side. They careen down the alley and past Nivia's shop, arms pumping, minds racing.

Chemight shoots past them.

"They're going to kill us," Ulrich shouts. His breaths hitch when a spark of chemight hits his sleeve. He pats it off, breaths frantic. "I'm getting too old for this," he hisses. He raises a hand to hold his glasses in place, the things slipping up and down with each slam of his feet against the pavement.

"Your house." Eledar skids to a stop and veers left.

"By the power of Winloc, stop," one of them yells.

*Sure, give me more reasons to kill Aquim.* Eledar grits his teeth.

"This way," Ulrich manages. He cuts into an alley.

Eledar glances back.

Artemis rounds the corner.

Ahead is a crowded square of Scraps and Utilities. A symphonic is set up at their center, strumming the tune of a fast-paced song. "Head toward the crowd," Eledar yells.

Ulrich nods and pivots.

They stumble into the mass of chemi as Alchemight's sun pinches into its three moons. The sky goes dark, and their pursuers' chemight sparks through the air in flashes of color. Eledar knocks his way through drunks and street performers. Then he checks behind him.

Green Hair and Artemis are at the edge of the crowd.

Eledar lunges for Ulrich and brings them to a stop. "Walk normally," he hisses. "Blend in."

Ulrich heaves large breaths, one arm clutching his stomach. "You broke into a shop?" he growls.

Eledar grimaces. "Vellene and I needed cloaks."

Ulrich matches his pace to some passing Scraps. He scowls, ruby eyes darkening.

Eledar draws his hood up. "What?"

"Vellene?" he growls. "That's not a common name in Scorus. I've only known two Vellenes my entire life." Ulrich shakes his head. "And one of them died fifteen years ago." He eyes Eledar. "The other is a Winloc."

Eledar releases a slow breath. "She can be trusted."

A brash laugh cracks from Ulrich's lips. "My family is done."

Eledar curses, finds a shadow, and pulls Ulrich into it. "I mean it, Vellene can be trusted."

"How dare you put my daughter's life on the line when you have our target as a sidekick?" Ulrich hisses.

"She's Imperial, and yes, a Winloc—but she wants change, Ulrich." Eledar checks for Chemibreakers, then takes his shoulders. "We put her under a death oath. *Mortello fusum.*"

"That's messy Scrap chemight." He shakes Eledar off him. "It probably didn't even bind."

"But if it did, then she'll die if she diverts from her will to help us or at the end of her contract." Eledar wipes sweat from his brow. "The thought of death is enough to keep her loyal."

Ulrich crosses his arms. "Vellene Winloc wants to kill her family?"

"Yes."

Ulrich's face remains twisted in discomfort, but he doesn't try to leave. He looks away, studies the Scrap crowd for the Chemibreakers. "I don't like it."

"Soffesa isn't a big fan either." Eledar rubs his arm. "But I can vouch for Vellene. She mended me when I washed up from Dalbian's Abyss, and when she had the chance to tell Chemibreakers—even her Surveillant—what we are planning, she didn't."

"Maybe not to your face. How can you be sure she didn't talk the moment she was with her father?" he argues.

"Because we're still alive." Eledar nods to a set of posters plastered to the alley's wall. "All those Scraps are wanted for unlawful doings, but I'm only up there for this cloak." His nostrils flare with annoyance. "Aquim is a proud chemi. He wouldn't let an assassination attempt go without repercussions. He'd be thrilled to make an example out of us."

"But you don't know for sure." Ulrich rubs his temple.

Eledar hesitates. "I guess I don't. That's why we need to get her a message."

They fade into the crowd of Scraps and make their way back to Nivia's. Eledar clutches his cloak around him, unable to spare the energy for another chase. He runs his thumb over his wrist, over a scab screaming to be picked away, but he holds his shame at bay at the sight of Soffesa and Ferula.

They moved back outside Nivia's, Ferula's hand tucked into his sister's. They both brighten at the sight of Eledar and Ulrich in one piece.

"What did they want?" Soffesa asks.

Eledar rubs his forehead. "Turns out the cloaks Vellene and I stole were worth more than I realized."

Ulrich grabs his daughter into a hug.

"You scared me," Ferula whispers.

Ulrich kisses her cheek. "But Soffesa kept you safe."

"Yeah." Ferula looks up at Soffesa with a grin. "I like her."

Eledar smiles as his best friend blushes. "That's a good look for you, Soff."

Her blush deepens, but she clears her throat and straightens. "Uzax came and went. They were scheduled for a second shift."

Eledar rubs the back of his neck.

"I relayed the message. Nivia—" Soffesa stops when the weaver walks out of her shop.

"Nothing to worry about, dears. That letter will go undetected," Nivia reassures them. Her eyes flit across their faces, then land on Ulrich's. A pleased smile blooms on her face. "Oh, look what the parduseus dragged in. It's the master of thieves, himself."

Eledar and Soffesa turn a shocked look to Ulrich.

Ulrich laughs, but the sound is brittle and anxiety-ridden. "Those days are long past me, Niv."

Nivia cocks a brow. "I don't know about that." She gestures to the group. "You're hanging around these devils."

"Master of thieves, huh?" Eledar crosses his arms. "You could have mentioned your resume of accomplishments."

Ulrich waves it off, adjusts his wired frames. "I'm an intellectual."

"What he means is he's a smart thief," Nivia points out.

"No," Ulrich insists, "I left that life behind."

Soffesa takes a step forward. "I knew that carriage crash was too good to be true."

Eledar's brow furrows. "You mean the clay?"

Ulrich slicks back his hair.

"You know, Master typically means you were instructing others," Eledar continues. He sighs and shrugs. "I would know."

Nivia raises a hand. "That would be me."

"And me," Ferula beams. "Mama and Uncle Uzax, too."

"Retired," Ulrich insists. "All of us."

"And you just so happen to be involved in our plans?" Soffesa persists.

Ulrich sighs.

Eledar clears his throat. "I guess, but I certainly want to hear more." But he's distracted. As the adrenaline from the chase fades, his mind wanders to Ulrich's explanation of Infusion, of knowing the truth about what happened between him and Vellene. There's no other explanation for why their formularies were drained. The tug he felt toward her—it makes sense.

Soffesa clears her throat. "We should meet at your shack in the morning, Ulrich. I think The Bloody Cloth isn't much of a meeting ground with what happened today. Eledar and I can sneak in and out, but four chemi is too many to maneuver past Chemibreakers."

Eledar turns away, draws mud from his elbow as his mind frizzes. A strong sense of possession fills him. Someone else is trying to claim Vellene. Take her. Infuse with her. His shoulders tense, and he blinks back blind rage. He curses and massages the back of his neck as he paces. He feels his sister's gaze, but he ignores Soffesa and steps away from the group.

"We'll keep a lookout and drop our wards when you arrive." Ulrich takes his daughter's hand.

Soffesa nods. She waits for them to leave before she yanks Eledar around to face her. "You're doing that thing." She looks down at the mud as it goops out of his elbow. "Abyss, Eledar." She licks her lips. "I'm no good at mending."

Nivia steps over and grabs the wound. "Here." Her natural chemight weaves around his skin and stitches it together.

Soffesa gives her a nod of thanks.

"I have clients," Nivia says. She gives Eledar's wound a tap. "Come by later. I'll outfit you to cover that."

Her eyes roam over his exposed skin and find all the remnants of various scabs and scars. "And anywhere else you might want to avoid scratching at." Then she and Soffesa exchange a goodbye, a quick kiss to each other's cheeks before the weaver heads into her shop.

Eledar stares past Soffesa, stares at nothing.

"Eledar?" She grabs his hands and keeps him from mutilating himself. "Snap out of it."

He looks down at her. "Sorry?"

She heaves a breath and runs her thumbs across his knuckles. "You need to sleep, brother."

But he clenches his fists until his nails bite into her palms.

She yanks back. "Eledar," she hisses in pain.

He clutches his cloak. He needs *lumis*, needs to forget, needs to run and hide and break and drown and—

"I'm going to have to disallow one-night stands," Soffesa grumbles and pushes past him. "I'm assuming that's where all this anxiety of yours is coming from."

His heart races. "The Drinking is only a week out, and we effectively have no plan to get inside Winloc Grove."

Soffesa presses her lips together. She knows. He knows she knows, but neither of them addresses the obvious: Vellene. Instead, she lets go of a breath. "Wait for a letter. If she's still on our side, then she'll write back. I asked her to look for that pouch taken from Imaex."

"Okay. Okay." Eledar wraps his arm around her shoulders. His chest heaves. "I need a brew."

"Not sleep?"

"No." He leans into her. "I need something else. Anything else, Soff. There's something wrong. I feel—I don't—"

But before he can take another step, before he can give in to the roar of sleepless nights swimming between his ears, Eledar falters. A jolt of pain radiates from his torso. He clutches his stomach, fingers splayed to catch the clay sure to leak free. He falls to his knees, eyes wild as he searches for a wound. He barely registers Soffesa's panic, her hands roaming his stomach, trying to find the source of his pain, too.

Then he hears it—an exhale that isn't his, the thud of a heart that will never be his own.

"Vellene," he whispers. He drags his gaze up to Soffesa's frantic face. "Vellene is hurt."

## Chapter Twenty-One

# *Vellene*

Vellene wakes to the thunder of a shard storm. She rubs the bleariness from her vision and sits up in her bed.

She frowns, confused. She shifts and pain radiates from her stomach. A groan slips from her as her fingers find where her corset was removed, her stomach exposed, and a cloth wrapped around her breasts to keep her modest for whichever Utility worked on her.

Formularies weren't enough. The wound was too deep. She trails her fingers over the surface of her stomach, where a ridge of puffy, swollen skin is stitched together in a line six inches long. Chemight can mend most wounds, but if it's not wielded quickly, especially for harsher injuries, scars can be left. *Another for the collection*, she thinks as her fingers find the scar on her thigh.

Why is she still alive?

A throat clears in the far corner of her room. A shadow shifts.

Vellene jolts when her Chemibreaker escort with the frightening red eyes steps forward. She clutches her comforter to her chest. "What's going on?"

"My name is Uzax." The Chemibreaker stands. They tangle their fingers with a nervous clearing of their throat. "I didn't mean to startle you." They're tall and thin, face and body an accumulation of sharp edges.

"Then don't sit in the dark of my room while I'm sleeping," she snaps. Her eyes travel to their hands. In them is a rolled piece of parchment.

They look down at it. "I'm supposed to give this to you."

"What is it?" she squints.

"A message." Uzax licks their lips.

Vellene straightens. "From who?"

They hesitate, then step to her bed and hand the message to her. "I promise I mean no harm. You've been asleep for a few hours. I thought I'd leave and come back, but I was afraid I wouldn't make it back in without being seen."

Vellene narrows her eyes, traces their frame.

They're older. Maybe late thirties. Their Chemibreaker uniform is crisp, clean, but their shaved head and oily skin tell another story—one of poverty, of little to no access to a bath or primitive formularies. Their face is earnest, however. The fingers of their left hand tap a rhythm on their pant-leg.

"How long have you worked for my family, Uzax?" she asks.

They ignore her, their eyes curious. They gesture to the message. "It's from The Silent."

*Soffesa.* Vellene focuses on the piece of parchment, unrolls it.

> Be ready. Next move: The Drinking. Also, look for a maroon pouch. If found, report back with location. - The Silent

Vellene frowns. While the vague description of a 'maroon pouch' troubles her, their next move being at The Drinking gives her greater anxiety.

It's an ancient ceremony. It occurs yearly between Imperials—usually for both Scorus and Frales. However, since her father took control of the source, he's held The Drinking in private with only his trusted Scorian allies.

The last one to occur, Vellene wasn't invited. Meanwhile, Imperials she barely knew got a chance to drink from the source. This year, her sister took control of the planning, and the ceremony falls on Vellene's birthday. Knowing Mogaell, the date is deliberate—a message. Vellene will die, and Mogaell will celebrate.

"This is all there is?" Vellene asks.

Uzax nods but flicks their ruby gaze to her window. "How did you, an Imperial assassin and a Golem get involved?"

Vellene shifts out from her covers and lifts her robe off her bedpost, slipping it on. She grits her teeth as pain radiates through her lower abdomen at the movements. "You may leave, Uzax. You don't need to be pulled further into this."

Uzax snorts in disapproval. "You're locked in here."

Her eyes shoot to her door.

"And I have the keys," they continue. "So, don't try to deter me. My brother has a daughter, and if their lives are at risk, then I have a right to know everything."

Vellene moves to her closet and rips out a random gown. She tries to ignore the fact that no gift was left by Kadir. It doesn't make sense. Why would she be healed? Locked away? Her father's pride would leave her to bleed out. She hadn't expected to live and she didn't care. Not in that moment. Nothing mattered except protecting Kadir.

She glances back at Uzax. "Mind turning away?"

Uzax nods with a grimace. "Nothing to worry about. I prefer older chemi," they say but turn their back anyway.

Vellene manages not to hiss in pain as she slips into a loose-fitting, periwinkle gown. She doesn't bother with a corset, knowing it will make her injury far worse. "When

I met The Silent and Eledar," she says, "there was no one else."

"Well, Ulrich has a propensity for trouble. Always has." Uzax drifts to her fogged-over window, the night beyond frigid and dark. They draw in the condensation, pulling back and watching as random lines drip and melt into something sad.

"You can look now," she says, reaching for her boots.

Uzax sighs but remains focused on the window.

"Why am I here?" Vellene asks. "In my room?"

"I only get orders." Uzax finally looks at her but frowns at her gown. "That looks like a grand sack of nothing."

She waves the comment off and tugs on a boot with a stifled groan, one arm clutching her stomach. "What happened to Kadir?"

"He went with your father to his office." They fold their arms. "Rathmore's guards lined the hall. Your father would be a fool to try something if that's what you're worried about."

Vellene's heart races. She forces her foot into her other boot and ties the laces. "What other orders did my father give you?"

"Just to lock you in until the parade." Uzax swivels the key to her room over their index finger.

The parade. She squeezes her eyes shut. Of course. There's only one thing that trumps Aquim's temper—his ego.

"Are you in pain?" Uzax asks.

Vellene swallows. "Some but it's manageable." She hesitates and stares at her palms, her memory of the fight flooding her. She'd never felt power like that or seen any chemi wield such a thing.

Curious, she reaches for what she assumes was her natural chemight. She blows out a breath when nothing comes. No golden light. No golden flames.

"Are you sure you're alright?" Uzax asks, concerned with her silence.

She shakes her head. "I did something, and I don't know how I did it."

Uzax raises their brows, either disinterested or anxious. She can't tell. Maybe it's both.

Vellene licks her lips. "Can I trust you?"

Uzax considers her, but they extend their wrist, their jaw clenched with apprehension. "As long as my family remains unharmed, you have a friend."

Vellene stares at their wrist, then she pushes aside her reluctance. Now is not the time to be picky about an alliance. She needs every chemi in her corner she can get. She clasps their wrist for a moment before they step back.

Vellene reaches for a candle and lifts Soffesa's message to its flame. She lets it flutter to the floor and wither into ash, the smoke a comforting embrace. "You're staring," she murmurs and slowly lifts her eyes to the Chemibreaker.

Uzax steps carefully to the last piece of the burning letter and places their boot over it. “That gleam in your eyes,” they say, their voice tight. “I’m taking a chance putting faith in a Winloc, but it doesn’t mean I trust you fully or ever will. Tell me of your character.”

She fidgets. “What does my character have to do with it?”

“Everything.” Uzax studies her face. “You are young. I won’t hold that against you, but I also know youthful views of the world can be idealized in a way that simply doesn’t work for those actually living in it.” They tilt their head, their ruby gaze darkening. “Idealized and warped sometimes beyond saving.”

“You don’t know me,” she bites out. She meets his gaze then. “Let me ask you something.”

They nod.

Vellene rubs a hand over her chest. “Have you ever been so hurt that it’s impossible to see yourself as anything else?”

Uzax wavers.

“Youth is innocence. It’s looking in the mirror and seeing a kid, wishing to be an adult.” She combs her fingers through her hair with a grimace. “But what if you were never innocent, always wrong, because you were born from monsters? What if when you look in the mirror you see a beast desperate to be a kid?”

She rubs her shoulder and looks away. “And so you keep breathing and you keep shielding, and you hope by some miracle you’ll look into that mirror and the kid you never got to be will smile. She’ll smile, and your chest won’t feel empty, and that beast—that thing that makes you feel powerful but also makes you starved—” She shakes her head and paces to her window. She stares out into a shard storm, at the mist and tar that makes her whole. “So starved you know that if you feed the beast even just a bite you’ll never see or know that kid.”

Her voice cracks, and she stares at her reflection in the window—her golden eyes lit with flames. “You want to trust me, but I don’t even trust me, Uzax. I need to kill my family, but I can’t promise I won’t need to be killed, too.”

A soft grip slides over her shoulder, and she meets Uzax’s sympathetic gaze in the reflection.

"Youth is nothing among monsters except a feast, and I was served to my mother and father long ago.” She gently leans into their grasp and reaches up to give their knuckles a light squeeze. Her lips wobble into a tight smile. “I’m sorry. I know that isn’t the answer you wanted.”

“Maybe not but it was honest.” Uzax turns her toward them. “Darling, whoever told you there’s no joy in growing old, in finding your voice—they deserve to die.”

Her throat thickens with grief.

Their eyes glisten in the faint candlelight. “You asked how long I’ve worked here. Years.” They slowly turn her away from the mirror and level their gaze with hers. "Years, Vellene. I've seen what they do to you, how they've stolen you piece by piece."

Her stomach rolls.

"I couldn't help you, or I told myself I couldn't. Not if it meant putting my family on the line." They shake their head. "I was afraid you were too stripped bare by Aquim, made into something he could use on a whim, but you questioning yourself tells me you want to be better than him." Their eyes waver. "In this life, that want is everything."

"I couldn't betray you even if I wanted to," she admits, her voice thick with shame. "I let them use *mortello fusum*."

"I know." Their jaw clenches. "I don't agree with it. If I was there, I would've stopped them."

She nods but pulls from their grasp. “I must assassinate my family.”

"Yes but not in that." They exhale and move to her closet, rifling through the garments. "I've spent enough time with Nivia—she's a Utility, by the way, who's joined our cause—to know the power in clothes." They hum until their fingers settle on a gown wrapped in plastic. "What you wear matters. My uniform, despite my upbringing, gives me authority among Scorus. You need to wear something that makes you feel that way. Take power in everything you do, Vellene." They drag the gown out of the plastic and smile softly. "Why are you hiding this?" Its skirt glimmers in radiant sparkles—flecks of yellow, orange and red coming to life like embers.

“My mother gave me it,” she says. She runs her fingers over the fabric. “It was the last gown she made for me before she died. It’s meant for my 18th birthday.” Vellene clutches the fabric. “I’ll be dead by then. It’ll be my father, or it will be the death oath. Either way, I’ll be wearing this to my funeral. Not to my inauguration to the Convocation like she hoped.”

Uzax gently tugs the dress back to her closet. “A different one, then.”

But Vellene snags its skirt and tugs it from them. “No, I want to wear it.”

Uzax gives her a small smile. “It’s a beautiful dress. You should enjoy it. At least for a night.”

She chews on her lip. It deserves more than the parade, but if it's all she has, then maybe they're right. She should enjoy it. Uzax moves back to the window and she slips into the more elaborate design. If she stands still, it’s an elegant black gown with a fitted bodice and plunging neckline. If she moves, it comes to life with colorful flecks. The bodice puts pressure on her wound, but she chooses to endure the pain, to give the gown a chance to live. "Good?" she asks, a shake to her voice. Grief overwhelms her over the loss of her mother. She shifts her weight and clears her throat.

Uzax turns and their smile widens. "Beautiful."

She steps to them, to thank them, but they both freeze when her door bangs open.

Aquim's eyes land on the Chemibreaker, and his nostrils flare. "What are you doing in here?" he growls.

Uzax recovers expertly and gives her father a fast bow. "Sir Winloc, I came to have your daughter get ready for the parade."

Aquim takes a threatening step toward Uzax, and Vellene quickly draws his attention, even if it means pain. "Why am I going to the parade? I figured I'd be put in my cell."

He turns to her, and Uzax mouths a silent *thank you* before they hurry into the hall. Her father glares at her, barely holding back his rage. "You die when I say you die. For now, I need you to uphold your duties as my heir."

Vellene smooths out the skirt of her gown and lifts her chin. "What did you do with Kadir?"

Her father slips into a sly smile at that, and Vellene's stomach squeezes in discomfort. "I made a deal."

Vellene frowns. "A deal?"

"He will make the Convocation back off on taking the source, as well as support my rise as conqueror of Alchemight," Aquim says. He drags out his words with a puffed ego, "As long as you come to no harm by myself or your sister."

She looks away in confusion. "Why would he give up so much?"

Her father's eyes glint with satisfaction. "He is young and seeks recognition, and I seek to be rid of you. Infusing you to him is a way to have both. I will recognize him as an ally, giving him a prosperous legacy, and you will bear him as many heirs as he pleases."

The sick feeling growing inside her makes roots. "I thought the Infusion proposal was a ruse. I thought you wanted him dead."

"No, daughter. It was a back up plan, and after your failed attempt at killing him, I have no choice but to give him what he wants. I won't risk a Fralian army coming to Scorus just to save *you.*" Aquim's face darkens. "Tonight, you will remain obedient. You will join your new partner on the Winloc float, and you will show all of the Scorian Imperials that a powerful alliance was made." His voice tightens with the threat. "Tomorrow, you will be his problem. Not mine."

Did Kadir really agree to this? Maybe he came to Scorus with the intention of killing her, but something changed. He had his chance—multiple chances—to take her down and he didn't. "He's coming to the parade?" she asks.

Aquim chuckles darkly. "Look at you. So desperate for love and attention." He clicks his tongue and gestures to the doorway. "Take it, daughter. Consider it a gift."

Her eyes trail his gesture, and she stills as Kadir steps into the doorway. His face is as cold as her father's. Every ounce of the pain she witnessed when he was hit with her father's formulary is pieced into a tidy, grim expression. "Love," he says, and his voice has never been so sharp and bitter. He extends a hand, gloved like her father's.

Standing next to each other, their darkness could be replicas, and a quiet horror fills Vellene. Had this been Kadir's plan all along? Had he never wanted to save his nation and instead only sought an advantage with her father? His admission floats back to haunt her: *I'm not here to live. I'm here to conquer.*

"Go." Aquim grabs her bicep and forces her from one monster's grip to another's.

Kadir secures a strong arm around her waist, tugging her to his hip and dragging her into the hall. Vellene winces as his fingers curl into her side. Painful bursts of ice zip through the bodice of her gown from his touch. She despises the way he touches her as if he's claiming her like some prize. She stiffly walks down the hall, tries to tug away, but Kadir's grasp is relentless. "So, this was your plan?" she mutters through gritted teeth.

"Be grateful," Kadir sneers, "I just saved you from rotting in a prison cell."

Vellene glances back. Her father vanishes into his office as they pass it. She rips from Kadir, and this time he lets her. "What's going on?"

He takes her hand in his and intertwines their fingers.

"Take a hint," she growls and shakes her hand free, but she slows when she notices the small weight of an orb in her palm. She pulls open her fingers, but Kadir clasps his hand over hers, tugging her back to his side as they step through the double doors and outside.

"Humor me, Vellene," he says, voice low as the wintry chill of Scorus encompasses them.

She swallows but holds his hand. The orb pulses with power in her palm.

He directs her down the hill of Winloc Grove to where the floats for the parade rest. There are several. Most are decked out with accessories and drunken Imperials. They're all lower bloodlines, of course—the Vonners and Pineskys gaping like fish in Winloc Grove's front hall. Nevertheless, the Imperials are dressed lavishly, sipping on honey-colored brews and blanketed in furs.

Kadir tugs her toward the float at the front of the procession, and she scrutinizes the anger in his eyes as he watches Imperials flaunt wealth and jeer at each other.

"Are you on my side?" Vellene asks softly. Her breath makes clouds in the night.

Kadir's face reveals no sign of sympathy, but as they drift through a group of Imperials waiting for the parade to start, he squeezes her hand.

## Chapter Twenty-Two

# *Eledar*

Winloc Grove sits like a malevolent shadow at the end of a coiled street of chateaus. While Imperial families hang colored banners, string orbs up like lights, and keep their lawns manicured and bright, the Winloc residence stands dark, shrouded by barren trees, their disjointed limbs crossing, intertwining, *reaching* for something better—only for it to never be found. The grass and bushes of vibrant flora are matted with tar, but Chemibreakers work on the house, wielding primitive formularies to clean the muck off windows. The mansion whispers of the darkness within, of the chemi brimming with unkempt anger at the center of his fortress. Aquim.

Eledar crouches behind a tree in the yard, knees trembling after hours of watching. He shifts his weight, scans the shadows, and spots Soffesa leaping between the trees, gray chemight streaming around her. It stabilizes her and keeps her as silent as the breeze as she moves through the branches—a specialty he's always been jealous of.

"Anything?" he calls, careful not to be too loud.

Soffesa lands beside him, her chemight puffing around her. Then, it seeps into her skin, and she joins him in a crouch. Her face scrunches in discomfort.

Eledar's fingers trail over his stomach. He checked it a thousand times for a wound, but the pain that radiates there is unwarranted. One moment, nothing. The next, he swears he heard Vellene cry out. Swears a blast of chemight tunneled through his torso. "Is she okay?" he tries again.

Soffesa ducks her head behind her veil of orange hair. "She's in bed."

"That doesn't answer my question." His hands clutch the grass beneath him.

Soffesa turns her eyes to his. Her lips press. Her brows draw together. "She's hurt. There was a Utility in there mending her stomach. Looked like it was slashed open. It'll probably scar."

His spine straightens.

"That's not all I saw," she continues, her voice low and wary. "There are Rathmore carriages stationed out front."

He lifts from the ground.

Soffesa slowly mirrors him. Her hand clasps over his wrist. "Lazar's son. The resemblance is uncanny."

Eledar steps out of hiding.

Her grip tightens, and she yanks him back. “Eledar, you can’t.”

He turns a glare to her. “Vellene is hurt. Kadir Rathmore is alive and well.” He rips his wrist from her. “More than that, she’s rumored to be Infusing with him. Against her will. You can’t stop me from going in there.”

Soffesa blocks his path forward. “If you charge in there, not only will you die, but you’ll ruin any chance we have at securing the source.”

“Vellene is part of our crew,” Eledar hisses. “She deserves to be saved just as much as anyone else. We never should have sent her back into that hell hole.”

“Vellene was willing to kill her family, Eledar. We didn’t force her to go back,” Soffesa insists.

“Is that how you keep your conscience free of guilt? Lie to yourself?” He shoves past his friend and strides across the lawn.

Soffesa trails him. Her hand snaps out and grabs the back of his shirt. “Stop.”

“I held her down after you drugged her.” Eledar shakes his head. “It’s our fault her stomach is torn open.”

“This rage—it isn’t you.” Soffesa pulls herself around him a second time and slams her palms into his chest. “What’s going on? Is it your feelings for her? How did you even know she was hurt?”

Eledar grits his teeth. “My feelings?” He barks out a short laugh. “You mean how I can feel the pain of her wound twisting up through me and striking against a heart I don't have? How I can feel Vellene's rage as if it were my own?"

Soffesa grabs his arm and tugs them into a shadow. "What are you talking about?"

Eledar rubs his forehead and leans into a tree. "I can feel her, a piece of her, with me. There was a moment, after our night together, where chemight moved between us. Our orbs drained."

Soffesa's lips pull apart with a question, but all she manages is a sharp intake of breath.

"Ulrich thinks Vellene and I are Infused. Maybe not completely, but enough to be connected somehow." Eledar's gaze drifts to Winloc Grove. "I need to get in there. I need to know she's okay."

"Unbelievable." Soffesa takes a step back.

He focuses on her. "I know."

"What happens to you when she dies?" Soffesa asks, her voice tight.

Eledar shakes his head. "If she dies, I imagine it will be painful."

"Oh, she will die, Eledar." Soffesa grasps her head and paces before him. "The odds are stacked against her. We put her under a death oath, her family wants her gone, and now she's to be tethered to a Rathmore."

"That can't happen, Soff. She's already Infused with me," Eledar explains, but doubt creeps through him.

"You said you two didn't sleep together," she argues.

"We didn't." He stares at Vellene's window. "It was only a moment, but it was enough."

Soffesa wraps her fingers behind her neck. "There's no rule book for Infusion. Most of what we know about it is interpreted from passed down stories." She stops pacing and glares at him. "Who knows what will happen to you once she's forced to Infuse with Rathmore?"

"I'm not worried about me," he explains. "I'm worried about—"

"Everyone else," Soffesa growls. She steps toward him and thrusts a finger into his chest. "It's always everyone else, Eledar. You never protect yourself, and I am always left to pick up the pieces. We're talking about a Winloc and a Rathmore. They're made for each other." She drops her hand and rolls her shoulders back. "Let Kadir have her. Let them Infuse, then let our death oath kill them both."

Eledar stares at the darkness crawling across her features. "You want me to sacrifice Vellene?"

"We already did." She shakes his shoulders. "We sentenced her to death weeks ago. You've just been too scared to admit it to yourself."

He flexes his fists. "I can't just give her up without a fight, Soff."

She folds her arms with a scowl. "If you want inside Winloc Grove, then you'll have to go through me. No exceptions."

"Don't do this." He steps toward her.

She moves into a lunge and raises her fists. "I mean it, Eledar. I won't let you ruin our chance at securing the one thing that could free us all."

"She's in pain. Please, Soffesa, I can feel it. It's stronger here. Maybe because I'm closer to her. I don't know. But I can feel her rage, and it's not something we should let go unchecked. It could be dangerous. For all of us. Source or no source."

Soffesa presses her lips together. Chemight blazes out of her knuckles.

Eledar grimaces and looks away.

Footsteps. Slow and soft.

Soffesa tenses, searches the clearing.

Two shadows sneak up the hillside toward them. He lunges toward Soffesa and tackles her to the ground.

She gasps in surprise, the breath knocked from her. "Get off me, you crazy bastard—"

"Shut up," he growls. "We've been spotted." The light of a candle flickers to life beyond Vellene's window above, and a shadowed figure stands in a tall silhouette. "She's awake," he whispers.

Soffesa groans and knees him in the groin. "I said: get off me."

Eledar chokes in surprise and rolls off her to the side. "The abyss was that for?"

She sits up and slicks off tar from the back of her leather dress. "Your priorities need serious adjusting, Eledar Lirik, and I refuse to give you any pity until they do."

"I've never asked for your pity." Eledar pushes onto his knees and scans the hillside. The tension in his shoulders relaxes when the moon's light flashes against a head of pink and purple hair. "It's just Ulrich and Ferula."

"Good. Maybe they'll talk some sense into you. Clearly, I'm no good at it." Soffesa pulls from the ground and ties back her hair.

"Why are they here?" Eledar scratches the scab at his elbow.

Soffesa slaps his hand away from the wound with a pointed glare. "We've been on watch all day. They're here for the night shift."

His fingers twitch at his side. "I'm not leaving. Vellene's hurt. More than that, my abuser's son is in there doing only the Guardians know what. I have every right to storm in there, Soffesa. Kadir has it coming. He sat by as his father created Golem. Sat by as myself and my chemi were tortured. Don't ask me to go back to The Bloody Cloth, because I won't."

She blows out a breath, then grabs his shoulders. She levels her eyes with his. "Vellene is Imperial. They have every resource to mend her."

"I'm less worried about her stomach wound and more worried about everything else I can feel now that I'm closer to her." Eledar licks his lips and shrugs Soffesa's hands off. "She's going to implode, Soff."

"Hey." Ferula tilts her head and studies them. She frowns at the tar smudged across their clothes.

"Everything okay?" Ulrich asks. He rests a hand on Ferula's shoulder, keeps her from taking another step toward them.

"We're fine," Eledar insists.

Soffesa scoffs.

Ulrich raises a brow. "Well, we're here for our shift."

"No more watching," Eledar says. He lifts his eyes back to the window. "It's time we get inside."

Ferula bounces onto her toes, and Ulrich adjusts his glasses. "That sounds—"

"Idiotic." Soffesa gestures to Winloc Grove. "the parade is tonight. Every chemi in there is on high alert preparing for it."

"What if I give you a better reason than Vellene or Rathmore to break in?" Eledar asks. A plan unfolds in his mind.

Soffesa shakes her head. "I wouldn't buy it."

"You said it yourself. Tonight is the parade. That means, pretty soon, everyone leaves." Eledar shoves his hands into his pockets and shrugs. "If we want the pouch those Chemibreakers took from Imaex, there won't be a better time before The Drinking to try and locate it."

Soffesa glares at him.

Ulrich clears his throat. "It isn't completely terrible. We can use the time to map the halls."

She huffs, her nostrils flaring in frustration. "You can't be serious, Ulrich. I thought you were supposed to be the 'smart' thief."

Ferula waves a hand and chemight sparkles over her fingertips. "I could break apart the wards on the place." She squints at the massive house. "Looks simple enough."

Ulrich gives her shoulder a soft squeeze. "And I can veil us. It will be tricky. I'll need a few formularies to amplify my ability. It's never worked well on moving targets."

Eledar's lips curl into a smile. "See, we get in. We get out. Easy."

Soffesa gawks between the three of them. "Do I get any say in this?"

"Whatever Eledar's motivation," Ulrich explains, "it doesn't make him any less right. If there's something we need from Winloc Grove before The Drinking, then tonight is the night to try and get it."

"They've got the floats set up in the street down the hill," Ferula explains. "They'll be far enough away to give us plenty of time to escape."

Soffesa chews on her lip.

Eledar offers her a sympathetic grin. He gives her shoulders a gentle, playful nudge. "I know you can't say no to a heist."

Her eyes darken.

"C'mon." He reaches for a loose strand of orange hair hanging in her face and tucks it behind her ear. "This is a win-win, situation. I get what I want, and we secure an advantage."

"If any of us gets hurt," she starts.

But Eledar shakes his head and his smile falls. "I won't let that happen."

Soffesa's shoulders slump in defeat. Her eyes trace his face for a long moment before she waves the crew forward. "Fine. This way."

They weave through trees, the four of them slipping from shadow to shadow. Utilities pass, mindlessly cleaning the grounds of the tar from the shard storm.

Eledar outstretches an arm, presses Ferula and Ulrich back as Soffesa darts ahead. "She'll give us a signal."

Soffesa stops at the last tree before an open expanse. Across from her rests a ladder. It sits against the side of Winloc Grove, left behind by a Utility wiping windows clean. She looks back at the crew and gives Eledar an annoyed nod.

"I don't know what you did, but she definitely has plans to murder you in your sleep," Ulrich whispers as the three of them sprint across the lawn.

Eledar smirks. "I bring out the best in her."

They chase after Soffesa, then careen toward the ladder.

Ulrich's ruby eyes light with a forgotten but cherished wildness as he presses a kiss to his daughter's forehead, then pushes his glasses up his nose. "Stay hidden. If anything happens, get back to the tavern. Understood?"

Ferula gives him a delighted smile. "I know."

"Good." Ulrich kisses her forehead once more, then turns to Eledar and Soffesa. "Shall we?"

"Go ahead," Ferula insists as she crouches behind a bush and presses her palms flat against the brick of the building. She squeezes her eyes shut as chemight pours from her. "I'll have the wards broken soon. Looks like the fools are using simple ones. Probably think everyone's too scared to try anything. So much for the rumors of it being notoriously well-warded."

Soffesa tests a rung, then shoots up the ladder. She stops at the top and tentatively reaches a hand out.

"Now," Ferula says through clenched teeth. "I can't hold these wards open long without formularies."

Soffesa thrusts the window open. Then, she disappears inside.

Ulrich goes next, as quick as any Scrap learns to be.

Eledar nods to Ferula. "Stay safe."

"Protect my father," she returns. A sweat breaks out on her forehead. "And hurry up, will you?"

Eledar chuckles and fumbles up the rungs. The ladder creaks under his weight, but he makes it to the window. The curtains whip around him as the wind thrusts at his back. He throws a leg over the sill and ducks inside. Then he stiffens as he scans the room.

Soffesa takes slow steps through it, lights a few more candles on the bedside table with her natural chemight. Flames dance.

But Vellene isn't here.

Ulrich moves to a heating box on the dresser, then steps up onto the bed and reaches for the chandelier on the ceiling. "All the orbs are cleared out of this room." He hops down with a scowl. "I can't shield us without them."

They all tense when the door squeaks open.

Uzax steps into the light. They freeze at the sight of Eledar, Soffesa, and Ulrich, then they laugh. "You just missed her. She's off to the parade." They shut the door and cross to their twin. The two embrace quickly.

Eledar runs a finger over the quilt crumpled at the end of Vellene's bed. Then he gingerly touches the spines of a pile of tomes on her bedside table. His chest warms as he stares at her life, but it occurs to him how little he truly knows about her.

"I delivered your message about the pouch to her," Uzax explains. "She hasn't had time to look if that's why you're here. I planned on searching rooms during the parade."

"I saw her hurt," Soffesa explains. "Eledar wanted to speed things up."

Eledar searches Uzax's face. "Is she okay?"

Their eyes dart to their brother. "Speed things up?"

"Is Vellene okay?" Eledar pushes and steps toward them.

They hesitate but nods. "As okay as she can be, considering the circumstances."

Eledar inhales and rubs his cheek. "You mean the Infusion with Rathmore."

"No." Uzax crosses their arms. "I mean you." They turn to Ulrich. "Us. The way we're using her to our advantage."

"She agreed," Eledar tries.

"She didn't have much of a choice, did she?" They ask, their voice hollow and their eyes dark.

"She's a Winloc. We needed insurance," Soffesa snaps. She strides past them and yanks open Vellene's door. "We came after that pouch. You can either help and get a piece of the source, or you can continue to contemplate our trustworthiness."

Ulrich scowls. "It doesn't matter. We need to call this off. I don't have access to formularies."

Eledar rubs his jaw. “I’m sure we can find some in another room.”

“I’m not stepping into that hall without them,” Ulrich says. He looks at his brother.

Uzax sighs and gives the orb pouch at their waist a pat. “I have some.” They pull out four orbs filled with natural chemight. They swirl an intense gray, like small, captured storms. “Here.” They hand them to their twin.

Ulrich rolls the orbs around in his palm. “No formularies?”

Uzax runs their tongue over their teeth and procures ingots—one nether and two marvels. “You can make your own.”

“I’ve never—” Ulrich starts, uncertain.

“I’ve got it.” Eledar scoops up an orb from Ulrich’s palm and takes one of the two marvel ingots from Uzax’s. “What formulary do you need?

“Morph.” Ulrich looks to the ceiling in thought. “Shouldn’t matter if they’re marvel or nether, as long as they can bend to my will.”

“And the last orb?” Soffesa asks.

Ulrich sighs. “As good as any Scrap’s chemight, I’m afraid. I can hold the cloaking spell over you, just as I did with my house. But my house doesn’t move, doesn’t breathe. It will be far harder without morph formularies to stabilize it.”

Eledar whispers wishes and curses to the orbs, the ingots melting around the little glass spheres until they accept it and brighten with newfound color.

"A Golem thing?" Uzax asks, brows raised in surprise.

Eledar looks up from his work with a crooked smile. "Sometimes a Golem thing. I've met Scraps able to accomplish it over the years, but it's a rarity." He continues with two more orbs, formularizing them with the last two ingots. "Are you okay to channel these without chemight deposits?"

Ulrich nods. "It's been a while. I'm a little rusty. But I've done it before."

"Good." Soffesa looks to Uzax. "Ulrich will cloak us but not you. I want you to go toward the Surveillant's room, stop near it, then keep walking. Don't look back. You're too valuable for us to lose. We need you here, inside Winloc Grove, for The Drinking."

"Idus?" Uzax asks about the Surveillant. "Why him?"

"He handles Aquim's dirty work," Soffesa explains. "If anyone knows about that pouch, it's him."

Eledar steps into the doorway. He peers into the hall, then glances back. His eyes fall on the tidy drawers, the small pile of clothes, the unmade bed, the tomes towering on the dresser. He swallows. He needs to make things right with Vellene.

Soffesa moves beside him as Ulrich murmurs soft words of hope. She side-eyes his profile with a grimace, but she takes his hand anyway.

Eledar squeezes it as her breaths come quick. "To fight is to live," he says and runs his thumbs over her knuckles.

"To live is to fight," she returns.

Silver chemight spills out of Ulrich. It umbrellas over the three of them, his ruby eyes locked straight ahead as he concentrates. His mouth moves with repetitive shapes. Small words he repeats like a mantra: "Hold on hold on hold on."

"Can you see us?" Eledar asks.

Uzax shakes their head. They step past everyone and into the hall. "Let's go."

Eledar holds his breath and keeps his stride in line with Soffesa's, careful not to breach their shield of invisibility. It shimmers around the three of them, waves of power rippling across it.

Uzax leads the crew through the halls. The further they go, the more Chemibreakers they squeeze past. They slow as they enter barren quarters made for Utilities that stay on the premises—the most loyal of Aquim's slaves.

Uzax stops outside a door, clears their throat, then pivots and heads back toward Eledar, Soffesa, and Ulrich. Uzax doesn't look toward them. Instead, they manage a single nod before they round a corner and disappear.

Soffesa moves to the door, sucks in a breath, then shoves it open. It gives way to a small eight-by-eight room. A single bed is smashed against a wall, a dresser next to it. It's just as barren as the hallway. In fact, it doesn't look lived in.

Ulrich gives a mangled groan as he lets go of his shield.

Eledar shuts the door. His nose crinkles when a foul smell hits him. "What is that?"

Soffesa's face twists. "No idea."

Ulrich heaves a breath as he collects himself and his power. He settles onto the edge of the bed and braces himself on his knees. "I'm not sure how long I'll be able to hold it when we need to leave." He lifts the orbs for them to see. Two are completely drained, leaving one with a formulary left and another with only natural chemight.

Eledar ignores the issue for now and moves to the dresser. He runs his fingers over its dust-covered top.

"Is it just me, or does this place look like it's never seen a living soul?" Soffesa asks. She steps to the wardrobe and gives it a sniff before she lurches back. "Abyss, that is foul." She pries open one of the doors.

Eledar gets on his knees, looks under the bed. Nothing. He frowns. "We'll have to try Aquim's quarters."

Ulrich shakes his head. "It's too risky. I don't have enough chemight."

Soffesa jumps back as the second door to the wardrobe falls open.

A body topples out. A headless body.

Eledar covers his mouth and nose as he nudges the body's robes with the toe of his boot. "Guess that explains the dust."

"He's been dead for at least a month if not longer," Soffesa says, crouching beside their severed neck and surveying its decay.

"Only one chemi I know of cuts heads off," Ulrich says with disgust.

"This wasn't Aquim," Soffesa says. "He'd have the guy's head on display."

"Who's to say it isn't?" Eledar asks.

She slips to the wardrobe and pushes the hanging robes out of the way. "Exhibit A."

Eledar peers in, then takes several steps back. The Surveillant's rotting, severed head lies on the floor of the wardrobe, a disgusting liquid pooling beneath it. He's seen his fair share of rot and decay, been trapped between piles of bodies, but something about this unsettles him. He looks around the room.

"We need to move on." He shakes his head. "This is clearly a dead end." He clears his throat. "Pun not intended."

Soffesa pushes a strand of hair out of her face. "We don't know for certain Aquim left for the parade."

"We need to try." He clenches his fists and crosses to the door. "Or I'll go alone, but I'm not leaving empty-handed." He looks between her and Ulrich. "We'll be okay."

Soffesa hesitates. "I know you're worried about Vellene, and this certainly doesn't help." She gestures to the dead Surveillant and cringes. "But Uzax said they delivered our letter. Maybe we should give her a chance to look for the pouch."

"We have three days until The Drinking," Eledar says. "Yes, I'm worried about Vellene, but I'm more concerned about going into that ceremony blind."

Ulrich tosses the two empty orbs onto the bedspread and takes his final two out of his pocket. He clenches them with a grimace. "We'll need to move quicker. I only have one formulary left to work with. The last orb with natural chemight is hardly usable for this."

Soffesa bites her lip, then looks Eledar up and down. "Are you sure about this?"

"Do you know where Aquim's quarters are?" Eledar asks her. She gives him a solemn nod, and he flings open the door. "Then lead the way."

He moves into the hall and glances back at Ulrich. "We'll use your shield in increments." Soffesa leads them forward, and he stops behind her at the corner of the hall.

She peers around it, then juts her chin. "We're good."

They hurry down the next hall, then another. All is quiet, most Utilities and Chemibreakers away at the parade.

Then at the next corner, Soffesa throws herself back into Eledar's chest.

"Now," he hisses at Ulrich.

The cloaking shield wraps around them as a group of Chemibreakers passes by. They wait for the guards to move on to another hall, then Ulrich lets his chemight go with a shudder of exhaustion. They rush forward, Soffesa at the lead.

The further they go into Winloc Grove, the more wealth drips off the walls. Portraits of generations of Winlocs. Chandeliers lined with strings of empty orbs that refract candlelight. Velvet chaises. Fireplaces lit for the evening. Intricate rugs woven with silver spideria.

Soffesa stops at a pair of double doors. This time, she doesn't hesitate. She pushes them open and strides inside.

Aquim's room is a large oval, a bed at its center, a fireplace in the corner, a table and chairs set to the side. Navy and light blue—the signature Winloc colors—cover every visible surface. Even the ceiling is painted a crisp, sky blue with an elaborate mural of spideria among the trees at its center. The room sits empty, its cruel chemi and his tyrannic whims out for the evening.

Eledar grabs the nearest box, turns it over, shakes it out. "Quick. Look everywhere."

They move through the room, turn it upside down. Objects break, clatter. The more they overturn, the greater Eledar's heart pounds.

"It's not here," Ulrich says, his voice strained.

"No." Eledar goes to the dresser. He kicks it and bottles of fragrance clink together furiously. "It has to be here."

"Eledar, stop." Soffesa grabs his shoulder.

He shakes her off, fists clenched. "I am not leaving without that pouch." He wrenches open the dresser's top drawer. His muscles tighten at the sight of several colorful orbs. They fill the entirety of the drawer, glimmering with an array of formularies. He reaches in to snatch—

"Who. Are. You?"

A chill runs over Eledar's body. He spins around.

Soffesa and Ulrich step back.

Aquim stands in his doorway, three Chemibreakers at his back. Chemight blazes up his arms. He looks around at his room, its disarray, and his chemight whips up to his shoulders in fury.

Eledar shares a frantic look with Soffesa. "Go."

Aquim growls and lunges toward him.

Eledar ducks as a weaponized primitive formulary barrels where his head had been. He pops back onto his feet, yanks a fistful of formularies from the dresser, and summons—

A blow cuts through his pants, sears into his thigh. Eledar cries out in pain, clutches the wound as mud oozes free, and falls to a knee. He glimpses Soffesa and Ulrich fighting their way through the three Chemibreakers as his vision fuzzes at the edges.

Aquim closes the distance. He opens a fist. His chemight pools into a wavering ball. He scowls at the mud leaking from Eledar's thigh. "Golem." His chemight vanishes, and he wraps his hand around Eledar's throat. "Abomination." He squeezes it, relishes Eledar's panicked attempt at a gasp for air. "That's unfortunate for you." Aquim's lips slither into a smile.

Soffesa and Ulrich tear down the last Chemibreaker. His best friend's eyes widen at the sight of Aquim's hand around Eledar's throat.

Ulrich grabs her arm, forces her away, then wields the last of his orb's chemight. The ward sparks up around them, then locks in place—the space where they stood now empty.

Eledar stares at where they vanished, mouths a final, "Go," before Aquim conjures a flash of chemight, and the world goes dark.

## Chapter Twenty-Three

# *Vellene*

The Winloc float is a thing of navy frills and banners of false hope. On the ground below, Utilities move into position, four to each corner. They summon chemight, large pouches strapped across their chests filled with orbs to keep the float in the air and moving. Vellene and Kadir approach, Chemibreakers in tow. A piece of her tension drifts into ease when she spots Uzax among them.

Kadir continues to hold her hand as they step onto the float. His thumb absently runs across her knuckles, fidgets with her nails. The anxious nature of the motion contrasts with his stern expression. Ice continues to prickle through the contact, but the longer he holds onto her, the more it feels like a cool wash of water across hot, aching skin.

Vellene bites her lip, tries not to think about what the sensation could mean—if anything—and spots her sister.

Mogaell stands at the back of the float's deck. She fixes her hair, then throws a demand toward the closest Utility.

"I need to speak with her," Vellene mutters. She looks at Kadir and finds him watching her closely, his violet eyes dipping from her face to her stomach. "What?"

His jaw flickers with tension before he lets go of her hand and steps to the front of the float without another word.

She stares at his back, her brow furrowing. She clasps the orb he pressed into her palm, turning it over between her fingers before she places it into a deposit behind her ear. She needs time alone with him, enough to determine whether he's an enemy or ally. *One problem at a time*, she reminds herself and moves toward her sister.

When it came to Aquim's blows against their mother or vice versa—Vellene always made sure to stand between them and Mogaell. Now, sometimes she sees her sister, and she wishes she hadn't. It's a sick thought, but she wonders if Mogaell would be different. If her sister would be more than a mirror of their father.

"You look fine," Vellene notes and leans into the railing next to Mogaell as her sister continues to fidget with her hair.

Mogaell snorts. She keeps her gaze forward, lips curled with a sneer. "I don't need your flattery."

Vellene eyes her neck. Could she slit it? She imagines the blood, the sputter of her sister's last words. Part of her would enjoy wiping the smirk off Mogaell's face, and that part of her makes her hands shake. She grips the railing. "I don't suppose you missed me when you thought I'd left for good?"

"You failed to run away, and then ruined our father's only chance to get rid of that Rathmore bastard." Mogaell pins her with a dark gaze. Something there is darker. Flashes of black before they fade to navy. She settles onto a cushioned throne and clasps her hands in her lap. Then her voice lowers and that darkness returns. "I haven't missed you all my life, sister. Why would I start missing you now?"

Vellene expects Mogaell's words to hurt, but there's nothing more than a dull ache now. The energy she used to waste on her sister—it's spent. With a tired exhale, she shakes her head. "How did we fall so far apart?"

"I ask myself that all the time." Mogaell crosses her arms and leans back into her cushioned seat. "Then, I look in the mirror and understand we were never two halves of a whole. Only two wholes in the way of each other."

Vellene grimaces. Their values never aligned. Even when there was peace between them, it had its boundaries. Love for Winlocs has always been conditional, hers and her sister's more so than even their parents. If Vellene shielded Aurora, it meant leaving Mogaell open. It was an impossible choice until Aquim began to favor the younger Winloc. She'd be a liar if she didn't admit Aquim's favor of Mogaell didn't make her jealous. Vellene is a body of bruises and scars. Mogaell is extravagance and care.

Her sister studies her nails, plays with their edges.

Vellene swallows. "I wish..." she trails off. She rubs her arm.

"I don't," Mogaell finishes for her. "Whatever your wish is: I. Don't."

Vellene glares at her. "What if my wish was for you to be the prettier sister?" she asks with a sneer, unable to keep herself from resorting to pettiness.

Mogaell fluffs one side of her hair and bats her lashes. "That wish would be impossible because it's already true." Then, she looks over at Kadir. "Are you truly to Infuse with him?"

They watch as Geralt, the Rathmore Chemibreaker, steps onto the float and hands Kadir a cloak.

"Thank you," Kadir says, his voice surprisingly grateful and kind as he plucks the cloak out of the Chemibreaker's hands.

Then Geralt leans in to whisper something to Kadir, who gives the chemi a terse nod.

"Tell them my partner and I will be ready to leave after The Drinking," Kadir answers.

Mogaell turns smug, and Vellene tenses, ready to flee. She forces herself still, to follow through, the faintest sting of poison sparking through her with her brief indecision. She holds back a wince.

"Everything okay?" Kadir asks. He looks between them and clasps his cloak into place, a second held in his gloved fists. He holds it out in a silent offering to Vellene when neither sisters answer him. "Come." He rests a hand on her lower back and guides her away from Mogaell's prying eyes. "Please tell me, love," he grumbles when they stop at the end of the float, "what the point of this atrocious parade is?"

Vellene eyes him. "Aquim claims it keeps morale up. Gets Imperials excited for who he will choose to join him in The Drinking ceremony."

Kadir scans the street. Large mansions and chateaus line it, light shining in the windows. Imperial families fill the sidewalks beyond their homes, all dressed lavishly and enjoying the night.

"Kadir," she says, straining with the weight of her question, "what's going on?" She brushes the orb he gave her behind her ear.

He drops his hand from her waist, leaning into the side of the float. "Don't worry about it."

But she forces his eyes to hers, slanting her body toward him. "I'm going to worry about it. You don't think I'll actually Infuse with you, do you?"

He shakes his head. "I meant it when I said I wouldn't force you into doing something you don't want to." Then, he hesitates, unable to find the right words, which is strange. He always appears so well-prepared. "But I also don't buy your father and sister leaving you alone. Not after you displayed your power."

"I know. Why wouldn't he want to know why my chemight is different?" Vellene wonders. "He didn't even ask."

"Because it would show he doesn't know why himself." Kadir grips the rail of the float. "You caught him off-guard, and I don't think your father liked that very much. He soothed the situation with this false Infusion, but I don't doubt he's scouring Scorus for an answer. I'm afraid of what will happen to you when he finds it."

Vellene leans into the float, then winces when it puts pressure on her wound. Her hand flies to her stomach as pain zings down into her knees.

A soft hiss releases between Kadir's teeth. Concern laces between his brows before he gingerly replaces her hand with his own. "Here, allow me." Pink steams from his palm and seeps beneath the bodice of her gown.

"It's not as bad as—" She stops herself, not sure she's ready for Kadir to know the extent of her pain, her vulnerability. His chemight soothes the wound, despite the fact the five words she uttered cast his face into a scowl.

He removes his hand from her stomach, a question in his gaze.

"It's not the first scar," is all she gives him, too ashamed to look at him.

"Don't do that," he orders. The violet of his gaze turns fierce. "Don't cower away." He holds her stare for a moment, then he turns and runs a hand through his hair.

They fall quiet, their breaths steady.

As Vellene stares out, his eyes trace her profile. She shivers and moves to say something about it, but then she spots someone out on the street. In the shadows—behind the circus of wealth—is a hooded figure in red leather. *Soffesa.* The Silent stands behind two Imperials, hood drawn back and the ink along half her face unmistakable. Something about the way she holds herself, however, is crooked. Vellene's breath catches with realization. Soffesa's hurt. She scans the shadows for Eledar or the others, but the assassin stands alone.

"Are you okay?" Kadir asks.

She jumps at his voice.

"I'm sorry, I didn't mean to startle you." He rests a hand on the small of her back. "You just look like you've seen a ghost."

She turns her gaze back to Soffesa, but The Silent disappeared. "I think I did." As she studies the crowd, she finds a robust chair built like a throne stationed with a few Imperials and Chemibreakers. She recognizes it as her father's seat, but it's empty. Vellene reaches for Kadir's hand out of instinct. She laces her fingers through his and relishes the comfort the action brings, the heat threatening to burst from her skin cooling enough to let her think clearly.

Kadir stares at his fingers intertwined with hers. "It's not stabbing me in the thigh," he says softly, "but I like it." His lips slip into a half smile, one of his dimples creasing.

Her heart beats faster at the sight of it, at the flicker of something like desire in his eyes. "I can't leave Scorus," she pivots the conversation.

He levels his gaze with hers. "I thought you wanted to be whisked away from all of this?"

"I need to stay." She chews on her lip. If she overheard his conversation with Geralt correctly, then he doesn't plan on leaving until after The Drinking. While that works in favor of Eledar's plan, there's so much more to it now. Her mother deserves justice. Her sister needs to be pulled away from the violence of their father before it's too late. Her nation needs to mend. Her responsibilities are stacking up. She can't ignore them. Not anymore.

He lowers his voice. "Are you going to tell me why?"

"It's not safe to talk here," she murmurs.

He squeezes her hand and his eyes flicker with wickedness. "Then, perhaps we could ditch this monstrosity?" Kadir lifts the bottom of his shirt and reveals chemight deposits, along with a swooping portion of his family crest on his right abdomen.

Her face heats as her eyes trail the sharp v above the line of his trousers. She moves to look away, but he gives an orb a tap. In it glows white, sparkling chemight—the same formulary he pressed into her palm and now sits behind her ear. He smirks as goose bumps rise across her Winloc crest. "Just don't let go of my hand." He runs his thumb over hers.

Adrenaline and anxiety war within her. She doesn't know what to expect from the formulary or whether she can trust him in the slightest, but she needs to take risks if she's going to move forward. "I'm ready."

He taps her knuckle. "Wield it. Now."

She concentrates and tugs on the formulary behind her ear. White chemight swirls around their intertwined hands. It curls up their arms, their biceps, their necks, their cheeks—and just as Mogaell vaults across the deck toward them, the chemight covers their eyes.

Vellene gasps as all of Alchemight takes a large inhale. It sucks her body in through its mouth, each of her organs pressing inward. Then, it spits them out.

They stumble onto asphalt across from the float, from Mogaell's wild expression, from the Chemibreakers staring in confusion at where they went.

Kadir tugs on her. "Run."

They sprint down the street and through the Imperial gates—past closed shops and bewildered Utilities. Vellene pumps her arms, heart in her stomach at the idea of running away. Again. Laughter zings toward her ears, and she turns a frantic expression to Kadir.

He sprints, the same as her, but he charges with laughter, face giddy, chest heaving. There's something so innocent about it that it brightens his face, shows his real age. His youth. It radiates off him as he takes larger and longer strides. Every meticulous detail of his outfit rumples with the wind.

*He is strange*, she decides, but her smile spreads wider across her cheeks. A laugh erupts from her chest, and she spreads her arms, lets the wind whip through her hair.

But Kadir's laughter fades. He skitters to a stop.

Vellene slows between piles of garbage to catch her breath, surprised when Kadir stoops beside a small Scrap girl.

She's curled in a fetal position on the pavement, teeth chattering, a soft cry escaping between bloodied lips. She wears nothing but pants, her top half covered only in dried tar.

Kadir kneels. "Hey." He swallows and reaches to the clasp of his cloak. He undoes it and lies the thick fabric across the girl.

She looks up at him with wide eyes before she clutches it against her.

"It's yours." He nods to her, gives her a reassuring smile.

Vellene makes her way back to them, heart in her throat. In all her life, she's never seen anyone—especially an Imperial—give a Scrap a personal belonging.

Kadir stands. He hugs himself as a frigid breeze whistles through the alley.

"That was—" she struggles to find the right word.

"Decent?" Kadir shakes his head and looks at her. "Isn't it sad that being kind—of all things—is a shock to you?"

Vellene looks away, embarrassed.

He watches her for a long moment, then he sighs and glances over his shoulder. "We should keep moving."

She blows out a shaky breath, her heart thumping from their sprint, thankful to change the conversation. "Where to?"

He slips from the darkness of his thoughts and forces his lips into a smile until his face brightens and his dimples show. It's a completely different face from the one she's come to know. The darkness is there, ready to be wielded, but the hints of deviousness and charm she's witnessed now take up permanent space.

It strikes her then how easily he slides between faces, as if he owns many of them and wouldn't dare pick a favorite.

Unease blossoms through her chest, but he grabs her wrist and pulls her down a street. "C'mon, there's a great place around the corner."

## Chapter Twenty-Four

# *Eledar*

Chemight jolts into Eledar's body. His eyes peel open. He gasps and sits up, muscles tense as Aquim tosses a ball of chemight. It slams into his chest. His mind sizzles and veins buzz as he's electrocuted.

Imperials stand and gawk. Several cheer in approval, and Aquim's fist lights with another attack.

"I'm. Awake," Eledar manages through gritted teeth. His shoulders tremor, but he braces against the ground and allows his surroundings to sink in.

He sits on Winloc Grove's front lawn. Behind him, Utilities work to free a dead Scrap from one of three lynches, presumably to make room for him. He swallows and drags his eyes over the crowd.

They hone in on the clay leaking from his thigh. It flows heavily enough that he worries it won't mend. But the skin around the wound itches. His natural chemight continues to pour forward and attempt to heal the gash. There aren't a ton of advantages to being a Golem these days, but being able to heal without the need for a formulary, even slowly, is a huge one. He sucks in a breath to steady himself and focuses on his opponent.

Aquim stands with a smug expression. He tilts his head and studies Eledar. "Give me your name."

Eledar presses his lips together.

Aquim chuckles darkly. Chemight streams into his other palm and forms a third blast to throw with the second. "You'll come to learn I get what I want, Golem. Eventually." He throws his arms out.

Power snaps forward and pummels into Eledar's stomach. Pain lances through him as he doubles over. He lets out a low groan and heaves a breath. Everything in him wants to fight back, to tear Aquim apart here and now. *Wait*, he tells himself. *Make him sweat.*

Eledar forces a smile.

The Winloc leader's smug expression slices into cold fury. "How strong you must think you are." He summons a new formulary, and his fingers light with navy flames.

"I'm built for abuse, Aquim." Eledar laughs bitterly. "You can't break me like you would your other captures. Your daughter."

The crowd around them falls into a silent hush. Several lean into Eledar's words.

He bites his tongue, realizing too late his mistake.

Aquim takes it in stride. "And which daughter would that be, Golem?"

Eledar spits mud on the ground.

"I'm being generous to you," Aquim says. His chaos formulary dances across his knuckles. "Tell me which of my daughters have you made friends with?"

"Generous?" Eledar laughs. "There's nothing generous about you. I'm sure Scorus agrees."

A sharp gasp strikes through the crowd.

Eledar grins. "See, no one is even bothering to speak up. To tell you of your greatness."

"Trust me, you're being treated like a king." He swivels his fingers, and the navy flames grow into long, winding tendrils. They swim toward Eledar. "But I can easily change that."

Eledar tugs onto his feet. His knees shake, but he holds himself tall. "I won't tell you anything."

"Then, I have to kill you."

He lifts his chin. "So be it."

Aquim tilts his head. "I must say, I'm surprised. I thought you cared about Vellene."

Eledar chills.

Aquim leans toward Eledar and lowers his voice. "She's a Winloc, Golem. Did you think I wasn't watching her? That I didn't know where she was the entire time she 'ran away'?"

"But you didn't know I was a Golem." Eledar looks at him, incredulous.

A wide, winning smile tugs across Aquim's face.

Eledar shuts his eyes and takes in a ragged, tortured breath. He was bluffing.

Aquim laughs. "She's been uncharacteristically obedient since she got back. Chemi don't just change." He frowns then. "I suppose I'll need to kill her, too." Then, low enough no one in the crowd can hear. "Although, I've been planning that for quite some time now. I guess I should thank you for providing me with a public and valid reason to do so."

"No." Eledar goes rigid. Chemight flashes to life in his palms. "Don't hurt her. It's my fault she's involved."

Aquim's features slither into contentment—a look of victory. "What exactly is my daughter involved in?" His chemight probes against Eledar's face, slinks toward his nostrils, his ears.

Eledar flinches from the mist, but it's no use. Aquim closes a gloved fist, and the chemight shoots into him. He coughs and stumbles back.

Aquim turns to face the crowd. "Let's give this Golem a proper Scorian welcome, shall we?"

The crowd bursts into applause, and Aquim grins.

Eledar sinks to his knees. He clasps his head, eyes wide as his life flashes before him. Bodies and death and betrayal. He squeezes his eyes shut. "It's not real it's not real it's not real it's not real."

"Oh, trust me, Golem—this is as real as it gets," he growls. Aquim stoops down to his ear. "The visceral, unrelenting pain of every failure, every hopeless dream for a better future." He digs his fingers into Eledar's wound, pulling out a glob of mud and letting it seep between his fingers with a cruel smile. "Enjoy the past. Until I'm done with you, it'll be all you have."

# Chapter Twenty-Five

## Two Years Before

# *Eledar*

The shambles of Frales rattle with an explosion. Eledar ducks into a tunnel and waves Niam forward.

Soffesa's father takes precarious steps. The fire of his orange eyes is long ago darkened with the deaths of his wife and son. His face is haggard, older from the weight of the pain—a constant reminder that this is it.

Niam is all Eledar has left to save.

"Eledar," he says, voice scratchy and raw from weeks without proper nutrients.

"Don't say my name like that." Eledar grabs the chemi's bicep and throws them both to the wall of the tunnel as a blast of chemight barrels forward. It slices in an iridescent purple—a formulary.

*Not good*, Eledar thinks. He swallows and tugs Niam around a corner and out of the tunnel.

At first, a stroll through Frales meant setting off mines, stepping over body parts, wondering if the black puddles on the ground were melted tar from a shard storm or pools of blood. Now, it's smoke and ruins. Chemibreakers hunt. Scraps and Golem scream. There are rumors of a resistance group forcing Imperials back, claiming the shore of Frales as a refuge. Eledar hopes to get Niam there. They're out of formularies, just like the rest of Frales, and Eledar has no way to continue shielding their shack.

"*Eledar*," Niam tries again. Alchemight's three moons light up the ruins of Frales.

"My name is not a goodbye." Eledar pulls them down into a crouch beside the crumbled remnants of a Scrap shack. "So quit saying it like one."

Niam shakes. "You need to leave me. Get yourself to safety."

Eledar turns to face the chemi. His eyes sink to the place on Niam's side that gushes blood. "Guardians help us," he murmurs.

"Eledar."

He scowls, prepared to argue, but as he meets the chemi's dimming eyes he remembers there's never an end to time, only lives. "Don't you dare," he growls, grasping Niam's face and giving it a shake. "Four years I've kept you alive and kicking. Four. Years."

"And I'm grateful. Eternally." Niam manages a pained smile. "You got Soffesa out. Now, that's all that matters. My life is a worthy sacrifice to keep my daughter safe."

"She'll never forgive me," Eledar whispers. Already the deaths of Soffesa's brother and mother weigh his conscious. He can't take on a third. Not Niam's. *Not Niam*, he begs.

"I don't have much time." Niam settles against a wooden crate propped against the debris, one of his hands pushed against his wound. It does little to nothing as blood rushes between his fingers.

"Don't talk like that." Eledar places a hand over Niam's, putting all his weight into stopping the wound from leaking any further. Instead, blood runs sticky into Eledar's palm. "I will kill every Imperial," he promises between gritted teeth, anger ripping through him.

Niam's breath runs ragged as he rifles through the pouch at his waist. He fumbles as he pulls out an orb filled with a strange formulary. "Give this to my girl. Promise me."

Eledar sucks in an uneven breath and takes the orb. In it, the formulary flashes auburn with small, golden flecks. "What is it?" he asks, eyeing the orb with curiosity. He swallows and looks down. "Niam?"

The chemi blinks furiously, face twisted in panic and fear. "Eledar." Niam reaches a weak, bloodied hand to Eledar's face and his eyes glimmer with a final flame.

"Son." And it's a goodbye. It's a featherlight whisper among the cries of battle and the thunder of falling buildings. It's a word of gratitude flung into a world filled with too much death.

Eledar catches Niam's hand as it falls from its place on his face. It goes limp between his palms, slipping over the orb nestled there like a final promise.

Niam's body collapses in on itself, gray mist curling into the night and bubbling tar swamping the spot he'd lain.

"Goodbye," Eledar whispers and his last reason to remain in Frales fades into the night.

## Chapter Twenty-Six

### Present Day

# *Vellene*

"How do you know where a great place is in Scorus?" Vellene asks as Kadir tugs her along.

"I make it a point to know great places." He pulls them into Scrap territory.

Recognition fills her. "This great place wouldn't happen to be a tavern, would it?"

"Why? You know it?" His brow twitches with apprehension.

"Don't look so surprised. I get out," she says. When she forced an escape. Takes on a death oath. Seduces a Golem. A nervous laugh leaves her, and she yanks her wrist from him and crosses her arms. "Don't pretend like you know me."

Kadir nods, pries her hands into his, and walks her to the porch of The Bloody Cloth. "You're right. I can only imagine what judgments you hold of me."

She stares at the tavern. *Eledar.*

"Nothing?" Kadir's smile falters.

Vellene turns her attention to him, fishing herself back to the present. "You're something, for sure."

He nods, eyes to the sky as he mulls it over. "I guess something is better than nothing, and nothing would be a great shame."

Vellene stares at those doors. She can almost taste the brew. Taste Eledar. She swallows. "Are we going in?"

Kadir grins. "Well, we've come all this way." He drags her up the porch and through the swinging doors. "Besides, I want to hear all your secrets."

Her eyes survey the dark tavern. The symphonic sets up on the stage. Some Scraps mingle about the tables, but it's not quite late enough for full-on festivities. She bites her lip, but she spies no familiar emerald eyes.

"You want a brew?" Kadir asks.

She nods absentmindedly.

"Okay, want to grab a table?"

"Actually, I'm going to use the bathroom." She eyes the staircase.

A shadow stands on the third step.

Kadir brushes his fingers against hers, then he moves to the bar.

Vellene makes a beeline for the stairs. She pulls onto the first step. "Eledar?" She fills with so much want and hope at the idea of seeing him, even when another part of her wishes to torture him for using her, manipulating her. She struggles between the two emotions, but her small smile dies when the shadow draws back a hood.

"Oh." Vellene stares at Soffesa.

Soffesa scoffs. "What? I'm no good?"

She peers around the assassin. "Where is he?"

The Silent scowls. "I thought you knew."

Vellene narrows her eyes on Soffesa's face. Welts of blue and black are painted across the assassin's un-inked cheek. "Are those bruises?" She looks at the way The Silent holds all her weight on her left leg. "Are you hurt?"

Soffesa's face softens from her usual scrutiny and into worry. "You really don't know?"

"What?" Vellene stares at her. "What don't I know?"

"Vellene?" Kadir's voice startles her.

She swivels around. He stands at the bottom of the stairs, brows furrowed and a mug of brew in each hand. "Kadir." She shifts her weight. "Um, this is—" She glances behind her, but Soffesa is gone, the stairs empty.

Kadir peers into the dark.

"Sorry, I think that transport formulary of yours messed with my head," Vellene says and feigns dizziness. She feels ridiculous as she white knuckles the banister, but she has no other idea to cover the truth.

His face softens. "Oh." He glances down at his full hands, then looks around for a place to set the mugs. He leans to a nearby table, drops them, then steps to her. "May I?"

Vellene clutches his shoulders. Pretends to be off-balance with a soft sway. Her fingers dig against the coarse muscle beneath the thin fabric of his shirt, her eyes dipping to his from where he stands below her. Her breath catches, his face open and raw as he looks up at her. They inhale at the same time, their eyes combing each other with matched wariness. It's then she knows he must feel it, too. A connection. Her core tightens.

"I'm okay," she whispers, but he wraps a tight arm around her.

Gently he lifts her from the stairs and settles her into a chair. Then he kneels and presses a hand to her forehead, concern etched across his face.

She watches him watch her, and for a moment, she relishes it. Being taken care of. Then comes guilt. She tenderly removes his hand from her forehead. "You know, after how my father treated you—after how I treated you—I figured you'd never be this nice to me."

Kadir lifts from the floor and settles into the chair across from her. His face flickers with the darkness he keeps at bay. "I don't believe kindness should be rare."

She tilts her head. "You're different."

He grins and leans back into the chair. "Don't worry, love. I can still pester you if you'd like."

"It's just—" Vellene stumbles for the right words. She thinks of how he let her stab him, of the way he smiled against the chaos formulary. "How can you be so trusting of me? We barely know each other," she whispers, searching his eyes for some sign of his allegiance.

"I think we know each other better than you think." Kadir lowers his voice and leans his chin into his fist. His gaze betrays nothing but an intense, genuine openness. It's like she's seeing him truly for the first time. "Fathers with the inclination to have power above all else. Growing up among a society of the brainwashed." His face hardens. "A loneliness no other could ever comprehend."

She measures her breaths, weighs his words.

He runs an idle finger over the scar on his neck. "You had something to tell me, Vellene. On the float."

She looks down at her hands. "It's dangerous for you to get involved."

"Hey."

She hesitates but lifts her gaze to his.

"You can trust me." His lips curve into a soft smile, his dimples dark in the low light of The Bloody Cloth. "I understand you. I see you."

A certain validation fills her. She sucks in a breath as it warms her. It's new, almost unrecognizable, but it's—wonderful. She matches his smile. "I see you, too." And she thinks she does. This him, here in this tavern, is real. The smile, the nerves, the want to soothe her. He cares more than he lets on.

Kadir adjusts in his seat, folds his hands on the table, and stares at his thumbs. Vulnerability fills his features, an emotion he's quick to hide, but she memorizes it, takes solace in it. He clears his throat, swallowing and fixing his face into a careful mask of calm. "Why can't you leave Scorus, love?"

She sucks in a breath, scans The Bloody Cloth for Soffesa. What would the assassin think of her revealing their plan to a Rathmore?

The symphonic starts. The tavern fills.

"We'll be seen," she says, and her muscles tense.

Kadir frowns but pushes from the table and offers his arm. "We should get back. Before they worry too much or disturb these lovely Scraps' night of indulgence, anyway. We can talk on the way."

Vellene accepts his arm and loops her hand into the crook of it. As they walk to the door, she glances back at the stairs, but she finds them empty. Some part of her thought Eledar would come after her, but she wonders if there was more truth to his words than he said there was. *Actions*, she reminds herself. Words are pretty, but actions speak far louder. Kadir may be cold, but he's never forced her to do something she hadn't wanted to.

She tightens her grip as he leads her outside. A frigid chill curls around them as they sweep down onto the street, and Kadir shivers. His arm shakes with the cold, and she watches him closely. She expects regret, to find those masks slipping away to anger over giving a Scrap his cloak.

Instead, he returns her curious gaze with something warm and affectionate, his lips tipping up with a small smile. "At least that Scrap won't freeze to death."

Without a thought, she unhooks her arm from his—

"What are—"

—and wraps it around his waist. She pulls him close, the chill between them forcing sharp inhales among the already frigid night.

Kadir trips over himself, a look of surprise on his face as he looks down at her. He chokes on his embarrassment and cocks a brow.

Vellene grins, stifling a laugh behind her clenched teeth. She gives his side a squeeze, and he flinches. The strange cold of their touch binds around them, but unlike Scorus, she finds that sense of comfort again. "You seem nervous," she notes.

Kadir clears his throat. "I'm not great at this. I don't exactly have much company in Frales."

She narrows her eyes. "I thought you were everybody's type?"

Kadir shrugs and gives her a humored smile.

"So, is this you?" she wonders, eyes tracing that smile. Those dimples. She shivers.

Kadir's face darkens in habit. "I wish."

She frowns, his answer drawing more questions. "Since we're alone—"

His lips curl. "I like the beginning of that sentence."

She knocks her shoulder into his. Her cheeks heat. "I'm trying to be serious."

"Why? It's so dull." Kadir slows their steps.

Vellene bites her lip. "What happened to you?"

The muscles along his arm tighten. "What do you mean?"

"You were supposed to be dead," she says. Then, quieter, "and your scars?"

Kadir glances down at her. His violet eyes harden, and his jaw clenches. He grimaces, every ounce of his brief happiness wiped away.

She immediately regrets asking, but at the same time, if she's going to trust him, then she needs to know him. "If you can't answer that, then can you at least tell me why you're siding with me? Why you never killed me?"

Kadir stops and turns to her. For a moment, he says nothing. His eyes trace her face, but his mouth twists with hesitation. He wavers but offers, "You're not what I expected, Vellene Winloc."

"Neither are you," she admits. Her arm falls from his waist, but he catches it and gives it a soft tug. Vellene takes a careful step forward. "What is it?"

Kadir holds onto her arm, channeling a deep chill beneath her skin as he runs his thumb along it. Then, he inhales, his eyes glistening in the moonlight, and hooks her arm around his neck. He takes her waist and clasps her other hand in his free palm.

Vellene recognizes the embrace as he pulls her toward him—the starting position of an Imperial dance. "What's happening?" she asks.

Kadir gives her a playful grin and pushes her into the first steps. "What, you can't hear it?"

She tilts her head, listens. "Hear what?"

"The music?" His grin widens. "It's a tune only for us."

A laugh shocks her when he twirls her, then she falls into his grasp with a heavy exhale. "What does it sound like?"

Kadir ponders it, pretends to listen. His eyes drift to the sky, then back to hers. He holds her gaze, and he drags her closer until her stomach presses against his.

He studies her face, and his smile fades into something relaxed and thoughtful. "It's sad and dark," he whispers. "But it picks up." He forces them into a quicker pace. "It picks up into an elegant rhythm of hope and brightness."

"It sounds beautiful," Vellene says softly, face tipped toward his as they dance.

Her father. Her death oath. Every obligation fades as she stares at him, sees herself in the hopeful glint of his eyes, the sad smile of his lips.

"It is beautiful." His eyes trace her face, linger on her lips. "More beautiful than I ever knew a song could be," he mutters.

Their dance turns into a sway—a tempo that's patient. Worthwhile.

"And it's ours?" she asks him, uncertain.

Kadir blinks and levels his gaze with hers. "All ours."

A blush sneaks up on her, colors her cheeks, tangles with the ink of her Imperial crest across her chest. Vellene looks away, stares at the pavement. Her fingers play with the hair at the nape of his neck, her thoughts wandering to the last arms she was held in. Her face twists in discomfort as Eledar's goodbye echoes through her mind, slithers through her veins. She hates that it poisons this. That she allows it to poison this. Anger thrums through her but so does wariness.

She was so quick to be lured in by Eledar's charm, so desperate to know his touch. She fiddles with her lip, her brows drawn. Does it make her naive to trust again? Or is having the capability to openly trust the one thing keeping her from tipping into the darkness?

Kadir gently takes her chin. He moves her face back to his, everything about his expression drooped with worry. "What did I say?"

Vellene shakes her head. "Nothing wrong."

"I can sense that's not true."

She clutches the back of his neck and sucks in a breath. "There was someone else. It's part of what I wanted to tell you."

Kadir lets go of her chin. His fingers slide from the base of her neck and rest on her shoulder. There's a tremble to his movements as if he's readying to break away from her. "Was?"

She could tell him no. Tell him Eledar is still part of her future, still sticks to her dreams at night. She could close off their connection and build an alliance based on mutual friendship. But inside her is a desire she can't say no to.

With Eledar, it was a spark.

With Kadir, it's a flood.

A flood of being seen, truly seen. Of having a future that isn't one-sided but reciprocated. *A future.* One away from her father. She brings her eyes to his, finds a question there. He wants her. She can see it in the way he looks at her, feel it in the way his heart pounds against her chest.

How is it even a question? Eledar forced her into a death oath. No matter his apology or their connection, she knows she deserves more than that—even if everything in her life has told her the opposite. She lifts her chin in resolution, her heart set on claiming something that's her own. Not a fabricated choice by the manipulations of others, but something of hers she can hold onto until the end. "Was," she whispers.

Relief passes over his features. Kadir moves his hand from her waist to her back. He wets his lips, and his dimples deepen with a nervous smile. Much like everything else tonight, his expression is pure and honest. No hidden agendas. No snide comments or smirks.

"Would it be okay," he asks, voice low, "if I kissed you then, love?"

Vellene grins. It's the first time he's called her 'love' that it hasn't sounded like a threat or a joke. Its sincerity drives her fingers to tangle into his hair and grip the back of his head. She tugs him toward her, and Kadir's violet eyes glitter in victory.

Then he lowers, his dimples never leaving as he dips his lips to hers. It's a soft, careful kiss. Timid in the best way.

Vellene melts toward him, and their muscles tense in unison, eyes squeezed shut. It's everything she wishes her kiss with Eledar was. Her stomach flutters as he clutches the fabric at her waist and presses closer. The tension in his shoulders and arms lessens when she moves her hands to the sides of his face, runs her thumbs along the outline of his jaw. Ice wraps around her, funnels into her veins, and douses every flame and flicker of pain.

They stay like that, lips pressed together, bodies intertwined for ten heartbeats. And, for a moment, Vellene swears she hears it—the tune of their song.

It's sad. She breaks from him, stares at him in awe. But it's the kind of sad you yearn for. The kind of sad you never want to forget.

She brushes a finger down the length of his scar—from the middle of his forehead to the left side of his jaw. Under Alchemight's moons, it's stark white but hardly sinister. It carves the definite beauty of his face into someone stronger, refined by years of strife. Then she trails her fingers to the scar across his neck.

Kadir sucks in a breath to steady himself, fists clenched into the fabric at her waist. The longer he stares at her, the more his dimples fade. A storm breaks free, shadowing beneath his eyes and drawing together his brows.

"What?" she asks.

He pries his fingers from her waist and pushes her away from him.

"Kadir?" Her eyes search his face. A face as tired and scarred as she feels on the inside. Her heart flutters as she looks at him, really looks at him, and she knows the face she sees now is his true self. No wickedness. No playfulness. Instead, his features drift between disasters. Handsome plains of sorrow, of rage. She wants him to be more than a play in her father's game, more than leverage against her death oath.

"Kadir," she whispers and hovers her lips before his. Any strategic moves she planned implode. What she feels for him isn't desperation. It's respect. The beginning of something solid and real. "I don't care about the scars. I never will."

His breath intertwines with hers. "Maybe you should."

She shakes her head. "You can tell me about them if you want, but it won't bother me either way."

Kadir tucks a strand of hair behind her ear. "I'm going to need you to quit talking to me like that."

Her brow furrows. "Like how?"

"Like you care," he breathes.

"Maybe I do." Vellene drops from her toes, rests her hands on his chest, and clutches the soft fabric of his shirt. "Would that be so bad?"

Kadir's gaze flashes and his face twists with uncertainty.

Vellene lets out an amused snort. "For someone so confident in their ability to make others swoon, you sure seem shocked right now."

Kadir's face brightens. "I admit, I didn't think it would actually work."

"Well, it did. Maybe that makes me a fool—" she worries aloud.

But Kadir covers her comment with another kiss, this one deeper. He drags his teeth over her bottom lip, then smiles against her. "I'd call you anything but a fool, love."

She grabs his shoulders, pulling them into the darkness of an alcove. She wants to forget for a while, and she wants to feel that power again. The confidence that comes with control.

His body tenses, eyes go wide. “What are—”

She covers his mouth with a hand and pushes him to the ground with a wicked smile. Triumph burst through her at the shock in his features as she straddles him, wraps her hands around the back of his head, and pulls his lips to hers. Her heart skips a beat, and she latches to the small bit of confidence she’s been granted.

But Kadir’s breath hitches, and panic flashes through his expression.

Vellene pulls back. For a moment she thinks she imagined it, but then it's there again—a nervous twitch of his left eye. She stares into his eyes, and she immediately lifts from him. "Kadir," she says softly.

His chest dips at the sound of his name. He shakes his head and takes her wrist. "Come back."

But she knows that panic, has felt it every day of her life. He slides into an easy smile, but it doesn't fool her.

His eyes glisten beneath the moonlight, and he inhales deeply. "Love, you shouldn't look so close," he murmurs and pulls her gently back into his lap. "You won't like what you find."

She shakes her head. “Do you want me?”

He lets out a soft groan. His forehead falls against hers, creased in exasperation.

“If you don’t want me, that’s okay.” She tucks one of the loose yellow strands that frame his face behind his ear, and his lips part with a shudder. "We can just sit here for a while."

He blows out a breath and closes his eyes. All of his masks flicker across his face until they wipe away and the only thing left is—

Desire.

Her breath catches as she stares at him, as he stares at her. Alchemight tunnels into darkness around them, until all they can see is each other. "Do you want—"

Kadir crushes his lips against hers. A breath and he encloses her in his arms. He squeezes her tight against him—the kiss not timid or soft, not desperate or hungry. It asks nothing of her in return, demands no response besides her being present and feeling whatever this is with him. Being terrified. Together.

His mouth captures her with a deep, unrivaled passion, both sincere and haunting. It matches the rhythm of their song, the thump of their hearts. He lays back on the gravel and takes her with him, his grasp around her as if she's an anchor to a different life, and he is hers.

Vellene sinks against him and tentatively reaches for the edges of his shirt. She slows when a shudder passes through him. She thought it pleasure at first, but she recognizes it for what it is. She releases his hem and traces her fingers over the fabric. Then she slips from his mouth to his cheek, his neck, pressing small kisses against the tension in his jaw and the pound of his pulse. His breath stutters, and she leans back to watch him, running a finger over the curve of the Ravian wing that slopes down and across his torso, careful to stay above the sheer fabric.

His eyes are closed, his arms still locked around her in a desperate attempt to keep her close. To be safe. But then his lashes flutter open, and when he meets her gaze, she thinks she would burn the realm to erase the pain she sees.

His throat bobs with a hard swallow. Then he offers her a grin and cups her cheek, drawing her mouth back to his. He kisses her with more urgency and takes her hand, directing it back to the hem of his shirt.

They break their kiss for the second it takes to pull it over his head, their chests heaving, before they come back together, thoughts as one, movements fluid.

She almost doesn't see it—the soft shimmer of colored wavelengths curling around them. Her mind can hardly focus on the power gushing in and out between them as it had with Eledar. Instead, she latches to him, runs her fingers down his spine to his waist. She slips them beneath his waistband without shame, too curious not to. Her heart hammers as she slides her palm down the sharp curve of his hip.

Kadir groans and rolls her over, braces his elbows on either side of her face. He deepens the kiss and presses against her. Every movement is jagged with need, his desperation growing like a twin flame to her own. His teeth slide over her ear, her neck as if he's discovering the same freedom she found briefly with Eledar. Then he runs a hand over her corset and fumbles with the strings until they unravel. He tosses them to the side as he moves to its clasp. His movements smooth into a slow rhythm when the corset clicks open, and she gasps at the momentum of air that fills her lungs.

His fingers press against the exposed skin of her back. He moves his free hand to her face, lips parted with a question—as if he isn't sure they should continue, if she wants him to—but Vellene pushes him up from his elbows, moves her lips to his, and flings her corset across the alley.

The soft, sheer fabric of her slip does little to hide her. She expects to feel a flame of embarrassment. Instead, she feels the opposite. Safe—as Kadir runs a hand over her collarbone and deposits. Secure—as he cradles her with an arm, muscles tense and grasp light but firm. Incredible—as his lips follow the trail of his hand, from her chin to her neck to the spideria above her breasts.

"Vellene," he murmurs her name like a prayer and tugs her slip down until her chest is exposed.

She arches into his mouth with a shudder. "Kadir," she answers and tugs him back to her lips, sinking her tongue against his.

He matches her need, his hands tangling into her hair and his hips dropping between her thighs. Then he traces her body with his mouth until he tugs her dress down further, exposing scar after scar. With each he finds, he kisses in remorse, his eyes filled with the understanding he promised and not the pity she despises. When he reaches the fire wound on her stomach from their fight, he wields the softest pink of a remedial formulary and drifts his fingers over the jagged, ugly scar. The itch of the wound soothes, and he presses a long kiss to it.

"I'm so sorry," he whispers.

Vellene shakes her head, unable to find the words to tell him not to be. She arches her back toward him, stretches her arms above her head. Her eyelids flutter shut. Every press of his lips against her skin sends a tingle through her. She no longer feels the cold air that tunnels through the alley and wraps around them. Just his chill. Her fire. The rush of power passing between his orbs and her own.

He kisses his way back to her lips, breath hot and heavy. "Moan for me, love," and his hand slides up her inner thigh. "Come undone with me." The words are a ragged request.

Vellene smiles against his kiss and moves her fingers to the clasp of his pants. Her heart races as they give away to a soft click, her hand—

A scream unfurls through her skull, tears through every ounce of her being, and the chemight wrapped around them in iridescent coils shatters.

# Chapter Twenty-Seven

## Eight Years Before

# *Eledar*

Around him, Golem lay about, chests rising and falling. Most curl into each other upon the stone floor, seeking warmth against the winter's chill. It's a necessity in their stone prison. Without a roof, they must shield themselves from the elements.

He blinks a few times, eyes adjusting to the dark.

"Eledar," a young, feminine voice hisses.

"What?" he asks, voice groggy. He swivels his head around to the grate in the wall.

Two orange eyes and a half-inked face are lit beyond its bars.

He pushes up from the ground and tiptoes around Golem, careful not to step on someone or to wake the Imperial on watch. He reaches the grate and grips the bars, pulling onto a crate often used as a stool. "What are you doing here?"

Soffesa's small face widens with a smile.

Closer now, he can make out cuts across her non-inked cheek, bruises along her neck. The cloak around her shoulders is a simple patchwork of rags all sewn together. Grease slicks the orange of her hair into a darker auburn. Her nostrils flare, and her eyes widen. "I'm breaking you out, Golem boy."

Eledar glances behind him, worries his lip. "I could get in trouble," he whispers.

"Aren't you always in trouble?"

"My Master could have me beaten."

"Aren't you always beaten?"

Eledar bites his tongue and looks back at the assassin-in-training. He met her a week ago, and since then she's done everything she can to befriend him—even despite his reluctance. He doesn't understand why, only that she may feel as lonely as he does.

Soffesa pushes her thin hand between the bars and flicks his forehead.

"Ow," he growls and swats her away. "Don't do that."

"Then don't be boring." She bends, disappearing from his view for a moment. Then she pops back up with a hook attached to a long rope in her hands. "I'll throw the hook over the wall. Catch it, so it doesn't make any noise, then hook it to these bars. I'll hold onto the rope and keep it still so you can climb up and over." She takes a few steps back and twirls the hook and rope. "Ready?" Her tongue sticks out in concentration.

Eledar tucks his hair behind his ears. "No."

Soffesa grins, then sends the hook flying.

He curses under his breath and throws his arms up. The hook descends from their roofless prison. It plummets toward the stone wall, inches from clattering against it and waking the rest of the Golem. He heaves a breath, jumps, and snatches the hook before it can do so. It scratches into his palm, and he hisses in pain as clay seeps free.

"C'mon," Soffesa insists. "Hook it here." She grips the rope in one hand and motions to the bars with the other.

Eledar hooks it slowly, careful not to clang its prongs against the iron bars. Once it's leveraged, Soffesa tugs on the rope, securing the hook in place. She nods to him. "Okay, now climb."

Excitement courses through him. He grips the rope and pulls back on it, pushing one foot into the wall to start his ascent.

Soffesa groans on the other side. "Abyss, lay off the stews, will ya?"

Eledar bites his tongue against a laugh and pulls himself up. He's halfway when a body rustles below. He stiffens, eyes wide as he looks down.

The Imperial on watch wakes in her chair in the corner. She clears her throat and stands to survey the Golem.

Eledar holds his breath, then realizes she can't see him. Not unless she looks up. Muscles in his arms and legs throbbing, he cautiously takes another step up the wall. Too afraid to breathe, too afraid to move any faster, he continues forward. One more, he thinks. He will make it. Just one more step.

He plants his feet, lifts a hand for the lip of the wall—

The rope slackens, and Soffesa curses on the other side.

Eledar fumbles, losing his foothold and grip. He cries out as he falls and slams into the stone floor with a loud crack. If he had a spine, it'd be broken.

Golem rise from sleep in shock. The Imperial charges toward him. "The abyss do you think you're doing?" she shouts at him.

Eledar coughs and struggles onto his elbows. He glances to the bars and catches sight of a blur of orange—Soffesa darting off into the dark. He scowls and looks up at the Imperial, just as a chemight leash sprawls from her palm. "No," he says, breathless as he scrambles back.

But the leash whips forward and winds around his neck, the chemight a visceral emerald in the night. The Imperial pulls it taut and tugs him to his feet. She forces him through the crowd of waking Golem and marches him to the exit of the prison. "If you didn't want punishment, you should have thought about that before you tried to escape."

"I wasn't," Eledar tries.

The Imperial laughs. "Do you think I'm a fool?" She slams open the door and thrusts him outside before locking it shut and dragging him toward Rathmore Manor.

Eledar swallows hard against the leash. He sucks in a breath and summons his natural chemight—his formularies taken from him after he finished his shift cleaning the property. Gray mist pours from his palms.

The Imperial glances back, and her face twists with disapproval. "Golem," she curses and uses her free hand to wield a second formulary. It slings outward in a zap of red, then captures his hands in a weaponized remedial formulary. The chemight spreads over them until it encases every finger, both palms, and his wrists, his natural chemight sputtering out in defeat. "You'll pay for that, too," she promises.

"Tella," a low male voice says from the shadows of the manor's front porch. A long, lanky body creeps out of the dark until Alchemight's three moons set the dark plum of his suit ablaze in a lilac sheen. Golden hair waves down the chemi's neck, his violet eyes drifting from the Imperial guard to Eledar.

Eledar fumbles against Tella's formularies to drop down to a knee. He lowers his head in a bow. "Sir Rathmore," he says, unable to keep the venom out of the words.

"Kid tried to escape," Tella explains. The Imperial straightens but gives a small bow of her head to her leader.

Lazar prowls down the steps of the manor, his stride strong and confident as he approaches Tella and Eledar. He stops before Eledar and reaches a single finger below his chin, lifting Eledar's face toward his. "Rise, Golem."

Eledar stands. His eyes dart to his left and right, searching with hope for a head of orange hair among the shadows.

"He tried to climb over the wall," Tella says. "I didn't catch the Scrap helping him."

Lazar steps back and looks Eledar up and down. "And why would you try to run?" He tilts his head. "You know it would do no good." His lips curl into a lazy smile. "All I have to do is tell you to *break*."

TUG—and a bone he doesn't have—a bone imagined by his Maker and Master—cracks inside Eledar. A strangled cry bursts from him as he falls back down to his knees.

"Break," Lazar purrs.

TUG—and Eledar's arm twists against Tella's chemight restraint, snapping at the elbow.

"Or I could say no demand." Lazar picks at a fingernail, his expression unmovable from a cold hardness. "And have you guess what happens next." The violet of his eyes brightens.

TUG—and Eledar's unbroken arm scrapes free from Tella's weaponized formulary, his natural gray chemight rising from his palm into the sharp shape of a shard. His will turned against him by Lazar, Eledar plunges the shard into Tella's neck.

"No," Eledar cries. His hand shakes as Tella's blood pours out and over his knuckles in waves of black. It sputters between her lips, her scream strangled as Lazar forces him to tear the blade free.

Tella falls to the ground, her body writhing as she scrambles for a breath. The chemight leash and cuffs she holds on Eledar vanish.

Lazar steps to her. He flicks his gaze to Eledar. "I don't like being disappointed."

Eledar trembles as he stares at Tella's lifeless body. He's been pulled every which way, but murder was never one of them. Lazar releases his hold, and Eledar immediately douses his chemight, the gray shard drifting apart into hundreds of small sparks. He drops beside Tella and clasps his hands over her neck. Her blood seeps slow and thick.

"She's dead, Golem."

Eledar presses harder. He grits his teeth.

Lazar grasps his shoulder and wrenches him back. "Enough," his Master demands.

Mist steams from Tella as her skin droops and drags into tar.

"She will return to the mist and tar she came from," Lazar says, his voice cut with less of an edge but sharpened nonetheless.

Eledar clenches his fists, Tella's blood trapped beneath his nails, tacked between his fingers.

"Her soul will continue to the next life." Lazar lets go of him. "But her chemight belongs to Dalbian's Abyss." He tugs on Eledar's strings as he walks to the porch.

Eledar clenches his fists, tries not to follow his Master, but his feet don't belong to him. They never will.

Lazar settles into a wooden chair on the porch and forces Eledar to stop at the bottom of the steps. "From mist and tar, we came. Of mist and tar, we are. For mist and tar, we live. All of it—power."

He locks his gaze with Eledar's. "But you are nothing but clay and chemight. Power diluted by command. You will never be a full chemi, no matter how much you may wish. You may think yourself brave. You may think yourself worthy of more. But you are what I say you are. When you die, you will return to the mound of mud you came from. Your soul will not carry on. Your chemight will not return to Alchemight. You serve no greater purpose during your life, and that will continue beyond your death."

Lazar leans forward, face stern. "I repeat, Golem: you are nothing. To think yourself more is to be melted down and made into a more obedient slave. Do you understand?"

Eledar manages a grim nod.

"Good." Lazar sits back and crosses his long legs in satisfaction. "Then you will walk yourself back to your prison, you will sleep through the night, and you will wake in the morning to continue your duties." His violet eyes sharpen. "You will do it all without being forced because you will carry with you for the rest of your useless life the truth."

His teeth glitter in the moonlight, as sharp as any predator's. "For mist and tar, my kind lives. For mist and tar, your kind will forever serve."

# Chapter Twenty-Eight

## Present Day

## *Vellene*

Vellene jolts upright. She grasps her head as shock pricks down her spine.

Kadir picks himself off her, his face moving from worry to alarm as she rakes in heavy gasps of air. "What?" He kneels beside her. He fastens his pants, then picks up her slip and corset from the ground, helping her cover herself. "What's wrong?"

A second scream rings inside Vellene. It's deep, guttural, and this time, pain accompanies it. She grinds her teeth, squeezes her eyes shut.

"Vellene, you're scaring me." Kadir pulls her to his bare chest, tucking his arms around her.

"Abyss," she curses, "I don't know what's happening. I think—"

The third scream confirms it. *Eledar*.

She scrambles out of Kadir's arms and yanks on her slip. Her heartbeat thrums to a newfound panic at the scream's bravado, its familiarity. She doesn't bother pulling her gown back on or trying to fasten the corset. She tears her cloak from the ground, steps out of her gown, and shivers in her slip.

Vellene moves into a sprint as Soffesa's words from The Bloody Cloth come back to haunt her. A fourth scream rushes through her, spirals into her toes. She picks up her pace, arms pumping, legs throbbing with each slam of her feet against the pavement.

"Vellene!" Kadir shouts after her. He chases close behind, pulling on his shirt as he goes.

Her mind seeps back toward his arms, and a sharp sense of dread curls through her at the thought of never being back in them again. She glances over her shoulder. "I need to get back," she calls, not stopping as a fifth scream occurs, fainter than the others as if Eledar fades somewhere past the point of return.

She charges through the streets, breaths ragged as she passes through the Imperial Gates. A crowd of Imperials and Chemibreakers stand at the edge of Winloc Grove. They face the prison.

Vellene shoves her way through until she reaches the front. Everything in her stills at the sight of her father's sword. The sword that severed the heads of the Vonners and Pineskys. The sword that was never wiped clean of blood. The sword that now drips with globs of clay.

Aquim's knuckles are white around the blade's hilt. In his opposite hand, he wields the tight navy ball of a chaos formulary. It's her father's favorite, and as it seeps in long tendrils into Eledar's head, Aquim smiles.

Eledar sits upon his knees on the ground, head down, arms outspread with a chemight lasso attached to each wrist. Chemibreakers hold the formularies, keeping Eledar from making any sudden moves. Clay drips in globs from his face. His shirt and orbs are removed, his torso sliced and cut, mud seeping out.

Vellene's lips part to say his name. Her muscles beg to drop to his side, hold him, shield him from Aquim's blows. But she's no idea why he's been caught, and she can't alert her father to their involvement. Anger surges through her. "What is this?" she shrieks, eyes wild with fear.

Aquim releases the chaos formulary and turns toward his daughter.

Eledar snaps his head up in the same instant. He rakes in heavy, sorrowful breaths until he sees her. The dark emerald of his eyes brightens for a split second, but then it all falls. His brow furrows in anger, his eyes fill with regret, his lips part with the beginning of an apology. Angry at himself.

Her heart beats a frantic rhythm.

Aquim rolls his shoulders back. “This Golem threatened our well-being—your well-being.” He gnashes his teeth. “He’s tried to steal our power from us.”

Vellene fights the urge to roll her eyes. Her father’s reasoning is for the sake of the gathered crowd. Aquim would never care about her well-being. She pushes back her fury and moves her features into confusion. “A Golem? He just looks like a Scrap.”

Several in the crowd nod their agreement. A few even scoff, downing a lilac-colored brew with annoyance. Tonight was meant to be nothing more than a mindless parade. Now, it’s a Golem being reaped of his chemight. *Inconvenient*, their eyes seem to say.

Aquim’s navy gaze narrows with rage. “He's a threat.”

“What proof do you have?” Kadir steps through the crowd and places himself next to her. His voice slices through the tension. He pieced himself back together—hair smoothed back and face manipulated into a hard expression of stone. He doesn’t glance her way. Instead, he focuses his attention on Aquim, eyes cold and deadly.

Aquim straightens. “Rathmore, you don't need to worry about this trivial matter.”

“If it's so trivial, then why do you beat this chemi to a pulp in your yard?” Kadir’s brow knits together. He gestures to Eledar. “This is cruel, Winloc. If he's a threat, then he can be executed. No one deserves this humiliation unless they've made an active attempt against your life, and even then, it's archaic." He rolls into a confident chuckle. "Please, Aquim. How much harm can he do locked in your prison, anyway? Surely you don't want such a meaningless creature to ruin tonight's celebration."

Vellene stares at Kadir, sure her father will kill him where he stands. *I'll miss you.*

But a brief flash of embarrassment crosses her father's face, and he clears his throat, his chemight disappearing. He adjusts his cloak but grasps his sword tighter and lifts his chin. "This is below me." He glares at Eledar. "Execution is all this thing deserves."

Kadir offers her an encouraging smile. He slips his hand into hers and gives it a small squeeze.

Vellene blushes, then panics.

Eledar stares at their intertwined hands. He grimaces and plasters his eyes to the ground.

Vellene swallows and wrenches her hand from Kadir's. He tenses as she does so, but she ignores him and steps toward Aquim. "Father, why don't we go inside? Kadir and I had a nice evening and—"

"Yes, you ran away again." Aquim's anger returns with ease. He clenches his jaw, then kicks dirt at Eledar.

Eledar coughs, spits.

"Cage the animal," Aquim sneers toward his Chemibreakers. He shoves past the crowd and walks toward the house.

Vellene follows, Kadir in tow. She glances back toward Eledar. *I'll be back for you*, she wants to tell him, to at least make a notion toward, but he keeps his gaze to the ground, lips pressed together.

Kadir matches her stride. "How do you know him?" he asks, voice low.

She grits her teeth and puts his question to the side. "Thank you. Aquim never would have listened to me." She looks at Kadir.

His face is solemn, a certain resignation in the way his eyes stare ahead. He gives her the smallest nod of acknowledgment.

Vellene heaves a breath and turns her gaze to her father's figure as they walk inside. She thinks back to her brief exchange with Soffesa, to the assassin's limp and bruises.

"I need to get back to Frales."

Vellene stops her chase after her father and turns to Kadir.

He rubs the back of his neck. "We can stay until The Drinking, but we leave the morning after."

Vellene hesitates, then touches his bicep. "I may need to stay longer. I know I should've explained, but we got…distracted."

Kadir folds his arms and clenches his jaw.

She shakes her head and steps close to him. "I'm sorry. It's just that the Golem is—"

Kadir pushes her hand off him and takes a step back. "Attend to your business, Vellene," he cuts her off. He takes another step backward, expression schooled into indifference, then turns and leaves. He hurries back to the guest room without another word.

She stands there, scowling in confusion, hand left mid-air where he pushed it.

"Vellene?"

She startles and pivots to find Uzax. They stand with their hands clasped before them, their eyes concerned. She blows out a breath and drops her hand. "What do you know?"

"They snuck in. Were after the pouch mentioned in their letter. My brother, niece, and The Silent got away." Uzax frowns. "Aquim and Eledar—well, you saw."

She presses her lips together. "Wait for my say, then come to my room."

Uzax nods. "I will."

"Thank you." She shakes her head. "Oh, and do me a favor?"

Uzax rolls their shoulders back. "Sure."

"Kadir Rathmore is in our guest room." She gestures down the hall. "I need you to guard him."

Uzax looks down the hall. "Is he in danger?"

Vellene scowls and crosses her arms. "Under my father's roof? With Eledar captured and being forced to tell Aquim only the Guardians know what?" She chews on her lip. "We all are."

## Chapter Twenty-Nine

### Present Day

# *Eledar*

Aquim's gloved fist wrenches around Eledar's neck before he thrusts Eledar to the stone floor of the Winloc prison. Two figures stand on either side of him. The first is Mogaell, Vellene's younger sister and a spitting image of Aquim. The other is an imposter in the disguise of Vellene's Surveillant—the dead Surveillant. Both wear matching scowls, expressions dark as Aquim kicks Eledar in the side.

Eledar grunts but remains somewhat upright. He spits out a mouthful of clay and smiles at Aquim. "I knew you were greedy, Winloc, but this is just plain desperate."

Aquim growls and slams his boot into Eledar's ribs a second time.

He falters but clenches his fists. Natural chemight steams from his battered and bruised fists.

"Careful, Golem. Dirty chemight gets you executed," Idus warns. He stares at Eledar with a disturbing set of eyes—white through and through. The only evidence of pupils is a pair of off-white smudges.

Eledar merely smiles at the Surveillant.

"I'm bored, father," Mogaell complains. She taps her foot for emphasis.

"As am I," Aquim agrees. He yanks him upward. "I made it clear Vellene's life depends on your transparency. So, I will only ask once more. When does my eldest plan to assassinate us?"

Eledar steadies himself with a shallow breath.

"Mogaell," Aquim demands.

The younger Winloc steps forward. With a flick of her wrist, something dark pools into her palm. It doesn't sparkle or drift forward as natural chemight or a formulary would. Instead, it glistens with darkness.

Eledar tugs back, but Aquim's grip tightens on his shirt collar. "What the abyss is that?"

"The abyss precisely, Golem," Aquim answers.

Mogaell's lips thin into a sharp smile.

"Give me something," Aquim continues, "or I will have my daughter fill you with tar."

Eledar's eyes narrow on Mogaell's mass of slick black chemight.

She turns her wrist in a slow half-circle, and her power slithers forward, the navy of her eyes darkening to an endlessly cold black.

Eledar's own chemight rises. It curls to his biceps and drifts forward, reaching tentatively toward hers. Then it snaps back and panic laces through him. Her tar slinks toward his mouth, his nose, his ears. "She'll kill me, and you'll know nothing," he growls at Aquim.

Aquim pulls his snarl down to Eledar. "When will my eldest strike?"

Mogaell's chemight presses between his lips. He wrenches away, but it weights his tongue, carves down his throat. Eledar chokes and her eyes glisten with sick triumph.

Idus takes a step forward. He gestures with slight alarm toward Eledar. "He's our only source," the Surveillant reminds them. "We cannot kill him yet."

Aquim grimaces but raises a fist.

The motion halts Mogaell, and she gives her arm a small tug backward. Her strange chemight flies out of Eledar's mouth and sinks into her palm.

"When will my daughter attack?" Aquim presses.

Eledar looks between the three of them.

"Tell me, Golem, or I promise the next hit will be to Vellene."

Eledar sucks in a breath, then looks to the floor. His face tightens. His stomach twists. "The Drinking."

Aquim straightens. He glares at Eledar. "You'll rot in this cell for committing treason. As will my daughter."

Eledar strains to his knees. “Hurt her, and it will be the last thing you ever do,” he threatens, but Aquim and Mogaell already have their backs turned. Idus trails after them.

The false Surveillant glances back for a moment before the stone door of the prison slides shut, and the harsh glimmer of electric wards wraps around the entire building. They thrum against the walls, then climb around the bars of Eledar’s cell. As they lock in place, the chemight cuffed around his wrists vanishes.

He stares into the dark before he slams his fist into concrete again and again, the rage that leaves him echoing between stone.

## Chapter Thirty

# *Vellene*

Vellene stares out her window at the prison where Chemibreakers stand guard. Alchemight's sun pinches into its nightly moons. The landscape falls into an eerie light. Trees of shadows. Flora of a dark valley. Spideria scramble across stonework.

She presses her cheek to her window and waits.

Aquim steps out from their chateau and crosses the yard. Chemight streams from his knuckles as he forces his way past the Chemibreakers guarding the prison and inside to Eledar. It's the only thing that tells her Eledar may still be alive.

Now she just needs to figure out why.

A knock echoes from her door—distinct, urgent.

She strides across the room and flings it open. She hopes to see Kadir, but that seems lost. Instead, Uzax waits in the hall.

"Any change?" they ask and step into her room. They carry their orb pouch, newly filled with as many formularies as they could pluck from chandeliers without notice. They dump the orbs onto her bedspread.

Vellene shuts her door and stares at her reflection in the mirror. "No. You?" Dark circles hang around her eyes. Not a surprise considering she hasn't slept in the 48 hours since Eledar's imprisonment. She tightens her robe, chemight deposits peeking out. She reaches for the formularies and slips them into her deposits, inhaling with the strength they bring to her tired bones.

"No word." They exhale and move to the window, stare out at the prison. "He should be dead."

Vellene swallows. "I know."

"So, why isn't he?"

She grimaces. Too many horrible scenarios fill her mind. None of which are in Eledar's favor, least of all hers.

Uzax looks at her. "We need to find out what Aquim knows, if what's meant to go down at The Drinking is even worth pursuing. I'm not doing this if he knows what we're up to."

She shakes her head. "Eledar wouldn't give us up."

But Uzax folds their arms with a pointed look. "He might if it means saving you."

"No." Her stomach fills with unease. "He values the end of Aquim's wrath more than his own life. We need Kadir."

They scrutinize her.

"He would believe in our mission," she insists. "He also has sway with my father. He may be able to convince Aquim to let Eledar go, or at least work off his supposed crime instead of die for it."

"That doesn't mean Kadir should be part of this." Uzax counts on their fingers.

She furrows her brow. "What are you doing?"

"Six lives, Vellene, including you and I. That's how many of us are on the edge of a cliff, right now. Do you really want to add a seventh?" Uzax eyes her, something like a challenge in their eyes.

Whatever the challenge is, she's sure she's already failed. "I do if it means we get out of this mess."

Uzax shakes their head. "I don't like it."

She crosses to her door and yanks it open. "You don't have to, but it's what needs to be done to save Eledar."

"Please."

She shoots a glare over her shoulder. "If he dies in that prison, and we don't make a move to get Kadir on our side, can you tell me you won't have any regrets? Eledar is the leader of our mission. He is the reason we stand any chance against my father. I can't sit idly by, nor should you."

Uzax presses their lips together. "I think you're discrediting your own value, Vellene."

"I can't control my power," she disagrees. Her lips press together before she strides into the hall. She charges down it, heart beating fierce within her. Chemibreakers eye her with suspicion as she passes. Utilities scramble out of the way, arms full of decorations for The Drinking.

Everything with Kadir left her with little to no time to plot her family's deaths. At this point, she's glad she got to wear the gown her mother gifted her, even if she did leave it in that alley. It deserved better than her death.

She pushes through the guest wing of the chateau. Everything gets brighter as she goes—more candles, elaborate chandeliers, brilliantly woven rugs, elaborate statues. Pretenses. She frowns and approaches a room guarded by six Chemibreakers, each of them wearing Rathmore cloaks. Two of them hold up their hands, red chemight swirling in their palms.

"Mistress Winloc," Geralt says. He straightens. "May we help you?"

"I need to speak with Kadir," she demands, breathless. "I thought you all were heading back to Frales?"

The Chemibreakers exchange wary looks.

"I'm afraid Sir Rathmore is indisposed," another says.

Vellene reaches for her chemight. "Move, or I'll do it for you." It ignites with her desperation. Still, the Chemibreakers stand firm. She scowls. "While I don't like to flaunt it, I am a Winloc. I belong to the most powerful Imperial bloodline between our two nations." She lifts her chin the way Soffesa taught her, hoping to exude power she rarely uses.

The Chemibreakers eye each other with uncertainty.

"A life is at stake," she tries, the edges of her voice frayed with concern.

Though a few of the Chemibreakers look sympathetic, they keep their mouths shut.

Frustrated, Vellene thrusts her hands forward, and the chemight slams the guards back like two strong arms pushing them aside.

The Chemibreakers gasp and groan. Geralt curses.

"I warned you," is all she mutters as she steps through the path she created and shoves open Kadir's door. It falls shut on the Chemibreakers' protests as they try to tug fee from her chemight's grasp—but they're hers until she wields them otherwise.

Vellene strides into the guest room and stops at the bed, stares at it, the covers pulled back, Kadir's clothes in a bundle on the floor. A pang of want thrums through her. The want to go back before Eledar's screams. The want to trace Kadir's frame, to look in his eyes, to know him. Shame creeps over her in a swell of heat.

A faucet runs.

Vellene spins to the bathroom door, prepares to fling it open, then thinks better of it. "Kadir?" she calls.

A splash emanates inside, as well as a grunt of surprise.

Vellene steps back as a shadow moves beneath the door.

It pulls open, and Kadir peeks through, torso bare and slick with water, cloth wrapped around his waist. "Vellene?"

"Sorry." Her strength falters, along with her hold on the guards outside.

Geralt bursts open the door. "Sir, we tried to stop her," he heaves, sweat across his forehead from thrashing against her ward.

It gives her a pang of pleasure at the sight of his despair.

Kadir takes her in, her winded and frazzled state. "Why are you here?" His tone is stern, but there's a certain torment in his eyes. As if he, too, wishes to go back to the alley, to wrap around each other, to indulge in anything except the truth of their realities.

Vellene chews on her lip.

Kadir leans into the door frame.

She sucks in a breath. "You haven't stopped by." It's not the first thing she wishes to address, but it's the thing that sticks to her mind and hollows out a hole in her chest.

He grinds his teeth. "You broke into my room, disturbed my bath, because I—what—haven't followed up on our brief interaction?"

*Brief interaction?* She rubs her shoulder, unsure of his alliance, of the night they spent together. There was nothing brief about it. How could he write it off? What changed? A flicker of fury lights within her at the belittlement.

Kadir sighs and looks at his guard. "I'm okay, Geralt. Thank you."

"Of course, sir," Geralt says. He looks at Vellene with suspicion, his eyes darting to the places she could conceal a weapon, but he leaves.

Kadir gestures to himself. "Could I have a minute?"

"Yes." She shuffles away. "Sorry." She moves to the middle of the bedroom, back turned. She focuses her thoughts on the alliance she needs to secure here and now. No time for charm. Only truths. *Eledar. How much time do I have left to save him?*

"What's going on?"

Vellene turns to him.

Kadir stands in a pair of simple pants. He dries his hair with a cloth, face twisted in annoyance. "There's more going on than you're saying. It's all over your face."

Her eyes trace the Ravian etched across his chest. She remembers running her hands over it, remembers the pulse of his heart against her palm. She clenches her jaw and brings her eyes to his, his words scorching through her mind and blurring her vision: *brief interaction.* So business-like. So without feeling. "Did I do something?"

His eyes soften. "No, Vellene." He moves to a chaise across from her and grips its back. He looks down at his fingers. "It's obvious to me the Golem your father imprisoned is a friend." He raises his gaze to hers. "Maybe more. Maybe that 'was' you mentioned before we—" He clears his throat. "You know."

She takes a step toward him. "Just a friend," she lies. Worry creases her features. "And I'm very concerned about his well-being."

Kadir studies her, wary.

"Can you help me?"

He bites his lip.

"Please," she whispers.

Kadir looks away. "Of course, I'll help you." He grimaces.

"That wasn't very convincing."

He straightens. "What do you want me to do?"

She clasps her hands. "Could you convince Aquim to let him go?"

"Why can't you?"

"Aquim can't know I know him."

"Why?"

"It's just better that—"

"Why, Vellene?" Kadir grits his teeth, stares at her.

She holds his gaze, rolls her shoulders back. "Eledar and I are part of a plan."

"A plan?"

"Yes." She squeezes her hands.

"What kind of plan?"

"One where some may not survive."

Kadir's face remains stone cold. "An assassination."

Vellene hesitates, then nods.

His eyes trace her face. "Who are you trying to kill, Vellene?" Then his expression hardens, the answer coming to him as the words leave his mouth.

Her fingers tremble.

He steps up to her. "Why are you helping the Golem?"

She clenches her skirts.

Kadir runs a hand through his hair, looks to the ceiling.

"You won't tell anyone, will you?" she asks.

He looks back at her. "And implicate myself somehow?" He scoffs. "No." He steps away from her, paces. "I mean, you're talking about assassinating a powerful—if not the most powerful—chemi between our nations." Kadir shakes his head. "I don't understand how you got tied up in this." Then, his eyes narrow. "Last night, we were interrupted. Somehow, you knew Eledar was in trouble. How?"

She waves the question off, even if she has been wondering the same thing. "Don't you want Aquim gone?"

"Actually, no."

Her heart drops.

"I don't believe unnecessary violence is the way to solve anything." He glares at her. "Frales has been in a constant war for more than five years, and we're not even close to the end of it. No one will sit down, negotiate, or talk things through. They automatically result to vengeance or a show of power." A bitter laugh forces itself between his teeth. "And if you think murdering your father will solve anything, you're wrong, Vellene."

"And Mogaell."

He stops pacing, tenses. "Your sister?"

Vellene bites her lip.

"Are you serious?" Kadir stares at her. "She's just like you—nothing more than a girl following orders."

Her forehead creases, his words slicing through her. *Is that really all he thinks of me?* She shakes her head and shoves the thought away. "It's part of the deal."

"What deal?"

She steadies herself.

"Vellene?"

"*Mortello fusum.*"

Kadir's eyes widen. He grasps his head, turns away in frustration. "A death oath?"

"The chemi I'm working with, they thought it was the only way," she tries. "That might be why I could sense his pain last night."

He snorts in disapproval.

"You don't get it. You don't live with Aquim, Kadir. You don't watch him kill Scraps for something as simple as looking at him the wrong way," Vellene rambles, her nerves curling through her. "You don't see how he poisons everything he touches. He had my mother killed by my *sister*. He destroyed the only good in my life, the two chemi worth—" Her voice catches. Her body shakes. "Killing my father is not unnecessary. It is vital. He deserves it. My nation deserves to be free of him." Her voice cracks. "I deserve to be free."

Kadir closes the distance between them and lowers his face to hers.

She stiffens but brings her gaze to his, everything in her uncertain.

"Vellene," he says, voice soft but stern. "I understand your grief, your need to avenge your mother's death, but you're venturing down a path you will never be able to come back from. I don't care what they've done. They are your blood. More than that, they are living, breathing chemi."

Vellene turns her face away, but he grips her chin and forces her gaze to his.

He searches her eyes. "Have you ever killed anyone?"

Vellene grimaces.

"I didn't think so." He releases his grip. "We need to reverse that oath."

Pain creeps into her heart, physical pain—the poison writhing to life. She clutches a hand over her chest with a gasp. "No."

He presses his lips together. "Okay." Kadir rests his hands on the back of his neck. "But I won't help you. Not if it means this plot to ruin your life continues."

"What do you care? You admitted what happened between us was nothing," she snaps, voice breaking.

He frowns.

Vellene shakes her head in annoyance. "I'm doing what I'm doing for our nations. Don't you care about that?"

"Maybe that's what you tell yourself, what your so-called assassin friends led you to believe." He scowls. "But it's your self-preservation driving you to do this. That Golem—Eledar—he knew that, and that's why you're under a death oath."

A bitter laugh cuts through her teeth as her heart thrashes in her chest. "Is that what it is? Are you jealous?"

Kadir laughs back. "I couldn't care less. You can be with anyone you want."

"Really?" Vellene closes the gap between them with a stride, grasps his sides, and tugs him toward her.

His breath catches, body freezes. His mask falls into surprise, his lips parted and a shudder running across his shoulders.

"Do you care now?" she snaps, then pushes him away from her. She scowls, her heart thumping hard against her chest. "If I crawl into your lap and kiss away all your fears, will that make my freedom worth your time, Rathmore?"

He stumbles back, fingers clenched into fists. "You're deflecting the conversation."

"Maybe you're the coward, Kadir. Maybe your will to act without a fight is because you're terrified of what it may cost."

His eyes darken. "I am terrified. I fear what it will mean for our nations if we keep fighting anger with more anger." The violet of his eyes turns wild, his voice breathless as he cripples with the weight of it all. "From mist and tar we were created, and I fear of the day that's all we become. We must be beyond our makings. If not, then we might as well wade into Dalbian's Abyss and never look back."

Vellene grabs her hair in frustration. "Peace doesn't just show up and knock on the door one day. We must take action."

"How does more bloodshed equal a better future? How does the death of a son, a daughter, mean anything more than death, Vellene?" he questions, voice infuriatingly calm. "Do you even hear the words you're saying?"

"Do you?" she cries. "You want me to sit by? Watch Scorus fall into the same mess you let Frales collapse into? Let Eledar die?"

Fury slashes across Kadir's face. He lowers his voice, words slow. "Say what you want about me, about Frales, but don't pretend, even for a second, what you're doing is a solution, because it's not, Vellene."

Her chest heaves. "Help me, Kadir."

He levels his gaze with hers. “I care about you too much to say yes.”

She sucks in a breath. *Fine*. She strides past him to the door.

“Vellene.”

She yanks open the door—

“Be careful.”

—and slams it shut. She shoves past his Chemibreakers and careens down the hall. Her blood boils as she spots Uzax.

They wait at the end of the hall, arms crossed, expression bored. They straighten at the sight of her. Their face falls to concern. “What happened?”

Vellene grits her teeth and continues past them.

Uzax jogs to keep up. “Vellene?”

“He’s not with us,” she spits, eyes narrowed on the path to the prison. “We need to break Eledar out. Now.”

## Chapter Thirty-One

# *Eledar*

The door to the prison slides open. Light streams inside behind a tall shadow.

Eledar grunts and lifts onto his elbows, fully prepared to feed Aquim every lie. It's what he should have done from the beginning. Instead, he gave the bastard too much. Too much Eledar can't take back.

He swallows and steels against the guilt. He forces a cocky smile, but it fades when the shadow steps inside, face scrunched in concentration. Chemight pools from between her knuckles and outside to Chemibreakers who lie unconscious. Eledar tenses. "Vellene?"

She gnashes her teeth, and he's never seen anything more beautiful. The mess of her curls. The desperation of her face. The intensity to the gold of her eyes. Something deep within him vibrates with need—a need to touch her, to be close to her, to feel the beat of her heart beneath his palm.

Eledar drags himself off the ground. He steps to the bars of his cage as something inside him winds tight. Any moment and it will snap. Not unless he kisses her, saves her. The wards waft toward him, and he grips his hands behind his back, careful not to touch the chemight imprisoning him.

Uzax steps inside behind her. Circles, almost as dark as Vellene's, hang below their ruby eyes.

Eledar hesitates. "You shouldn't be here."

"Uzax," Vellene manages between clenched teeth. "Chemight."

"Right." Uzax pulls orbs from a pouch at their waist. They reach to the dip of Vellene's robe, where the orbs in her chemight deposits fade of all color. They pop them out and replace them one at a time. Their fingers tremble as they go, tongue stuck between their teeth and eyes narrowed on the task at hand.

As her chemight deposits refill, Vellene relaxes. Her eyes take Eledar in. "I was worried you were dead."

He peers past her. "I'd love to chat in length, but I'm sure Aquim will be back." His eyes soften. "Although, I did miss you."

Vellene looks away. Guilt sharpens the hollow nature of her features.

Eledar bites his tongue, remembering her holding Kadir's hand. He hoped it was part of a scheme, but her shame tells him otherwise.

"What does my father know?" she asks and avoids his gaze.

Eledar wets his lips. "He came to see me before he dragged me outside and beat me. He didn't leave me a lot of choice—"

"Get to the point, Eledar," she snaps. The muscles in her neck strain as she douses the Chemibreakers outside.

Uzax shifts their weight, uncomfortable.

Eledar grimaces. "He knows there will be an attack during The Drinking." He cringes, then looks at the floor. "And he knows you're involved."

She curses under her breath.

"He threatened your safety," he says and twists his fingers together behind his back. "I was trying to protect you."

"I'm dead either way. You're a fool," Vellene spits.

He flinches.

She flexes her fingers at her sides and bites down on her lip. "I'm sorry. These last two days—"

"I know." Eledar meets her gaze.

She holds her chin high but has yet to master the stone-cold calculation Soffesa and he spent years cultivating. Little pieces of her torment burn through—to a twitch in her brow, a flex of her jaw. He wishes nothing more than to take that torment away, especially if he's the cause of it.

"So, we call it off then?" Uzax asks.

Eledar heaves a breath and shakes his head. "No. We don't need the element of surprise to win this."

"Since when?" Vellene nudges Uzax, and they replace her orbs again.

Eledar measures his breaths, never looking away. Never wanting to ever again. "I think I know where the source is."

Vellene straightens. She blinks a few times. Her brow makes a small indent.

He almost forgot that about her. Now, he lets it take up permanent space in his mind. He slicks his hair back. "There was another Golem in Scorus, Imaex. He killed himself so your father couldn't use him for information on Golem. A Chemibreaker showed up, took nothing but a maroon pouch. The rest of Imaex's research was in Golem script, something only I can read." Eledar manages a weak grin. "It's in the abyss."

"Dalbian's Abyss?" Uzax asks, brow raised.

"And you found it, can access it?" Vellene questions.

His grin falters. "Well, not exactly, but it has to be nearby. Aquim will go to it before The Drinking." He eyes Vellene. "Follow him."

A frustrated, strangled noise leaves her lips. "You don't think I've tried that before?"

Eledar rubs his neck. He actually hadn't considered she tried to find the source before.

Vellene's shoulders slump. The confidence she wears as a mask falls into disbelief and weariness. Her eyes trace his face. "This is done, Eledar," she says. "I'm sorry, but there's nothing more we can do." She takes a step back toward the door.

Uzax moves to replace her orbs, but she lifts a hand and shakes her head. "We're leaving." She sucks in an uneven breath. "I'll find a formulary to break your wards, and I'll help you escape, but the original plan is off the table."

He steps closer to the electrified bars. "You'll need to send word to the others."

Vellene nods. "I will."

"Vellene."

She hesitates.

"I need to tell you I'm sorry." He wavers on his feet. "For doubting you."

Vellene glances over her shoulder at him. "Just try not to die, okay?"

He nods. "You, too."

"We've got company," Uzax hisses. "Aquim."

Vellene peers out from the prison. She bites her lip, then grips Uzax's arm. "Find your brother. Deliver the message. Don't come back."

Uzax squeezes her shoulder. "Remember your value," they say softly. "Good luck." Then they sprint out and into the shadows of nearby trees, avoiding where Aquim and a set of Chemibreakers storm forward.

Eledar's eyes widen. "Run," he demands, but Vellene holds her ground. "He'll kill you, Vellene. He said he wouldn't lay a finger on you if I told him what he wanted to know, but I doubt that applies if he finds you here."

She shakes her head. "Anywhere I run, I put others at risk. He won't go after Uzax, but he will go after me." She heaves a careful, heavy breath. "I was doomed since I met you. Might as well embrace it."

"Now is not the time to be courageous," he argues.

Aquim fills the doorway. Scorus bustles with howls of wind behind him. They rip into his cloak and it whips at his back. His expression is fierce. Eyes hungry for victory, lips curved into a knowing smile.

Vellene rolls her shoulders back, and in that moment, she masters the mask of an assassin. Every falter or twitch Eledar noticed moments before slates into determination. Her lips curl into a snarl, her eyes shine with rage, and he knows then he's never been in love before. Not until her. Not until that face.

Then her father's chemight unfurls.

## Chapter Thirty-Two

# *Vellene*

To live is to fight.

To fight—as her father knocked down her mother.

To fight—as she wrote *Never Forget* on the wall of a prison cell as an eight-year-old girl.

To fight—because she is so tired of dying. Slowly. Endlessly. At her father's whims.

Vellene's hands slam to the pavement as she catches herself, Aquim's blast of chemight narrowly missing her. She rolls to the side, clenches her biceps, and tugs her elbows back. A weaponized remedial formulary tugs from its orb on her chest and funnels into crackling red light within her palms. Everything in her buzzes with newfound energy as if her muscles understand: this is it. This is the fight she's bid her time for.

"Vellene. I knew it was only a matter of time." Aquim analyzes her, mouth twisted in supreme disgust. He prowls into the prison.

Her chemight remains hot in her palms as she eyes his movements. "You've known about my involvement with Eledar for how long, father? At least 2 days." She tilts her head in question. "What? Too lazy to capture me at my room? Needed me to do the work for you?"

"I wanted to see who else was involved." He nods outside. "Seems you're alone."

*He didn't see Uzax.* Vellene hides her relief. "I don't need anyone else to piss you off. I've done well enough on my own."

"Just a lowly Golem." Aquim's lips twist with distain. "How futile."

"Say what you want." Her power begs to be free, to strike Aquim down. "We almost killed you."

"*Almost*," he sneers. Blue chemight steams from his knuckles. "My own flesh and blood. Working to destroy the chemi that puts a roof over her head, cares for all her needs."

"Don't lie, father." Vellene narrows her eyes. "You've never cared. I bet part of you is glad. Now Mogaell can have your throne."

Aquim eyes her chemight, and his snarl relaxes into a soft smile. "Oh, poor, silly child. You are a fool. A sad. Lonely. Pathetic. Fool." He takes sly steps toward her, and Vellene backs up, wary. "I knew you'd be a failure the moment you became your mother's favorite. I'll relish ridding Alchemight of you." He steps closer, his smile savage as she takes another step back. "Keep going," he whispers.

The words string along her spine as sharp as razors, and before Vellene realizes what he's done, before she can comprehend the shout that comes from Eledar behind her, her back hits the ward of the prison cell.

Vellene gasps as the electric chemight in her palms reaches toward the wards. Her body slumps, and her knees give out as her chemight turns against her, the wards wielding it toward its intruder. She blinks and fires off a blast to where her father stands above her, smirking, but the blow lands nowhere near him.

Aquim slings his hand back, then whips it forward. His chemight sharpens from knife to anvil and slams into her chest. Her mind fries, thoughts obliterated, will destroyed. She moans and hits the stone of the floor, drifts toward darkness as her father leaves with a satisfied laugh and his Chemibreakers rush in. She forces the darkness from her vision, tries to fight, fight, fight.

But her eyes slam shut.

## Chapter Thirty-Three

# *Eledar*

Vellene's shrill cry pierces through Eledar, echoes through his skull in fine pricks of pain. He shakes as he feels an echo of her cracked ribs within his own.

*No.* Panic rises. He grabs the cell bars without thinking, and a shock wave funnels through him before the wards throw him back.

Eledar falls with a groan, his vision blurred. He lies on his side, one arm outstretched toward Vellene, her body lying limp on the other side of the cage. He blinks as the colored wards fade, as the door to his cell pops open and Chemibreakers roll her inside.

He fumbles to pull himself up but he falls flat against his shoulder. His anger and concern dip toward exhaustion, but he reaches an arm toward her and twists a strand of curls between his fingers. "Vellene?" he asks, throat sore, mind frantic. "Answer me."

She lies still.

"Vellene, please," Eledar begs through gritted teeth. Dark blots disperse across his vision. He drops her curls and stretches for her neck. He presses the tips of his fingers to it, feels for her pulse, but a shiver of exhaustion ripples through him. He groans. *Stay awake.* He forces himself upright, braces his hands on the cold stone beneath him. He wracks in frantic breaths as his hand reaches for the bare spot in his brow.

Eledar picks at the hair. Then, he pinches the loose skin at his elbow, picks at a scab, and reopens the wound. He blinks back drowsiness as mud grimes his fingers, and the stone door of the prison once again opens.

"What more could you possibly want?" Eledar growls and scoots closer to Vellene. He tugs her into his lap and wraps a protective arm around her. "Get back," he says, voice hoarse.

A shadowed figure rushes to the cell at the sight of them. Light hits his face as he stoops and peers through the wards. Kadir Rathmore. Eledar shudders, a long-forgotten panic seizing him at the sight of those violet eyes. There are differences—his scars, the white of his hair—but it's like seeing the violent ghost of his past.

"You," Eledar seethes with bitterness. "It's too late for you to come play hero." As the words leave him, so does his strength. Too much strength. His fingers tremble, his veins burn. He smooths his expression, tries to hide his exhaustion. Some of it must come from Vellene, the pain she has, and the injuries forcing her unconscious.

Kadir focuses on her. He wipes sweat from his brow, the violet of his eyes like glass. Concern knits across his brow as he summons chemight, despite the clear exhaustion darkening his eyes.

Eledar scowls, realizing what he's trying to do. "Don't—"

Kadir's chemight hits the ward but refracts back. It slams into his chest and shoots him across the room and into a wall. He gasps in frustration, eyes wide, and hair disheveled. He slicks it back into place and scrambles across the room before he drops to a knee. He peers past the blur of the wards at Vellene, then—slowly—he brings his eyes up to Eledar's and anger settles across his features. "Tell me she's alive, Golem."

Eledar runs his fingers along her cheek, brushes hair from her face, trails them to her neck. Her pulse is soft against his palm, and it strangles him. "Barely," he whispers.

"How could you do this to her?" Kadir's jaw clenches. He's the portrait of wounded too deep to comprehend.

Eledar recognizes the look, the need to protect her. He swallows. "I didn't do this. It was Aquim."

Kadir stands, scoffs. "Your selfishness is the reason she's in that cage with you."

“Selfishness?” Eledar scowls. “You don’t know me, and you know nothing about my plan.”

“*My plan*,” he repeats. “Are you too dense to realize your plan was never something she wanted? I know you’re not because you put that abyss-damned oath on her.”

“Are you here to help?” Eledar asks. “Or to rub my failure in? Because I’ll be honest, I’d prefer help.”

Kadir looks hesitant but his anger dips back to concern. “I can’t break you out. Not without knowing which ward formularies were used. But she needs to mend her ribs.”

Eledar tenses, those words confirming his worst suspicion. He drags Vellene closer. “There are chemi that can get through without the original formularies.” Eledar hesitates. “I can tell you where to find them, but only if I know you won’t turn around and imprison them.”

“I’ll do anything to help her. She doesn’t deserve this.” Kadir’s brow furrows.

"You feel her pain," Eledar whispers. He can feel the pain of her ribs keenly, like a blade stabbing along his abdomen.

Kadir wavers, his hand ghosting over his own ribcage. "Let me help her. Before it's too late."

Eledar manages a solemn nod. “There's a Chemibreaker, Uzax. Vellene sent him into the city to find the others and call off our plan. I’m not sure exactly where they all are, but one of them will be at The Bloody Cloth. She always is."

He grips Vellene. It's possible Rathmore only plays at affection. He grits his teeth and studies the son of the man who created Golem. The son that sat in his wing of his father's manor while Golem were melted into nothing and war in Frales erupted.

Then Vellene's pulse flutters against his fingertips. He licks his lips. "I want to help Vellene, but I need to know you're trustworthy before I hand you names."

"Kadir Rathmore." Kadir says quickly, his eyes never leaving Vellene. "I've recently joined the Convocation to—"

"I know who you are."

Kadir draws his eyes to Eledar's with reluctance.

"Your father was my Master." Eledar grits his teeth.

Kadir hesitates. "I was a boy when he began Golem imprisonment."

Eledar bites his tongue as fury surges through him.

"I understand my last name carries infamy." Kadir swallows. "But I want to change that. I want peace for Frales." He gestures to Vellene. "But I don't think now is the time to address politics. She needs mending, and I can't give her that with these wards up."

Eledar's eyes slide over him. The Rathmore crest peeks above Kadir's shirt collar. It has the same sweeping lines as Eledar's. As if they're one and the same. "How did you know she broke her ribs?" he presses.

Kadir looks away, blows out a long, steady breath. "I don't need their names. I'll just search for Uzax." He gives Vellene a once-over look of worry, then he stands to leave.

Eledar squeezes his eyes shut. He knows what he must give up. Knows he can't take it back. Knows if Kadir is anything other than who he says he is, the list in Eledar's pocket will lose its last remaining name. "Soffesa," he calls after the Imperial. Her name slices through his throat with the hot acid of betrayal.

Kadir turns back, unsure.

Eledar runs his fingers through Vellene's curls. "Go to The Bloody Cloth. Ask for The Silent."

Kadir hesitates. "The assassin?"

Eledar nods.

"Is this a trick?"

"No. Not when it comes to her." Eledar's shoulders slump. "You're right. She doesn't deserve this."

Kadir raises a brow, surprised at the admission. Then he nods and breaks into a jog away from the prison and toward the city. The moment he slips out, Chemibreakers guarding the prison move the stone door back in place, eyes blank, and Eledar heaves a shuddering breath as his exhaustion subsides enough to clear his head. Kadir wielded chemight their entire conversation, and somehow Eledar hadn't noticed. He clenches his jaw, then freezes as Vellene moves.

She gives a light moan, face twisted in agony.

"Hold on," he whispers to her, the pain rupturing through him feeling more real than anything about himself ever has. "Please."

## Chapter Thirty-Four

# *Vellene*

The moment Vellene opens her eyes is the moment her body sets on fire. She gasps and flings to her feet, heart frantic at the memory of her father, of the wards and chemight that struck her down.

But her knees tremble. Her body wilts toward the ground. Pain—*poison* —sizzles through her veins.

Vellene shoves her arms in front of her to catch herself, but someone else does that for her. Strong arms wrap around her. She slumps into their chest, her vision dotted in red blotches of pain. A sigh of relief fills her left ear as their grip tightens.

"Never do that to me again. *Never.* Do you understand, Vellene Winloc?" his voice is soft in her ear. He presses a firm kiss to her cheek, then nuzzles into her shoulder.

"Kadir?" she manages, both syllables a strike against wavering vocal chords.

His grip loosens, face pulls back. He's silent for a long moment. Then—"Eledar, actually."

Somewhere in Vellene is a morbid flash of embarrassment, but the twinge of poison in her veins pummels it into submission. She groans, falls from his grasp, and clutches her stomach. “I’m going to be sick.”

She winces and crawls to a corner as the first hack ripples over her body. She coughs, and liquid spurts and splatters from her lips across the stone. She blinks rapidly as her vision fades in and out. She brings her fingers to her lips, pulls them back, and stares at the black that stains them.

Blood. Panic sets in. She's coughing up blood.

Eledar steps beside her. He reaches his hands down, pulls her hair from her face, and kneels. He looks at her fingers, at the blood she stares at. “Abyss.”

Vellene nods.

“Listen, just lie down. Relax. Kadir went to find Soff. She’ll get Ulrich and Ferula to come break these wards, and then we can get you mended.” He says it hurriedly, voice breaking every few syllables with a lack of confidence.

Her face falls. “This can’t be mended.”

“Aquim used what appeared to be a nether chaos formulary. It shouldn’t be too difficult to—”

“Aquim didn’t do this,” Vellene snaps toward him. “You did.” She makes out his face in between moments of blurred reality. “This is your death oath poisoning me from the inside out, Eledar. We called off the assassination. Aquim trapped me in this cell with you, and now I'm the one paying the price."

Regret crashes across his features. His nose wrinkles in displeasure and distorts his freckles. The humor that's always a blink away is gone. Everything about him is stern. Filled with contempt. "We had to do that, Vellene."

"No, you didn't." Vellene shakes her head. The poison plunges through her abdomen like stabs from sharpened chemight, Eledar's hand at the hilt. "I was with you from the beginning. You just had to trust me." A bitter laugh seeps from between her lips. "And you did, but not until you made sure I'd die if I wronged you. That's not trust. I was naive not to see it." She stares at him. "I was a scared Imperial with the right connections. You saw that and took advantage of it."

Eledar frowns. "You're hurt, in pain. We can talk about this when—"

"No." Vellene pulls to her feet and leans into the wall for support. "I am so tired of being pushed around. First my father. Then you and your crew. Even Kadir has his own agenda. I can't do it anymore. I won't." She shakes her head. "I'm paying now for others' decisions."

Eledar balls his hands into fists. "Alright, Vellene, I'll give you that maybe Soffesa and I took advantage of you with the death oath, but there were plenty of chances for you to back out before then."

"And have you kill me?" she shrieks. "Because those were my choices, Eledar." She spits blood at his boots, and he flinches.

"You told me you wanted to kill your family," he says hoarsely.

"I told you I wanted to be free." Hot tears drench her cheeks. Vellene wipes them in frustration. "Now look where I am." She throws her hands up in defeat and shakes her head. "I'm back in this cell, probably until my last breath."

Eledar steps up to her. "You know what, Vellene? Fine. I used you. Is that what you want me to say? I saw an opportunity to avenge the deaths of hundreds of Golem, of thousands of Scraps, to free myself from an eternity of doing others' bidding—and I took it."

His eyes trace her face. "But you don't get to fault me for your inability to take action. You waited years to get away from your father, and when you finally did, you found every excuse to stay. You didn't have to help me. You didn't have to follow me back to The Bloody Cloth." He rubs the back of his neck. "I'll take the blame where I am to blame, but I won't shoulder your own pathetic regrets." He lowers his voice, brows furrowed in anger, eyes alight with shame. "And despite both of our faults, I care for you."

Vellene grasps the stone of the wall. His words slam through her. *Pathetic. Inability to take action.* Her chin trembles, and she reaches a hand up to cover it.

"Vellene," he softens.

She holds up a hand to keep him from coming closer.

"I'm sorry. That was harsh." He blows out a breath.

She clutches her stomach as the world drifts away below her feet.

"Let me help you sit. You look weak." He reaches for her.

Vellene shoves his grasp away. "Don't touch me." Then she slams her hands into his chest. "Stay away from me."

His hand drops to his side, his emerald eyes glistening with sorrow.

"I don't trust you, Eledar." She sucks in, then slides down the wall and settles onto the ground. "You're right. I was scared to take action, and that's my own fault, but you manipulated me. Maybe you didn't think about it like that. I hope it wasn't on purpose—"

"No, I never wanted to hurt you, I—"

"—but you did manipulate me." Vellene lowers her gaze to her boots, unable to watch the crumple of his face.

The cell falls silent.

Eledar moves to the opposite side. He settles onto the ground and runs a hand through his hair. "Yes," he admits. "I did."

Vellene tilts her head back against the wall. She squeezes her eyes shut as misery zips through her.

"I'm sorry," he whispers, eyes cast down.

She struggles to pull away from the pain. "I'm sorry, too." Her eyes drift to him. "I shouldn't have hit you like that."

No poison plagues Eledar, yet his face wavers with the same torment. He pulls a knee to his chest and grips it. His muscles strain with the urge to jump up, to cross the room to her, but he plants himself to his side of the cell, forehead creased in concentration.

"It seemed so simple," he mutters. "Come to Scorus. Get the source. Avenge the deaths of everyone Aquim's tyranny stole from me." He picks at his forearm. Then he digs his nails into his flesh. Mud pools up, but he continues to scratch.

Vellene frowns. "Stop that."

Eledar blinks, looks at her. "What?"

"That," she nods to his hand picking at his arm.

He looks down and flushes with embarrassment. He grunts and shifts his weight, clasps his hands around his shin, lacing his fingers.

Vellene stares at the mud. Her eyes then trail to the other wounds marked across his bare chest. Most healed, but a few remain open. Each time he moves, a bit of clay dribbles out. It's strange to hink that's all he is.

He notices her judgment and adjusts to keep his wounds out of sight. He glares at the floor.

Vellene pierces through the pain of the poison. It's hard to look past her anger, to see Eledar in the moments where he cared, but he did. She knows he did, and she knows she reciprocated. She bites her lip. His words from The Bloody Cloth float along a current of loathing and sink into her skin: *What I should have said is you're beautiful and extraordinary, and if we had the time, I'd give it all to you.*

She shivers and grips her biceps. For a moment, her vision sharpens. The way his silver hair slicks back over his head from days being trapped in the prison. The slight indent in his left cheek and a dark, angry bruise. His skin littered with bruises and lashes from her father's torture. Concern filters through her. No matter their differences, he's been here, under Aquim's care, after fighting to retrieve something he thought would free him. Isn't she trying to do exactly the same?

Vellene opens her mouth to say something, anything other than a curse or foul words toward him, but it's too difficult. More than that, there's something different about seeing him, being near him. It's as if her senses align with his, as if her heart beats in his chest. She itches to move closer to him but forces herself still.

"Can I ask about Kadir?" Eledar's words are slow and unsure. He keeps his gaze on the ground.

Vellene rubs her arm and blinks away tears as the poison wiggles through her. "My father wished for me to get close to him and kill him."

Eledar looks up at that. The darkness of his face brightens just the slightest. "It was a ploy? Your relationship with him?"

Guilt confronts her. She hesitates. "At first."

His hope dampens.

The memory of their kiss twists through Vellene. It rams into the night she spent with Kadir, the night that would have gone much further if it hadn't been for Eledar's screams. Screams she heard despite the distance. She bites her lip. "I didn't think there was anything to hope for between us," she admits. "And I was angry at you. For the death oath. For not trusting me."

His shoulders slump. His eyes slant with bitterness. "I suppose that's fair."

She studies him. "I feel a connection with Kadir."

Eledar clears his throat. "Alright."

She bites her tongue. "But I felt one with you, too. That night."

He cringes. "Felt."

She frowns at her lie. "I still care."

"But as a friend."

Vellene looks away. She's not sure she can even call him that. Too much bitterness has built up inside her. Just looking at him makes her fists curl. But there's also a piece of her rooted to him, connected.

Eledar blows out a breath.

"I'm sorry," she manages.

"Don't." He laughs and hides his disheartened expression behind a false smile. "It's not like it was a big deal. We made out, and you went on with your life. As did I. It was a bit of fun. Nothing more."

They fall silent at that—at the understatement. Power thrums between them like chords tethered from one body to the next.

Vellene twists her fingers together.

"Are we good?" he asks.

She meets his gaze. Her answer traps against her tongue. She wants to say yes, to face death with Eledar and the assassination behind her. But she wheezes and rubs her throat.

"Vellene?" Eledar drops his leg. He presses his palms to the floor, ready to push himself up.

"Breathe," she chokes on the word. She trembles onto her knees and palms as she attempts to wrack in breaths. Her lungs sob.

Eledar crosses the room in two strides. He bends to her and wraps an arm around her shoulders. "Poison or panic?" he asks.

Vellene coughs and blood sputters out of her lips. "Both," she croaks.

Eledar forces her into his arms. "Lean into me."

She presses her ear to his chest and warmth pulses between them. Her heart slows. Her eyes flutter shut as the thinnest amount of calm channels from him to her. She tightens her grip around him and relishes the reprieve.

"Just relax," he says, but his voice breaks. He rocks her and lies his head against the top of hers. "They'll get us out, and Soffesa can try to undo the oath. Just hold on."

Vellene clutches a hand over her heart.

"I can't stand this." Eledar squeezes her. "You've no idea how much I hate myself, right now."

She grits her teeth.

"I never should have let Soffesa put this oath on you. It was immoral." He runs his thumb over her bicep. "And honestly, it's not something I would have normally done."

"I'm not in the mood to assuage your guilt, Eledar." Vellene shivers as a cold sweat breaks across her skin.

His next words are soft. "You hate me, don't you?"

"Right now?" Vellene clenches her jaw against the pain. "A little bit."

They freeze as the stone door to the prison grinds open.

Kadir steps in, four shadows behind him. His face scrunches behind a gold mask that covers his eyes. In formal Imperial attire, he rushes to the warded prison cell, then gestures to the shadows behind him. "Hurry.

There may be a party going on, but I can't hold off these Chemibreakers forever." The muscles in his neck tense as he says the words, eyes drawn to Vellene in Eledar's arms.

She blinks up at him and eyes his clothes. The Drinking. Her birthday. Her stomach squeezes.

"How is she?" Kadir's brows furrow along the top of his mask. "She looks worse than I expected."

"It's the oath." Eledar turns his gaze to Soffesa.

The Silent steps into the prison dressed in a gown of red and black. The half of her face covered in tattoos is trapped behind a mask of black lace.

Behind her are Uzax and two others. Vellene stares at an older chemi with similarities to Uzax and a young girl. They must be Ulrich and Ferula. Both Uzax and Ulrich are outfitted in Chemibreaker uniforms—likely courtesy of Uzax.

Soffesa shifts her way forward and beside Kadir. She peers past the warded cell, her eyes finding Eledar first. Her lips curl into a snarl at the welts on his skin. "Aquim's death has never been more deserved," she sneers.

Eledar grunts as Vellene becomes heavier in his arms. "Soff, I need you to reverse the oath."

Soffesa tenses. "I can't do that."

"Can't or won't?" he growls.

"Can't," she insists. "Death oaths are binding chemight. Nothing breaks them once they're spoken."

Eledar's muscles flex around Vellene as if he can squeeze the poison out of her. Vellene squirms, and he slightly relaxes his grip. "She will die," he says, voice tinged with guilt and pain.

Soffesa says nothing, her face as calm as ever, but one of her fingers twitches.

"One problem at a time," Kadir says, but his voice is as torn as Eledar's, if not more so. He motions to Ulrich and Ferula. "Can you break these wards?"

Ferula steps up to the cell. The small girl wears her pink and purple hair twisted into a high ponytail. A plum mask of lace wraps around her eyes, and she's dressed in Imperial evening garments—an elaborately decorated corset, stiff white pants, and flowing petal-like skirts. She tilts her head as she examines the wards. "This is going to take a lot of chemight. They must have upped their game after we got into Winloc Grove so easily."

"Whatever you need," Kadir answers.

She holds out her hands to Uzax and Ulrich. "I'll need to borrow yours."

"Of course." Ulrich takes his daughter's hand, and Uzax takes the other.

"I'm going to need you, too," Ferula tells Kadir.

Kadir winces. A sweat breaks out across his brow.

Vellene's eyes find his hands. Light blue chemight glows faintly as it twists from his palms and drifts beyond the prison doors, where Chemibreakers lie unconscious.

"If I refocus my chemight, then we'll have about eight minutes before those Chemibreakers regain consciousness." Kadir looks to Eledar. "Can you carry her?"

Eledar keeps his arm around Vellene and nods.

Kadir looks to Ferula. "Ready?"

Ferula grins, the young chemi's face filling with eagerness. She bounces up on her toes. "Ready."

Kadir closes his eyes for a moment, then grunts as he pivots his energy from the Chemibreakers to Ferula. He takes hold of Ulrich's free hand, eyes never leaving Vellene's. "Go."

Ferula concentrates on the wards. Silver chemight sparkles from her palms. It encompasses the hands of Ulrich and Uzax, then funnels over their chests and down into Kadir's fist. Chemight surges forward, pools against the wards.

Eledar shifts his grip on Vellene. "Hold onto my neck," he tells her.

She must, because then one of his arms slips above her waist, while the other grabs beneath her thighs. Her lips part with a shallow breath as he lifts her and cradles her against him. His eyes find hers, and as her fingers curl into his hair, real fear widens his eyes.

"Just breathe," he whispers. "We're almost out."

An unconscious Chemibreaker shifts outside the prison, their armor clinking.

"We're losing time," Kadir hisses.

Ferula's chemight tunnels through the wards, slow and steady. "One second," she snaps.

The wards slither into a crackle of little sparks. Every formulary trapping Eledar and Vellene within the cell simmers into steam before they disperse altogether.

Ferula sucks in a heavy breath, and the four of them let go of each other.

Kadir's the first to rush to the cell's door. He yanks it open and strides to Vellene in Eledar's arms. He grabs her face and looks into her eyes.

Vellene swallows. "Hi."

Eledar shifts uncomfortably.

Kadir ignores him. "How are you feeling?"

Her breaths are labored. "Not great."

"Why can't the oath be reversed?" Eledar pleads with Soffesa.

"It's an *oath*, Eledar." Soffesa grimaces. "I wish I could help her, but I can't."

"Then we finish the job," Kadir says. He lets go of her and steps back. "We kill Aquim and Mogaell."

Even in Vellene's blurred state of reality, his words shock her. She wants to tell him no. She wants to tell him destroying his values over her life isn't worth it. She wants to tell him to look at her and know she did exactly that, and that's why she's like this. Not because of Eledar. Not because of Soffesa.

She chose to go to The Bloody Cloth. Chose to sacrifice her beliefs and play the good daughter. And now—now she's dying. There's nothing that can be done, and she doesn't want him to become her. She doesn't want his goodness to sour into something no one can salvage.

She'd beg him to let her die if she could.

But the words won't come. Her breaths thin.

All she can do is reach for him and try not to focus on the way Eledar's chest tightens beneath her ear as she does.

Kadir takes her from Eledar in a swift movement, moving out of the cell in quick strides. She peers between her lashes at Eledar as he grips Soffesa in a hug, everything about his face pinched in darkness.

"We've got Chemibreakers waking up out here," Uzax calls from outside.

"I've brought you a carriage," Kadir whispers to Vellene.

She lies there, head against his chest. She's never felt so small. So weak. So vacant.

"Is your poison not listening? We're going to carry on with the original plan and keep you alive."

The thrum of poison slowed. It slowed the moment the wards on the prison cell broke apart, but the damage is done. Vellene tilts her head back to look at him. She hates the anger on his face. Even behind a mask, violence comes to life in his eyes. "That's not what you wanted."

He carries her across the lawn, pace quick as shouts erupt from semi-awake Chemibreakers. "What I want is peace, Vellene. You're a big part of that."

Vellene manages a brittle laugh.

"You are. You're the rightful heir to your father's seat on the Convocation, and you have a good head on your shoulders for right and wrong." He glances down at her. "Your assassin friends missed the solution, and it was right in front of their faces."

"What is it?"

His intensity softens into a charming smile, both dimples exposed. "You, love."

They pull to a stop beside a carriage, the door flung open. Everyone climbs inside. Two Rathmore Chemibreakers man the driver's bench, one of them Geralt. They both nod to Kadir.

Kadir lifts her into the carriage, then pulls himself up before slamming the door shut. He lets out a breath. and the carriage moves toward the tree line of Winloc Grove.

Vellene slumps into him and blinks back a haze.

"Eledar," Soffesa whispers. Her hardened face twists into recognition. "It's time."

Eledar stares at Vellene. His eyes waver with panic.

"Time?" Kadir asks. He follows Eledar's gaze to her face, to the way her eyelids flutter shut, to the slow movement of her chest.

*It's a strange feeling to die*, Vellene thinks as her name shouts from the lips of everyone in the carriage and turns into an impenetrable silence.

A silence so dark she believes she will forever sink.

## Chapter Thirty-Five

# *V*ELLENE

*I wonder if this is how mother felt within her last breaths.*

The thought makes a spark in the darkness. *Will I finally see her again?* Vellene smiles to herself, wades into a low tide of rolling fog. It sticks to her, drags her down, clings to her shoulders. *Am I in Dalbian's Abyss?* She extends her arms, gently pulses them, watches as the fog parts at her movements. She looks down at her feet, where the fog continues. *I can't be. There's no tar.*

"Vellene."

She squints at a figure cloaked in navy. They wade through the fog toward her, a gloved hand outstretched. Her eyes widen as a strange light pierces the veil of the fog and shines down upon long purple waves of hair, their tips tinged in green.

"Mother?" she whispers and sinks to her knees in shock as Aurora's hand slides over her shoulder.

Her mother's face is sickly pale, but she's beautiful nonetheless. Her full lips spread into a smile as she looks upon her daughter, her golden eyes just as Vellene's. "All my wandering in Nowhere, I never expected to find you among the lost souls." Aurora takes Vellene's chin and forces her back to her feet.

"Nowhere?" Vellene asks, her voice calm and steady. Whatever effects the poison had, they've vanished in this strange place of gray.

"Tell me, my child. How long have I been gone from Alchemight?" Aurora asks, her face curious. She drops her hand from Vellene's chin, but she fastens it to the thin fabric of Vellene's robe as if her daughter may vanish if she lets go for too long.

"Almost six months," Vellene whispers, still in disbelief. "I don't understand. What is this place?"

"Six months," Aurora mutters. Her pale face twists in pain. "It's felt like years."

Vellene clings to her mother. Tears threaten to break through as she wraps her arms around Aurora's cold body. "Am I dead?" Vellene asks, her voice breaking.

"I am." Aurora hugs her back. "I'm sorry for that."

Vellene pulls away to look at her. "I ran."

Her mother smiles, broad and bright among the gray. "Good girl."

"But," Vellene hesitates, "I went back. To kill him."

Her smile fades.

"And now I'm here." Vellene laughs bitterly.

The sharp edges of Aurora's face soften into sadness. She cups a gloved hand to Vellene's cheek. "Oh, my beautiful daughter. You won't be here long. Don't worry."

Vellene's heart gives a quick thump. "What?"

Aurora reaches down and picks up Vellene's right hand. She holds it in between hers and splays Vellene's palm open. In it is a shimmering of colors, a web of orange as warm as the sun and of blue as cold as a dream. Colors Vellene has seen only twice before.

*Eledar*, Vellene thinks, warming at his name. She bites her lip. *Kadir.*

"I'm glad you went back, even if it does fill me with terror." Aurora's dark brows furrow. "My mistake all these years was trying to tame your father's greed. I should have known he was too great of a beast."

The colors in Vellene's palm swoop up her wrist, wrap up to her elbow. They smother her nerves and fill her with a sweet feeling of remorse and desperation. She frowns, unsure what to make of it. She looks up at Aurora. Her eyes widen as her mother's pallor becomes translucent, her grip on Vellene's hand less solid. "Mother?"

"Fight back, Vellene," Aurora says, and her voice sounds distant. "Never forget the power you have. Sharpen it. Wield it."

*Never forget.* Vellene swallows as the color from her palm encases her body, liquefies her bones.

Then light. Too much light.

She lifts her hands to cover her eyes as it breaks through the mist, strikes through her chest. Energy radiates through her, and she rockets from Nowhere's grasp.

Vellene's eyes slam open. She sucks in a large gulp of air as she jolts awake. She lies on the floor of the carriage, the colorful chemight that brought her back fading from her sight. Ulrich, Uzax, Ferula, and Soffesa peer down from the benches, hands on their knees.

But Eledar straddles her, chest heaving, face beaded with sweat. He slumps into Soffesa's legs, his eyes tired, body weak.

Vellene flexes her fingers and strength courses through them. A hand gently touches her back, and she turns her head to find it in Kadir's lap.

He gives her a small smile, his golden mask removed and his face as exhausted as Eledar's. He tucks her hair away from her face and lets his forehead fall to hers, his shoulders shuddering. "Thank, Alchemight," he whispers. He lifts his face away to meet her gaze. "How do you feel?"

Vellene pulls out of his grasp. "I was dead."

Eledar swallows. His chest heaves as he catches his breath.

"Not all the way, it seems," Soffesa grumbles in annoyance. She keeps a protective hand on Eledar's shoulder.

"They saved you," Ferula says. She beams at Eledar and Kadir, her face flush with excitement. "Can you teach me how to do that?"

Eledar manages a slow shake of his head, and Kadir looks away.

"I'm afraid it's only between the three of them." Ulrich pats Ferula's head, but his voice is strained, his face haunted as if he witnessed something he hasn't seen since another lifetime. He stares at Eledar and Kadir for a long moment before he gives them a solemn nod.

Eledar focuses on his breathing. His eyes meet Vellene's for a second before he looks down at his hands. They shake, and he clenches them into fists.

Kadir squeezes her shoulder and lifts onto the bench beside Uzax. "You didn't think we'd just let you go, did you?"

"I don't get it." She eyes them. "How could you have possibly channeled enough chemight to heal me." She feels for the poison in her veins. It tickles—*still there*. She presses her lips together. The death oath is still in place.

"You know, you could say thank you," Soffesa bites. She glares at Vellene.

Vellene touches Eledar's ankle where it rests beside her. She flinches back as a shock spreads between them. She curls her fingers away with a grimace. "Soffesa's right. Thank you." She finally gets him to bring his eyes back to hers. "We're okay."

Eledar gives her a small nod. His lips slip into a slim smile.

"Thank you," she says, turning to Kadir.

He clears his throat and places his mask back on. "As much as I wish we could cherish your return to the living, love," Kadir says as he peeks out the window, "if we're going to kill the Winlocs, we need to do so soon. I don't want you falling back into the clutches of that oath."

Vellene tugs up from the ground and settles onto the bench with Kadir's help.

Beyond the thick tree line, lights of The Drinking twinkle. Imperials arrive in throngs of sparkling gowns and intricately embroidered vests. They make their way to the Observatory, its giant glass doors open wide.

Kadir reaches for a bag squished into the corner next to Uzax. He opens it and pulls out formal wear—some for Vellene and more for Eledar. "Get changed. Courtesy of your friend Nivia." He smiles at Vellene, but it doesn't reach his eyes. There's an anxiousness to it.

Unease settles in her stomach, but it wipes away as Kadir's face falls into the perfect picture of concern.

"I won't lose you again," he breathes, then drops a kiss to her cheek.

Vellene plucks a gown from the bag and drags it onto her lap. "Nivia?"

"A recruit," Eledar offers, his eyes plastered to the place Kadir kissed her and his jaw tight. "She's a messenger Utility and has great gifts in weaving."

Vellene clears her throat and sighs. "Alright." Her eyes drift to Eledar's again, and this time, he doesn't look away. "I'm ready."

If an Imperial evening garment were ever built for murder, it'd be this one. Skirts light, pants form-fitting for easy mobility, intricate holes designed into the pattern of the sleeves and corset to allow simple access to chemight deposits. Vellene adjusts the small hat she was given, and its veil shields her face.

Tonight, Winloc Grove is alive. She tucks behind an outcrop of trees, Kadir's carriage, and the rest of the crew camouflaged by the dense foliage along the perimeter of the property. Beyond, Chemibreakers line the walkway to the double doors of the Observatory. Every curtain of the chateau is drawn back—a rare sight. Every face behind a mask holds a wicked smile. Every conversation ends in forced laughter.

The Drinking. Vellene's mind struggles to see anything behind the extravagant display of wealth other than poverty. A poverty of grace. Of beauty. Of decency. Then she spies her sister.

Mogaell clutches to passing arms, whispers sweet nothings, upholds the Winloc name. Every movement is calculated, every touch leverage. Even from the distance Vellene stands, she sees Mogaell's true nature. A power-hungry Winloc hidden behind the soft smile of a seventeen-year-old chemi.

Tonight her family will die. By her hands or by the others. The thought brings relief and peace followed by shame. what does it make her that she craves their deaths? Vellene taps her pant leg nervously as Kadir passes around a bag of orbs.

"Fill every deposit. Scraps, fill your pockets. You can still draw from the orbs' chemight. It just won't be as potent or as reliable without deposits." He pops new orbs into his own deposits as he speaks. "If we're doing this, we're doing this strategically and with little to no mess. I want everyone walking out of this alive." He holds himself straight, muscles tense, eyes dark.

She rubs her arm and thinks about Kadir's want for a peaceful negotiation. She wants to tell him to leave, to take his Chemibreakers back to Frales until Aquim and Mogaell are gone. There's no reason for him to stain his hands with this.

But she knows they need him and she knows Eledar and Soffesa will never let a Rathmore walk away that knows their plans. More than that—and maybe it's selfish—she needs him. All of them.

"I'm sorry," Soffesa growls. "Did I miss the memo where you were put in charge?"

Kadir sets his jaw. "Follow me, or I turn you in."

Soffesa presses her lips together, and the group falls silent.

Vellene lifts a brow, surprised by the threatening tone of his voice. Another inkling of unease unfurls through her chest.

Kadir finishes filling his deposits and looks at her. "Are you ready for this?"

She chews on the inside of her cheek but nods. "Everyone will be in the Observatory until The Drinking. When that happens, they'll move to the dining hall, and Aquim will go to retrieve his bottles of the source." She looks at each of them. "I'll take care of Aquim." Then she looks to Eledar. "But I'll need you to take care of Mogaell. I'm not sure I have the stomach for it."

Eledar nods. "Soffesa and I will take her, but you should have backup against Aquim."

"I'll go," Kadir volunteers.

"No." Eledar clears his throat. "You and your Rathmore attire will grab the attention of every Winloc Chemibreaker. You said it yourself. We want to walk out of this alive."

"And without suspicion," Ulrich adds. He keeps a protective arm around his daughter. "Where do we fit in?"

"Be ready at the exit," Uzax suggests. "When we come through, place a ward to keep others from following." They look at Vellene. "I'll come with you. I may not be the strongest fighter, but I know how to use Imperial chemight as well as any other Chemibreaker."

Vellene nods and offers them an encouraging smile. "Okay." She sucks in a breath. "That's it then."

"Blend in where you can. The masks will help us, but Eledar and Vellene escaped from prison. Chemibreakers will be on edge and on the lookout." Kadir sucks in a slow, steadying breath. "Meet back at the carriage in an hour."

As they disperse, Vellene veers toward the back entrance of Winloc Grove, Uzax at her side. Her only consolation is the way her death oath's poison recedes into nothing with each step she takes toward her home. She wonders what it will feel like to be the last Winloc, wonders if it will be enough to put the beast inside her to rest.

Her ears tune to the smush of grass behind her, and she slows as Kadir jogs up next to her.

"One second," he says and takes her hand. He pulls Vellene to the side, away from Uzax and the others.

She eyes him, unable to see his nerves with his mask but feeling the small shake to his fingers as he grasps her. "Everything okay?"

Kadir eyes Eledar and Soffesa as the two enter the Observatory, then studies his eyes flick over her face. He reaches his hand to her cheek and presses his palm against it.

Vellene swallows.

His lips part. Then shut.

"What?" she demands.

Kadir grimaces. "Nothing. Just." He grabs her hand and gives it a quick squeeze. "Be careful, love." He sucks in a breath, turns, and heads for the crowd of Imperials without another glance back.

"You, too," she whispers after him. Her nostrils flare in confusion. The indent between her brows throbs. She rubs her forehead.

Uzax walks up to her, arms crossed, face dark. "You look in pain," they note.

Vellene pinches the bridge of her nose. "I've got two idiots pining for me, my family to kill, and poison waiting to cut like a razor through my bloodstream." She grits her teeth and strides toward the chateau. "How else should I be, Uzax?"

They shrug and match her stride as they move to the back of Winloc Grove. "There's a bit to appreciate there, I think."

She raises a brow in question, eyeing them with frustration.

"They care about you, first of all." Uzax stops at the back door. "You're finally getting rid of the people that have sent you down this path of hurt. Plus, if none of it works out, you get the reprieve of death." They smile at her.

She grins. "I guess I should take what I can get."

"Of course." They study her, face crinkled in concern. "It may have gotten lost in all the bumps along the way, Vellene, but remember what happens when we accomplish this."

*Never forget.* She readies herself. "Honestly, I can't envision the future. I just see the plan and what needs to get done."

"Freedom, Vellene." Uzax sweeps the door open, the eyes behind their mask glinting with hope. "For you. For me. For everyone."

She bites her lip.

"Where should we try for Aquim first?" Uzax asks.

Vellene straightens and redirects her gaze to the front doors of Winloc Grove, the hallway lined with heads waiting on the other side, the pedestal marked with her name, and the sword that hangs above it. "Actually," she says and pivots away from the back entrance. "I need to grab something first."

## Chapter Thirty-Six

# *Eledar*

Eledar braces himself as he enters the Observatory, Soffesa at his side. He touches the fabric of his mask, ensures it's secure. He swallows, shoulders hunched as he winds his way through Imperials. They fill the Observatory like a herd of creatures, every conversation a prey to overpower and eat alive.

Imperials laugh, one hand grasping a brew, the other waving about mid-story. Their skin bears one or a variation of the six family crests. Across chests, biceps or exposed torsos is the double-diamond-shaped body and spindly legs of the spideria for the Winlocs. Descendants of distant power—hardly threats and likely why they were invited. Wearing the skeletal skull of the canisoss for the Pineskys or the beetle-like body of the scumtis for the Vonners would mean a quick death. Beyond the Winloc spideria, the other Scorian crests may as well be extinct.

"Just look at them," Soffesa hisses, the exposed portion of her face etched with disgust.

"Oh, I'm looking," he whispers in discontent.

Among the crowd are Fralian Imperials. The etched feathers and crude beak of the ravian for the Rathmores, the spotted feline face of the parduseus for the Caligari, and the swooping snout and sharp whiskers of the rodenti for the Stones. The intricate ink of the crests twists around chemight deposits, each filled with an orb. The further the descendant is from the main six bloodlines, the more variation put into their crest as a child chemi.

Soffesa's eyes narrow as she scans the crowd. "Guess Vellene's proposed Infusion with Rathmore means Aquim is playing nice with Frales, or at least faking it."

Eledar follows the flow of the crests, searches for those that glow with more wealth than others. He picks at his elbow as he and Soffesa maneuver through the crowd, then catches himself. He can't go shedding clay. Not in this crowd. He sucks in a breath, steadies his nerves.

Soffesa brushes her hand against his. "What is it?"

Sweat prickles at his hairline, the nape of his neck. He asked himself the same question. His mind trails to Vellene limp beneath him, his chemight streaming out of his body and into hers. He wanted so desperately for her to live. He never wanted anything more, and as soon as he placed a careful kiss on her forehead—certain there was no amount of chemight that could wake her from wherever her soul ventured—electricity crackled between them.

That was when Kadir knelt on the ground, when he placed his hands against her shoulders.

Thin ribbons of swirling colors twisted between the three of them, and every ounce of Eledar's energy drained—just like the first night he and Vellene kissed at The Bloody Cloth.

Now, even with the refuel of chemight from the orbs Kadir provided, Eledar's fingers tremor. The further Vellene goes from him, the weaker he feels, as if some tie between them is on the verge of snapping into two.

"Eledar," Soffesa whispers.

He clears his throat. "I'm just recuperating."

"Is it Kadir?"

He presses his lips together. He knows Kadir and Vellene must be Infused, even if it's only at a small capacity. Vellene needed both of them to wake up, her power stretching between them.

He knows. That doesn't mean he wants to think about it.

"We can talk about that later." Eledar searches the crowd as sweat trickles from his forehead and down his jawline. His gaze snags on Vellene's Surveillant. He elbows Soffesa and nods in Idus' direction.

Soffesa tenses and swallows. "Back from the dead?"

"More likely, it's his murderer in disguise. Probably using a morph formulary."

"That body was at least a few weeks old." Soffesa crosses her arms. "You think this imposter was here the whole time? Fooling even Vellene?"

Eledar frowns, remembers how Idus stood to the side during his interrogation in the cell like a silent shadow. "Yes."

The imposter crosses through a throng of masqueraders and stops before Mogaell. She stands to the side of the crowd, arms crossed, face bored. The navy and black strands of her hair tie into a crown of braids, accenting the sharp lines of her cheekbones. She straightens at the sight of Idus.

They drop into quick whispers before Idus reaches a hand to her bicep and gives it a tight squeeze. He turns and strides away, robes billowing around him with a flourish.

Eledar's fists clench as he remembers the younger Winloc's abilities, the tar-like chemight that choked him into submission. In all the chaos, it receded to the back of his mind. He shakes his head. "Before we take out Mogaell—"

"What was that?" Soffesa interrupts. "Did you see that? Their conversation looked personal."

Eledar eyes the fake Surveillant.

Idus disappears around a corner, moving quicker than any elder should be able to.

"I guess we should add that to the list of things to deal with," Soffesa mutters.

Eledar's focus pulls back to Mogaell, on what needs to happen next. Even with his anger for her, a sense of dread fills him. This is Vellene's sister. He worries Vellene will never look at him the same if he takes Mogaell's head. He remembers her request during their night together—to make it quick, painless. It's the only thing he can give her. He must.

Soffesa tugs on him, seeing his apprehension even behind his mask. "It's going to be fine."

"Are we sure she needs to be part of this?" he asks.

Soffesa grits her teeth. "Now isn't the time to change the plan." Then with slightly less venom, "If you want Vellene to live, then her sister must die."

Vellene's lifeless body flashes in his mind. Eledar grinds his teeth. He reaches for comfort. The kind that comes with rules to follow and tasks to complete. A rigidness he abided by as a Golem, and then again as he became a soldier in war. His jaw tightens, but he nods and continues forward.

Mogaell rips away from the crowd. She ventures into the darkness of a nearby hall, her hardened gaze and cold snarl glancing over her shoulder once, before she disappears.

Soffesa and Eledar exchange a look, then follow.

A pit forms in his stomach as the hall stretches before them, Mogaell at its center, her small frame fragile. *I can't kill her*, he realizes as she opens a door. He stiffens, his steps disjointed. He's killed before out of necessity. His hands are as stained as any others from Frales. But Mogaell is only a few months younger than Vellene. His fists clenched. He won't come back from this.

Soffesa looks at him, knows he can't. She pulls away. "Stay here."

Eledar studies his sister. "You shouldn't have to do this alone. I'm here."

"You can't do this, Eledar." Soffesa blows out a breath, then gives him what may be the most sympathetic look she's ever possessed. "Let me do this for you. You protected my family and gave them more time than they were meant to have. You helped me escape the war and took on that burden alone." She grabs his shoulder and squeezes. "The least I can do is return the favor."

The shake of his fingers worsens.

"I may not like her," Soffesa says. "But we all saw what happened in that carriage. You and Vellene are tied to each other—for better or worse. If she dies from our death oath, then I lose the most important chemi in my life."

Eledar glances away.

She squeezes his shoulder tighter. "You, Eledar. Even if Vellene dies and it doesn't kill you, it will kill a piece of you. A piece I'm afraid will never come back."

He sucks in a breath, then wraps his arms around her. "I don't deserve you, Soffesa Fedelis." He tucks his chin against the top of her head.

"You're wrong," she whispers into his chest. "There is no realm where you and I aren't two parts of a whole."

He tightens his hold on her.

"I need to do this for you," she pleads softly.

He pulls away. His eyes trace over her half-inked face. "That's fine, but I'm coming with you."

Her face twists. "No. If you help kill Mogaell—"

"I ruined things with Vellene," he says.

Soffesa steps out of his grasp. "I doubt that. But if you do this, you will."

He looks to the double doors Mogaell vanished through. "Maybe," he says carefully, calmly, "I don't care." He clenches his fists. "I can't care. She's in love with someone else."

"Are you sure?" she demands.

He inhales, then plasters on his falsest of smiles. "Let's kill a Winloc."

# Chapter Thirty-Seven

# *Vellene*

Vellene moves between the shadows with Uzax on her heels. The halls she grew up in. The halls that close in around her, make her breaths run ragged. She continues forward, one hand gripped around the hilt of her father's sword.

Crusted over with the blood of the Vonners and Pineskys and holding the promise of reaping her own, the ingrained spideria flashes beneath her fingers on the hilt. She's careful to keep the blade hidden between her skirts and pantleg, holding the fabric up and around it as she hurries forward.

They trail her father to his quarters. Gloved hands clenched, shoulders hunched, his protective detail left behind—Aquim moves through the halls as conspicuously as Vellene and Uzax, certain not to draw attention as he goes after the source. He stops outside his room, glances around, then ducks inside. The door falls shut with a soft click.

Vellene takes Uzax's wrist and pulls them against the wall as her father's most trusted Chemibreakers file into the hall. "They'll be looking for me."

Uzax nods and straightens their uniform before they step into the open. They furrow their brow and look at the Chemibreakers. "What are you doing here?" they growl.

The Chemibreakers look between each other with frowns.

"Sir Winloc descended to the party almost ten minutes ago," Uzax hisses. "Are you really about to tell me no one is protecting him? There are criminals on the loose!"

Their frowns replace with nerves.

"Well?" Uzax shoos them in the direction of the party. "Go!"

Vellene presses against the wall and holds her breath, thankful for Winloc Grove's natural darkness as the Chemibreakers charge past her. She waits for the last cloak to turn the corner, then she exhales and strides toward Uzax. "Thank you," she whispers.

"A piece of advice," Uzax says, their voice concerned. "Don't chat. Just strike." They turn the door handle. "Good luck."

She readies her father's sword, and the door swings open. Her father's quarters sit like a beast dressed in dark and light blue fabrics. High archways mimic the tips of blades. She scans the room, and the indent in her brow flares. *It's empty*, she realizes. She takes cautious steps forward, slowly lowering the sword. She peers into the bathroom, then the closet. "Where are you Aquim?" She grits her teeth.

Uzax pops their head in through the doorway. "Anything?"

"Close the door and stand watch," she demands, her eyes scouring every inch of the room.

Uzax closes the door, and what little light came from the hallway vanishes in a blink.

Vellene stands within her father's darkness, and her heart aches. The room screams of Aquim. Gaudy decor to match his absurd outlook on Imperialism, on the grandeur of power and wealth. She moves with slow steps, checks every corner, and flings open the wardrobe door. She steps around to the other side of the bed, kneels, lifts the bed skirt. She reaches for courage, then looks beneath.

Nothing.

Vellene moves to pull herself away. Then she freezes.

A single box rests against the back wall. The smallest amount of light creeps between the box's woven structure. It sparkles and glistens with the alluring shine of formularized orbs.

Vellene sets the sword down and tugs the box out from under the bed. She bites her tongue, then yanks its lid off. Several orbs rest inside. Within them, auburn chemight swirls. She picks one up. It weighs heavy in her palm. She pinches it and brings it to her eye level.

Subtle, shining specks of yellow sparkle within the auburn.

Familiarity curls across her shoulders as they tense. She remembers the strange orb Eledar had when she met him, the same one—and the only one—that didn't drain after their shared moment together.

*What are you,* she wonders and reaches up to her neck. There's only one way to find out. She pulls an orb free and sets it on the ground before she inserts the strange one. She forces her shoulders to relax, steadies her pulse. Then she tugs on the orb's chemight.

In a breath, Aquim's room shatters—splinters into three, twenty, thousands of indecipherable slices.

Vellene's hand shoots out for the sword's hilt on reflex. She moves to yank the orb from her deposit, but she's not quick enough. The room folds away like a set of curtains and settles into a hazy darkness. Black ground fans outward before tar swallows it.

Then the dark land trails into the peak of a hill where a figure stands, navy cloak billowing among a throng of gray vapor. *Aquim.*

## Chapter Thirty-Eight

# *Eledar*

Remorse. Anxiety. Guilt. They slam through Eledar as Soffesa thrusts open the double doors to the Reading Room. The floorboards creak under their weight as they take slow steps into the center of a large, open area of sofas and shelves. He tears the mask from his face and scans every shadow, every space between tomes.

"Oh, what do you know—it's a hero." Mogaell slips from behind a shelf. Her slender, small frame moves quick and fluid. Her navy eyes sharpen. Her lips curl.

Chemight sparks from Soffesa's palms. She plants her feet as it lengthens into twin daggers.

Mogaell tilts her head, then she smiles. "The Silent, I presume. I must say, I've wanted to meet you for some time. Leading my father to the heads of the Vonners and Pineskys? My favorite sellout, here in the flesh."

Soffesa matches her smile. "Talk all you want. I'll slit your throat soon enough."

Mogaell's eyes flash with delight. She lifts a hand and spins her fingers around in a summon. Her tar-like chemight threads up and down from her palm.

"Eledar," Soffesa says with distaste, "What is that?"

"It's just chemight," he mutters.

"Oh, it's more than that." Mogaell presses her lips into a smug expression as her chemight solidifies into a tall staff, both ends sharpened into blades. "It's a gift from the Guardians, and I plan on using it to its fullest extent."

"Cut the intimidation tactics," Eledar says. He pulls on a weaponized remedial formulary and a crimson sword extends from his palm. "You know why we're here."

"Actually, I don't." Mogaell grips her chemight tighter. The veins along her knuckles sprout into black tendrils. They crawl up her arm, sprout across her bicep. "My father—I get. He lacks the ability to create a better future. He's too blinded by his lust for power. Honestly, I want him dead, too."

Eledar and Soffesa exchange a confused look. He scowls. "If that's the case, then why align yourself with him?"

"Who said I did?" Her eyes glitter as the darkness sprouting through her takes control, sucks every ounce of color from her irises. Her lips stretch into a feral smile as she nods behind them. "Your turn."

The floorboards creak.

Eledar spins to the doorway as a shadowed figure flings their arm out. Chemight encompasses Soffesa, but it leaves Eledar untouched and exposed. He reaches for his sister, then yanks his arm back.

The chemight around her crackles with a ward.

Eledar manipulates his chemight sword. He tugs on his deposits, power zinging through his veins—

"I wouldn't do that. You'll only hurt yourself." The figure in the doorway steps into the light.

*Idus.* Eledar frees his chemight despite the threat. It pulses in red waves off his fists.

The false Surveillant pulls off a golden mask. Features etched in age, milk-white eyes carrying the weight of the world, Idus runs a hand over his long, silver beard. "Mogaell, you may go."

Without hesitation, Mogaell shoves past Eledar. Her chemight slithers back into her palm as she goes. She gives him a playful wink. "Have fun, hero," she says, then stalks out of the Reading Room.

Eledar moves to follow her, but Idus blocks the doorway. His eyes run over the false Surveillant with distaste. "The abyss do you want?"

Idus hides his hands within the folds of his sleeves. "Eledar Lirik, leader of the Fralian uprising, a chemi made of clay, and apparently, someone who isn't afraid of consequences."

Eledar narrows his eyes. "Release my friend, or I'll be forced to attack."

"I'm afraid I can't do that." Idus flicks his gaze to Soffesa, who bangs her fists against the bubble surrounding her. "But I also don't wish to fight."

The red fury of Eledar's chemight ripples up his arms and circles his biceps.

Idus paces to a shelf, runs a crooked finger over dust-covered spines. "Don't worry. Vellene will kill Aquim," he states, his tone certain.

Eledar frowns. His eyes drift to the mask Idus ripped off. *Why does that look familiar?* His chemight flares. "I'm sorry to strike down an elder—even if you're only posing as one—but I can't wait any longer to chase after Mogaell. She'll ruin everything."

"Mogaell is not a threat." Idus takes a single step forward, levels his gaze. "She's with me."

Eledar shifts his weight. "And who are you?"

Idus smiles softly. He clicks his tongue, tilts his head.

Confidence blooms within Eledar. He steps forward. "I'll admit, I'm curious. Who pretends to be a middle-class Surveillant only to partner with the throwaway Winloc?"

Idus holds his ground, lifts his chin. "Oh, she's no throwaway, Lirik. She masterminded most of our plan. I'm just here for the source." He clasps his hands with a smile. "Vellene will kill Aquim, and I will use the source to cure her death oath. Both Winlocs will be with me."

The white of his eyes goes stark. "The question is, will you join me as well?" He chuckles darkly. "Although, with your annoying interference, I'm not sure I want you involved."

"I won't ask again." Eledar raises a fist. His chemight roars upward. "Who are you?"

The false Surveillant takes slow strides and paces. "Mogaell and I wore masks for weeks." He lifts his mask for emphasis. Its gold sheen reflects in the candlelight of the Reading room. "Not much unlike these." He looks between them. "Mogaell pined for Aquim's seat. I watched after Vellene." He relaxes his shoulders. "I originally sent you here in the hopes of avoiding the dirty work myself, but things changed. I called your mission off, and yet you decided to go after the source anyway."

"You." Eledar grits his teeth. "The leader of Equilibrium."

Idus smiles.

"Show me your true face," Eledar demands.

The false Surveillant lifts a brow. "Revealing my identity is not part of the plan." A wrinkled hand snakes out from his robes. Chemight flashes to life on his fingertips. It dances in an emerald green. "I'll take your apology now."

Eledar scowls. "I owe you nothing. You terminated our contract."

"Then you proceeded to go after the one thing you know I need." The resistance leader plays with his chemight. It swivels in and out between his fingers, sparks across his knuckles. "Not only that, but you put a death oath on someone I want alive."

"You're just trying to hold us off." Eledar wields his chemight toward the barrier wrapped around Soffesa, but the ball of electricity tightens around her.

Soffesa's eyes widen. She shakes her head. "Don't," she hisses. "I don't care what happens to me. Don't do what he wants, not unless he's going to give you what you want."

"Ah, yes, your Master," Idus says.

Eledar's veins light with rage as he draws his chemight away from the ward around Soffesa.

The Surveillant tilts his head. "With a single flick of my index finger, I could squeeze your pet assassin into oblivion." His white eyes darken with pain as the words leave his mouth, but his expression is schooled into cool confidence.

"Let her go," Eledar demands.

Idus waves the demand off and lowers his voice. "Great chemi are all forged the same. It doesn't matter where you come from, as long as you have power to wield, formularies to sharpen, and a mind for deception."

Idus clicks his tongue in dissatisfaction. "I watched you from a distance when we were children. I watched Lazar dote on you. Sure, he beat you into submission, but he also gave you so much attention. From that, you grew. A Golem, yes, but a chemi more so than his brethren. You deceived your enemy and freed those you cared most about. That is, until they all died. Under your watch."

Eledar's biceps tighten. "You've been watching me? All these years?"

Idus's fists clench. "You accepted my offer, came here. Gave yourself a mission to kill. Hoped to find purpose beyond the guilt. The guilt that—I might add—will never recede. Never. I want you to listen to me, Golem. Listen hard." The false Surveillant licks his cracked lips. "My plan remains the same, despite your disloyalty. Equilibrium will possess the source. We can split it evenly among ourselves and become leaders."

Eledar grimaces. "It's not disloyalty when you freed me of the mission."

"A deal is a deal. Contract terminated or not. Maybe you think me cruel, but I'm not. I ended your contract, but I still intended to provide you with your Master. For a price."

"A price?" Eledar growls.

"I'm curious. Who did you plan on using to fill Aquim's seat on the Convocation once you murdered both Winlocs and stole the source?" Idus questions. "I would have thought Vellene, but—no—you made sure that couldn't happen without crippling her first. Was that a conscious decision? To poison her?" The older chemi's face surges with anger.

Eledar clenches his jaw. "Hurting Vellene was never intentional."

"Don't tell me you didn't think about it." Idus straightens, ignoring Eledar's comment. "The convocation would have become yours. A chemi with experience working and living within all class systems."

Eledar swallows. "I don't want that. I just want my freedom."

Idus clasps his hands. "We could redesign the whole system together. Do away with orbs as a currency and equally distribute the power."

"I told you before, and I'll tell you now: that sounds too good to be true." Eledar's chemight sparks. It demands to be wielded.

Something in Eledar tugs toward Idus, toward the man lying underneath the guise of the elderly chemi. He shivers at that tug—a tug he hasn't felt since he left Rathmore Manor. The truth scorches through his mind. "Enough of this. Reveal yourself, Lazar. Let us chat face-to-face."

"Oh, I'm not Lazar." Idus's withered skin shakes. "I killed him years ago. Had to." He grunts as his robe shifts and assembles into a familiar dark tunic of crisp lines. "I never intended to pull your strings like he did. I still don't want to, but we're running out of time. I should have been able to hold this disguise until I'd already fled."

His silver beard sinks into his skin until it disappears. His withered hands revert into that of callused palms and black-painted nails. His stark white gaze intensifies into an electric plum, and his shaved head fills out into carefully adjusted white, two yellow strands drooping at both sides of his face.

Where his suit dips, the smooth ebony of his chest glitters with filled deposits and the ink of a ravian—the Rathmore crest.

"I must admit," Kadir says. "It does feel good to be myself after so long pretending." His purple eyes alight with playfulness, but even now he wears a mask. Nothing is genuine about him. Ever. And Eledar was a fool to think otherwise.

"What about Vellene?" Eledar asks, his words sharp as daggers.

Kadir rolls his shoulders back. "She is extraordinary, don't you think?" His face flickers with lust.

Eledar growls and latches to his adrenaline. He pulls on a nether chaos formulary and slings it.

But Kadir lifts a hand and catches Eledar's chemight with ease. It funnels into a ball of green in his palm. He smiles at it, eyes glistening in triumph. "Amazing, isn't it?" His gaze darkens as he looks from the chemight to Eledar. "The moment I sliced my father's throat, I felt your strings of obedience attach to me. You will do well to remember I am your Master, Eledar Lirik. Your chemight cannot be used against me." He tilts his head and smirks. "More than that, you know as well as I that we are connected to Vellene. Hurt me, and you hurt her—one way or the other."

Kadir drops the ball of chemight, and it dissipates against the ground. He adjusts his cloak. "I think it's best you come along now." He smiles but his eyes remain dark. "We only have a few minutes."

"A few minutes until what, Rathmore," Soffesa snarls, the words muffled but fierce through the wards.

The room shakes beneath them. The barrier around Soffesa evaporates as Kadir braces himself against one of the marble pillars. He lifts his brows. "That," he says with a grin. "I gave you your answer, Lirik. Now, here comes the price."

A blast booms from the Observatory and funnels into the Reading Room. Tomes rain from their shelves. Portraits clatter to the ground.

Soffesa and Eledar stumble back, as Kadir crouches and absorbs the shock.

Eledar trips and takes Soffesa down with him. He grunts and pulls on his chemight, but a second blast sends him back to the ground. He rams into Soffesa, and she hisses in discomfort.

Kadir stands, brushes off his suit. He pulls an orb from his pocket and places it in a deposit. “This is the smallest of victories to come,” he sighs as he looks down at them sprawled on the ground. “Last chance, Golem.” He extends his hand. “Join me. We can end this war.”

"Never." Eledar channels chemight toward Kadir. “If you want me so badly, then pull my strings. Be done with it.”

Kadir eyes Eledar’s palms and grimaces. “I meant what I said, Lirik.” His face draws taut. “Equilibrium wants equality. That doesn’t involve forcing the chemi I want to my side. The choice needs to be yours.”

“No,” Eledar hisses. He sucks in a sharp breath and shoots off his attack.

It catapults toward Kadir. his Master, the son of his Maker—

But white light spirals and encompasses Kadir’s body. In a blink, his frame distorts and vanishes as Eledar’s blast hits the shelf where he stood.

Eledar’s chest heaves, his breaths panicked, and Winloc Grove shakes with a low, haunting sob.

## Chapter Thirty-Nine

# *Vellene*

Vellene clenches the fabric of her pants and climbs the hill, breaths shallow as each gulp fills with mist. In every direction, the fog stands like gray walls separating this piece of land from the rest of Alchemight. The abyss. She's sure of it, but it doesn't matter where she is. It matters that she ends this. Now.

Aquim tenses at the sound of her boots. He turns, but his face remains stone. "Vellene. I thought that might be you."

She tears off her hat and veil, tossing the contraption to the ground. "Father." She raises his sword. Its iron is heavy in her palm, but it wields as light as air—a weapon proud to be in an unforgiving hand. She summons chemight from a nether remedial formulary. The weaponized mending chemight lights her knuckles in streams of red.

"My daughter." Aquim shakes his head in disappointment. "Here to kill me." He rolls his shoulders back. "What would your mother think?"

"She'd be glad," Vellene spits, remembering Aurora's words when they stood in Nowhere. "Since you had her murdered."

"I did," he admits and gestures to Vellene. "Mogaell forced the poison down her throat right where you're standing."

She trembles and looks down at her feet. Everything in her hollows into a deadly calm. The beast in her gut yawns to life, and the embers in her veins blink into existence like quiet, furious stars.

Aquim grunts.

Vellene's gaze snaps up, realizing her mistake, as purple chemight in the shape of shards zips toward her. She drops into a crouch and throws her fist forward. Her chemight attacks the shards with a slash. She shields her head and braces herself as the two formularies combust. Mist explodes outward, nothing but a shadow with her father's wicked grin on the other side.

Vellene stands, her embers lighting—one at a time. *Spark spark spark*, and her veins pop with fire.

He tilts his head. "I'm almost proud." He extends his left arm and amber-colored chemight sharpens into the length of a blade.

"You should be." She mirrors him with the sword. A shimmer of her natural gold chemight mists from her palm and slinks down the blade. "I learned from the cruelest." She grips its hilt as the fire within her roars to life. Her chemight deposits run hot against her skin, and the gold chemight around the sword blazes into furious flames. It burns brighter and brighter as it licks and chars the years of dried blood on the blade.

Cruel, she makes herself. Cold, never. She burns with rage, explodes with the prospect of freedom. She gives his sword a slow twirl and anchors herself to the confidence that blooms through her chest.

"Any last words, daughter?" Aquim asks.

A slow smile curls her lips. "You've no idea how long I've wished to speak freely in your presence."

"By all means, now is the time." Aquim adjusts his gloves.

A million questions thrash through her, all valid, all needed—and yet only one sticks. She licks her lips, hesitant, then locks her eyes with his. "Did you ever love me?"

Her father's brow lifts in surprise before he sneers. "Always so desperate."

"Answer the question," she bites out.

Aquim sets his jaw. "How could I love the thing holding me back from becoming everything?" He steps forward, his careful mask of stone shifting. "You have always been and will always be my greatest disappointment."

Vellene narrows her focus on his prowl forward. She swallows and forces her fingers to steady, pulse to calm. He thinks he has the advantage. He thinks these insults will delay her reaction time. She grips the sword and her flames dance across it, happy to breathe, to wish, to curse. She levels her weight between her legs, her feet firm against the ground.

Then Aquim shoots forward with a roar. He swings his chemight toward her neck in a large arc.

Vellene grits her teeth and blocks it with her blade of death and flame. Sparks erupt into waves of fire. Her muscles clench as Aquim thrusts his weight into his chemight blade, forcing her to her knees. She stares into the storm of his face, but she does not waver.

She will never cower again.

"Relinquish your chemight, daughter," he snarls down at her. "You have lost."

Vellene's lips curl into a sinister grin—one that threatens to be worse than his own. She lets it free, every ounce of darkness, and her adrenaline spikes. She strains to balance his weight with one arm as she frees her other and yanks it back.

Aquim's gaze narrows on the movement. His weight against her blade lessens as he moves to fire another attack—

Vellene pulls as fire licks up her spine, burns through her mind. It flings from her palm in a lash of gold. Like a serpent of fire, it blazes into her father's stomach, teeth and claws first. Power unchained.

Aquim cries out. His chemight blade vanishes into tiny sparkles in the air as he cups an arm around his torso in agony. "It's not real," he tries to tell himself as he drops to his knees in pain.

Vellene lifts from her knees and stands above him. Her beast devours her father. It continues to leak from her palm and shoot into his abdomen, searing holes in his attire, then his skin. She allows it to burrow into him, dig its way through the one who kept it suppressed all these years.

In her other hand, she raises the Winloc Sword. Her flames burn away the last drop of blood marking its steel. She delights in the way her fury devours the promise of her head on his pedestal. It burns and burns as her father screams—until even her rage exhausts itself.

A deep, impenetrable hollowness wastes within her. Her skull flashes with every moment he dared to leave marks on her skin. The memories flood the hollowness, fill it to the brim as she stares down at her father.

He drops to his side, writhes with death. He attempts to summon multiple formularies, his palms sparking between emerald, blue, violet, and crimson.

"I expected this to be more of a fight." Vellene hovers her blade over Aquim's chest. "I also expected this to be harder."

Her flames evaporate as she raises the sword. Nothing but blade. She will take his head, and he will rot into nothing. Just as he did to the Vonners and Pineskys. Just as he planned to do to her. "Then again, you spent so much time making me hate you."

Aquim's breaths become labored. He looks up at her, eyes filled with true fear.

Something twists in her. She wants it to be remorse, but it's heavier than that.

Pleasure.

She chooses to focus on his fear, on how it was her own. Chooses to hold onto the pain, to the way her hollowness swoons into a brush fire, ravages against her heart. Her face reddens with heat, wavers with disappointment. "All I've done is wait on you to change. Hope to have a father." Her arms shake.

Aquim focuses his gaze.

For a flicker of a moment, there's something like love tucked in his features. Mistaken love. Love he shoved aside for too long and cared about not long enough. It dissipates into self-preservation, into the eyes of a chemi looking up at not his daughter, but someone else. Someone he ignored too often to recognize.

"The source—" His voice strangles as his body convulses with a wave of agony.

*Enough.* The fire inside Vellene reaches her eyes. Tears burn down her face, slope along the curves of her cheeks, linger against her lips. She tastes them and their salt withers on her tongue.

Then, she arcs the sword down upon his neck.

Vellene gasps, eyes wild as Aquim's head rolls a foot away. She steps back. Her chest heaves as she drops his sword with shaky hands.

His body is limp. No spasms. No last breaths. Just blood as black as tar oozing from where his head was. The orbs embedded along his neck and chest—a replica of her own—fade from formulary to mist then to nothing.

She sways as her hammering heart slows. Her adrenaline evaporates, and the blood rushing in her ears tunes to the silence of the desolate isle. She rubs the circulation back into her face, cheeks raw from the wind that zips across them. Her eyes glue to her father's lifeless form, and her gut twists with uncertainty.

She wishes she made him suffer.

Vellene kneels and pulls aside his cloak, trails her fingers along three large bottles strapped to the interior. One is filled with chemight from the source. The other two remain empty.

She tugs free the full one and studies it. The chemight within looks as any summoning orb would—naturally as gray as the mist of Dalbian's Abyss. Up close, however, it carries the same yellow specks as the orb that got her here.

Vellene yanks the orb from her neck. It sits empty, whatever transporting formulary it held now drained. She frowns and looks around for a way off the barren island, but only tar and abyss surround her. She hesitates, then pulls on its chemight, hoping it may transport her as the other formulary had.

Nothing.

She's trapped—poison tingles through her—and her sister is still alive.

Vellene sucks in an uneven breath and drops to her knees beside her father's corpse. "Hurry, Eledar," she whispers.

## Chapter Forty

# *Eledar*

Eledar hugs Soffesa as the Reading Room crumbles. Tomes topple off of shelves. Candles tilt from their perches and set flame to rugs. He blinks back dust as the ceiling cracks and rains debris, then scowls at the spot Kadir stood. His Master. The leader of Equilibrium. All of this—the mission to get the source in exchange for his Master—was a ploy. Kadir could've given it to him on day one.

Somehow it's worse that Rahtmore hasn't pulled his strings. No—Eledar's been fool enough to cause this destruction all on his own.

"We can't lose him," Soffesa shouts. "As long as Kadir is alive, he can—"

"I'm aware." Eledar eyes the corner of the room, where a pillar shakes. "We also can't die, Soff." He takes her hand. "Let's just hope Kadir's too busy to use his hold on me."

They sprint down the hall. Imperials—those that can walk—flee the Observatory. Several, however, lie on the ground unconscious as Winloc Grove falls apart around them.

Eledar slides to a stop, forcing Soffesa to halt, too. He grabs the sleeve of an Imperial trying to run. "Help," Eledar growls.

The Imperial's face twists in disgust before she yanks her sleeve from his grasp and continues her escape out of the chateau.

"They're Imperials, Eledar. They're not worth risking our lives for," Soffesa argues, eyes sharp as the glass of the Observatory's ceiling cracks.

He grimaces but lets Soffesa pull him forward. They shove through the crowd, then pivot as a piece of the roof caves in. Eledar grabs his sister and tugs her back, narrowly missing it. Blood spatters across his face, hot and thick as the Imperials ahead of them smash into the floor.

"Eledar!" Uzax runs toward them, dirt and debris covering their Chemibreaker uniform.

His gaze swings behind them, and dread curls across his shoulders. "Where's Vellene?"

Uzax curves around the remains of the ceiling and sprints forward. Worry etches across their face as they survey the river of blood, black as night, streaming out from beneath the debris.

"Uzax." Eledar grits his teeth. "Where is Vellene?"

Uzax shakes their head. “I lost her. I hoped she found you.”

The muscles along his back tense.

“We got rid of the Chemibreakers guarding Aquim, but they came back when they realized I lied to them,” Uzax says. They rake in a large breath and rub their throat.

The three of them huddle and move down the hall.

“Then this started happening.” Uzax waves a hand at the crumpling chateau. “The Chemibreakers left me, and when I checked Aquim’s room, Vellene was gone. She must have run out during the explosion.”

They step onto the front porch and hurry down the steps. Imperials stand in groups outside, some injured but all angry. Their voices mix into a frenzy of chaos, shrill above the dismantle of Winloc Grove.

Eledar glances back at the chateau, at the way it falls in on itself. His stomach flutters as he surveys the crowd a second time in search of purple, green, and blue curls. *Where are you?* He scans every face, hopes to find Vellene waiting.

He should’ve known that would be too good to be true.

He pivots back toward Winloc Grove. The building barely stands—one foul gust of wind away from caving in.

Soffesa eyes him, then straightens. “Don’t even think about it.”

He hesitates but strides to her and kisses the top of her forehead. "I'll be back."

"At least let us see that she isn't outside," Soffesa argues.

"Look around." Eledar holds out his arms. "Vellene isn't here."

The glass ceiling of the Observatory shatters. The sound carries through the air like a broken chord.

His shoulders tense. "Vellene could be unconscious on the floor."

"I'm coming with you," she says.

"No." Uzax steps up between them. "I should go. I lost her. It's my responsibility."

Eledar nods. "Okay." He looks at Soffesa. "Please stay here. Vellene could already be—" His words strangle. But he would know. He would've felt her die. He's sure of it. He presses a hand to Soffesa's shoulder. "I need to know you're safe."

Soffesa's eyes glisten. "You better come back to me, Eledar Lirik. Otherwise, if Vellene isn't dead, she will be."

Eledar forces a smile. "Don't worry." He pulls himself into a backward jog. "It takes a lot to kill clay."

Uzax joins him.

"Just stay away from fire then!" she shouts after him. "I can't be friends with a puddle."

Eledar offers an encouraging nod, then turns and sprints up the steps into the destruction of Winloc Grove.

## Chapter Forty-One

# *Eledar*

Dust curls around Eledar as debris shakes from the ceiling. He coughs but charges forward, arm up to shield his eyes. "Vellene!" he yells. His muscles tighten as he steps over severed limbs.

"This is bad," Uzax mutters. They drop to chemi, check for pulses. "They're suffocating."

"I need to find her." Eledar's throat restricts as thick smoke slinks down it. A fire blazes in a far-off hallway. Orange flames lick up tapestries and devour screams.

Uzax points down a hall to their right. "Aquim's quarters are that way."

They cross through the front hall, the heads of the Vonners and Pineskys free. Their pedestals sit among the rubble, their glass cases shattered. The skulls' gray, rotting eyes stare up from the ground, mouths open in their constant, silent screams. Tonight, however, they're screams of elation, of victory, of freedom, while those who imprisoned them wail for salvation.

Chunks of ceiling, small bonfires of furniture and rugs—they block their path forward. Every step, a scream. Every breath, a last plea. Every blink, fear. Moonlight streams through cracks in the ceiling, a spotlight on the dead, on the pools of blood spilled.

Agony strikes through Eledar and his mind races. *You've felt nothing*, he tells himself. *She must be alive.* He repeats it like a mantra and maneuvers around the decay. Cracked tile crumbles under his boots. Blood splatters onto his shins. Winloc Grove groans as fire drenches the path forward. It sears flesh, turns moans into blood-curdling screeches. His hands shake as he lifts his palms and summons a marvel primitive formulary. Uzax mirrors him, and they both douse the flames in a soothing emerald—a heavy blanket of chemight to suffocate the flames' hunger and soothe the last moments of the wounded.

Steam erupts and bites into Eledar and Uzax as they wade forward. Uzax hisses. Eledar sets his jaw. *Alive*, he repeats. *Stay alive. Vellene is alive. Live.*

They move around a corner, and the hall tunnels into darkness and quiet—free from party-goers and casualties. Eledar and Uzax climb over a pile of bricks before Eledar slams into Aquim's door.

Smoke encompasses them, the curtains wrapped in flame. Eledar douses them, then sucks in a breath. His chest rattles as he steps around the corner of the bed, sure he'll find Vellene unconscious.

Instead, Mogaell lifts from a crouch with a box in her hands. Her eyes flick to them, and her furrowed brow wanes into smooth confidence, chin lifted and lips pursed.

"I take it you passed on Kadir's offer." Her gaze trails across Eledar before her lips slither into a smile. "Shame. I think we could have had some fun."

Eledar lunges toward her and whips out a blade of weaponized chaos. It glistens navy as he shoves into Mogaell and raises it to her neck. They take several steps back until he thrusts her against the wall. "Where's Vellene?" he questions.

Mogaell's eyes darken. Black veins sprout from her eyes and down her cheeks as she wields tar between her and his blade. It oozes over his formulary before she flicks her wrist and forces the blade away from her neck.

Eledar struggles to push forward, to resist against her chemight's grasp. "Do you truly care this little for your own blood?" he spits.

Mogaell flinches and closes her fist on her chemight.

Eledar's formularized sword shatters in his grasp, and he stumbles back as the power leaves him.

Beyond the room, the echo of screams falls into the everlasting silence of death. The only sound comes from the building itself, its death-plea vibrating the tile beneath Eledar's boots.

Mogaell whips her chemight into her palm and keeps her hand steady on the wooden box. "You shouldn't question things you know nothing about." She tilts her head. "You, of all chemi, do not get to question my intentions for my sister. If she dies tonight, her blood is on your hands."

Eledar pulls on his chemight. A weaponized primitive formulary rises through his veins, then drips from his palm into a lasso. If he has to haul her out through the window, he will. "What's in the box, Mogaell?"

Something shines within the box's loosely woven structure. Orbs.

Mogaell smiles but grasps it tighter. "Wouldn't you like to know?" Her natural chemight creeps over the box and weaves itself between its gaps. It moves quick, snaps from her palm like the bite of a serpent until it severs the life of whatever light lived within.

Uzax clenches their fists beside Eledar. "What are you doing?"

Mogaell levitates the box, her tar spinning it in a slow circle. "I think it's obvious," she says, her voice soft but lethal. She sharpens her eyes toward them and offers a murderous grin. "I'm finishing the job."

Her chemight swallows the box, its tar compressing the shining orbs within. She throws it toward them and leverages a formulary as she sprints for the window and *jumps*. She vanishes in a blink of violent, bright white light and—

The box explodes.

Eledar lurches backward. His head snaps against tile, and his vision darkens. He hacks, his breath knocked from him as he strains to get back to his feet. "Uzax?"

Dust and smoke form a thick haze. A foundational beam creaks loose above.

Eledar scrambles out of the way as it crashes toward him. It slams into the space he'd been. "Uzax?" he shouts between large inhales. His hands fumble over the fallen beam as he stumbles forward. He falters when his boots collide with flesh. *No no no*—he drops and wrenches Uzax's head between his hands. "Uzax, wake up," he commands.

Uzax sputters. Their eyes roll back, and Eledar shakes their head again.

"Wake up," he growls. He carefully drops Uzax's head and braces against a concrete slab. It lies across their lower half, crushing anything beyond their knees. Eledar roars as he shifts all his strength into the slab, but the smallest movement of the concrete only manages a low groan of pain from Uzax.

"Winlocs," Eledar curses as he bends and places his hands beneath the slab. He grunts and heaves it upward. Muscles rip along his biceps, tendons cry around his wrists, but the concrete remains unmovable.

The building trembles with a long screech as debris rips down from the ceiling.

Eledar kneels beside Uzax and holds the chemi's head with a hand. "Can you move?" he pleads. "At all?"

Uzax blinks through delirium and terror, eyes hazy. They give a slow shake of their head no before their brow scrunches in pain. "You need to leave me before this place collapses."

Eledar glares at them and grips the back of their neck. "You clearly don't know me very well."

"Staying makes you a fool," Uzax says.

"Then I must've been born a fool," Eledar mutters as he surveys their trapped legs. He grunts and shields his head as small pieces of ceiling rain down on him. They cut into his forearm. Clay escapes, but he wipes it away and concentrates on his orbs—what little chemight he has left.

*There's no other way*, he resigns, his eyes plastered to the place where blood bubbles between Uzax's legs and the concrete slab. "A fool that's going to save you," Eledar amends and glances down at their face.

Their eyebrow twitches. The ruby light of their irises dims into a deep, dark crimson.

"No," Eledar says and gives Uzax a slap, "don't do that."

Uzax blinks awake with a scowl.

"I'm sorry," he says with a grimace, then he pulls on his power, and a weaponized remedial formulary slices from his palms into a thick, sharp blade. "We'll grow them back later."

"Grow back—what are—" Uzax's eyes widen.

Eledar grits his teeth and slams the blade down below their knees.

Uzax screeches. Blood streams out from the halves of their legs.

Eledar searches his deposits for marvel remedial formularies, the last three he has. He tugs on all of them, and pink streams forward. Blood gushes between his fingers as he pushes his hands over the wounds to cauterize them.

Uzax lifts onto their elbows, forehead sweaty. "You Fralian bastard," he grumbles. "Couldn't you just let me die?"

Eledar smiles and grabs Uzax's arm, lifting it over his shoulder, then grunts as he moves the chemi into his arms. "After all that fuss? Maybe next time, I will."

"Guardians help me if there's a next time," Uzax curses.

The room gives a loud groan. Walls shake. Furniture topples over. Smoke slinks across cracked tile from too-close fires.

"Hold onto me." Eledar summons every drop of courage within him.

Then he jumps out the window.

The ground comes fast. Too fast. His legs *snap* beneath him. He hisses as he falls to his stomach, dropping Uzax.

*You don't even have bones*, he curses at his legs. Agony radiates through him in response. He digs his elbows into the dirt and drags himself forward, Uzax at his side doing the same.

"What about Vellene?" Uzax shouts over the sound of Winloc Grove screaming.

Eledar falters. "I just need to mend. Then I can go back in and—"

A massive boom thunders behind them.

They press to the grass and cover their heads as glass and concrete fling across the lawn. Eledar looks over his shoulder at the pile of stone that was Winloc Grove.

Torment strikes through him.

Not from his broken legs.

Or from the multiple wounds mud seeps from.

Pain.

Pain that isn't his.

A death screech that pummels through his soul, vibrates his being.

*Vellene.* His adrenaline wilts, tears creep into his eyes. He pushes them back, pushes every feeling back—but the pain is persistent. It digs through his bones, scrapes through his veins. He stares at the rubble, and he *feels* her die. Feels the heart he only had with her wither. Four beats falter into two. Then—silence.

An unbearable silence.

He furiously digs his elbows into the ground. Yells, as he drags himself forward, as he claws at concrete. Sound rips from his chest, but it never reaches his ears. He drowns in her silence as the pain *fades*. "No," he whispers, cries, *screams*.

"Eledar." There are hands on his shoulders, then arms around his waist. They pull, tug, force him back. "Eledar, please. We have to move."

A roar wrenches from him—no, not just from him. From someone else. From hundreds. Eledar shakes as he pulls back from a slab of stone. Clay leaks from long cuts, each of his fingers sliced and torn.

"Heal." And it's Soffesa. It must be—her orange hair a beacon against the dark sky. She reaches under his shirt, presses orbs into deposits. "Heal your legs."

"Vellene," he manages, and his vision flashes red.

"We can't help her until you help yourself." Soffesa turns to Uzax. "What happened?"

"My life was saved," Uzax mumbles. They blink rapidly, pupils dilated, throat bobbing.

"She's dead," Eledar whispers.

Soffesa rests a palm on his cheek. "You don't know that."

He stares at her, past her.

"Eledar, you don't know that." She presses her lips together.

His shoulders fall. Exhaustion curls up his spine, loosens it. He pulls on the remedial formularies she placed into his deposits. Rose-colored chemight pours from his palms, licks the wounds on his fingers, and slides to his legs. He grunts and inhales sharply as his bones shift and snap into place. False yet torn tendons melt and mold. Ligaments intertwine. The chemight that makes him more chemi than Golem mends. He shudders with the final snap, then tests his legs, bends them at the knees.

Another roar signals from their left as the sky rumbles with the thunder of a shard storm.

At the bottom of the hill, where Winloc Grove begins and Imperial estates line cleanly paved and plucked streets, Scraps set it aflame. Torches raised, mouths gaping in battle cries, their ragged cloaks whip around them in a vortex of fury. They charge toward the Imperials who escaped Winloc Grove, cutting through their bodies like shards of wilted grass. Formularies leak from them—power they shouldn't have—and their leader stands at their center.

A chemi drenched in plum. A smile as wide as Alchemight's three moons. A Rathmore polishing the bones of his prey.

Eledar lifts to his feet. His eyes lock with Kadir's.

"We need to leave," Soffesa insists.

Kadir's smile sharpens, his meticulously placed hair tousled as chaotically as the chemight that thrashes out from his palms and demolishes Imperial homes.

"We need to stop him," Eledar growls.

"No." Soffesa grabs his wrist and yanks him back. "We need to get Uzax to the carriage. Ulrich and Ferula are counting on us."

He turns his anger toward her. "You can't expect me to watch him tear Scorus apart."

Her orange eyes flare as she dips and wraps one of Uzax's arms over her shoulders. "We can only take on one problem at a time. Right now, Uzax takes precedence."

Eledar looks back at Kadir. A new line of rage tunnels through him as Kadir vanishes. White light flashes as his body disperses into the wind. "He and Mogaell need to pay."

Soffesa grips his shoulder and gives him a frantic squeeze. "Please Eledar. I can't lift them alone."

He bites his tongue but drops to Uzax and takes on their weight. A thread of worry tingles through him at Uzax's pallor, their eyes closed and breaths shallow. His focus drifts to the rubble of Winloc Grove, at the hands and legs that stick out in strange angles.

He looks up at Soffesa. "Okay."

She nods, the dark sky overhead shooting her orange hair into a flag of fury. "Okay."

## Chapter Forty-Two

# *Eledar*

Scraps charge up the hillside, Scorus lit in flame at their backs. They loot as they move forward, drag bags full of Imperial wealth, then slam them into any Imperial that twitches with life.

Starved, they pummel lives away as if they may restore every second stolen, every night gone hungry, every word lost to terror.

For power—they ravage.

Carrying Uzax, Soffesa and Eledar sprint across the lawn as Kadir's carriage careens toward them.

Its door flings open, and Ferula hops to the ground. Her small frame tightens as she extends her hands toward the approaching mob. Chemight streams out of her palms, her arms, everywhere in waves of gray. It reaches across the first line of Scraps and encases them in a ward. "Go!" Ferula cries. Sweat carves down her face, her lips parted in frantic breaths.

Ulrich swings out of the carriage and shoots up an umbrella of invisibility. The carriage vanishes except for the open door to its interior. "Get in," he growls. His hands shake as he juggles formularies, no place to nest them without deposits.

Soffesa and Eledar lift Uzax into the carriage, and Ferula backs up to the door. She shudders as her chemight fades, the orbs tucked in her fists exhausted and her natural chemight on the brink of snapping.

The barrier between the carriage and the Scraps breaks apart, a crackle snapping through the air. Makeshift weapons fling through the torn seam before digging into the ground at Ulrich's feet.

Ferula climbs inside and gives her father a squeeze on his wrist before he follows suit and slams the door shut. He propels the carriage forward, one arm out the window, a primitive formulary streaming down to the wheels, orbs clutched in his other fist.

"Uncle, your legs." Ferula's face turns dark as she wraps her hand in Uzax's. She studies Eledar's weary face, and her lips thin into a frown. "Vellene?"

Eledar clenches the bench beneath him, and Soffesa shakes her head.

"And the task?" Ulrich's expression hardens.

"Mogaell escaped," Eledar breathes.

Soffesa rubs her chin. "We don't know if Aquim is alive."

"So we have nothing?" Ferula asks, her voice small in the cramped quarters.

"It was all Kadir. I couldn't stop him. His father was my Master, and when he killed Lazar, that power transferred to him." The words are hurried as panic settles in his chest. Eledar picks at a scab unable to focus on anything besides the deafening silence within him. Dead. He digs his nails into a wound. Vellene must be dead.

Soffesa lays a hand over his and clutches his fingers. It stops him from opening another wound, clay tacking between his knuckles. He swallows and stares at the floor.

"We've no idea where Kadir and Mogaell went," Soffesa says softly, her usual grit and determination replaced with weariness and concern as she watches her best friend.

Eledar's chest heaves. "You need to let me out."

The words echo between them all—their certainty, finality.

He meets Ulrich's gaze. "My actions are not my own. Not anymore."

Ulrich's nostrils flare with reluctance, but he slows the carriage.

Soffesa scowls. "What are you doing? We can't afford to slow down."

Eledar avoids her glare, chews on his lip. He hates that this is how it ends, that after five years of fighting his way back to Soffesa, he now has no choice but to leave her again.

"He's right," Ulrich answers her. The carriage stops, and he pops open the door. "Kadir could pull Eledar's strings at any time. We're all in danger with him around, especially when we don't understand Kadir's motives."

Eledar digs his nails into his knees, remembers Kadir at the helm of the Scorian Scraps. There was no ounce of remorse in his expression. He wore the smile of a victor. "He must have the source." Eledar twists his fingers. "How else would he have been able to provide those Scraps with enough power to take on the rest of the Scorian Imperials? He's too powerful to ignore that he has influence over my decisions, actions."

"I don't care if he has the source," Soffesa says. She places a hand on Eledar's knee, desperate. "He's family." Her eyes dart around the cabin in earnest before they glue to Eledar's face. She shakes him. "Look at me. You're family."

Eledar runs his tongue over his teeth.

Soffesa squeezes his knee. "Eledar, please." Her voice trembles on the words.

He lifts his eyes to hers and wishes he hadn't.

Sorrow sits like an old friend against Soffesa's slumped shoulders. Her eyes flash, lips parted in protest at the resolution permanent across his face. She turns a frantic expression to Ulrich, but her body retreats into the corner of the carriage. She knows, just as Eledar does. There's no future when his life is tied to another's.

Ulrich sucks in a breath. He fastens a grip around Ferula and Uzax.

She shakes her head. "What about rebuilding your wife, Ulrich? Eledar is the key to that."

Ulrich scowls. "I want Ester back, but not if it means putting the rest of my family at risk." He grimaces. "I let my need for my wife cloud my judgment once before. I can't make that mistake again."

Soffesa's hand drops from Eledar's knee, her mind making peace with the situation before her words. "You're not leaving me."

"I'm sorry." Eledar memorizes her face, then peels from his seat.

Soffesa's eyes water. She blinks back tears in frustration. "You don't have to apologize if you stay."

Eledar takes in a breath and drops to the road. "Close the door, Ulrich."

"No." Soffesa forces her way toward the door, but Ferula grabs the edge of her gown, and Ulrich positions himself in front of the opening, blocking her path forward. "Move," she growls.

"I'll find you when I'm free," Eledar tells her, hopes it's not an empty promise.

Her face contorts with fear. "I can't do this again. I just got you back."

"You still have me." Eledar gives his chest a thump with his fist. He nods to Ulrich. "Go."

Ulrich summons chemight and thrusts his hand out the window, willing the carriage to move forward.

"I will claw your face off," Soffesa yells at Ulrich, her voice carrying through the window before it's swallowed by the whoosh of the carriage shooting forward.

They steer around a corner.

*Alone.*

The carriage disappears.

*Again.*

Eledar wavers. Wind whips around him. It picks up with a wail, black clouds percolating in the sky. The first shards of a storm slice down and across his cheeks, through the fabric of his cloak.

Tar sticks to his hair, puddles at his feet. He closes his eyes as the shards open new wounds and old. Mud leaks from him, slops to the ground, and mixes with Alchemight's tar. Thunder rumbles with anger, echoes through his toes to his mouth until he's falling.

Falling as he presses his hands into tar.

Falling as every fault pummels against his heart.

Screaming at himself. At the excruciating wave of loss and grief he's ridden too many times.

And Alchemight swallows it all.

Then there's an abandoned ship docked at the shore. There are crates of *lumis*. Crates.

Then. Then. Then.

There's nothing he wouldn't give to see their faces in the mist, in the sun, in the moons. The faces of everyone he's lost. Even if it is false—it's still those he loves returning to him within tricks of light and shadow. For now, he needs *lumis* to be enough. For now, he must forget every touch, every look, every solid thing. He must be blood and clay. Nothing more. Nothing less.

He must grieve—falling, screaming, drowning.

Eledar drags himself through the shard storm, each step heavier, either from the tar tacking to his boots or the weight settling across his shoulders.

The cargo ship's crew has departed, likely Scraps and Utilities who ran to join the uprising. The crates sit exposed to the elements, tar shards thunking into their thick wood before melting across.

Clay oozes across his face, arms, and legs as Eledar grips the top of a crate and throws it off.

*Lumis* twinkles within. Glass orbs filled with enough light to brighten his soul. For now.

He reaches for his deposits and empties them all. He lets filled, vital formularies clink to the ground and roll toward Dalbian's Abyss. In their place, he secures *lumis*. Every deposit, he fills and fills. Warmth spreads through him, and his next swallow of pain is lighter. His next breath—easier. He inhales deeply, the darkest moments of the last several days brightening through his veins. He relaxes into the side of the crate, tilts his head to the sky.

Shards scrape and scrape, but that's the thing about harboring pain.

It's all numb, in the end.

"Lirik."

His neck snaps in the direction of the voice, but his vision blears into white edges. All he makes out is a purple cloak. "Rathmore," he rasps.

Kadir stands on the dock, face shrouded by his hood. "Filling your head with lies, I see."

Eledar turns and grips the crate, afraid to show weakness before his Master. He steadies, the wobble of his knees subsiding as he places his weight into the side of the crate. "Lies are your specialty. Not mine."

Kadir steps onto the ship's deck and stops next to the open crate. He peers inside, then pulls back as he crushes one of Eledar's discarded formularies. He lifts his boot and stares at the colored mist rushing free beneath. "You turned me down." Kadir lifts his head. "For this?"

"It's all I have because of you." Eledar maneuvers forward, prepared to make a threat, but he misplaces his footing.

Kadir latches onto his shoulders, steadying him. "What an existence you must live, blaming everyone else for the damage you cause. To think, I used to admire you," he mutters.

Eledar rips from Kadir, and his back hits the sharp edge of one of the crates. He rights himself, ignores the pain. All pain.

"Take the *lumis* out," Kadir commands.

Eledar freezes, expects to feel a pull on his strings but nothing comes. He grimaces.

Kadir lifts a hand and drops his hood, despite the shards of the storm. Tar mats his hair as shards slice into his scarred face. The violet of his eyes is sharp and certain, his mischievous glint replaced with a fair amount of apprehension.

Eledar peers at the chemi. "Do you ever show yourself? To anyone?"

Kadir rolls his shoulders back. "No one cares who I truly am." He wipes blood away as it pools from a wound on his cheek, sliced open by a shard. "That includes myself. I will be who I need to be. That's all that matters." He licks his lips and nods to Eledar's torn vest. "Remove the *lumis*."

Eledar's biceps tense. "No."

Kadir looks to the side. Annoyance strikes through his carefully crafted confidence. His jaw ticks. "Don't make me do this."

"I don't hold that kind of power," Eledar argues. "Not with you around."

Kadir's nostrils flare with an inhale, then he raises his hand.

Panic flickers through Eledar as he recognizes the motion—fingers open to the sky before they curl into a fist. *TUG.* He shudders as his arm yanks up to a deposit and forcefully removes a *lumis* formulary before depositing it back into the crate. *TUG*, and it happens again and again, each formulary removed accompanied by darkness. Cold, it smothers him, takes over his mind, sobers every hint of blissful ignorance.

"Stop," he growls, but Kadir's back is turned, his purple cloak waving off him as he steps down onto the dock toward an approaching ship.

*TUG*—Eledar follows. He grits his teeth, hisses as pain shoots through him the more he resists.

The last shard falls. Alchemight's moons peer between clouds like leering, watchful eyes of the Guardians. As he's yanked forward, Dalbian's Abyss shifts. Mist curls around black sails, an hourglass—shaded equally on both ends—shines in crimson thread. Its bow pokes forward, and red letters blaze in the moonlight: *Huntress*.

Rathmore Chemibreakers descend the hillside of Scorus. They clap and whoop, faces bright with smiles and the blood of their enemies. Several shed collars and reveal ink of the Equilibrium symbol. It's then that their gaunt faces, jagged walks, and chemi-made weapons make sense—Fralian Scraps dressed in Chemibreaker disguises.

*TUG*—and Eledar forces through their reverie. He sweats, combative against Kadir's hold. He opens his mouth to rage—*TUG*—and his lips seal shut. His hands wind together behind his back, cuffed by his Master's command.

With each step, the Scraps of Equilibrium quiet, their victory drowned by the enslaved Golem before them. Their eyes turn to Kadir, their leader and victor, await for an explanation, a speech, anything to understand the irony—how the very chemi who single-handedly caused the uprising in Frales and paved the way for a group such as Equilibrium now fights to run and disappear into the *lumis* crates behind him.

Kadir says nothing as The Huntress docks. He climbs aboard and nods to a female Scrap waiting on deck. All the while, he wields a marvel remedial formulary. Rose-hued chemight drifts up from his palms and seals his wounds from the shard storm. It stitches together his smile, grim but satisfied, as he turns his gaze to Eledar, to the crowd.

For a moment, Eledar swears there's something more to Kadir's unmovable face. Swears the bags beneath his eyes darken, the white of his scars brighten. He swears, *swears*, there's a crack in Kadir's smile, a twitch in the corner of his lips that could be a hint of fear or panic or sorrow.

Eledar leans into hope, believes maybe he was wrong. Maybe there's remorse behind Kadir's mask. Maybe, in the next breath, Kadir will let Eledar go free.

But time doesn't still.

The next breath passes—

*TUG* —

And his hope drowns as his body becomes anything but his own.

**JINAPHER J. HOFFMAN** IS AN EPIC DARK FANTASY AUTHOR BUILDING A MULTIVERSE OF FEMININE RAGE KNOWN AS WRATHOS.

SHE IS AN AMAZON #1 BEST SELLER AND MOTHER TO TWO ADORABLE BUNNY RABBITS. SHE LIVES IN CALIFORNIA WITH HER HERO AND PARTNER AND SPENDS MOST OF HER DAY ORGANIZING MULTIVERSE PLOT HOLES AND BUILDING MAGIC SYSTEMS.

LEARN ABOUT JINAPHER'S UPCOMING RELEASES BY VISITING HER WEBSITE: WRATHOSBOOKS.COM

**TO SUPPORT JINAPHER, PLEASE LEAVE A WRITTEN REVIEW ON AMAZON + GOODREADS.**

## GLOSSARY

### World Building

**Alchemight** (/aL - Kuh - my -t/) – one of the realms in Wrathos, a multiverse of feminine rage; two nations known as Scorus & Frales

**Chemight** (/Ki - my -t/) – natural, mist-like magic founded in a discipline of wishes & curses

**Chemi** (/Ki - my/) – humanoid beings made of mist, tar, & chemight

**Formulary** (/F-orm-u-Lay -er -ee/) – chemight infused with nether (weapon) or marvel (healing) ingots (metals) within glass, marble-sized orbs to create more potent magic

**Imperials** (/uhm-pee-ree-uhls/) – wealthiest faction of chemi, likely belonging to one of six bloodlines

**Chemibreakers** (/Ki-my-brAy-kuh-s/) – soldiers of the Imperials

**Utilities** (/you-til-uh-tees/) – middle class chemi that typically specialize in rare abilities or work as indentured servants to Imperials

**Scraps** (/s-kuh-rah-ps/) – lower class chemi with typically low stores of natural chemight

**Golem** (/Gal-um/) – an enslaved subset of Scraps in Frales, who are made of mist, clay, & chemight. They can be controlled by their Master, or the chemi who created them

## Name Guide

**Vellene Winloc** (/Vuh-lih-n Wihn-lah-k/)
**Aquim Winloc** (/Ah-ck-we-ihm Wihn-lah-k/)
**Mogaell Winloc** (/Moh-gahl Wihn-lah-k/)
**Aurora Winloc** (/Ah-roar-uh Wihn-lah-k/)
**Eledar Lirik** (/Ehl-uh-dahr Lih-rih-k/)
**Kadir Rathmore** (/Kuh-deer Wra-th-Ma-or/)
**Lazar Rathmore** (/Luh-Zahr Wra-th-Ma-or/)
**Soffesa Fedelis** (/Soh-feh-suh Fuh-duhl-Ius/)
**Ulrich Eni** (/Uhl-rih-k Ih-nee/)
**Uzax Eni** (/Ooh-zah-x Ih-nee/)
**Ferula Eni** (/Fuh-roo-lah Ih-nee/)
**Surveillant Idus** (/Sirh-vAhl-ihnt Ih-dihs/)
**Evanora Stone** (/Eh-vuh-nor-uh Stuh-ohn/)
**Xenos Caligari** (/Zay-nohs Cahl-uh-gar-ee/)
**Vonner** (/Vah-ohn-uhr/)
**Pinesky** (/Pihn-es-kee/)
**Nivia** (/Nih-vee-uh/)
**Dally** (/Dahl-ee/)
**Bian** (/Bee-ihn/)
**Imaex** (/I-mah-x/)

## Creatures & Crests

**Spideria** (/S-pi-deer-ee-uh/) – large spider-inspired creatures; double-diamond, hourglass shaped torso; multiple legs with pinchers; crest of the Winlocs [Scorus]

**Ravian** (/Rah-vee-ihn/) – raven-inspired creatures; crest of the Rathmores [Frales]

**Canisoss** (/KAhn-ee-sah-s/) – dog-inspired creatures that are skeletal in nature; skull-like heads with hollowed out eyes; crest of the Pineskys [Scorus]

**Rodenti** (/Roh-dihnt-i/) – rat-inspired creatures; razor-like whiskers; blazing red eyes; fang-like teeth; crest of the Stones [Frales]

**Parduseus** (/Pahr-dihs-ee-uhs/) – leopard-inspired creatures; crest of the Caligaris [Frales]

**Scumtis** (/Skuhm-tihs/) – poisonous beetle-inspired creatures; crest of the Vonners [Scorus]

## Types of Formularies

**Primitive** (/Prihm-uh-tihv/) – green; for basic necessities

**Remedial** (/Ruh-me-dee-uhl/) – red; for mending

**Chaos** (/Kay-ahs/) – blue; for altering the mind

**Morph** (/Muh-ohr-f/) – purple; for altering physical attributes

**formulary colors can vary off the primary color*

**formularies can be weaponized when melted down with a nether ingot, or they can be used for good/basic purposes when melted with marvel ingots. Ingots are metals derived from a mortal form of white gold.*

**a specialized formulary may need to be used with a name, much like when casting a spell, but these are incredibly rare - only a few in existence. Examples include 'lumis' and 'silgis entris'.*

Made in the USA
Las Vegas, NV
29 November 2024